Wishes and Stitches

Also by Rachael Herron

HOW TO KNIT A HEART BACK HOME
HOW TO KNIT A LOVE SONG

Wishes and Stitches

A Cypress Hollow Yarn

RACHAEL HERRON

WILLIAM MORROW
An Imprint of HarperCollins*Publishers*

WISHES AND STITCHES. Copyright © 2011 by Rachael Herron. All rights reserved. Printed in the United States of America. No part of this book may be used or reproduced in any manner whatsoever without written permission except in the case of brief quotations embodied in critical articles and reviews. For information address HarperCollins Publishers, 10 East 53rd Street, New York, NY 10022.

HarperCollins books may be purchased for educational, business, or sales promotional use. For information please write: Special Markets Department, HarperCollins Publishers, 10 East 53rd Street, New York, NY 10022.

FIRST EDITION

Library of Congress Cataloging-in-Publication Data has been applied for.

ISBN 978-0-06-184132-3

11 12 13 14 15   OV/RRD   10 9 8 7 6 5 4 3 2 1

*To Cari Luna, for reading my first drafts
and for believing in me anyway*

Acknowledgments

Thanks go to my amazing editor, May Chen, for helping me up the learning curve so gracefully; to the fantastic agent and friend to whom I probably owe my firstborn child, Susanna Einstein; to her assistant Molly Reese, who rocks; and to everyone at HarperCollins who makes being part of the team so wonderful: Carrie Feron, Pam Spengler-Jaffe, Amanda Bergeron, Christine Maddalena, Tavia Kowalchuk, Megan Traynor, Shawn Nicholls, thank you for believing in my little town of Cypress Hollow. Thanks go to my family for telling everyone they know about my books, and to Lala, for putting up with me when I go crazy eyed and start writing nonsense sentences on the insides of matchbooks. Thanks to the PensFatales, for being my writing family, and to A. J. Larrieu, for reading my work at the drop of a proverbial dime. Thanks also to Gwen Alcázar, for knowing many things, and to Eddie Dwyer, again, for providing me with the specifics. And huge thanks go to Eliza Carpenter, my imaginary friend who's become more real than I could ever have imagined, and to Rosemary Hill of RomiDesigns, who designed the shawl I could not (and that Eliza *would* have, had she thought of it).

Wishes and Stitches

Chapter One

A knitter completely devoted to her task never drops her stitches, never makes a mistake, never miscrosses cables. She's also probably not as much fun as the distracted knitter.

—ELIZA CARPENTER

In Tillie's Diner, Naomi's scrambled eggs were cooling fast. She stared with blank eyes at the crossword puzzle tucked under her cup, the coffee ring on the ink spreading each time she set it back down.

Come on. Focus. These jangled nerves and distracted thoughts weren't like her. The diner was normally a place of calm where people nodded to her, but didn't bother her—the townspeople talked among themselves, letting her work the puzzle in peace as she eased into the morning, writing down the last word before leaving for the office.

But today Naomi's thoughts flew everywhere, all over the place, most specifically to the one thing she was trying not to remember.

"How you doing, hon?"

Naomi jumped. "Fine, thanks." Shirley was a good waitress, fast and accurate, and one of the few friends Naomi had made in this first year of living in Cypress Hollow. On days off, they went to the movies or walked the coastal trails while Shirley scanned the beach for people engaged in shocking behavior, which she pointed out at the top of her lungs. But she wasn't usually much for checking back in with Naomi after she'd served her breakfast. She'd just cruise by her table, refilling her coffee cup, never spilling a drop, already moving on to the next table. Shirley wasn't big on small talk. That was fine, Naomi had never been great at it herself.

But today Shirley lingered, the pot still hanging over Naomi's cup. "You look different," she said. "You get a haircut?"

Blinking, Naomi reached up to touch her curls. "No . . ." She suddenly felt shy. "But I'm using a different conditioner—"

"Nope. Something else." Shirley set the coffeepot on the edge of the table and crouched so she was on Naomi's eye level. She lowered her voice. "You got some."

"Excuse me?" Naomi stiffened.

"Action. At that conference you went to. I can tell you got some, because you got this high color right here." Shirley pointed to the top of her own cheekbone. "And because you're *way* less uptight than normal."

Naomi shook her head. "I can't—no, you must be imagining that."

"I don't mean no offense by it, you know that. I'm just saying. You look good." Shirley puffed a breath of air as she hauled herself back to standing, using the edge of the Formica for purchase. "Did you have fun, though? Just tell me that."

Naomi felt the spots of color Shirley had noticed burning on her cheeks. "I . . . yes." *Yes. I had the best time of my life and I can't stop thinking about it.*

"Good girl. Keep it up, then." Shirley walked away, taking the coffeepot with her.

Did a one-night stand really show like that? Was Naomi wearing the equivalent of a neon sign? Was it flashing above her as she walked? *Got laid. Best sex ever. Ask me how.*

Oh, damn. She would *not* think about it. Instead, she fiddled with her phone, staring at it with unseeing eyes until she almost dropped it on her plate.

Her normal booth in Tillie's was the one farthest from the door, next to the entrance that led to the side room where the old ranchers sat in the morning. It was the booth no one else wanted—the vinyl was torn in such a way that it always poked her legs uncomfortably, and the center table leg tilted, even though it was bolted down. Naomi was used to resting her newspaper so that it covered the burned stain on the Formica, and she didn't set her pen on the tabletop lest it roll off the table. Again.

At least Naomi normally *got* a booth. Half of it was luck, the other half was getting there early enough. It seemed as if everyone in Cypress Hollow came through Tillie's in the mornings, and lots of people had their favorite seats that no one else would dream of sitting in. Mayor Finley sat in the booth closest to the door, saying hello to everyone, local and tourist alike. She was tall, always dressed in yellow, and reminded Naomi of a pencil. Officer John Moss, who Naomi thought looked like he should be working for Boss Hogg, sat on the stool nearest the cash register, peering into open wallets as if he expected a tip.

She tried eavesdropping on the room next to her, her favorite part of Tillie's. The ranchers gathered there—tourists were strictly not allowed, nor were townsfolk even, normally. Naomi loved to hear the rhythm of the stories they told, the way they held on to vowels longer than anyone else in town. She couldn't quite hear them, though. Dang it.

If only that group back there would come into the new health clinic.

She drew small circles along the bottom of the paper, and then made a note to remind herself to call the paper to advertise the free blood sugar check she was offering next week. Maybe that would bring a nibble or two.

A nibble. Like she'd gotten along her jawline, the curve of her neck. . .

That fling had *not* been like her. She would never have one in Cypress Hollow, that was for sure. Word would spread like a seasonal virus, and Naomi valued her privacy above all else. But at the medical conference in Portland last weekend, in a city where she knew no one, it had turned out to be as easy as tripping over the uneven curb in front of Tillie's.

Naomi had seen him when the conference attendees moved from the opening session over to the bar. His eyes met hers across three crowded tables. Next to the men who had typical doctor-style clean haircuts and ties neatly knotted under their chins, he'd looked rugged. His dark brown hair was a bit too long, parted unevenly, as if he'd just run his fingers through it after showering, and he leaned against the hotel's tall iron and glass table as if it were a tree. The long planes of his jaw were softened by a mouth that was perhaps a little too big, but the proportions worked—he stood out from every other man in the room. The others looked like they were in soft-focus black and white to Naomi. He was drawn sharply in color. He'd taken his tie off, if he'd even had one on that day, and the top two buttons of his soft blue shirt were open.

His eyes, dark and smoky, met hers and he grinned at her. His expression told her he'd caught her—he knew she'd been checking him out. And the wink he'd dropped, the one that made Naomi's heart race, told her he liked it.

After watching each other from their respective circles of acquaintances for an hour, they finally met in the bathroom line.

He said, "You have gorgeous eyes. I don't think I've ever seen greener eyes in my life."

"Nice line," said Naomi, smiling and leaning back against the wall. She was trying desperately to remember this game, but it had been a long time since she'd played it.

"Rig," he said.

"Seriously?" She couldn't help it. Of *course* his name was Rig. If he got into trouble in here, he could probably jump off the hotel roof and land on his waiting black horse and ride off into the wilderness. She shook the thought from her head and said, "Sorry. Naomi."

"Can I buy you a drink?" he asked.

"Sure," she said.

"There's a minibar in my room."

Naomi swallowed her gasp and nodded as coolly as she could.

They never got around to opening the minibar—there had been other, more relevant things to open: her blouse; his slacks; her skirt; and then, her legs.

Even though she hadn't planned it, Naomi had remembered how to get what she wanted, and Rig had known how to give it to her. Those long, sensitive, *talented* fingers would be wasted on a GP; he had to be a surgeon. But that was yet another question she didn't ask. In the dark, they didn't ask many.

After round two and more kisses, she'd felt the warm flush of pleasure that had nothing to do with where his hands were going. She *did* still know how to work this—thank God. It had been one of the most interesting things she'd studied in medical school, the sexual act and how people could fit together physiologically.

If only everything else was as straightforward and easy to control.

She'd flown home feeling the heady flush of a new secret. She kept picturing Rig's fingers, kept feeling the shape of his mouth on hers. She held the knowledge of him carefully to herself, something to bring out later and remember when her spirits needed a lift.

Naomi sighed, moving her coffee cup slowly across the Formica. She doodled on the edge of her paper. She needed to get Rig's hands off her mind. She could think about them later, but not here, where Shirley was still glancing curiously at her. Hopefully Shirley wouldn't tell anyone. She trusted Shirley, yes. But Cypress Hollow was a small town, and it was difficult for the residents to sit on good gossip.

It was such a close-knit town that it had been hard for Naomi to gain her footing, to make friends. She had Shirley, of course, thank God. And Lucy Bancroft at the bookstore was sweet—they'd had coffee twice, and Naomi kept meaning to call her again, but time had slipped away from her while she was working on opening the health clinic. Every once in a while one of the locals would notice that she was sitting in Tillie's and would nod or give a half smile, but no one stood next to her table chatting like they did over by Mildred and Greta's booth. No one impeded the flow of customer traffic while catching up on *her* week. Mrs. Irving had never laughed while standing at her table like she did at others, her head tipped back, lipstick on her teeth, laughing so that her belly shook under her blue plaid dress.

It was okay. Naomi had known it would take a while to fit in here, and that was fine. Besides, she was awful at small talk. Terrible. She was the opposite of her mother, who could charm a bluebird out of the sky, and just like her father, who'd thought meaningless chat was a waste of time that could be better spent elsewhere.

"Hey, you!" a happy voice said from behind her as someone gripped her shoulder. A smile crept onto her face as she turned her head. Maybe, just maybe, today it would be different? She'd get that casual chitchat right?

Elbert Romo's engineer's cap bobbled on the back of his head, and his blue denim shirt was missing a button. "Sorry," he said to Naomi. "I lost my balance there for a second."

"Oh," she said.

Elbert steadied his hand on her table. It wobbled precariously, spilling her coffee. She didn't mind the new puddle. "How are you?" she asked.

"Oh, sorry," he said again to Naomi, not looking at her. "I'm just trying to get his attention."

He pushed off and wobbled on his cane toward the front of the diner. "Hello there!" he called. "Over here!"

Naomi dropped her eyes back down to the table, then picked up her phone again and checked for nonexistent e-mails that she knew hadn't come in since the last time she'd had it in her hand.

Okay, so she hadn't broken into Cypress Hollow society yet.

She stole a glance toward the front where Elbert was pumping the hand of a man who dwarfed him. The brown, scuffed cowboy boots caught her eye first—the man wore them just like everyone else in this town did, and they looked great on him. His legs were long in his well-worn jeans, and his chest was broad under a red plaid shirt. His dark brown hair was thick and a shade too long and it stuck up in places as if he'd just woken up. He had a scruff of beard on his jaw. If he yelled "Timber," she'd believe him.

And she was damned if he didn't look exactly like . . . Rig.

Chapter Two

*What is lace but a series of attractively arranged holes?
They'd be mistakes anywhere else.*
—E.C.

N aomi sloshed even more coffee onto her paper as she set her cup back down, and she gripped the handle tightly.

What the *hell* was he doing here? She hadn't said where she lived, and she hadn't asked him, either. One-night stands did *not* show up at breakfast the next week. Oh, God. He'd see her . . .

"Good to have you here," she heard Elbert say. "Come on back, and meet everybody."

Meet everybody. In a year, she'd never been invited to do that. How on earth did Rig rate?

Elbert introduced him to Mayor Finley, who nodded and said something to him that Naomi couldn't catch. Mildred and Greta both leaned all the way out of their booth to stare at Rig's rear end after he passed their table. Mildred's ball of sock yarn bounced out of the booth and down the aisle, as if chasing him.

Elbert didn't glance at Naomi as he stomped past, but Rig did. He smiled and nodded, and somehow didn't look surprised, the way she knew she did. The corner of his too-wide mouth twisted, eyes crinkling as he paused next to her.

Naomi was too flustered to smile back. She had the same thought she'd had in the bar when she'd first seen him: He didn't look like a doctor. He looked like he belonged on a motorcycle, illegally crossing borders.

"In pen, huh?"

She'd forgotten how deep his voice was. She nodded and twiddled the pen's cap.

"I would have guessed that about you. I use erasable pen, myself," he said. He reached out one of those huge, gorgeous hands—yep, it really was him—and touched the edge of the paper.

"Why not just use a pencil, then?" she asked. Her voice felt like it would shake, embarrassingly, but instead it came out strong.

Rig shrugged, and Naomi noticed again how broad his shoulders were. "Not as much fun that way."

"So, stalking me already?" Was it possible that she was flirting again? Just like that?

He laughed. "That's me. Stalker guy. Considering I didn't even know what state you lived in, I think I've done well, don't you think?"

Naomi bit her bottom lip as she grinned. She'd forgotten how easy conversation was with him. "What are you doing here? I mean, besides the obvious stalking thing. Surf's up?"

"Yeah, that's me. Dr. Hang Loose. Hang ten. However that goes."

His tone was light, but she could imagine it, actually: his wide thighs and broad chest in a black wet suit, his hair slicked back, face turned to the sun as he rested on the waves, waiting for a set. . .

Naomi said, "They say the surf's great here. There are always people out there, even at night."

"Maybe sometime I'll get a chance to try it."

"You'd be good, I bet. You're strong." She felt color rise to her cheeks, but she held his gaze.

This was fun. She still had no idea why he was here, but Naomi was glad that he was.

His eyes turned serious. "Naomi, I didn't plan on this. My brother lives here, and I just found out yesterday that you—" He stepped forward as if he was going to say more, but her phone buzzed, clattering on the table. He looked at it and then looked at Elbert who was yanking on his sleeve.

Picking up her cell phone, trying to act cool, Naomi said, "We can talk later. Go with him, he wants you."

Rig nodded. "Soon. We'll talk." His voice was a promise. Then he was herded toward the side room, and Naomi flipped open her phone.

The message was a spam e-mail advertising Viagra. Naomi's scrambled eggs were stone cold now. No hope for them. She pushed the plate away and looked around for Shirley. More coffee was the only thing she needed. But Shirley had followed Elbert and Rig into the ranchers' room, and if Naomi leaned her head back a little, she could just hear what was being said.

Elbert introduced him, and a volley of greetings was exchanged.

"Rig Keller!" said Pete Wegman, one of the old ranchers. "You're Captain Keller's brother, ain'tcha?"

A mumble of something Naomi couldn't quite hear. Dammit. She wanted to catch this.

"That's Jesse, and Landers, Hooper's over there. That's Cade, on the right."

"Howdy." Naomi recognized Cade MacArthur's voice. She'd treated him for a knee injury a few months ago. He'd been what she privately termed an im-patient, but his wife, Abigail, had seemed kind. Naomi had ached, then, to tell Abigail who she was, but it hadn't seemed like the right time.

Naomi missed something else from the back room, and then heard, "Nah, it's just a dumb nickname my brother gave me when I started working on the oil derricks. But it stuck, and I kind of like it now." Then he said something she couldn't hear, and an appreciative wave of laughter rolled through the ranchers' room.

Good lord, what if he stayed?

Naomi missed something under the clatter of Shirley picking up dishes and putting them in the bus tub, but then she heard Rig go on.

"No, not with my brother. Staying with Shirley here, actually."

Shirley? She hadn't mentioned she'd rented out her back unit, although Naomi knew she'd been advertising it. Not that she was required to tell Naomi anything, really, but . . . Naomi heard Shirley, sixty-five years old next month, giggle like a schoolgirl.

"Oh," said one of the older men. "We were sure sorry about your brother's wife a few years back."

The rumble of a trash truck going by the window covered Rig's response, and Naomi suddenly felt guilty for eavesdropping. She wished for the hundredth time that she was comfortable knitting in public, but she wasn't. That's just the way it was. So she fiddled with the cord of her headphones—she never listened to her iPod while she was at the cafe, knowing that would be too antisocial, but she kept the device near her. One of these days, with the way she worked the cord between her hands, she'd end up finger-knitting it into a tiny plastic noose, and what then?

So what if he was in Cypress Hollow? So what if he'd been introduced to the ranchers, and she had never actually met any of them in person, just knew them from eavesdropping? Dr. Pederson and she were going to hire a new doctor soon, and then she'd watch that person, see if she or he fit into the town better than she did. Until then she'd try not to worry.

Old Bill trundled by, rag in hand. Naomi couldn't remember if she'd ever seen him anywhere but behind the cash register. She hadn't really been aware that he had legs.

Naomi disentangled her fingers from the headphone cord and held out a hand. There was no time like right now to be friendly. Right? It had been easy with Rig—maybe it would be with the owner of the diner, too.

"Bill?"

Old Bill stopped, stock still, eyes still forward as if he didn't quite believe she was speaking to him.

Naomi's pulse fluttered at her throat, and she felt breathless. But she spoke anyway. "Hey, if you're going back there, would you mind telling everyone that I'll be having a free blood sugar check on Friday night? At the health clinic I just opened next to my office. They might . . ." She ran out of smart ideas. "They might want to get that done. You, too."

Old Bill stared at her. "You sayin' my food isn't healthy?"

Naomi sucked in a breath. "Oh, no, that's not what—it's just that—"

"Because I buy them free-range eggs from Hooper. That's good cholesterol. And if them boys want bacon, I figure they've worked hard enough in their lives to deserve it."

"But . . . low fat isn't a bad—"

Looking ahead deliberately, the conversation obviously over, Old Bill moved forward. In the back room, she could hear the introductions being made all over again.

Swallowing hard, she filled in eleven down. Eight letters, one who is a foreigner. Easy. *Stranger.*

She wrapped the headphone cord around her iPod, put her phone in her pocket, folded up the paper, left correct change and a healthy tip on the table, and walked out, leaving her eggs behind her.

She didn't look back to see if Rig watched her go. One night was one night. And that night was over.

Chapter Three

For lace, don't be ashamed to use plenty of stitch markers. We all forget where we are sometimes.
—E.C.

As Naomi pushed open her front door at the end of the day, she heard the home phone ringing. She sighed and threw her purse and briefcase on the couch, and then kicked off her Danskos. Bending over, she rubbed the arch of her foot and waited until the rings stopped as the call went to voice mail. The silence wouldn't last. She might as well make the most of it. She poured herself a glass of water and took it along with the phone to the sofa, where she sat with a *whump*. It was a good couch. No, a great couch, red and soft, so inviting . . . She could just close her eyes for a few minutes. . .

No. Naomi straightened herself and waited for the phone to ring again. She picked up her knitting, working a few stitches. She'd finally started the wedding shawl pattern written by Eliza Carpenter, and Naomi was making it for herself, something to throw over her shoulders on cold mornings. The creamy white fiber was so fine, so soft, almost as lightweight as the sunshine they'd sat in that day when Eliza spun it. And she loved the pattern, although it some-times got confusing. Good thing she was on the—no, wait. Had she been knitting back on the wrong side? Confused, she tried to read the lace. She'd screwed up somewhere. Again. Also, no surprise. This pattern was going to kill her.

Naomi sighed. Lord, it had been a long day. Pederson had been out again. No surprise there—Naomi was used to seeing both her patients and as many of his as she could fit in. They'd had a shared partnership ever since she'd bought her way out of direct employ-ment after Pederson's original partner retired two years ago. It made accounting easy—they split both the bills and the profits although Pederson still had a larger share.

But in the last six months, even though they split the income, they sure as hell hadn't shared the work. Today, Naomi had spent the day seeing patients, but not really *seeing* them. And she hated that—the patients were the best part of the job and when she had to shuffle them like cards, it frustrated her. She knew she'd treated a woman for athlete's foot, and another man had a rash that looked like classic poison oak, as well as twenty other patients, back to back, as fast as she could shoehorn them in and out. They came from as far as forty miles out in the countryside, and women who drove that far to be told it was just a virus weren't happy people. But if some-one had asked her to match their names to their symptoms or, God forbid, their faces to their names, she wouldn't be able to do it.

At least her grumpy jack-of-all-midlevels Bruno helped with that. Nurse and office staff all wrapped into one wide, scrubs-wrapped package, Bruno always had the right file at the right time, all the labs ordered when she needed them, and he even vacuumed before the cleaning crew came in. Even though he rarely cracked a smile, he didn't need to—he was probably the best thing Pederson had ever contributed to the practice.

She stared at the lace chart, her eyes unseeing. Her hand moved to the phone resting next to her thigh. It hadn't rung again yet; her mother must be leaving the message to end all messages.

Okay. She tried again, pulling the fabric away from the needles to look more closely at it. In the previous row, had she missed a yarn-over? Could she fake a fix for that? She glanced at the pattern she'd placed in plastic page protectors in a binder. Did she have to rip back? Oh, great. That would be the capper for today. To say that ripping lace never went well for Naomi was an understatement. And since she rarely remembered to use a lifeline, hoping for the best, the yarn always, always won.

Times like this, she missed Eliza the most.

The phone rang again. Yep. Right on schedule. Naomi didn't need caller ID to know who it was.

"Hi, Mom."

"Sweetheart. How are you?"

"Fine." Her mother never wanted an actual answer—she just needed to ask.

Her mother sighed. "Oh, sweetheart. She called again. Can you believe it? And you know what she wanted?"

"Money?" Naomi tucked the phone between her ear and shoulder, leaving her hands free to start knitting. She'd just forge ahead not knowing where that yarn-over had gone, believing everything would be okay. Like Eliza would have. Even though Naomi never quite believed it herself.

Her mother gasped. "How did you know?"

She should really get one of those cordless headsets like Bruno had at the office. Naomi knitted three stitches before she answered. Maybe she could redeem today a tiny bit. "Because Anna never calls you, Mom, and when she does, she needs money. It's not that hard to do the math."

"She wouldn't tell me where she was. That kills me, you know it's killing me, right?"

"Yes, Mom."

"You'd tell me if you knew where she was?"

Naomi made a face she was glad her mother couldn't see. "She never calls me, you know that."

"She might one day, though. And if she does, just do your best to find out where she is, and Daddy and I will drive or fly out anywhere and get her. We'll bring her back, and we . . . we can fix her, I'm sure we can."

"Anna's a big girl now. She's all grown up." Naomi dropped another stitch and, stifling a curse word, paused for a moment while she caught it.. "You've done all you can, now she's going to live her life." Even if that meant stripping in seedy bars and having inconsequential affairs with inappropriate men. Naomi thought her little sister had made some pretty crappy choices, sure, but Naomi, at least, had given up years ago trying to save her sister, even when she wanted to. Anna was just Anna.

"But her life is *awful*," said her mother.

Naomi heard the low rumble of her mother's husband's voice in the background. "What did Buzz say?"

When Naomi was five, her parents had divorced, and she'd gone to live with her father. By the time Naomi was nine, Buzz Maubert was Maybelle's second husband and the newborn Anna's father. Both times Maybelle had married, she'd gone for men with good jobs who pulled in enough money to keep her in her name-brand clothes: first a doctor, then a lawyer, even though Naomi couldn't think of too many men more different from her fastidious father than Buzz. Before he'd retired, when Buzz left his office, he'd roared away on his Harley, and he hadn't been just a weekend warrior—he loved everything about motorcycles, including fixing them, getting the grease under his nails. Now that he could stay home and work on them all day, Maybelle tolerated the dirt he tracked in with his leather riding boots because his retirement package allowed her to hire a housecleaner.

"He's saying his program is starting. *I'm on the phone, Buzz!*"

"So what's new with you two?"

As if she hadn't heard her, her mother went on. "I didn't give her the money, though. Even though she cried."

"Of course you didn't."

"I said I'd bring her the cash, and she refused. But maybe I *should* have wired the money like she asked. Then I'd know where she was, right?"

"She'd take off," said Naomi. "Just like she always has, she'd get the money from Western Union and then she'd run off, and you and Buzz would spend a thousand dollars traveling and staying in hotels, looking for your adult daughter who by then would be in a different state. Same story, different day."

Her mother sighed heavily into the receiver. "Oh, it's just so hard. You couldn't understand."

Naomi turned her work and started back. The lace was simple when it came right down to it. A triangular scarf, garter stitch on both sides, lots of knit stitches, no purls at all—meant to be easy. Meant to be made from one skein of laceweight or sock yarn. At least that's what Eliza Carpenter's pattern said. But Naomi would end up having to use different yarn if she kept having to rip it out like this. The yarn would pill before it was even worn.

Naomi had considered giving the shawl to her mother next Christmas if it turned out well, but at the moment, she didn't feel very inspired to give it away.

Maybe she could still redeem the conversation. "Hey, I finally opened the health clinic that I told you about."

"Buzz! Can you turn that down, please?"

"You know, like Dad had at his office. Remember? He'd love that

I'm doing this. I'm going to run it like he did his—I'll have free blood tests and blood pressure checks—"

"*Buzz!*"

That line of talk wasn't getting Maybelle's attention. Par for the course—no one listened to her about the clinic. "We might be getting a new employee at work." Naomi really just wanted to see if her mother listened when she spoke, if she'd remember the last conversation they'd had, when she told her that Pederson was making noises about hiring a third. "I'll end up losing money of course, for a while, until Pederson retires and we consolidate again, so I'm not happy about—"

"Oh, sugar, are you asking for money now, too? If the good daughter needs money, then I don't know how we went wrong. How can a doctor need money? We're retired now, you keep forgetting that. It's not that easy."

Would she go to daughter hell if she just pushed the red button with her thumb and hung up?

Her mother went on. "And ever since you moved to that godforsaken little town . . . You always were your father's daughter, never listening to a word I said. I can't believe you moved there, after everything I've told you about it. Podunk, *hick* town with a chip on its shoulder. When I lived there, no one talked to me, no one acknowledged my existence. And that's because I wasn't Cypress Hollow born and bred. And you *chose* to move there. I'll never understand."

Naomi could feel the pulse at her temples. "Mom. The fact that you happened to live here a million years ago and hated it isn't enough to make me hate it, too. I love it, in fact." She wondered if she was lying.

"And if you need money, well, that'll just—"

"I was trying to keep you updated on my life, Mother. I don't need money. That wasn't the point . . ." Her voice trailed off. Her mother wouldn't get it, and it shouldn't matter as much as it did.

"I just don't see how—"

"Mom, I gotta run. I have to get ready . . ." Crap. What did Naomi get ready for in the evening?

"A date? Do you have a date?" Her mother's voice was suddenly eager.

"Um . . ."

"You do. *Buzz!* She has a date! Oh, sugar, tell me all about it."

Naomi heard a sound of interest on the other end of the line as her stepfather said something.

"Daddy says that you should have a good time."

"He's not my father, Mom," she said on a sigh, unable to stop herself. Sure, Buzz was Anna's father, but even though he was a good father, he wasn't hers. He'd only really known her after her own father died of a heart attack when Naomi was seventeen years old, when she'd been forced to live with her mother for a year until she turned eighteen. Buzz was a heck of a nice guy, but she'd already had the best father in the world, and her mother had been unsuccessful in her attempts to make her forget that.

Her mother's voice was tight. "Fine. Please do not get murdered or raped, and make sure he pays the bill." The click signaled that her mother had hung up without saying good-bye.

Chapter Four

Lifelines are a lifesaver. I like to use floss, myself. It's stronger than yarn, and bringing it out to thread through your stitches always shocks the nonknitters.
—E.C.

Knitting didn't help calm Naomi down. She'd missed two yarn-overs on the last row while talking to her mother, and it was screwing her up. The windows had been shut all day to the summer sun, and it was too warm inside; the wool of the shawl made her hands feel hot and clumsy.

And now, frustrated from her mother's phone call, not knowing what to do but knowing she wanted to *do* something, Naomi played her game. Knowing it was silly, she reached for Eliza Carpenter's book *Silk Road*. Closing her eyes, she let the book flip open, and then she stabbed her finger onto the page. *When stuck in your knitting, there's always an answer around the corner. But you may have to wander to find it.*

That was *it*. Eliza was right again. A walk on the beach, that would do it. Wasn't that why she'd moved here? What a waste; she rarely remembered to go. Throwing her knitting into its basket, she changed into jeans and a T-shirt, put a twenty in her pocket, and left, locking the door behind her. Cash and keys, all she needed in her adopted town.

Her spirits lifted as soon as she started walking west on Clement toward the water. Only two blocks away, the beach had been what sold her on her house when she moved here. She'd had visions then of getting a dog, a big orange shaggy one, walking it every night, nodding to friends she'd made, and fitting in.

But as wrapped up in work as she was, as focused as she'd been on figuring out how to open the health clinic—the dream she'd finally realized a few weeks ago—it wouldn't have been fair to get a dog. And while she knew people in town from treating them as patients, and got along with them well in the office, she still missed the collection of girlfriends she'd had in San Diego and the easy camaraderie of late-night ice-cream talks, and weekend shopping trips.

Naomi had just never liked the city itself, had yearned for something slower, smaller. She'd grown tired of hearing sirens bringing people into the emergency room all night, and hated the way the traffic snarled and growled every time she fought her way onto the freeway. Cypress Hollow had seemed like the perfect answer.

Over the course of Eliza's treatment, the two-year time span of their friendship, Eliza had told Naomi everything about her beloved small town. Naomi knew that Pete Wegman went crazy if he drank tequila, and she knew that Mildred and Greta were the true town doyennes, their blue hair and fancy umbrellas notwithstanding. Eliza had also told her that Cypress Hollow would someday need a new doctor, and that they'd embrace her with open arms. She'd said that on her first day in town, Naomi would probably make friends she'd treasure above all others for the rest of her life. She'd said that everyone loved one another in her small hometown, and that she should apply to work for Dr. Pederson's private practice if he ever had an opening.

In love with the idea of becoming a small-town doctor, like her father had always wanted to be, Naomi kept her eye out for job openings. When the magic words "Cypress Hollow" appeared in her e-mail notifications, she applied for the position and won it, beating out fourteen other applicants who wanted to practice near the beach. And on her first day working in the office, the chamber of commerce's Don Beadle had stopped by bearing a fruit basket and a request that she move her car, since the street sweeper was coming by and she'd do well to remember that this happened on the third Monday of every month.

As she approached the water, the sunset turned ferocious. Hot pink ribbons and ridiculous splashes of red lit up the pale blue sky. A brilliant orange roasted the underside of the low clouds as the sun hovered an inch over the ocean. Seagulls wheeled above the pier, coming to rest on light poles, and children ran along the edge of the waves, darting back when the foam splashed too close.

Ahead of her by half a block, almost at the line of the sand, was a dark-haired man. Tall. Jeans and boots. Great backside. Naomi stumbled on a piece of broken sidewalk as she remembered: Rig was in town. Her one and only one-night stand was probably somewhere nearby, right now. Embarrassment warred with a low-grade excitement—was it him? Did she want it to be?

The man turned, and his profile was unfamiliar. She should feel grateful for that, right?

As Naomi passed the gazebo in the small grassy park across the street from the beach, she raised her hand in greeting toward the two women knitting on a bench. They smiled back and one waved, one called out something that Naomi couldn't quite hear. Naomi knew their faces, but not well enough to put names to them, and even though she longed to stop and touch their knitting, to talk about yarn, she was overcome by shyness, so instead she just gave them her biggest smile and hurried on.

As soon as her back was to them, Naomi's smile fell, and she pressed her lips together in frustration. If they'd been in her office, if they'd been patients, she would know what to say, how to be comfortable with them.

Knitting friends. Wouldn't that be nice?

Well, she'd had Eliza. No one could ask for much better.

Crossing High Street, she pulled back her shoulder-length brown hair with the rubber band she kept around her wrist for exactly this purpose. She hated the feeling of the curls hitting her in the eyes, and wondered for the hundredth time if she should just cut it all off.

Hitting the sand's edge, she slipped off her tennis shoes and parked them next to some ice plant. The sand was still warm, but when she got closer to the water, she could feel the cool wet sand an inch or two underneath the dry.

Naomi felt the muscles in her neck relax for the first time all day.

Eliza had been right about this. And about the knitting. Eliza had told her that the Cypress Hollow beach was the prettiest in all of California, and that knitting would save her sanity. Both statements had turned out to be true. Naomi had never seen a horizon like this, the breaking waves beating a perfect rhythm against the soft sand, and if it weren't for going home every night to her knitting, she'd feel even lonelier than she did already.

Small white terns darted in and out of the foam at the edge of the water. They moved as quickly as her thoughts, keeping her company as she walked.

The sun dipped almost all the way into the dark blue water, and just a sliver of orange floated on the ocean's surface. From the road out of sight, to her left, she could hear the occasional car going down High Street and taking the turn where the coastline came back, curving in toward itself along Beach Road. Voices carried to her ears over the dunes, a child's cry, a snippet of laughter.

Turning around earlier than she usually did, she headed back toward the pier and caught the last orange flare from the sun being swallowed by the sea. An elderly couple, arm in arm, nodded to her as they crossed paths. Two small boys shrieked their way across the dunes and darted around the pier pilings. Even the terns moved two by two.

But down there, just at the edge of the foam, stood one white heron. Alone. Proud. It looked content to be exactly where it was, and Naomi straightened her shoulders.

This was a good place to be.

When she reached the base of the pier, Naomi climbed the steps up to the street above, trying to make her legs feel long and heron-like.

"Watch out!" a man yelled. She looked up to see Rig racing forward, his arms outstretched. "Milo!"

A small child rode his bike directly into the path of an oncoming car.

With a screech of brakes, the purple SUV lurched to a sudden stop, but not quite fast enough—it hit the child, sending him to the pavement with a thud.

Chapter Five

It's natural to feel a touch of fear when knitting lace.
—E.C.

There was a moment of strange silence before the SUV's door flew open and the child gathered the breath to cry, and then all hell broke loose. Naomi sprinted forward as Rig raced into the middle of the street. The driver tumbled out of the purple SUV and slammed the door on the cursive writing that spelled PHROSTINGMOBILE. The owner of the local bakery, Whitney Court, wore a short, poofy black dress and ridiculously high heels. She put her hands to her mouth, her eyes wide.

"Did I kill him?" Whitney asked. "Oh, God, did I kill him?"

Naomi shook her head and brushed past her. "If he's screaming, he's breathing."

And he could certainly breathe—the kid was wailing bloody murder. Rig fell to his knees next to the boy. "Milo, are you hurt?" He moved his hands up the child's arms, then down his legs.

"No, don't touch him, don't move him," said Naomi. "You," she said to Whitney, who still stood next to her car, apparently frozen in horror. "Call an ambulance. Okay, let's check him out."

Rig barely glanced in her direction and then turned back to the boy. "Milo, buddy, I know you're upset, but quit crying for a second. I need to ask you to show me how your body works."

Milo caught his breath between screams. He hiccupped, giving the man an interested look. "What . . . do . . . you . . . mean? My body?"

"Can you wiggle your toes and move your feet?"

"No, keep him still," said Naomi, leaning over the boy.

Rig unsnapped Milo's helmet. He took it off, running his hands over the boy's head. "Milo, can you move your toes?"

"Yep . . . *hic*." Milo waggled them in his sandals.

"And can you show me seven fingers, buddy?"

Naomi held up her hand. "You need to stop. He could be injured internally. Please, we need to examine him without *moving* him."

"Really, I got it," he said, but his voice sounded shaken. "Milo, seven? Can you show me?"

The boy solemnly held up two fingers.

"Oh, God," wailed Whitney, her cell phone in hand. "He hit his head, didn't he? I broke him!"

"That's two, buddy."

"I was trying to . . . *hic* . . . trick you, Uncle Rig." Milo put up the other hand, showing five extra fingers. "That's seven."

"Hey," started Naomi.

"Let's get everyone out of the street." Rig stood and then reached down, picking Milo up under the arms. He held the boy with one arm, and with the other he picked up the bike. "Come on, big guy. You're okay now."

"I told you not to move him!" Naomi hurried to follow them. Why wasn't he listening to her? He was a doctor, for Chrissake. He should know he could hurt Milo without even trying. "Until he's examined, keep him still . . ." Her voice trailed off. Rig was already on the sidewalk, the bike at his feet. He held Milo against his shoulder. Curled into the man's bicep, the boy looked like he was about five, and thank God he wasn't presenting any obvious injuries.

But that didn't mean there weren't any.

"Would you mind very much if I looked at him, too?" Naomi tried a new tack. She smiled as broadly as she could. "I'd love to just make sure he's okay."

"My uncle's a doctor. For people," said Milo from Rig's shoulder. "Not for animals. If he fixed animals, then he'd be a vet."

Naomi shook her head to clear it, her smile slipping. "Yes. Sorry. But, Dr. Keller . . ."

Milo sniffled and burrowed deeper into his uncle's arms.

"But what? And come on, shouldn't you really call me Rig?" His smile was slow and warm.

She'd remembered him as good looking, but damn, she'd forgotten exactly *how* good looking he was. Some of the local young cowboys and ranch hands who came into Tillie's were handsome, young and sweet and pretty faced. Rig wasn't sweet looking. He was wearing lived-in jeans and a dark black T-shirt that strained over his chest. He was big and broad, his face still sporting that stubble. He looked like a cigarette ad from the sixties.

Milo wiggled in Rig's arms.

"You see?" said Rig and smiled back. "I appreciate your offer, though."

"He . . . could have a concussion."

"I don't think he does. Did you call that ambulance?" Rig asked Whitney.

"Y-yes. Do you really think he's okay?" said Whitney. She was pale, the blusher on her cheeks standing out, bright pink, a fine sheen of sweat at her hairline.

"I know he's fine. I saw it happen, and it wasn't your fault. Milo here," Rig patted Milo's back, "didn't look both ways. He just learned to ride his bike, so we're new at this. Two doctors on the scene, though, how lucky can you get?"

"But I *hit* him." Whitney sank down onto the planter box on the sidewalk. "I can't believe I hit him. I could have run right over his little body. Oh!" She put her hand over her mouth, the white of her face turning a pale green.

"Go ahead and cancel your call. We don't need an ambulance."

"Dr. Keller, I'm afraid I have to insist that—," said Naomi.

Rig didn't look at her as he kept talking to Whitney. "You didn't really hit him. You touched the back of his bike, practically a love tap. He hit the ground harder yesterday when he ran into a light pole. Kids bounce, huh, Milo?"

"I bounce!" yelled Milo.

"Are you sure? Really sure?" Whitney's face was a mixture of relief and tears.

"I'm sure," Rig said, and his voice was warm. Reassuring.

Naomi had to try one last time. "Can I at least help you get him home? To make sure that he's—"

"We're fine."

His voice was just as reassuring when he spoke to her, and she wanted to protest. She wasn't the one who needed help; that little boy needed to be looked after. "Peer to peer, then, I think he should probably take it easy the rest of the day. Don't you think?"

Rig's smile turned into something that looked like a grin. "Yeah, well, maybe I doctor differently than you do. A hug is the best medicine, right?" He kissed the side of Milo's head. "And besides, we have an appointment to play Frisbee on the beach. After he trumps me at that, we'll both have a lie-down; does that make you happy, Doc?"

"No." She shook her head. "Not really."

"You want to come?"

Naomi raised her eyebrows. "What?"

"To play Frisbee."

Milo turned his head and peeked at her again. "I throw good."

"God, no."

Milo hid his head again. Oh, crap. Her too-quick phrase wasn't meant for him—it was meant for his uncle. She started to raise her hand as if to touch him, but then she stopped, letting her hand drop. She didn't want to scare him. "I'm sorry, Milo, I bet you're great at throwing. But not today, thank you."

Rig shrugged and hitched Milo up a notch at the same time. "Suit yourself, Doc. It's good to see you again." His eyes were exactly the same dark brown as her favorite pair of ebony knitting needles, rich and warm. "And hey, I should probably also tell you I'm the new doctor in your office. Pederson and I finished up the paperwork yesterday. So I guess I'll be seeing you at work." He grinned and picked the bike back up with his free hand, looked both ways, and crossed the street.

Naomi gasped, feeling as if the wind had been knocked out of her. Pederson *wouldn't* have. He wasn't even in town, was he? It was true that when she'd been hired, it had been with a phone call and a faxed contract. Small practices sometimes played it looser.

But without consulting her? Pederson was the primary, and she knew he could make those decisions without her, but she'd bought in, and she was his only partner. He should have . . . Damn. Naomi balled her hands into fists.

Tomorrow she would figure out how to deal with it, tomorrow she'd fix it. Now she only wanted to be home with the afghan pulled over her knees, her needles in her hands, the stitches slipping like—

On second thought, oh, *hell* no.

With a burst of speed that felt foreign but right, Naomi sprinted across the street after Rig. She startled an elderly man driving a modified golf cart who shook his fist as he trundled by, yelling something she couldn't quite make out.

"Hey," Naomi said loudly. "What did you just say to me?"

"Go take the Frisbee up to the sand-dune hill, right there, okay, buddy?" Rig directed Milo which way to go, and then turned to Naomi. "I'm sorry Pederson didn't tell you himself."

"How could you finish up paperwork with him when he's out of the country?"

"Faxes and e-mails. We're livin' in the future." His smile was rueful. "And I had no idea my Naomi in Portland was the same as Naomi Fontaine, his partner. How would I have known that?"

She gaped. "*Your* Naomi? It was one night."

"One fucking great night."

On many levels, yes. "Whatever. You don't just come to a town and step into a *business* like that. My practice!"

He held up his hands. "I'm not trying to be a threat—"

"Stop." Naomi stepped forward and stood on a small rise in the sand. They were eye to eye, and words, instead of stuttering in her throat, came easily for once. "Look, guy. This is my town. This is my *life*. If Pederson's made a decision I can't reverse, then I'll handle it, but you should know one thing: What happened between us has nothing to do with my business. I love my practice and my patients more than . . . more than anything else I can think of, actually. I won't let that be compromised in any way, by anyone. No matter how hot that someone is."

The corner of Rig's mouth quirked.

"That's not a compliment," Naomi went on. "I'll do anything to protect myself and my way of life. Now go play with your nephew who should be lying down in a quiet room, go jar his little head by tossing around a Frisbee, and I'll talk to Pederson tomorrow. We'll figure whatever this is out. Just please know this: my work is everything to me." Her voice shook, just a little. This was so important—*this* was why she never mixed business with pleasure, and why she shouldn't have at that damn conference. "That can't change."

Rig nodded, and his voice was completely serious. "I get that. And I feel exactly the same way about my practice. And my patients."

"Fine then. Okay." She took a deep breath and straightened her shoulders before giving him a firm nod and then turning.

As Naomi crossed the street again, she felt her knees, so sturdy just seconds ago, start to quake. Her limbs felt made of rubber, almost as if she'd been the one hit by the car.

Whitney was still seated on the low planter. She sniffled and dried her eyes. "I should move the PhrostingMobile, I guess." She stood and abruptly grabbed Naomi's hand. "He's really okay?"

Naomi thought of all the ways the boy might not be okay. He could be bleeding internally. Even with the helmet on, he could have a concussion that wouldn't present for another hour or so.

But then she looked at Whitney's face, still green with splotches of pale pink. "I'm pretty sure he won't die," she said. Whitney looked more stricken and she realized she'd said the wrong thing. Again. "And his uncle's a doctor."

"Then he knows what he's doing, right?"

Naomi leaned against a street sign; her legs still felt unsteady. "I sure hope so."

Chapter Six

Sometimes, we are tempted to think of our knitting as a potential family heirloom. That puts a little too much weight on the yarn, don't you think? Right now, it can be merely your work-in-progress.
—E.C.

In his brother's backyard, Rig flipped a burger on the grill and then took a moment, turning in place to look around. When was the last time he'd barbecued outside with his family on a perfect summer evening? Too damn long. It had to be more than a year since he'd been off the rigs long enough to get to Cypress Hollow.

He wondered how long Naomi Fontaine had been in town. Shit, he should have known. When he'd been signing the paperwork, the thought passed through his mind—what if this Naomi was the one at the conference in Portland? Then he'd dismissed it. There were thousands of small practices in the world, she wasn't the only doctor named Naomi. They hadn't, during that incredible night, said one thing about their home lives. For all he knew, she was married with nine kids and a minivan.

Admittedly, today probably hadn't been the best way to spring it on her. He knew Pederson hadn't told her anything—he'd told Rig he hadn't been able to get in touch with Naomi yet. But Milo had set it up by jumping in front of that car, and he couldn't walk past her again, like he had in the diner.

He peeked under the edge of one of the burgers—not ready yet. Five-year-old Milo, who'd grown tall as a weed and just as skinny, zoomed by, and shot Rig with an unloaded water pistol. His earlier fall hadn't slowed him down a bit, and Rig knew he'd be shaking sand out of his ears for the next day—his nephew liked to tackle him in the dunes after a good Frisbee throw.

Milo came running back, yelling, "Oil rig! Oil rig!"

"I'm making burgers right now. Not a good time."

"I wanna play oil rig! I'm the worm!"

Rig checked the meat—it'd be fine for a minute. He moved away from the grill and grabbed his nephew, lifting him up and turning him upside down. Milo was getting heavier. At what age was he going to be too big to play this game? He lifted Milo up, bit by bit, holding him by the ankles. "What do you think, worm, you ready to get hoisted by the crane?"

"Worm! Worm!" Milo was always delighted when he got to play lead hand, the lowest position on an oil platform. Either that or he wanted to play driller, the head boss, and as far as Rig could tell, the game was the same no matter what position Milo took—Rig had to play crane operator and lift Milo up as high as he could before swinging him around by the ankles. Rig had been a doctor on the platforms a long time, and as far as he could tell, cranes never flew around 360 degrees and then kept going, but it thrilled his nephew, so he ignored the logistical problem.

"Hold on, worm! I think the crane is broken! You might fall—oh, no, it's gonna be bad . . . You're probably going to need a doctor.

Good thing I'm here!" Rig turned in place as fast as he could, and Milo screamed in delight.

"Hey, be careful!" Jake Keller came out the back door carrying a plate. "Don't drop him!"

"I'm not going to drop him." Slowing the spin, lowering Milo gently, Rig let him put his hands onto the ground so that they made a wheelbarrow for a second, and then Milo rolled onto his back and turned into a dying spider, his other favorite thing to do. He kicked, twitching his legs and arms in spasms.

It was late, and the sun was sinking rapidly, but the sky was still bright blue straight overhead. Jake put down the plate of sliced to-matoes and onions. No lettuce for the Keller men—just a waste of time and space, and they all knew it.

"He started it," said Rig, turning back to the grill. He picked up the spatula and pointed it at Milo. "Pow! You're a really dead spider now."

Milo squawked and flapped, and then ran toward the monkey-puzzle tree.

"Watch it! You could have hit him with hot grease."

Rig sighed. "I'm not throwing burning oil at your son. Never have, never will. Not unless he deserves it."

"Or you could get it on the clean concrete. Don't drip."

Was his brother serious? They were outside, for God's sake. "Really, dude?"

"Where's Dad?" asked Jake, sounding irritable.

"Dunno. Probably asleep in his room."

Jake straightened the red-and-white cloth on the picnic table. "You know, we poured that concrete ourselves. It's nice. I want to keep it that way."

Ah, there it was again. Rig knew better than to argue with his brother when the word *we* was involved. If it was something Jake had done with Megan before she died, it wasn't going to change. They still kept the baby-proof locks in place, even though Milo was old enough to know not to eat the ant traps under the bathroom cabinets. Milo knew how to undo the catches, and now he could throw his own trash away under the kitchen sink.

Jake still kept Megan's clothes in his closet. Rig had only asked once if he wanted help with cleaning it out, and Jake had nearly taken his head off.

She'd died three years ago, but Rig felt like the funeral was yesterday. Rig missed his sunny, always-laughing practical joker of a sister-in-law. Milo missed the idea of a mother, but Rig could tell his memories of her were almost gone. And Jake . . . The shadow of grief he'd seen that day in Jake's eyes had almost killed him.

But while Jake could remember the good times now, and even though every once in a while he laughed, usually when he was looking at Milo, the house was still a shrine to Megan, down to the last dishes she'd left in the drainer. Jake made them dry their dishes by hand and put them away, rather than using the rack, and he wouldn't use the coffee cup with the cow on it that sat in the drainer even though it had been his favorite, because he wouldn't move a damn thing she'd put down. Sometimes Rig wished that something would happen to mess up Jake's way of life and the perfect rows of vacuum marks on the living room carpet.

When their father had moved in six months ago after the heart attack, he'd hoped that it would shake things up in Jake's house, but Frank seemed to have slotted himself into the running of the house without creating a ripple, and the *People* magazines Megan had purchased before she died still sat in the dusty magazine rack in the bathroom. He knew it couldn't be easy for his brother to start moving on, and God knew there was precedent. When their mother had died ten years previously, Frank hadn't gotten out of bed for almost six months, and it had taken a combo of therapy, strong drugs, and some serious ass kicking from his sons to get him back to living life with any level of interest.

"You're on fire," said Jake.

"Huh?" Rig had spaced out. "Shit!" One of the patties had flared into flame, and the others were threatening to go the same route. Hitting it with the spatula until the flames died, then moving it onto the plate, Rig said, "Well, that one's mine. I don't mind a little char."

"Carcinogenic, you know," said Jake, his eyes following Milo as he climbed the small tree. "Careful, buddy. Not more than four branches, you know the rule."

Milo gave a high-pitched squeak and dropped backward out of the tree, doing a flip in the air and landing on his feet. "Ta-da! Did you see that, Dad? Did you see that, Uncle Rig?"

Rig whooped. "That ruled, buddy!"

Jake sighed. "Be more careful next time. I don't want you landing on your head."

Rig flipped another burger. "He landed on his feet. He's fine."

"I had to scoop up a kid the other day who fell off the parallel bars at his school. Broke his back in two places. He'll be lucky to piss by himself when he gets out of the hospital machinery he's cranked into."

"That boy's not Milo."

Jake nodded. "Damn straight. Not gonna be, either."

"Hey, thanks for asking about my first day in town. It was fantastic." Rig slid the last burger off the grill and onto another plate.

Jake gave a dry laugh. "Yeah, sorry." He put the burgers onto buns and lined up the mustard and mayo. "Hang on a sec. Dad! Milo! Dinner's on!"

Milo squeaked again, his recent favorite form of communication, and bounced onto the long picnic bench next to his uncle.

"So," said Jake, and Rig could see the effort he was putting into cheering up. "How did your first day go as a new town citizen?"

"I'm going to have to work with the hottest one-night stand I ever had."

Jake said, "Rig!"

Milo bounced once, hard, and said, "My nightstand is next to my bed. Where's yours?"

Chapter Seven

Patience is a virtue in life, but it's a godsend when knitting.
—E.C.

T he screen door to the kitchen flapped as Frank Keller came out, a highball in his hand. "Boys! Is it time for your patriarch to say grace?"

Rig sighed in relief. "Saved by the dinner bell."

Frank set his drink on the picnic table and raised his arms. Milo covered his eyes with his hands. "Dear Lord our heavenly father," Frank intoned. Rig waited for it. "*Damn*, you make good cows for eatin'. Thanks, God. Amen."

Rig knew his father actually meant his verging-on-sacrilegious prayers. He loved the boys' dead mother, God, his boys, and any drink that came with salt, in that order. Nothing to be done about him.

Rig felt a deep surge of something that felt like joy, and a pushing at the back of his eyes, like a yawn that wanted to happen. He took a deep breath and turned it into a grin instead. It was so *good* to be home.

He waited for Milo to be done with the ketchup before finally answering Jake's question. "Does everyone in this town really know everyone else? And are they all always that *nice*?"

"You've been here often enough over the years—I've introduced you to plenty of nice people. It's just a good little town."

"Emphasis on the *little*. There are probably fourteen people I haven't met, and that's including the kids who were in school. I don't even know how this town supports two doctors."

"You're exaggerating. Lots of people to treat." Jake finally had the trace of a real smile on his face. Maybe now that he was back in town his brother could relax a little bit, have some fun. It had been a long time.

"No, I'm not. Every single person I met, which was, as I mentioned, everyone, knew you. Had some story about you. I swear to God, most of them say they were saved by you from a burning building at some point or another."

Jake grinned. "Nah, buildings don't burn much anymore."

"Okay, then you saved their favorite cat from up a tree."

Inclining his head, Jake said, "I'll give you that one. I've saved lots of stupid cats who would have come down on their own given a can of tuna at the bottom of the tree and enough time. We even got a goat out of a tree the other day, I kid you not. Other departments mock. But we live to serve in the Cypress Hollow Fire Brigade."

"Can I have a cat, Dad?" asked Milo, mustard all over his face.

Jake shook his head slowly and patted his son's head. "You know we can't get a cat. Grandpa's allergic."

Rig frowned. "Since when are you allergic, Dad?"

Frank looked alarmed. "I am? That's too bad. I always liked cats. So did Margene, didn't she, boys? Always a cat or two knocking around the garage, bringing in a lizard or a half-dead bird."

Milo looked riveted. "Half dead? Which half?"

"Zip it, Dad," said Jake, gesturing with his burger. "You're just going to make it worse."

"Zip what?" said Milo. "I don't *get* it." He slapped his mustardy hand on the table and dropped his pickle.

Jake said, "I'm sorry, buddy. I was just trying to tell your grandpa to step off."

"He's sitting down." Milo looked even more confused.

"Figure of speech," said Jake and gave Milo another pickle. "Here, try this one. How did you get mustard *up* your nose, big guy?"

Milo sniffed. "Put it there."

Rig had a hard time not laughing out loud. This was where he needed to be. He didn't know how he'd been able to stay away so long as it was.

Being a contract doctor to a large oil company had been a bizarre way to use his degree, at first. If a guy broke his pelvis after skidding three stories off a hoist, they brought Rig in by helicopter. And as the years went on, Rig got better and better at it, got used to living out of one big duffel bag, and the roughnecks looked to him for all the medical needs the rig EMT couldn't handle. Only when someone was genuinely sick with a serious illness that required specialized attention did the guys head inland, and they usually cursed him out as they did so. He swore back and pretended not to notice when their eyes got wet. Roughnecks weren't quick to trust, and Rig never took that trust lightly.

He already missed them.

But this was the right decision. Family should come first, that's what he'd been telling the guys all these years. When they retired and went onshore for good, Rig was the first one to tell them how awesome it was going to be. "You can get a cheeseburger whenever you want one. You can give a girl in a bar all your best lines. You can walk up a hill. You can sit on grass. You can sleep and your bed won't sway."

Damn. Rig missed that swaying. But this burger sure was good. And thanks to Elbert Romo, a rancher he'd once pulled a nail out of while he was visiting his brother, who'd introduced him to Dr. Pederson, he was going to be able to stay and work in this small town. It wouldn't be like working the rigs, not in any way that he could imagine, but he could finally have a stable home. Unpack for real. And he could be with his family.

Something rough stuck in his throat. It was a moment before he could say, "I've missed you guys."

Jake looked up from wiping his hands on a napkin, then his gaze dropped to his plate. "We've missed you, too. We knew you were busy, though."

"Yeah," Frank said. "Busy with the ladies." He waggled a gray eyebrow.

"Nah."

Frank laughed. "I used to love the girls who weren't ladies." He paused and then added politely, "Before your mother, of course, who was always a lady."

"You don't get it. There weren't any girls out there, period. Well, that's not quite true. On two of the decks there were a couple of women, but they were spoken for. Big, mean-looking boyfriends. I kept my eyes down and my hands to myself. And I did meet a couple of girls onshore, but I'm just not into anything serious."

"So much for a Keller getting any in this century," mumbled Frank before he got up to wander over to the hammock.

Jake said, "What, are you waiting for perfect?"

"No. Just not interested in a relationship. I'll be a happy bachelor forever. Anyway, you and Dad found perfect and look how you turned out." He smiled to take the sting from his words.

"We didn't have perfect." Jake's face stayed drawn.

"Nah. You did. And I don't need that. I'll just cook burgers with you guys until Milo's sixty."

Milo's jaw dropped. "That's *old*."

"That's idiotic. Why the hell would you want it like that?"

Rig was surprised by Jake's sharp tone. "What do you mean? I thought you of all people would understand."

"I guess I don't. I'm supposed to be the wreck. You're the one who's still supposed to find the love of your life and make everything work out okay. And yeah, how were you supposed to do it on the rigs? And now, how the hell are you going to do it here? There are probably four unmarried women under the age of forty, none of them perfect because this is real life, and lots of single guys to go around. Your odds in Cypress Hollow aren't that great, I gotta tell you."

"Fine by me," said Rig easily. He dropped half a pickle into his mouth and enjoyed the crunch. The air was thicker now, and a sudden coolness was dropping into the garden as the first fingers of fog sneaked over the back gate. "If I date, it'll be casual. Nothing special. And it's okay if I don't date at all." An image of Naomi's curls flashed in his mind. He ignored it.

"So you're just waiting for another Rosie?"

Rosie had been pretty awful, Rig could admit that. It didn't help that Rig had actually thought he loved her. He'd almost proposed when she showed up at the bar they hung out at with a new man, a new ring, and a new tattoo that proclaimed JIMMY, all of which had broken his heart. And hell, he'd known that Rosie had her faults. That the heartbreak he felt was one-hundredth the pain his father and brother had gone through in losing their loves. It would take a lot more than just "better than Rosie" to get him thinking seriously about a woman again. If he ever did.

"Don't worry about me. I'm fine. We'll be the four swinging bachelors until Milo gets married."

"Yech! No way!" said Milo from under the oleander bush.

"Milo!" yelled Jake. "That's poisonous! Get out from under there. How many times do I have to tell you?"

Rig raised an eyebrow. "I think he'd actually have to eat a leaf or two to get poisoned."

"So?" Jake said. "It's only a problem if it happens once, huh? *Now*, Milo!" Taking a deep breath, he went on, "You settled in okay over there at Shirley's?"

Mouth full of his last pickle, Rig nodded. After he swallowed, he said, "Took about a minute to move in. Nice little cottage. Just had to put my clothes in the drawers and my books on the shelf. And hey, my bike fits in her shed, so I won't need to borrow your garage."

A frown creased his brother's face. Rig's hand rose to his own forehead. He was a year older than Jake. At thirty-five, did he have that same deep wrinkle?

"About the motorcycle." The crease on Jake's face got more pronounced.

"Oh, boy."

"You know how much I hate those things."

"I do."

Jake rubbed his temples. "Sure, you're a doctor and all, but do you have any idea what a motorcycle rider looks like at the scene of being hit by a semi? Have you ever witnessed people trying to get a helmet off a rider so they can do CPR when the helmet is embedded in his neck?"

Milo made a *vroom-vroom* noise and raced the ketchup past the mustard. "Want a motorcycle!"

"Dude." Rig glanced meaningfully at Milo.

"Don't worry about him. At least *he'll* never ride one."

Milo squeaked. Then his eyes filled and his body tensed. "Motorcycle!"

"You see?" said Jake. "He already hates them."

"I promise to be careful," Rig said. It was the best he could give his brother. He wondered for a brief second if Naomi Fontaine ever rode a motorcycle. That curly hair would get all messed up, get wild and tangled. And would she hold on tight, or lean with him easily into the curves?

Dumbass. Rig shook his head and started picking up plates as Milo launched himself into one of the full-blown fits he was getting better and better at lately. He loved his nephew, but damn, this was one good reason not to live in his brother's bachelor pad. His ears felt like they were bleeding. The best Rig could do was ignore it and keep clearing up while Jake cajoled, and Milo stiffened more and more, finally dropping to the ground, beating the grass with his fists, crying almost unintelligibly about motorcycles.

With flight in his eye, Frank trundled back into the house, empty tumbler in hand. "I gotta get on the computer. I swear to God you kids never did that."

Rig bet they had. And he bet that his mother had handled it, keeping their tantrums from his father. Keller women were saints, took care of their men, and then they died.

He was way better off not dating than chancing becoming a typical Keller man. He'd do well to remember that when he was around Naomi at the office, too. No matter how pretty that hair was, Rig was putting himself off-limits except for casual dates that didn't lead to anything. Like he'd had with Naomi that one scorching night in Portland. Perpetual bachelordom—it was better this way. Simpler.

His family, three other bachelors, was all that he needed, even if one of them was screaming like an injured sea lion right now. They were everything.

Chapter Eight

Knitters don't lie on purpose, but no one admits the full extent of her stash.

—E.C.

That should do it," said Naomi as she handed the prescription to Mildred, who then gave it to Greta, who put the paper in her purse.

They were her first appointment of the day. Both of them seventy-five if they were a day, they were attached at the hip. They always came in together, and Naomi was fond of them, even if they slowed down her average patient visit time. Eleven minutes. That's what Naomi thought was the ideal length of time to spend with a patient—that was time enough to chat, assess, and examine, if one was moving quickly, methodically, with economy of motion that usually still left enough time to make a connection.

But she couldn't do that with Mildred and Greta. There was always something just a little wrong, a bunion, a twisted ankle, a patch of dead skin, and even though these problems were easily fixed, the ladies liked their chat and didn't take hints to speed things up, even the broadest. Today it was a bout of insomnia. It was noth-

ing compared to the breast cancer Mildred had gone through before
Naomi had even moved into town. She was now eleven years in
remission and going strong.

Naomi went on, "Just one before bed, and I'd recommend not
taking them more than once a week. They're habit forming, but they
work well."

Greta clutched her purse. "You do have addiction in your family,
dear."

Mildred clucked. "I've avoided the gutter this far, I think I'll do
just fine. Now, Dr. Fontaine, what's this I hear about a new doctor
in town? Is he the fella we saw yesterday at Tillie's?"

Well, if the jungle drums had been beating, Mildred would have
heard the news on the first thump. Naomi slipped her prescription
pad back into the drawer. She bet Rig Keller told his patients to
call him by his first name. "I'd love it if you called me Naomi,
Mildred."

Mildred gasped and pressed a hand to her generous cleavage. "My
word! We couldn't do that. You're our doctor."

So much for that bright idea. "All right. But maybe you'll change
your mind. And yes, I'm thinking we might soon have a new doctor
here." For the hundredth time, Naomi wished Pederson would
answer his cell phone. "More important," she said, standing, resist-
ing the urge to usher them out like birds, "when are you two going
to start using Cypress Hollow's first health clinic?"

Mildred's eyes widened. "I don't know about all that. We see
you."

"It would be a perfect place to have your friends come in, have
blood pressure screenings, gather to talk about cancer risk or recovery. I usually staff it in the evenings, and it's always open to the
public when we are. Lots of free periodicals and informational pam-
phlets."

Shaking her head, Mildred said, "Folks in town don't need that.

We have enough gathering places. There's Tillie's and the Rite Spot, and the Book Spire for in between. And if I'm going to gather, I'd rather knit than talk about cancer. My word. That would just be another place for me to lose my umbrella. Speaking of which—"

"It's right here, dear," said Greta quietly. "I have it."

"Ah. Thank you." Mildred beamed at Greta, who bloomed in the gaze. Naomi shuffled her feet to move them, and they bobbed in front of her like slow-moving ducks.

"Would you just like to come look at it? I have time, I could show you right now. There's going to be a free blood sugar analysis later this week. And it's just next door, just a room away. It's the old dance studio . . . I added—"

Mildred interrupted, "But there really is a new doctor in town, then?"

Naomi felt another twinge of anxiety. She'd kept this practice alive for the last year while her partner took himself on three-month trips to places like Antigua and Tanzania. She was used to being in charge, used to answering questions without having to confer with another party.

At least, if it was a done deal, he'd be just an employee until Pederson officially retired. She'd still be in charge.

"Maybe," she said.

Mildred held open the swinging door that led from the back office to the front, and when they'd passed through she leaned heavily against Bruno's reception desk.

"The important question is this: if he's that handsome brute we met yesterday in Tillie's, is he single?" Mildred winked at Bruno, who stared back, straight faced. His pen was still tucked behind his ear, which in Bruno code meant he wasn't ready for talking. He turned back to the computer and tapped something in. Naomi let herself feel pleased for a short moment that the pen behind his ear was from the pack she'd bought at the drugstore—the expensive ones that she knew he loved but wouldn't order because he said the patients always walked away with them by accident.

Naomi cleared her throat. "I went over his CV." The one that she'd found in a quick search of Pederson's desktop, but she wouldn't mention that. "He's definitely well qualified for the position. No one will be disappointed."

"But ladies are already asking me. Is he single? And by that I mean, is he divorced or gay?"

Naomi blinked. "I have no idea." *Boy, was he not gay.*

Mildred flapped a hand. "Oh, you. No help at all. All right, we're off. We're going to Abigail's store next. Did you hear that her employee Sara is expecting? That makes three baby sweaters I have to make before the end of the summer." She took Greta's arm firmly.

But Greta didn't move. She looked up at Naomi. "Do you knit, Doctor?"

Naomi bit the inside of her lip and could feel the *yes* forming on her tongue. She was dying to tell them she did, to finally have someone in town to talk to about her hobby. . .

But then they might want to see her knitting. She couldn't do that. She wasn't a bad knitter, but she was nothing like the experts she saw knitting all over town, and these two were at the top of the knitting in-crowd pile.

"I know how to, but you know me." She laughed lightly. "Never time for anything but my patients. Don't forget to get to the pharmacy before you go home."

"You should come knit with us at Abigail's store sometime," said Greta.

Naomi's heart sang, *Yes, yes, yes.* Why, then, did it make her so nervous she could barely speak? Somehow, making friends in the big city had been easier. Most of her pals had worked with her—doctors like her, who didn't know how to bullshit, who cut to the heart of the matter without any wasted time. Women who weren't offended when she did the same. They were more casually formed, friends who came and went as interests and staff rotations changed. She'd always had a half dozen people on speed dial on her phone—she couldn't call any of them a best friend, but she could call them to go to the movies. Here, every connection made felt so important, so irrevocable.

"We'll see, won't we?" She watched as they wobbled together down the sidewalk.

To go through life together, side by side. What must that be like? Her heart twisted strangely and she asked Bruno for the next patient's chart.

She went on with her next few appointments, making up the time lost to Mildred and Greta, and it wasn't until she had mixed up a mother's name with a daughter's (one needed allergy medicine, the other needed birth control, and neither knew the other was there— it could have been awkward), did she realize the strange feeling in her stomach was nerves. Rig would surely come by today sometime, to get the lay of the land. That would only be natural, and it was nothing to be scared of. Obviously. Then she dropped her pen three times in the next appointment and couldn't find her stethoscope until Bruno helped her. Finally, Bruno told her she should take a break, and she heard the implied meaning: that she needed one.

In her office, sitting in her father's old brown leather chair, she took a deep breath. Eliza Carpenter would have told her to *have fun, with everything*. Easy for her to say. Of course, even sick, Eliza had known how to have fun almost all the time. Once, from her hospital bed in San Diego, where Naomi had treated her for two years for the cancer that eventually killed her, Eliza had grinned and asked her for a favor.

"I want to make a trip into the hills. When I'm out of here."

Naomi had nodded, not sure Eliza *would* get out; the cancer had spread and was invasive.

But sure enough, after Eliza had been released from her second hospitalization, she'd asked Naomi to drive her out to the low hills around the San Vicente reservoir. Naomi's strict rule of never getting involved with patients went right out the window and she felt wildly flattered to be picked. Everyone in the hospital wanted to be near Eliza—Naomi had routinely kicked out orderlies and cafeteria workers who'd flocked to her room, and she couldn't keep track of the number of nurses who wanted to be on Eliza's floor. Many of them were knitters and knew of Eliza Carpenter's fame. But others were just drawn to her because of her sparkling green eyes and the way they lit up with excitement just to have the curtains drawn open every morning. She was electric, and even when sick she was more *alive* than most people were on their best days.

That day, Naomi had picked Eliza up at the small independent-living apartment she'd been staying in for the last few years. They were small, joined cottages, and Eliza said that everyone who stayed there was a knitter, that it was a knitters' retirement home. Naomi hadn't quite believed it, but when she drove onto the property, she saw various light poles and bus benches covered with colorful bits of knit graffiti. A VW bug parked in a space marked for CARSHARE was clothed, roof to wheel wells, in a granny-square car cozy. Four women sat in a circle at a picnic table, all of them knitting, and she drove past a small yarn store attached to the property that was packed with elderly residents.

Naomi helped Eliza load a little folding spinning wheel and tiny stool into her car, and then tucked a bag of fiber behind the passenger seat.

Once they were sitting on a low green rise overlooking the water of the reservoir, clear, bright sunlight spilling around them, Eliza spun as Naomi set out their picnic. Between bites of *caprese* sandwich and sips of her favorite cream soda, Eliza's wheel flew. Naomi knitted a clumsy watch cap as she watched the thin cream-colored yarn dripping from Eliza's fingers like water. By the time they packed to go, as the sun was dropping into the wide bowl of dark water, Eliza had plied two bobbins' worth of cream laceweight yarn.

"Here," she said, "this is my last hand spun, from the sheep I loved best. Make two skeins, soak them, and dry them to set the twist. It will be enough for the simple wedding shawl in the third book."

Naomi had laughed. "I'm never getting married. I may never even manage a second date again."

Eliza looked at her sharply. "What about your mother? She married twice, didn't she? Maybe you're just a late bloomer. You never told me her name."

"Maybelle. Her maiden name was Skye. Why? Oh! Did you meet her, in that short time she lived in Cypress Hollow?" Why hadn't that ever occurred to Naomi before?

"Is she a knitter?"

Naomi laughed. "No, my mother pays people well to do everything they can for her. No matter how many times she ends up getting married, she'll never make a shawl."

Eliza's eyes dropped to the fiber on her lap she was predrafting. The soft wind lifted it, making it dance as she held on to it lightly. "Then make it for yourself, sweet girl, even if you never marry. It'll work as a pretty scarf. There's nothing wrong with that."

Suddenly overcome by a gift of hand-spun yarn from someone like Eliza Carpenter, Naomi said, "I couldn't. I'm not good enough at knitting."

"You are. You have clever fingers. Please, take this. You've made me happy, bringing me here for the last time."

Naomi remembered how bright Eliza's eyes had been, snapping with life and verve. That hand-spun wool, not a piece of knitting as the world would have predicted, was Eliza Carpenter's last finished object. But it hadn't been Eliza's last gift to her.

On Naomi's final visit to her while she was still conscious, Eliza took her hands and said in a whisper, "Your eyes don't belong here. You're not a city girl. The ocean is in your blood. Go to Cypress Hollow. Go, live there. Love there. For me." The way Eliza's hands had gripped her own had felt like a benediction, and Naomi had felt a rush of connection unlike any she'd ever known from a patient. *This* was why doctors had to keep a professional distance. *This* was why her colleagues couldn't remember their patients' names without stealing a glance at their charts.

Eliza had died an hour later. Naomi informed Eliza's inconsolable friend Abigail, who was waiting just outside the door. Abigail had then turned to the other grieving knitters in the cold hallway who'd been whispering prayers into the stitches of their sweaters and socks, and Naomi had taken herself home to mourn. She hadn't yet moved the yarn from the bobbins into skeins to set the twist. She was a terrible spinner, but she knew how to do this much. Tears in her eyes, she wound the skeins from her thumb to her elbow.

But at the end of one bobbin, taped to the actual wood itself, was a piece of paper. She hadn't noticed anything different about Eliza's spinning that day, but then again, she'd been knitting. Eliza had wound fiber all around this so it was completely invisible until now.

Hands trembling, Naomi used her yarn scissors to snip the tape and pull off the paper. She unfolded it carefully.

A ring fell into her lap.

A small gold ring, with a tiny diamond, the sides of which were held in place by what looked like platinum leaves. It was delicate. Perfect.

Eliza's dark script read, *This was my sister Honey's wedding ring. I have many people I love, but very few with the kind of eyes you have. You remind me very much of her, and I'm giving this to you (I knew you'd never have accepted it any other way—forgive my treasure hunt method). Knit the shawl in honor of her (not in memory of me, because we'll be thinking of each other no matter what). Thank you for being kind to me when I wasn't at my best. We are kin, my dear, with knitting in our blood. Wear the ring in joy.*

Naomi had slipped it onto her right hand. It fit perfectly, as if it had always been there. Eliza was right, she would never have accepted a ring from a patient. Ever.

But she'd accept it from a friend. If she was honest with herself, she could admit that she'd felt more connection with Eliza Carpenter than she felt with most people, her own family included. Eliza was blunt almost to a fault when she wanted to make a point, but could talk to anyone, anywhere, with a focus that made the other person feel as if whatever it was they were saying was the most important, the very *best* thing that had ever been said.

When Eliza had told her to knit, she had. And when the idea of moving had come up, remembering what Eliza had said about Cypress Hollow had made it the top town on her list.

And now, Naomi sat in Eliza's hometown, twisting the ring on her finger, looking out the window to the dunes across the street. She was building a practice, yes. But was she building a life?

Her intercom buzzed and Bruno's voice said, "Sugar Watson just canceled—you have twenty minutes until your next appointment."

Thank God for Bruno. He put the right paperwork in her hand, he restocked supplies, he filled cancelation slots, all while checking people in, getting their vitals. Even with his scowl, the patients seemed to love him. And though he rarely spoke, she knew he was key to the smooth running of the practice.

She should tell him so.

Naomi made her way through the office until she was standing behind him.

"Bruno," she started.

He swiveled, clearly startled that she was talking to him. The pen was behind his ear again as he typed, and she wasn't following his nonverbal clue. "What?"

"I just wanted to thank you for everything you do. You're the reason this place runs so well . . ." She stopped as Bruno turned away to retrieve a piece of paper off the printer. "Are you okay?"

"I'm fine," he mumbled as he removed the pen and set it on the desk. Then he turned sideways to fiddle with a loose cabinet knob.

"Really? You seem a little off."

He sighed heavily. "I'm okay."

Naomi kicked herself. She should have noticed something was wrong, but she'd been so busy all day . . . Pulling a small chair around the partition and into his space, she sat facing him. "Tell me what's going on. I'm sorry I haven't asked before."

"It's nothing, Dr. Fontaine."

"And about that, will you call me Naomi?"

He stared.

"I'm sorry that it never occurred to me." God, she sounded like such an ass. "But I'd really like it if you would."

"Okay . . . Naomi." Her name sounded round in his mouth, as if he was trying it out for the first time, which perhaps he was.

"Now, what's going on?" She took a stab in the dark. "Is it a girl?"

He went on staring at her. "What?"

"You know, girl trouble?" Naomi floundered. "Dating woes?"

"I'm gay," Bruno said flatly. "I assumed you knew that."

Several things clunked into place in Naomi's mind, including the man named Peter, who came to collect Bruno for drinks on Friday nights after work. "Oh, shit."

"That's your answer to 'I'm gay'? I'm gonna say that's probably not politically correct."

Naomi grimaced and dug her fingers into her thighs. "No, that's *so* not what I meant. I was just surprised."

"Wow."

"I—," she started. Maybe she could make it right. "So Peter is . . ."

"My boyfriend."

Naomi nodded. "He's very . . . he has nice . . ." What wouldn't sound bad, wouldn't sound as if she was stereotyping him? Shoes? Eyes? Hair?

"Do you have a problem with gay people?" Bruno's scowl was deeper than usual.

"Of course not. I'm glad you are." *God*, she wanted to hit herself in the head. She was glad he was gay? What did that even *mean*?

"Excuse me. I think I'm going to take a break."

"Yes, of course. Yes." Naomi scooted back in the chair to let him out. Then she dropped her head into her hands.

She didn't even know Bruno, did she? Naomi didn't know where he lived, had never hung out with him after work. She didn't know if he and Peter had pets. Lord, they could have kids and she wouldn't know it. That was inexcusable. If she'd ever had to treat him, if he'd ever been in front of her, as her patient, she'd know something about him—they'd have that small connection, the only one she was good at making. But out here, in the front office. . .

Maybe she could get him a gift certificate to something. A spa, something nice. Rubbing her eyes, she sighed. A gift certificate as an apology was ridiculous. It was something her mother would do.

And she couldn't think of anything else.

Chapter Nine

Flirt with your knitting like you'd flirt with a man—flatter it, pay close attention to it, find out its deepest secrets and desires.

—E.C.

Coffee. She needed more. Naomi's brain was screaming for it by the time she hung up with Pederson. It all seemed legit, the hiring, all of it. Pederson was going to pay the biggest percent of his salary, since he was still drawing equally from the partnership while not working. If Rig Keller worked out, Pederson would officially retire, and the new guy could step up and buy his share of the practice. That was, if Naomi approved of him, he said. Pederson had made it clear that she had the final say. "If Keller doesn't cut it, then we can talk about you buying me out. You can choose whether you want him as a partner or not in your own time, but I'll be retiring in the not too distant future, no matter what."

You already did, didn't you? Naomi wanted to ask, but she bit the words back. There was no way she'd be able to afford to buy Pederson out. She made good money, but not *that* much money. She'd had to finance her almost half of the business as it was. And she knew Pederson wouldn't be coming back. He'd called her from Puerto Rico, where he'd just bought a time-share.

The man she'd thought was just a one-night stand *had* to work out. She didn't have much choice.

Her intercom buzzed. "Doctor?" Bruno's voice sounded strangled. "We have a . . . situation in the front."

Naomi spun out of her father's old chair so fast it fell backward with a thunk. She'd never actually had a walk-in emergency, not yet, so they were overdue for one. Images flew through her mind as she ran through the office hall—burn? MI? Asthma attack, or anaphylactic shock?

She pushed through the swinging door into the waiting room at full speed. Bruno knelt on the carpet next to an older woman who was swaying, the curlers in her violet hair bobbing as she put her hands to her lined face. Naomi strained to look over their shoulders to see what they were leaning over.

"My baby, my baby, my *baby*! Oh, save her, please!"

An infant? Shit, they'd need an ambulance for transport . . . Naomi deliberately pushed down the frisson of fear that had always risen when she'd worked the ER—when the doors there had banged open, she'd gotten used to taking a deep breath and then *working*.

"Move aside, please, let me in." Her voice was regulated, even. Professional. "Tell me exactly what happened."

Bruno said, "This is Mrs. Archer, and she—"

"Oh," wailed Mrs. Archer. "I knew better than to give her that pork rib, but she was just starving, and her little eyes begged and begged. *Do* something, *save* her!"

The patient was a tiny brown dog.

A *dog*.

A Pomeranian, Naomi assessed, or maybe a long-haired Chihuahua, with a ridiculous-looking lion cut—fringe at the face and the tip of its tail—and one that wasn't breathing very well. The dog coughed and retched, its glassy eyes bulging. "She's choking?"

"Yes!" screeched Mrs. Archer. "Help her!"

As Naomi knelt and reached for the dog, she said, "You know I'm not a vet, right?"

Mrs. Archer clutched the neck of her purple sweatshirt. "You're a doctor, right? You took that oath! Now *do* something. She's my baby."

Bruno made a choking sound that echoed the dog's, and Naomi knew the only thing stuck in his throat was a laugh.

But the poor dog looked miserable. It was obviously able to breathe around the obstruction, and while Naomi saw the humor in the situation, she felt for the animal. "Let me see her. What's her name?"

"Miss Idaho."

Naomi bit back the smile. "A beauty queen."

"Careful, if you pick her up, just be—"

"I've got her. Bruno, come with me and lay a cover over that low filing cabinet." Naomi carried the hacking dog through the doors and into Bruno's space. No way in hell was she risking getting caught putting the dog on an examining table, but a table-height filing cabinet couldn't hurt, could it?

"Here," Bruno cleared the space and put down the paper. Naomi laid Miss Idaho down, her tiny sides heaving and tears leaking from her eyes.

She pried the small mouth open, grateful that Miss Idaho didn't seem inclined to bite. Naomi recognized Mrs. Archer from walks— she had two other dogs identical to this one, and one of them had once gone for Naomi's ankle. If she hadn't jumped into the rose bush next to the credit union, it would've gotten her. Instead, she'd received an undeserved stern shake of the head from Mrs. Archer and two puncture wounds from the rose bush.

Naomi couldn't see anything in the dog's mouth.

"Can you pull it out?" Mrs. Archer bobbled up and down next to her.

"I can't risk pushing it in farther."

Heimlich, then? As on an infant, with chest thrusts? Naomi risked a glance at Bruno. Staid, solemn Bruno, who never laughed at work, had the corners of his mouth tucked, and his eyes danced with what looked like mirth.

Only way to know was to try. Naomi fitted her thumb just below the wriggling dog's sternum, put her other thumb on top of it, and pushed.

Nothing.

One more time she pressed firmly, and the small piece of bone flew out, smacking Naomi wetly on the forehead before it dropped to the floor, and she was blasted by a sudden rush of fetid dog breath. "Oh, wow. Your dog could use some of those Greenies. Her breath is not quite . . . fresh."

Miss Idaho leaped into Mrs. Archer's open arms and began licking her face. "You saved her!"

"I did." Naomi grinned. "Another happy ending." Squirting liquid soap onto a wet paper towel, she prepped to remove the dog slime from her forehead.

Someone behind her clapped. "Well done," said a low voice that sent a quick shock of electricity up her spine.

Rig Keller.

Shit.

He stood at the swinging door, grinning as if he were a kid about to get on a roller coaster. Naomi had to concentrate on not rubbing off her mascara as she finished cleaning up.

"I apologize: you were busy when I came in and I didn't want to disturb the lifesaving. I didn't know this was what I'd signed up for, but I gotta tell you, I approve." He filled the doorway with his broad shoulders—how had she *not* noticed him coming in?

"What, this? Just another day in the office," said Naomi while drying her brow with another paper towel. She was relieved her voice sounded even. "We just saved a baby."

Bruno nodded with her, solemn again.

Naomi went on, "Mrs. Archer's baby. A real beauty queen, too. A tiny, hairy human baby who suffers from . . . lupidexederma, a *most* challenging skin condition. Also, advanced gingivitis."

Mrs. Archer frowned. "Will my insurance cover this?"

As Bruno took a relieved-looking Mrs. Archer by the elbow and steered her firmly through the swinging door, Naomi said, "I'm sure it will. We'll just bill them directly so you won't have to worry about it."

There. That was taken care of. Naomi blew a curl out of her face. Now there was just the man to deal with.

Rig came forward, his hand outstretched. "It's good to see you again, Doc."

"Naomi, please." That was it, it came out just the right way. Casually. Yes, they could stand here and talk as if they hadn't . . .

She stopped her thought. His hand was huge and cool to the touch and he shook her still-damp one firmly, with just the right professional level of pressure.

He put his hands back in his jeans pockets and smiled. "Naomi."

Jeans? He wasn't planning on actually working today, was he? Although she had to admit that he looked better in jeans than most men looked in expensive suits. The way they clung to his wide, well-muscled thighs. . .

"Coffee! Before all this, I was going to get coffee," she said, waving her hands idiotically. "In the break room, Bruno's probably made some . . ." She turned and led him into the office hallway, not watching to see if he followed.

But the carafe was empty and it needed washing. Normally she left it for Bruno, but not this time. She needed to get that spa certificate sooner rather than later. "I just need to rinse this." She turned the faucet on and felt Rig's eyes on her back. Neither of them spoke over the water, and she used the moment to take a deep breath.

When she'd started the coffee brewing and turned back around to face him, he said, "I hope this is an okay time."

"It's fine. I was on a short break before the walk-in emergency." She couldn't help grinning. A *dog*. "Do you want some?" She gestured to the pot.

"No, thanks. I'm fine. Do you have time this afternoon to go over some things? Maybe show me around? Or should I have called first? Did Pederson call you yet?" Rig jammed a hand into his thick hair, as if he was nervous, too.

She nodded. "I'll give you the nickel tour right now."

Rig looked relieved. Maybe this wasn't easy for him, either. She was, essentially, his boss, and she hadn't known about it till yesterday. For God's sake, his tongue had done things to her that she thought might still be illegal in some backwoods parts of the country. And now she had to be professional. Competent. Well, even if she didn't like it, even if she was furious with Pederson, she could be professional. None of this was Rig's fault. He was just the new guy.

She reminded herself that her father had raised a good doctor, not one who got flustered easily, dammit. She took another deep breath and smiled. Rig smiled back, and she felt something flip in her stomach.

"We don't normally work on animals on top of file cabinets, just so you know."

"Of course not." Rig's smile was like honey, slow moving and sweet. "I find filing cabinets often too high. That was a nice low one, though. Again, great job. I have to admit, I thought you were more of a by-the-book kind of gal, the kind who would have sent her down the street to the vet."

Naomi paused before speaking. She *was* a by-the-book kind

of doctor, and proud of it. She didn't have time to waste messing around with alterna-healing ideas, the kind of East meets West stuff that some of her colleagues were embracing. No. It had to be tested and proven true for her to subscribe to an idea. No chakra-energy centers for her.

Except she'd done the Heimlich on a dog.

She cursed the blush she felt rising. "Well. Yes. Shall we?"

Then she took a deep breath and led Rig around the office, showing him the records-management system, the computerized charts on each patient, the billing area, the examining rooms and their organized closets, and the small lab drop area. Naomi felt his approval with each step. Every time she pulled out a drawer, he asked intelligent questions, and he seemed impressed with the stock of supplies they kept on hand.

Bruno came into the back office carrying a case of paper.

"Bruno!" said Naomi. "You might have already gathered this in all the excitement, but this is Dr. Keller, our new hire."

"Hey," Bruno said, brushing past them.

"But you can call me Rig," Rig said.

Bruno nodded but didn't say anything. He opened a cabinet and started putting away the reams of paper, moving boxes of pens out of his way.

"Bruno's great," Naomi hurried to say. "I mean, he does just about everything around here. I couldn't do it without him. And he's gay!"

Bruno's hand froze in midair, still holding highlighters. Rig coughed.

Naomi wanted a sinkhole to open under her feet. She'd meant to sound cool, breezy, casual. Not like an asshole.

"Bruno," she said as he walked away from the box half emptied on the shelf.

"That plus the amusing but rather disgusting doggy Heimlich you did on my filing cabinet equals this: I'm taking the rest of the day off." He said the words over his shoulder, not waiting for confirmation or permission, and exited through the side emergency door.

Naomi slumped against the counter. "I didn't mean to say that."

"Didn't come out well," said Rig.

"Nope." Naomi sighed.

"Will he be okay?"

"I sure hope so, because I wasn't blowing smoke. He's essential."

"He'll be fine. Anyone who can walk out like that has a backbone, and that's a good thing." Was that a laugh she heard in his voice? She hoped not, because if it was . . .

"What's down this hall?" he asked. "Restroom?"

"Yeah. And . . ." Naomi straightened. She'd make it up to Bruno later, and she'd make it good. But now she had to handle Rig. "And . . . your office. It was Pederson's, but I doubt he'll need it now. You might as well take it over."

The grin almost split his face. "Hot damn. Pederson did say I should use his. You know, I've never really had one of my own. I always used the front seat of rental cars. Or perched high over the ocean in small metal rooms with bad lighting ."

Naomi opened the second door. "It's . . . well, you can see that he hasn't been around much."

Much? She was being generous. A thick layer of dust had settled on the edges of the bookshelves and on Dr. Pederson's framed certificates. When she'd been in here to find Rig's CV, she hadn't opened the windows. But when Naomi pulled back the curtain, an actual cobweb was draped over the glass.

"Oh, God, this is awful. We have a cleaner, of course, but he always said for her not to go into his private space, and I haven't had any need to." Naomi brushed her hands off, slapping away the coating of dust she'd picked up just by pulling out the man's chair. "I think I've . . . been in a bit of denial about him coming back.

Somehow I believed him every time he called to say he'd be back in a couple of weeks."

Rig, still smiling, pushed open the casement window. "Ah. That's better. When was the last time you saw him? In person?" Rig's dark hair fell forward as he looked outside. The man needed a haircut. Doctors didn't have hair like that unless they had a nickname that started with Mc and starred in a television hospital show.

Naomi blinked, hard, and brushed off a chair with a piece of Kleenex. "If you'd asked me yesterday, I think I would have said about a month. Being in here, I'm kind of thinking . . . It might have been Christmas. I saw him at church, and that's the only time of year I go."

"But it's the end of June."

Naomi shrugged.

"Wow. And you've been paying the bills with just your practice?"

"Mine, and I try to see as many of his patients as I can. As many as will see me. Some of them won't."

Rig came around the side of the desk so that he was in front of it, nearer now to her. The air got heavy, and Naomi noticed again how he filled up space in a way that seemed to have nothing to do with his height or breadth.

"You've been working a double practice. For six months."

Rubbing the back of her neck, Naomi nodded. Maybe that's why she was always so tired on the weekends.

"What do you do for fun?" He pushed a pile of papers back and perched on the edge of the desk.

"I work," she said as she thought about her knitting basket at home.

"And go to conferences?"

Naomi straightened her spine and tried to make her eyes chilly. Ice. "We won't mention that night. Okay? I wasn't expecting you here, but I'm willing to work with you if you can promise me that you won't mention the conference in Portland. That you won't even *think* about it."

As if she could stop thinking about it for even thirty seconds.

But the air felt clearer, and Rig nodded. "Fair enough. No problem. So what else should we know about each other? Did you always want to be a doctor?"

"It's the only thing I ever wanted to do." She took a sip of the coffee she was still holding, surprised by her own candor. "What about you?"

"Oh, hell no," Rig said. "This was the third thing down on my list to do."

"What were the other two?"

He picked up a pen and stared at it. "I always wanted to work the rigs—I could see their lights from my bed as a kid, and I wanted to *be* there, where they sparkled." He gave a half laugh. "They don't sparkle close-up, I can tell you that. And I wanted to be a cowboy in a rodeo. Only *then* did I want to be a doctor. But I managed to get that first goal in by working as a doctor on the rigs. The cowboy thing, it hasn't worked out yet."

"You were in the Gulf, right? I saw your CV. Why did you quit?" she asked. *Why are you here?*

"I've been trying to get here for years. Ever since my brother lost his wife to breast cancer." He paused and then said, "Wanted to be with my family. What about you? Any kids? Husbands?"

She laughed out loud and then looked at the floor, embarrassed. Did he really think she would have . . . ? "No," she said simply.

"Where are your parents?"

"My mother and her husband live in L.A. My father is dead." Even now, so many years later, it hurt to say.

"I'm sorry," Rig said. "My mother died ten years ago. It sucks, huh?"

It did, but she sure as hell wasn't going to talk about it.

"What about siblings?" he went on. "You have any brothers?"

"No."

"Sisters?"

"What's with the third degree, Hank?" She let the name fall into the room, listening to see if it would land with a whisper or a thud.

His dark eyes widened a bit, and then he blinked. But he waited for her to speak.

"Your CV says Henry Keller. You never went by Henry? Or Hank?"

Rig shook his head firmly. "Never Hank. In college, before the oil derrick work, I was Henry. My brother, Jake, started with Rig years ago, and it stuck." He paused. "*Never* Hank."

"So I'll only call you that when I'm mad at you, then."

"I'm not sure I trust you." But the hint of a smile broke along his jawline, and Naomi realized that she'd successfully teased someone for the first time in what felt like forever. Even if it was him. It felt good.

"Back to siblings," he said.

He was serious about this getting-to-know-you routine, wasn't he? "I have one sister."

"Are you two tight?"

Naomi rubbed the bridge of her nose. "I haven't talked to Anna since Christmas three years ago. She had green hair, two new tattoos, and a boyfriend named Slice who carried a gun. We don't have anything in common except trying to avoid our mother's phone calls."

Rig leaned back. "That's the saddest thing I've ever heard."

"Wow. You haven't heard many sad things, have you?"

He looked past her shoulder out the window and across the street to where a low sand dune rose. Beyond that, the edge of the pier was visible. His eyes were as dark as the water. "Nah. I've heard 'em."

Naomi didn't know where to look or what to say. She didn't have the right words. She never did. So it fell to her to change the subject. At least she was practiced at doing that.

"You have nice eyes," she blurted and immediately felt the color in her cheeks rise. *Shit*. "I mean, I'm not trying to flirt with you." Oh, God, it sounded worse said out loud. "But they're nice." She gulped audibly as she tried to stop her runaway train of a mouth.

But then Rig smiled, and it was like the sun coming out from behind a cloud. "Thanks. Hey, where does that door go?" He pointed out of the office toward the door that led to the health clinic.

Naomi felt a rush of relief. He was going to let it go. "Nowhere. I mean, somewhere, yes, of course. But I'll show you tomorrow, is that okay? You'll make yourself at home in here? I have a couple of things I need to catch up on before my next patient, and Bruno won't be here to help me because I'm a moron."

He laughed and Naomi let herself out of Pederson's, no, *Rig's* office, and made her way to the break room where she reheated her now-cooled coffee. She felt like she'd made a narrow escape—her palms were sweating.

She took a deep breath and leaned back against the refrigerator. What did he do to her? She was absolutely going to have to stop acting like a hormonal fourteen-year-old. Only one thing mattered. Only ever one thing. Like her father had always said, "The practice is more than just patients. It's about a community becoming whole. Someday you'll understand." He'd never known Naomi as more than a skinny teenager who studied hard—because she'd had few friends in high school to distract her—and brought home good grades. It still tore her apart to think that he'd died before she'd become the doctor he wanted her to be, the one he would have been proud of. But his legacy lived on—she made sure of it. Her practice, and now, the health clinic, was everything. It was all she needed.

Chapter Ten

If you hear a knitter scream, stitches are on the run.
—E.C.

After touring the office, Rig picked up Milo—Jake had to work an evening shift on overtime, and Frank already had plans that he wouldn't divulge to his son.

"Your dad's got a life, kid, and I can keep a secret or two."

Rig just nodded, not giving his father the satisfaction of the third-degree grilling he probably wanted to play to, and took Milo to Tad's for ice cream where they had sundaes for dinner. He'd sworn Milo to secrecy, coaching him to tell Jake that he'd had lots of protein for dinner, which was technically true.

Rig lay in the hammock he'd just put up in Shirley's backyard, while Milo snoozed off his sugar crash inside. Keller men, all of them, loved a hammock, and Shirley hadn't minded when he'd asked if he could string it between the tall acacias; in fact, she'd said she'd use it herself sometime.

It was still warm from the heat of the summer day, the sky still bright blue, not a trace of fog rolling in yet. Rocking in the hammock, gazing up through the boughs, he'd drifted off himself for a few minutes, and in his dream, he was back in the diner where he'd first seen Naomi, but instead of looking vaguely stressed and worried, she was laughing like she had in Portland, those big green eyes sparkling like dew on grass.

He reached an arm to the ground to lift his soda to his mouth. When he set it back down, the hammock rocked again, and he closed his eyes with the gentle sway.

What was it going to be like, working in such close proximity to a woman like Naomi? Rig was used to rig crews. The people he hung out with tended to spit and swear and get drunk on nights off and end up sleeping under truck-stop picnic tables. Rig could break up an onshore bar brawl as easily as he could set a broken arm. And he'd done both while drunk, come to think of it.

And when it came right down to it, Rig realized that not since his residency had he worked indoors with any regularity. He was used to taking helicopter rides to where his patients were, used to filling up his medical bag with anything he might need on a contingency basis.

This was gonna be cush. With Bruno there to answer the phone and check in patients, a closet full of samples right there at hand, a lab pickup, and a pharmacy and a hospital nearby, what more could he ask for? It was just good luck that Elbert had introduced him to Dr. Pederson, and that it had gone as well as it had.

Everybody had gotten what they wanted. Rig got a home near family, Pederson got a way out of town, and . . . Well, he wasn't sure what Naomi wanted. He could say with some certainty that it wasn't a new partner. Or was that just because it was him?

But he'd change her mind. She liked his eyes. He felt a warm glow in his stomach, remembering.

The hammock stilled, and he closed his eyes again. He let himself remember, just for a second, what she had looked like underneath him. He'd try not to remember it too often, but right now, he didn't stop himself. The way she'd kissed him, that first time, in the hallway outside his room. It had been a promise of so much more, and then she'd delivered. Boy, had she. Naomi had had the upper hand over him that whole X-rated night. He hadn't minded giving it to her, either. She'd been incredible, and she'd seemed more comfortable setting their pace. Until he'd kissed her that last time, when her hands had started to shake. She'd looked confused, and then, somehow upset. She'd bolted after that. Rig had just assumed she had a boyfriend or something at home, and had been hit by guilt. Or something. There'd been a change in her, in that last heated kiss, the one that had burned out of control and left Rig's head spinning.

There, she'd been so confident. Here, she seemed more . . . vulnerable. Well, he supposed anyone on their home turf was different from what they were when they were away.

A scream shredded the afternoon's stillness.

Milo. Rig flipped himself out of the hammock, landing on one of his knees. Had a bee stung him? Had someone gotten in the house?

Milo was still on the couch in the small sitting room, right where Rig had left him sleeping. He was sitting up, his eyes closed, his mouth still open in that ear-splitting scream that seemed like it would never stop.

"Milo!" Rig reached him in three paces. "What is it?"

He took Milo in his arms and rocked him, hard. Milo hid his head in the crook of Rig's arm and stayed there, breathing heavily.

A few minutes passed. Only when Rig felt Milo's shoulders start to relax did he speak. "Bad dream, buddy?"

Milo nodded.

"But it's over now. You're safe with me, you know that?"

Milo mumbled a noise of assent.

"What was the dream about?"

Silence.

"It helps if you talk about it. Makes it smaller. I promise. Give it a try."

"Mom."

"You dreamed about your mom?" Rig tightened his arms around him.

Milo nodded again. "I saw her, but she was far away, and I couldn't see what she looked like. And when I got up to her, her face was a monster." His voice shook. "A bad, mean, ugly snake monster."

"Hold tight, okay?" Rig scooted Milo off his lap.

Milo's fingers scrabbled to grab Rig's T-shirt. "No, don't go . . ."

"I'm only going over to the bookcase, okay?" He grabbed the album he wanted, tucked up on the highest shelf. "Okay, look what I got you."

It was the album Megan had made for Rig—the one of Jake and Megan's wedding. She'd made special ones for him and Frank, family albums. Such a Megan thing to do. He turned to the first picture, an eight by ten, a close-up of the bride. She grinned in that special Megan way, the kind of smile that lit up everyone else within a two-mile radius.

"Now tell me. Does she look like a monster?"

Milo stole a sideways look. "No, that's Mom."

"Dang right. You just had a bad dream, that's all. You want to see more? Go through this with me?"

"Yeah." Milo stuck his thumb in his mouth, and even though Jake had been trying to break him of this habit, Rig let him keep it. Everybody deserved comforting.

They paged through the album, stopping on every picture that featured the glowing Megan. In one where she posed by the water, Rig remembered the moment so clearly it was as if he was there again, watching his brother's happiness, wondering if he'd ever find the same.

"You remember those earrings she's wearing, buddy? Your dad

gave her those diamonds and she wore them all the time. She called them her magic sparkles."

"Don't remember."

"Do you remember a little bit? Her smile?"

"No." Milo turned the page with force, almost ripping the album.

"Easy, Milo. Don't pull." Did he really not remember his mother? Not even a little bit? Rig supposed that a five-year-old didn't retain too much of being two, although he'd thought with Jake's constant talking about her and showing him pictures, that something would have stuck.

"What *do* you remember?" He tried to keep his voice nonjudgmental.

Milo shrugged.

"It's okay. That's why we have pictures, right?" It wasn't okay, not really. But it would have to be.

He looked at the clock. Just after eight. Jake should be here soon to pick up Milo. He also wasn't planning on telling his brother about the late nap. Illicit sugar, thumbs, and naps. He'd give the kid his first beer at eighteen, and then he'd be the perfect uncle.

"Hey, Milo," he said. "You want to look at the pictures I took of you as a baby? I have those here, too."

Milo wiped his wet thumb on his pants. "Yes, please," he said politely.

As Rig pulled the right one off the bookshelf, he heard the distinctive squeal of his brother's brakes.

"Dad!" Milo jumped off the couch and parted the curtains. "He's not at work anymore!"

"Looks like you're right!"

Rig opened the front door and let Milo fly out, running across Shirley's carefully cut grass in his bare feet toward the side garden gate.

Something felt odd to him, and he let the strange feeling sit until he could identify it. As Jake scooped Milo up into his arms, as they turned to walk toward him together, Rig realized what it was.

Family had arrived at his house, and Rig was there to say hello. After years of living in hotels, moving from contract to contract, it felt right to be here, holding the screen door open.

"You're letting in flies," said Jake.

"Oh, yeah?" Rig grinned at Milo as they came up on the porch. "You two are flies? I should have known it by your big compound eyes. I suppose I'll let you flies in."

Jake kissed the top of Milo's head and squeezed him before setting him down. "Getting heavy, huh? You on a growth spurt?" Milo nodded and ran back to the couch to look at the album again. Jake was doing a good job. And Rig hoped like hell there would continue to be a place for him to keep helping.

"You off for the night?"

"Yeah," said Jake, jingling the keys in his pocket. "Got another guy to cover the rest of the shift. Dad would have been fine watching Milo, you know. He does it all the time."

"He said he was busy. And I wanted to," said Rig.

Jake nodded. "Good." A simple word, but it made Rig happy to hear it.

"You want a beer?" he asked.

"Hell, yeah."

As Rig walked into the kitchen to grab the bottles, he heard Jake say to Milo, "Whatcha got there, little guy?"

There was a pause.

Then Milo wailed, the same kind of scream Rig had heard earlier, when Milo had been having his nightmare. He hurried back to the living room.

"What happened . . . ?"

Jake stood next to Milo, clutching both photo albums. "We don't look at these."

What the hell? "But I thought—are you serious?"

"They're put away at our house."

Rig gripped his bottle tighter. "But you talk about Megan, and nothing *else* of hers is put away. He had a bad dream about her, so I thought—"

"You thought wrong. I was going to go through these with *my son* when I thought it was time. I would tell him each story the right way. He'd hear it from *me*." Jake stopped and took a breath. He didn't meet Rig's eyes.

Milo ceased wailing and dribbled off into sad whiffles. His eyes tracked back and forth from his father to Rig.

"I didn't know," said Rig.

"I'm sorry." Jake paused. "But you should have asked, then, instead of acting so impulsively. You know, you've always been like this. Doing whatever you feel like. Jumping out of helicopters. Rock climbing. Parachuting. Moving into town with a week's notice."

"But I told you, I just wanted to—"

"Things in my life aren't as easy as they are in yours. How long are you going to rent this place, anyway? You say you're staying, but how do we know that? You've never been around, not in Milo's whole life. Why now? This isn't your—"

Home. Jake didn't say it, but Rig heard it. Clenching his jaw, he said, "Fine. Message delivered. Copy. But you should know I'm not going anywhere. I'm here for you guys."

Jake rolled his eyes, but looked down at Milo, extending his hand. "Let's go home."

Milo, who had been standing on the couch, unlocked his knees and dropped, face-first, into the cushions. His narrow back shook.

Rig went back out to the hammock, leaving his brother to care for his own son. Screw Jake. He'd meant the best, and he didn't have to prove anything.

He took both beers with him.

Chapter Eleven

Sweaters and socks and hats are all good things to make. But every once in a while, indulge in the comfort of the weight and warmth of a blanket growing larger on your lap.

—E.C.

It felt good for Rig to go to the office the next morning, to *do* something. He went in extra early to find Bruno already scowling at the computer screen. On a whim he said, "Let's go get breakfast." Bruno took a moment before removing the pencil from behind his ear, then he looked up and said, "Yeah."

An hour later, they were back, both of them ready to go. Rig pushed open the office's door, glancing at his watch as he did. "Eight forty-five on the *dot*," he gloated. "Not bad!"

"I still can't get over that scorpion story," said Bruno, pushing past him to get behind the desk. "That must have been one wild night, bro."

Rig nodded. "It was also a really long time ago. We all do things that we regret, you know? We don't always remember the rules in the heat of the moment. You know, your guy Peter is just like my five-year-old nephew, testing his boundaries. He'll come around."

"Thanks for breakfast." Bruno grinned back at Rig, and he was pleased to see that Bruno looked *happy*. Breakfast was all the man had needed. Breakfast and being asked about himself. Really, Rig figured that's what everyone wanted.

Bruno handed a file to Rig. "You're pretty open-minded for a guy from the Gulf, you know?"

"What did you expect, some redneck asshole? Just because I wear shitkickers?"

Bruno shrugged, then nodded. "Well, thanks." He paused. "I guess I should talk to Dr. Fontaine."

Rig laughed. "She felt awful about what she said, the way she said it. If I were you, I'd just wait until she comes to you to apologize. Now, I'm going to—" As he turned around, he noticed that the swinging door to the back office was ajar. A face withdrew, and the door shut quickly.

He almost knocked Naomi over when he went through. She turned and pretended she was busy with something in a drawer. Then she accidentally whacked her hand on the drawer as she shut it.

"Dammit!" she said, cradling her hand.

Maybe the best defense was a good offense. "Insta-karma?"

"I wasn't eavesdropping." Her voice was low, and her cheeks flamed.

Rig took a deep breath. Naomi Fontaine couldn't be anything more to him than a coworker. His boss, in fact, until he could buy in. Even though she was sexy as hell with those wind-blown dark curls, there was something a little too . . . secretive about her. Rig didn't do secrets, and he'd lay good money on it that that was what he was to her: a secret, best forgotten.

Besides, he'd dated coworkers before, and it was usually a mistake.

But man, the way she'd treated that little dog, when she could easily have been affronted by being asked, that had been great. She could have sent the old woman down the street to the vet who had a big sign hanging on Main Street. The way Naomi had leaned over the dog and scratched its ugly little head when it was breathing well again, and the way she'd lied about billing the lady—that was sweet, kind, and well, hot.

But there was no way he should be attracted to her. Not now. He shouldn't even be thinking about her.

Then why was he moving to be closer to her? He didn't give himself time to answer the question.

"I apologize for talking about you to Bruno. I didn't mean anything by it," he said. Up close, she smelled like soap and sweet flowers. Gardenia, maybe. His head swam for a second and he shut his eyes to clear his thoughts.

"I don't need you to tell me when I need to apologize to someone, Hank."

He'd let that one go for what she'd overheard. But Christ have mercy. She wasn't doing a very good job of hiding those curves under the white coat.

"I'm sorry. I meant no offense. I was cheering up Bruno, but I went overboard, I guess. I just wanted my first day to start off on the right foot."

Naomi looked as if she was going to say something smart-assed, something to cut him down to size. Rig braced himself. But instead, she said, "How did you cheer him up?"

"I don't know. Coffee usually helps everything, so I bought him some of that. And eggs with a bagel on the side. And he didn't say no to that huge Rice Krispies bar at the counter."

"So you just fed him?" she asked incredulously. "That's all it took?"

Rig frowned. "And we talked. That's usually all it takes, right?"

Her eyes, green as sea glass, lifted to his as she shrugged.

"Interpersonal relations not your bag?"

She surprised him again, this time by laughing. "Believe it or not, I try." She again shook out the hand she'd knocked against the drawer and looked away.

Rig said, "Oh, I'm sure you do just fine," but he barely heard the words. She was close to him, just a foot away, and he felt intoxicated. *Danger, danger.* His head screamed at him to stop, but his hand moved forward of its own volition. He watched it move as if it were someone else's. He took her hand in his, opening it, palm up.

Why did he want to comfort her so much?

He heard an indrawn breath, and he wasn't sure if it was his or hers. It didn't matter. Her hand was small and impossibly soft, and he felt a knot forming on the back of it. Just the tips of her fingers were rough, as if she used them a lot. He doubted there was that much suturing to do in this town—what else was she doing with them?

Their eyes met again, and the way the bright summer sunlight streamed in through the window behind her, lighting her long brown curls to an almost maple color, made any more rational thought impossible.

Rig lifted Naomi's hand to his mouth. Until it got there, he had no idea what he'd do, but when her fingertips were close to his lips, he knew. He first kissed the injury, already bruising. She gasped. "What are you—"

"This is beautiful," Rig said. "Engagement ring?"

"No!"

He kissed the tip of her thumb, lightly, still not believing what he was doing. His mouth moved around the firm flesh at the base, and using his tongue, just the slightest bit, he tasted her skin in a flick, almost too quick for her to feel. But she felt it, he could tell. She kept her eyes on his, and any moment he was prepared to stop. To apologize. To be slapped. But instead, her eyelids fluttered in a way that made his insides clench.

Then as softly as he could, using almost no pressure at all, he bit the tip of her thumb.

He watched her as she fought with herself, the ice in her demeanor warring with the heat in her eyes. He released her hand regretfully.

Pulling her hand back as if it was her idea, Naomi said, "What the hell was that? I thought we weren't going to—" But her voice was too breathy to sustain the anger implied in the strong language, and Rig didn't apologize, even though he knew he should.

He shouldn't have done that. But he wanted more.

A buzzer screamed next to them, and both jumped. Bruno's voice came over the intercom. "Dr. Keller, Maddy Walker's your first appointment. I'll put her in three."

"Why did you do that?" whispered Naomi, holding her hand as if she'd sprained it.

"I don't know," said Rig. He could only be honest with her. "I couldn't help it."

"Well . . . *don't.*" She spun on her heel and was inside her office, the door slamming behind her, before he could draw breath to speak again.

Pushing the talk button on the intercom, Rig said, "I'll be right there." His voice sounded completely normal. But he couldn't get a full breath into his lungs, and all he could think about was how her hand had felt in his, how it had tasted—of antiseptic and a hint of salt, and something that was completely hers . . .

Oh, no. He wouldn't do this. Of course he wouldn't. He understood self-control. He was a grown-up. But God, he ached, both physically and mentally.

Damn, it had been a long time since someone torqued him up enough to get blue balls.

Chapter Twelve

Sometimes we knit the sweater of our dreams, forgetting that the seams will still have to be sewn at some point. Seaming is a small price to pay for happiness, though, don't you agree?

—E.C.

After Naomi's last appointment, she left without checking on Rig. She'd seen enough of him today just walking by half-open doors of patient rooms. Invariably, he'd been laughing, presumably at something the patient had said. What was this, comedy-club doctoring? Laughter is the best medicine? She rolled her eyes at the thought.

But he was a grown man, a doctor, with all the papers. She'd never owned this place—she'd just been spoiled for a while, and it had been nice.

She waved a good-bye to a surprised-looking Bruno—Naomi seldom left before he did—and went outside. She blinked in the sudden sun, and felt the unexpected warmth of coming out of an air-conditioned climate into the coastal summer. She turned right, and went immediately inside again, entering the health clinic from the front entrance, the one she rarely used.

It was an enormous room that had been used as a dance studio until it closed overnight, leaving small dancers outside, knocking on the glass. Pederson had been ready to sublet the space to a flower vendor who was looking for retail space on Main, but Naomi had talked him into letting her try the clinic. He'd never been excited about it like she had, but that's because he was on his way out, anyway. Surely that was why.

The mirrors still hung from its dance studio days—they made the space look even bigger than it was. Naomi didn't care for the harsh overhead fluorescents, but they were all she had to work with for now.

Around the room, she'd placed card tables covered with brochures on just about every medical problem imaginable. She'd added transitional flyers, ways to help a recently diagnosed loved one apply for Medicare, for disability, for hospice. Wooden chairs bought cheaply at an office-furniture sale sat next to the tables, and the whole center of the room was empty. But if the Red Cross agreed, as she hoped they would, this would be a fantastic place to hold a blood drive.

The thought of that actually gave her tingles. There was so much that could be accomplished here, why didn't people see it?

Her father would have. Gilbert Fontaine had been her moon and her stars while she was growing up. As soon as Anna had been born to her mother and stepfather, Naomi had realized it wasn't that her mother wasn't good at mothering—she just wasn't good at mothering *her*. But as long as she'd had her father's approval, she was okay. She could handle Maybelle taking Anna on shopping trips, bringing to Gilbert's apartment a bag of clothes that were either too large or too small for Naomi, because while they'd been shopping, Naomi had been lying on the rough orange carpet in Gilbert's office, using tracing paper to go over the diagrams and images in his medical books. When she tumbled into naps on long, warm Saturday afternoons, Gilbert had always picked her up and placed her on the office settee, tucking blankets knitted by his mother around her. When she woke, sometimes she pretended to be asleep longer than she actually was so she could keep her cheek on the scratchy, overstuffed pillow, listening to the drag of her father's pen across his notes.

Only once did she shame herself in front of him. She was just nine or ten, helping in her father's practice. He'd asked her to go next door, into his health clinic, and tell everyone waiting that he was almost done with his patients, and he'd be there shortly.

"No. They smell."

"They *what*?"

Naomi had made herself smaller as her father had grown taller, his face darkening with displeasure. But she'd said, "They don't smell good. Some of them aren't . . . clean. They should probably go somewhere and wash before they come here."

Gilbert had thundered, "No daughter of mine would say that."

Naomi had felt as if he'd slapped her. Her father had never said anything to her that wasn't loving or encouraging.

He'd said, "They don't *have* a place to wash. You think the people who come to the clinic *like* the way they live? You think they chose that? Out of all their options? Do you think they like having three kids before the age of twenty to a junkie dad who makes them work in a way I can't explain to you? Don't you *ever* look down on them. Don't you ever even *think* badly of them. What they've gone through, we'll never understand. They are, cumulatively, wiser than we'll ever be, and I'm ashamed of my daughter."

Naomi had bitten the inside of her mouth so hard she'd drawn blood, and then not only had she gone next door to tell everyone her dad was almost ready to come help them, she'd used her allowance to fill up the candy bowl that was fallen upon by the children who'd been playing in the kids' area.

Now, in the re-creation of her father's dream, the one that had become her own, she looked in the direction of her kids' area. Smaller, sadder than his, it hadn't been used yet. She'd never had a child come by with a parent in tow or not. But she would. It would happen. She had to believe that.

From behind her a low growl said, "Wanna dance?"

Naomi screamed and clutched her chest as she spun around. It wasn't until she'd hit Rig in the shoulder that she really knew who he was. "You *scared* me!"

"You socked me, woman!"

"Natural response. Right up there with the screaming."

Rig grinned, and his dark eyes danced as he held out his arms, and invited her to do the same. "Come on. That's what this old wooden floor wants."

Naomi backed up, her heart still racing. What if she *did* dance with him? Without music? Oh, God, she must be losing it. He might bite her again. She shook her head and said, "I was thinking it wants a good waxing. Hey, speaking of things that need a little shining up, are you going to keep dressing like that?"

He looked down at himself, at his jeans and dark brown shirt, and then back at her, his arms outstretched. "My jeans not tight enough for the cowboy lovers out here? I can get some Wranglers on the weekend, no problem."

"Jeans, though? And I know Dr. Pederson's white coat is too wide for you, since you don't have a beer gut the size of Oregon, but wouldn't it do for a couple of days until we get your own?"

He dropped his arms easily and moved to run his fingers over the bookcase she'd also picked up with the used office furniture. "I don't like to be fancy. People talk to me more when I'm not. My clothes are clean, I can assure you of that. On another subject, what the hell? Look at these books. Depressing. Cancer, cancer, oh, goody, myeloma and leukemia, more cancer, and some more cancer." He slid his hand over the second row of books. "And it looks like this is the death and dying shelf. Cheery. Matches the rest of the vibe in here."

Naomi spun around, looking at her creation. Yeah, maybe she hadn't decorated it enough yet. But it wasn't about the decorating, it wasn't about what it looked like. What mattered was what it contained, what was at its heart. It was suddenly vastly important to her that he got it. Pederson never had. But maybe Rig could.

"My dad always wanted a small-town practice, but he never got one. He worked in a neighborhood that straddled two districts of Los Angeles. All day his practice was full of rich clients, and he kept them healthy." It felt strange to talk to someone about it, but she kept going. "Next door, he opened a center like this for the lower-income community to come for advice. For resources. Under his watch, it turned into the community gathering place. They had lectures and classes, even dances sometimes. Everyone went there to get all their information, about stress, and health, and diet, and there was always someone, a volunteer or my dad at night, who was sitting there with all the answers. Free health checks. It was organic. Lovely. Everything free. He'd be so proud if he knew I was doing this." If she pulled it off. And maybe she wouldn't. *Shit.*

Rig looked seriously at her. As if he was really listening. "Who comes in here now?"

"Now?" Naomi grimaced. "No one. I've seen two people in here on the nights I've sat here with the door open, and they scuttled out as soon as they saw me."

"It does kind of have a Christian Science reading room feel, doesn't it?"

Naomi yanked the curl next to her ear. "Dammit. Really? I was hoping to avoid that."

"Yeah. I'm thinking people expect you to preach the word if you lie in wait behind that table. Why is this so important to you?"

Naomi couldn't say the words that mattered: *My father expected me to do more than just be a doctor, just make money. He expected me to help.* So she just shrugged.

Rig, though, was already nodding. "Yeah. We can make something out of this."

The words chafed. She'd already made something here. No one recognized it yet, that was all. "I don't think I need help, thanks. It's fine as it is."

"What about yoga sessions? There's so much room here."

"Really?"

Rig ignored her sarcasm. "Tai chi would be good, too. And acupuncture. All done at low cost, or free to seniors to get them in here. A real wellness, body and soul place. I'm all in favor of treating the whole body."

"East meets West, huh?" Naomi raised an eyebrow. No way. That sure wasn't what she had in mind. Naomi believed in treating people the way she'd been trained.

He went on. "Have you thought about having support groups meet here? You could even get the twelve-steppers."

Of course she'd thought about it. But had it happened yet? No. Did she know how to make it happen? Naomi wished she did, but she sure as hell wasn't going to ask him for help with it.

"You just leave the doors unlocked all the time?"

Naomi took a few steps away from him. "When the practice is open, yeah. The last person out, either Bruno or me, locks it up, unless I'm staying in the evenings. Which, like I said, hasn't been a popular feature." She paused, feeling color flood her face. Was it showing? Her desperate need for this to succeed? "I'm holding a free blood sugar testing next week, and I'm hoping people come by. I put it in the paper and everything." Her fingers twitched, and she yearned for her knitting. The yarn slipping off the tip of the needle would soothe this nervousness she felt. She twisted the hem of her shirt between her fingers instead.

"No offense, Doc, but a sharp poke in the finger? You really think people are going to line up to be told they should be healthier?"

Naomi's shoulders dropped. Damn. She looked around and tried to see it for the first time, with new eyes.

It wasn't just plain. It was *ugly*. Unattractive. Practically offensive in its nonoffensiveness. No personality. Who would like this? Who in the community would embrace this? Why would they?

"I'll figure it out," she said, trying to keep the defeated tone out of her voice. "Lock up behind you, would you? Uses the same key you already have."

He protested, saying something she couldn't hear over the roaring in her ears. In the sunlight, she blinked back the sudden tears that threatened to spill over. She walked briskly away from the office. Anywhere but here.

The practice sat on Main Street next door to the hardware store. Across the street was the boardwalk and the main parking lot for the pier. It was wide and flat, and public works kept back the encroaching sand as much as they could. The boardwalk had restrooms and several snack shacks—the most popular foods passing by in tourists' hands seemed to be chocolate-dipped vanilla cones and pink cotton candy. As Naomi crossed the street, she saw one round child about six years old had both, and his ice cream was in as much danger of falling off its cone as his face was of getting covered in the pink fluff.

She turned left at the boardwalk, walking along the south side of Main Street. The light slanted in that way particular to the coastal summer, still warm, but with a breath of coolness promised by the low-lying layer of fog that waited on the horizon. In a couple of hours, as the sun went down, the fog would race in and the cold, clammy air would wrap itself around the people still in tank tops and shorts. The locals could be identified by the sweatshirts wrapped around their waists. They knew come evening they'd need them.

Someone called her name.

Naomi paused and listened. She must have heard it wrong.

Then she heard it again: a woman was calling her name, and she sounded happy about it.

Chapter Thirteen

*Blow your wishes into your knitting, whisper your hopes
against the yarn.*

—E.C.

Toots Harrison, a local yoga teacher whom Naomi knew from
the charity auction for the SPCA, waved cheerily. Half a
block away and on the other side of the street, she was carrying a bunch of at least thirty helium balloons, and wore a toxic green
sweater liberally decorated with pink polka dots. She looked like her
own one-person parade. "Naomi! Hello!"

She jaywalked across the street with little regard for the two cars
that honked as she made them stop, and came up to Naomi as if she
was an old friend. For a moment Naomi pretended that she really
was. It felt wonderful, if bittersweet.

"Toots, you look like you're going to fly away."

"Oh, wouldn't that be marvelous? To go up, up, up and then float
around peeking down on people? I'd love that. How are you, Dr.
Fontaine? It's been a long time since we talked about my teaching
you how to knit. You know I'm happy to, anytime."

"And I appreciate that." Naomi hadn't actually lied—she'd only expressed interest in Toots's knitting at the auction, and Toots had assumed Naomi wanted to learn. "Where are you headed with those?"

"Lucy's birthday party! Oh, my dear, aren't you able to come?"

For just a half second, Naomi was tempted to say that she couldn't, that she had plans, and that's why she wouldn't be there, but Toots just had something about her that made it too difficult to be untruthful.

"I wasn't invited." The admission was even more painful than she'd thought it would be.

Toots's face fell and a balloon popped as it hit the light pole they were standing next to. "You're *kidding*."

Naomi shrugged. "I don't really know your daughter that well. We've done coffee, but that's about it." She smiled to hide the hurt feelings. No big deal. Just a party.

"Naomi, you simply have to come. The whole town is coming. Owen's throwing her a surprise party, the first she's ever had."

Naomi shook her head, but Toots overrode her, continuing, "I won't take no for an answer. It's at Abigail's yarn shop tonight. Oh, do you know where that is?"

Naomi, feeling mute, nodded. Of course she did. She'd been just once, when she'd first moved to town. She'd desperately wanted to see Eliza's home, to make that connection between the land and the patient she'd loved, but when she'd been there, the pretty little shop had been busy with a knitting group, full of loud women all having fun, and she'd been struck with a huge bout of confusion. Stay, and fail at polite chitchat? Run away and listen to them laugh as she went? When Abigail MacArthur offered to help her, she'd told her that she was lost, looking for a waterfall in the area. Then she'd received such good directions to the waterfall that she thought she'd made up, she had to drive by it afterward. And it was, truly, beautiful. But the falls hadn't been half as alluring as the sound of those women, all talking and laughing in friendship, their needles flying in their laps.

She hadn't reminded Abigail that they'd met twice already, in the hallway outside Eliza's room at the hospital in San Diego and then again at the funeral. Abigail had been crying too much to register anything else, including Eliza's doctor, who was also grieving.

It was good that Eliza had known love like that.

Toots pulled Naomi back to the present by saying, "The best part is the *way* we're going to surprise her. Abigail set up a ruse—she needs help sewing together a blanket, and would Lucy come out and help her? Of course, since it's her birthday, she might suspect something's up, but when she gets there, the shop'll be closed, only Abigail there, with work in her hands to turn over to Lucy." Toots leaned forward conspiratorially, and the balloons bounced with a rigid plastic tapping noise. "But we're bringing the party to *her*. So park on the county road out of sight of the cottage with the rest of us, right at eight. Then we'll sneak up, en masse, and barge in, screaming. Oh!" Toots clapped and let go of the whole bunch of balloons.

"Careful!" Naomi grabbed the attached weight and pulled the mass back down.

"So will you?"

"Oh, I don't think that . . ." What, was she scared? She was lonely and sad because the community didn't include her, and here was an invitation by a woman who was beloved by them, and she wasn't jumping on it? It didn't matter that she hadn't been on the original invite—Naomi was being ridiculous.

"Yes," she said, her voice tight. "I'd love to."

"Oh, *good*," said Toots. And she sounded like she really meant it. "Bring that new doctor you have, too. He could meet the whole town tonight in one swell foop, as they say." Giving a cheery wave, Toots and her bunch of balloons made their way down the street.

Rig? No. Not him. The last thing he needed was help with being friendly.

Naomi could use a social outing, she knew it. It probably wouldn't kill her.

Right?

Chapter Fourteen

A nonknitter is not ignorant. She is simply uneducated as of yet.

—E.C.

Rig felt exhilarated as he locked the door behind his last patient. He'd seen seven people today—not a large number, but since four of them were walk-ins and most of his day had been free, he'd been able to spend quality time with each. He'd learned about Mrs. Luby's corns, and Theo McCormick's snoring, and he'd been able to give them suggestions that actually might work, rather than just prescribing something. After he'd given Bart Harrison a referral to an allergist and explained the way a neti pot worked—boy, had that man's eyes popped wide when he realized what Rig meant—Bart had invited him to his daughter's surprise party. He'd left, thumping him on the back in parting. "My wife, Toots, will love you, son. You've got to come."

Rig turned out the front-office lights. Bruno had left fifteen minutes earlier, since there hadn't been anything for him to do. He'd jumped at the chance to leave early, and offered to have the time docked from his wages.

"Nah, man, get out of here. Go home and fix yourself a drink, and then call Peter, okay?"

Bruno said, "Why? He should call me."

"If you make the first move and it's not your turn, you get the credit for being the bigger person. It's just there, comes along with it. You'd be a fool to miss that opportunity."

"You brain-gaming me? I thought you were a GP."

"I haven't been single this long without playing the game a little. But connection is a good thing. Just do me a favor and do it, okay? Report back tomorrow."

"Fine," grumbled Bruno. "If you insist."

Now Rig stood in front of the window, looking out on to Main Street. He supposed any doctor would think this was a very fine view—sand and shore opposite, the pier reaching toward the horizon, pink clouds piling up to the southwest.

But for him, the water was so much farther away than normal. He was used to standing on the deck of a rig and seeing nothing but water for miles around. Water heaving below him, the sound of a thousand pieces of machinery grinding under his feet, and all around, nothing but the sea, the salt in the air staining everything he owned with a slight fine layer of white.

Rig jumped at a rap on the glass door. He'd been so busy gazing out past the pedestrians that he hadn't noticed one had stopped. It was a deliveryman, dressed in brown with features to match, a frantic look on his face.

Rig unlocked the door and pulled it open.

"Dr. Fontaine here? I got an overnight delivery for her, but I forgot to get it off the truck when I made my rounds earlier. I don't know if it's something really important for the office or what, and I didn't want to let it wait another day because of my screwup." The man's gangly neck swiveled up and then sideways, trying to look around Rig. He handed over the box. "I don't want her to be mad.

I haven't been doing this job very long. Is she here to sign for this? Or can you?"

The package was small and weighed very little. "I work here." The words felt strange. "I can sign."

The relief was obvious—the man's shoulders sagged, and his skinny chest rose with a huge breath. "Thank God. Would you . . . if you don't mind . . ." He looked at his watch. "Technically it's only a couple of hours late . . . I'm sorry."

Rig looked at him sympathetically. "Secret's safe with me."

"*Thank* you."

Rig relocked the door and took the package with him into the back. The return address said Koigu, with a Canadian address.

What if it was important? It had been overnighted—it was obviously something Naomi needed quickly.

It might be neighborly to take it to her.

Yeah. Rig quickly warmed to the idea. She'd be pleased he took the initiative, right? And if it was important, he'd only be scoring more points with his new boss/future partner, which couldn't hurt, right?

The alarm accepted the code she'd given him, and he locked the back door. He went down to Tillie's to see if he could find out where Dr. Fontaine lived. Would he really be able to get directions to a community member's house when he was this new?

Sure enough, Old Bill didn't ask questions, just scribbled barely legible directions on the back of a flyer advertising the chicken-turkey-bacon scramble, and Rig was on his way.

Naomi lived close by, on a street that looked well kept. Older houses on spacious lots had full-grown trees hanging over long driveways. The lawns were manicured, and in the front yard of every third house, someone was outside watering or pulling weeds, or chasing their children in a game of tag. It looked like something from a television ad for life insurance. People really lived like this? Even Jake's house, which was nice enough, set back on a quiet cul-de-sac, didn't look as ideal, as perfect as this street.

He counted down numbers until he reached hers.

Naomi's lawn was a little shaggy, overgrown with Bermuda grass and a cluster or two of short foxtail. It looked like she was fighting a losing battle with clumps of dandelions.

Looking around, he couldn't see evidence of a man. Rig didn't know he'd been wondering until he'd checked to see how her gutters were (dirty from the bottom, which meant they needed a good cleaning). The two camellia bushes were untrimmed and growing so high that they almost covered up her front windows. As he knocked on her front door and peered into the entry that could be seen through the side glass, he saw only women's shoes. No men's boots or sneakers anywhere to be found.

The gut feeling of satisfaction surprised him.

He would just drop off the box and go. Helpful, that's what he was.

He knocked again, a little harder this time. Maybe she was in the shower? Man, that wasn't the image he needed, but he let it play out for a second before he squashed it: Naomi, her curly hair wet and hanging heavily down her naked back, turning slowly under the spray, her breasts high, nipples tight against the beading water . . .

His *Playboy* movie fantasy was broken by the door jerking inward.

Naomi stood there, fully clothed in a blue T-shirt that looked as soft as it looked old and black workout pants, a portable phone held between her ear and her shoulder, shaking off her hands, which dripped water all over the entryway.

Her eyebrows went up when she saw it was him. "Mom? Mom. Hey, Mom! There's someone here. I gotta go." There was a pause while she listened, rolling her eyes. "Please, Ma. Okay. Fine. It is, okay? Are you happy? I've got to hang up. Yeah, bye."

She shook her head, staring at the phone, and then seemed to realize all over again that he was there. Stepping backward into a small living room, she gestured him in.

"How did you find me?" she asked.

"No hello?" He handed her the package. "Asked Old Bill."

"And he just *told* you?" Her voice was tight, and suddenly Rig doubted the wisdom of what he'd done.

"I'm sorry. I'm sure he only did it because we work together."

"Jesus. This town." She scrubbed her eyes with one hand. "I'm sorry. He probably thought he was helping." The tension was gone from her voice. "And my God, I'm sorry." She looked around the room. "This place is a mess. I've been too busy to . . . No, truth is, it's always kind of like this."

"It's nice," he said, and he was surprised to find that he meant it. More cluttered than he ever would have thought her house would be, it had a good feeling. Warmth. Comfort.

But she wasn't inviting him to stay. "I'll get out of here, then, now that you have that."

She looked down at the package. "My yarn!"

"Excuse me?"

"It's just yarn," she said, sounding more casual this time.

"Oh," Rig said. On the couch rested a basket, a ball of yarn, and some needles with something hanging from them. "Knitting?"

She half-smiled, and he loved how the softness played on her face. He bet she had no idea how pretty she was when she did that.

"Don't tell anyone."

"Secret vice?"

Naomi sat on the sofa next to the knitting, placing the box on her lap. "You have no idea. In this town, yeah. I'm totally in the closet." She paused again, and then said, "You want to have a seat?"

He did want to. He wanted to stay for a few minutes in this room that smelled like her, felt like her. "Sure." He sat in a green wooden chair.

The living room seemed to have no rhyme or reason, and no apparent thought had been given to the placement of things. The sofa was too close to the coffee table, and the lamps stood in awkward areas—the one nearest the couch was still three feet away, which must have made her knitting difficult at night when there was no natural light coming in from outside. Two antique-looking upholstered chairs sat facing each other, as if two people having an intense discussion had just left the room. Books were piled on every surface, medical texts he recognized, and ones with pink and red covers that he didn't. A large dust bunny lurked in the far corner, although the surfaces looked clean enough. It didn't appear that housekeeping was her strong suit.

But for all the awkwardness of the room, for all that it shouldn't work, the colors brought everything together. A deep red wall on one side touched an orange wall in which stood a doorway that looked like it led to the kitchen. The other side wall, opposite the red one, was bright yellow, and was decorated with a flight of blue butterflies that looked hand painted. It should have felt like a children's room, or a paint-demo area at a hardware store, but it didn't, it felt rich and warm. A brown lamp in the shape of an owl stood next to an improbable owl ashtray.

Only one picture hung on the red wall, a large, blown-up print of a brilliantly colored orange California poppy against a hillside covered with dry brown grass. The poppy's petals reached up, as if yearning for the strip of blue sky at the very top. It looked bold, daring, and shy, all at once.

It was a perfect setting for Naomi. Awkward. Leaving more, something hidden, to be desired.

"So," he said into the silence. "Yarn. You going to open it?"

Her face lit up again. "I was going to wait, but fine. Since my secret is out and all."

She ripped at the packing tape with her fingers, declining his offer of his pocketknife. Then the box flaps parted, and the last remaining tension in her face evaporated.

"Oh," she said in a breathless voice. "This is gorgeous."

The yarn she pulled from the box was pretty. Even he could see that. A mix of purples, blues, and reds, the yarn came in what looked like twisted hanks.

"Koigu," she said. "Worsted weight. I've been wanting this for a while, but this colorway was sold out for a long time. Actually, it might have been years since they've done this one."

"Years?"

"Doesn't it look like a sunset? Like the kind we have around here? Look at that pale blue mixed in, right here."

Naomi held it out, and he had to agree. It *did* remind him of the colors that lit up the western sky at dusk. "I've never seen anything like that, actually. It's pretty." *Just like you.* He didn't say the words.

Instead he said, "I used to knit, you know."

Naomi laughed, a sudden happy sound he wanted to hear again as soon as she stopped. "You did? You don't look like the type."

"Oh, yeah?" He picked up her knitting, careful not to drop any of the stitches. "My mom was always knitting, but I didn't try it myself until I was in college. My buddy said it was a chick magnet, and he was right. I could probably finish your . . . is it a scarf?"

"Shawl."

"I could probably finish up this shawl for you right now if you want."

Naomi crossed her arms but her smile remained in place. "You know how to knit lace."

"Lace?" Not a chance in hell. "Sure. Easy."

"Did you knit on the rigs?"

Rig couldn't help snorting. "No way, not on any of 'em. They liked me out there. I didn't want them throwing me to the sharks."

"Ah, so you know how to stay in the knitting closet, too."

"Oh, yeah. But it was always fascinating, making knots like that in a regular, prescribed pattern." He paused, and then said, "Sometimes putting stitches in a person feels the same way."

Naomi colored and she looked at her thumbnail. She nodded slightly.

He went on, "It always made my brain feel good. Even if I was just making a scarf for my mom. Who taught you? Your mom?"

"No way. She can barely tie her shoes without help. That's why she wears slip-on Prada loafers. No, I learned from Eliza Carpenter. As knitters go, she was famous. She was originally from here, actually; I knew her from treating her in San Diego." She paused. "But no one knows that here." She took the lace back from him, her voice softer than perhaps she meant it to be. Rig wondered if she knew how completely readable her face was—sadness and stubbornness warred, and then stubbornness won. He wanted to touch the curl that hung so softly by her right ear, but of course he didn't.

Naomi shook the needles. "This pattern is kicking my ass. Maybe you can show me how to do the tricky part? Right here?"

"Tricky part." Rig examined the lace with what he hoped looked like a knowledgeable eye, picking up one end of it. "No, I'm afraid you screwed the pooch with this one. Even I couldn't fix the mess you've made. You have holes everywhere, did you know that?"

She laughed again, and he felt like he'd won the lottery. When she laughed, she seemed open. He'd seen the same thing for a moment when she'd shown him the center, and then she'd closed off again.

This was better. He released the knitting carefully, suddenly worried he'd fuck it all up, for real.

Naomi seemed to collect herself. She sat up straighter and turned her knees so that she faced him more directly. "Do you want something to drink?"

"Um . . ."

"I'm going to have some iced tea. Would you like some?"

"Yeah."

She practically ran to the kitchen, leaving Rig behind on his wooden chair. He took a deep breath, and stuck out a foot. He examined the scuffs on his work boot and wondered idly if he should get a better pair, a nicer pair, for the office.

Then he wondered if she'd notice.

What would it feel like to kiss her again?

Was he truly as crazy as he was feeling? Maybe, if he was, he should prescribe himself some antipsychotics because he sure as hell never felt like this.

Rig leaned back and studied the poppy on the wall. It was perfect, blooming exactly where it should.

Chapter Fifteen

It's normal to feel nervous the first time you do something like stranded colorwork, even though it's actually easy as pie. Nerves happen at the most ridiculous of times, don't they?

—E.C.

Leaning against the refrigerator, Naomi raised a hand to her cheeks. What the *hell* was going on? Why was she so thrown by him? She opened the door of the refrigerator and stared into it blindly.

Fact: She had a new employee in her business.

Fact: Rig Keller was equipped to do the job and would be an asset to the practice, no matter how she felt about it.

Fact: She was more attracted to Rig than she'd been to anyone in years. In more years than she could count, actually. Was it because she already knew what he could do? Funny, it felt like she didn't have the slightest clue to what he was capable of doing to her.

Fact: It felt dizzying. And wrong. And just plain frightening.

The chill from the refrigerator made her shiver. Did she even *have* iced tea? She'd offered it before she'd thought. There, she had the bottled kind. She had no idea how old the bottles were—did they expire?—but at least she could pretend she was a hostess sometimes.

Whereas in reality, she never was. Not once since she'd moved here. Besides the cable guy and the two Jehovah's Witnesses she'd invited in one day because she was bored—boy, had *that* been a mistake—Rig was the first person to be in her house. The townspeople hadn't beaten a path to her door like she'd thought a small town would, and she never had to choose between social engagements.

Naomi twisted open the caps and poured the tea into glasses. Adding ice, she placed the glasses on a serving tray that she used to hold her frozen dinners when she ate in front of the TV. She shook some stale gingersnaps out of the Trader Joe's box onto a saucer and called it good.

She was serving him *tea*.

Dammit, one of the few places she'd ever felt confident in her reactions to people was in sexual attraction. Maybe it was because it didn't require language, which was where she was always tripped up in everyday interactions, but sex had always been kind of easy for her.

Relationships? That was a different matter—the men she'd been involved with always ended up telling her that they couldn't understand her because she wouldn't talk about her feelings. No relationship had ever lasted more than four months, maybe six, tops. Naomi had gotten over the hurt as quickly as she could each time, determined to pour all her energies into medicine. With patients, behind the closed door, where she had the knowledge that they needed—she could relax then. She didn't relax many other places, or with many other people. But then again, she'd never been in love with anyone as much as she was in love with pursuing her dreams.

She bet her father had felt the same way—maybe that was why he'd never dated after the divorce. She got her focus, her dedication, from him.

And now just look at her. Naomi was nervous, frantic butterflies in her stomach the size of the blue ones she'd painted on the wall in a fit of creative energy last year. She picked up the tray and swallowed, hard. Maybe she didn't understand how she felt around him, but that didn't mean it had to show.

In the living room, Rig stood staring at the picture of the poppy she'd taken years before, during the drive out to the reservoir with Eliza.

"It's good," he said. "Really good. Did you take it?"

Naomi nodded. The scrapes on the yellow-painted surface of the coffee table had never bothered her before, but they seemed to jump out at her now, and she placed the tray so that it covered as much of the damage as it could.

"Nice." Rig reached for a glass, and as he pulled back, their arms brushed. She felt the warmth of him, smelled the soap he'd used that morning.

If this was playing it cool, she wasn't doing very well.

"How long have you lived here?"

Naomi felt a sharp burst of embarrassment. Most people would have gotten around to buying furniture that matched. Sometimes she felt like such a fake grown-up. "Ever since I got into town a year ago. Doesn't look like it, does it?" She laughed lightly, but the sound didn't hit the right note.

"I like it. It looks like you. I never would have pegged you for the owl-collecting type, though."

Naomi exhaled as she fell onto the couch next to him. "I'm *not*. They're courtesy of my mother. Once, we were browsing in an antiques store and I said an owl figurine was cute. Since then, I haven't had a non-owl present from her, ever. I have an owl doormat, owl picture frames, even owl candle holders. And those are the things I leave out. In the hall closet I store all the other owl things I can't bear to look at—the owl clock that hoots on the hour, the owl bookends.

On the rare occasions my mother makes a visit, I make sure to put them all on display, even though it's kind of like shooting myself in the foot."

"But you don't really like them."

"I don't hate birds. That's about as much as I ever think about owls."

Another pause fell in the room, feeling heavy with something she couldn't name. "And I hear you're staying . . . with Shirley Bellflower?"

As if he was as conscious of the small talk as she was, he nodded and abruptly changed the subject. "What are you doing tonight?"

Naomi straightened. "I'm going to a party." It felt good to say. Tonight, she was going to a party. Just like everyone else.

"The surprise party for Lucy Bancroft?"

"How do you . . . ? Yes." Of course he knew about the party. Why was she even surprised?

"Me, too." He glanced at his watch. "In fact," he went on, "we should probably get over there if we want to be on time. Want to go together?"

The words sounded so easy for him, falling off his tongue as if he invited one-night stands to parties all the time.

Maybe he did.

Wouldn't that be a nice thing to be able to do?

Naomi thought furiously. She hadn't even glanced at her hair since leaving for the office this morning, and the ocean air had been whipping strongly as she'd walked home—it was a curled tangle, she could feel it. She'd never reapplied lipstick after lunch. She hadn't even *thought* about what she'd wear, and if she had, she was sure she didn't have the right thing.

And if she went with him, she might die of these nerves she didn't understand.

Forcing her lips to part, she said, "You know, I've got a thing, so I was going to drive myself . . ."

"A thing."

"Yeah."

It didn't look like he was buying it. "After, you mean?"

"Uh-huh."

He shrugged. "Okay then. I'll just see you there."

"That will be nice." Oh, she longed to slide sideways and bury her face in the pillow she held on her lap. *Nice?*

He reached for a gingersnap and popped it whole into his mouth. "It'll be good to go to a party," he mumbled around the cookie. "Get to know some more people in town."

Naomi chewed on her bottom lip until she told herself to stop. "I should probably change."

"Why?" Looking puzzled, Rig cast his gaze down Naomi's body and then back up. "I think you look great."

"You're crazy. I wouldn't go to the mailbox in this." She looked beat up, she knew she did. These were her oldest yoga pants and her most comfortable T-shirt, and both had tiny holes in inappropriate places.

Rig set his glass down on the tray. His mouth twitched as if he were swallowing a grin. "Um."

Naomi bristled. "What?"

"Like I said, you look great."

Oh, that low tone of his voice, so low she practically had to turn her head toward him to hear the rumble of his words. His voice sounded like a caress.

She stood, her knees a little wobbly. "Thanks."

He stood, too. "Just grab a jacket in case it gets cold and put on some shoes, and we're good to go. Please? Will you reconsider just coming with me? I'll take you by your thing later."

"No thanks." But Naomi's voice was weak, and the words were automatic. This was insane, this feeling of heat in her lower belly, this moronic groundswell of lust that was flooding her body. They just had good chemistry. *Really* good chemistry. Not her fault. That was all.

"I wish you'd change your mind."

"Um, well . . ." Lord, the man was so close. Naomi could just . . . she could . . .

She couldn't.

"So, I guess I'll see you there," she said.

Before she could see it coming, before she could move, Rig stepped forward and scooped her into a hug.

Chapter Sixteen

It's the little surprises in knitting that keep us going.
—E.C.

Rig hadn't bargained on how soft she would feel. Instantly, his head swam, as if he'd had too much to drink. She smelled of flowers and adhesive, like a rose-scented Band-Aid. He'd never known before that he had a favorite scent, but now he did. It was her.

It was a second or two before he realized the hug was completely one sided. Naomi wasn't hugging him back. She was stiff as a two-by-four in his arms.

He released her, letting his arms fall to his sides and stepping back. "Sorry," he said, feeling lame. "That was weird, wasn't it?"

Naomi looked up at him, those green eyes glimmering in a way he couldn't read. She swayed toward him and then took a breath. Dammit, he couldn't read her at *all*. She was nothing like she'd been in Portland—confident, secure, knowing. Now she was something else, almost fragile, and god*damn* he wanted to kiss her. But he couldn't. Wouldn't.

"Just one more thing," she said. It seemed as if she was deciding something, and Rig wished like hell he could tell what it was.

He moved the tiniest bit closer, and it was official—he was now completely in her personal space. "What?"

"This." Her cool fingers moved to his throat, and then trailed up to his cheek. Rig tried to remain as still as he possibly could, as if he didn't want to scare off a curious butterfly. He took a deep breath and held it as her fingers traced his jaw, then his chin. She was so close. If he wanted to, he could reach out and . . .

Naomi gasped and met Rig's eyes.

His hand slid down to her other hand, his fingers entwining with hers, and he tugged her forward as he stepped toward her, closing the final inches that had separated them.

His mouth inches from hers, she whispered, "I have no idea what I'm doing. And I hate that."

She went up on her tiptoes and pressed her mouth against his.

Naomi's lips were sweet—he could taste the slightest hint of ginger and rose and faintly, mint. She moved her mouth so that she pulled slightly on his lower lip. Something shifted inside him, and Rig went from turned on to completely over the top, on *fire* for her.

Putting one arm around her, he pulled her to his chest. As her soft breasts pressed against him, he tangled his fingers in those curls he'd been dying to touch since he last saw her. Cool as chilled vodka she'd been then, that morning as she'd dressed, iced over, with that outrageous hair that protested her outward appearance, implying everything he tasted in her mouth that night and again now.

She was heat, and fire, and he'd *known* he hadn't gotten this wrong. Feeling triumphant, he crushed her mouth with his and her lips parted. He breathed her in as his tongue dipped into her warmth. She tasted darker now, heady, like wine.

His hand splayed flat on her lower spine, and he didn't have to pull her closer—she pressed herself against him, and he knew she could feel his reaction against her stomach. Fuck, he was hard.

Rig wanted her.

She knew it.

And she was just going deeper into the kiss. Who *was* this woman? Liquid nitrogen to molten lava in less than sixty seconds. His head swam and he didn't think he could hold her any tighter. It was already hard to breathe, and so hot in the room he thought he might explode into flames if she pulled his tongue into her mouth like that one more time.

"Uh—" Someone cleared a throat and coughed delicately. It took Rig a few more seconds to realize that the noise came from behind Naomi, near the front door. Maybe he should relinquish the hold he had on her, but God, it was so difficult. One last crush of lips, and he lifted his head and looked over her shoulder.

A girl stood next to the lamp just inside the door, hot pink stripes in her blond hair, a suitcase in her hand. She wore a calf-length black skirt, and a green tank top that emphasized exactly how pregnant she was. She had to be about seven months along, if not more. The fabric of the tank strained across her belly, and her feet looked swollen in her green flip-flops.

"Hi," the girl said.

Naomi stiffened, freezing. Rig could practically feel her skin cooling to the touch. He let his hand fall from where it was twisted in her hair, and she spun, still halfway in his arms.

"Anna. Holy shit." Naomi's voice was flat.

"The door was unlocked." Anna gave a small, apologetic smile, and Rig saw the resemblance—they both had full lips and long, straight noses. Of course, Naomi's lips were a little fuller now, from his kisses. He hoped Naomi remained standing in front of him until he cooled off for a second. He didn't want the tent in his pants to scare off her little sister. This must be the one she'd said she never spoke to, never saw.

Looked like that was about to change.

"So you just walk in?"

Anna's smile wavered. "I didn't mean to interrupt. I knocked, but I don't think you heard. You're . . . busy. I can go out and come back later."

"You didn't interrupt anything."

Yes, she had. But while Rig minded that he wasn't kissing Naomi anymore, this was as good a reason as any not to be. He watched the reunion with interest. Why hadn't they hugged yet? Kissed each other on the cheek at least?

The girl looked over Naomi's shoulder. "Hi, I'm Anna."

"I figured." Rig stepped from behind Naomi—thankfully, he'd cooled off a little—and shook her hand. "Rig Keller. Pleasure to meet you."

Anna grinned. "He's cute, sister."

Naomi's mouth twisted, and it looked like she was biting the inside of her cheek. There was an awkward silence. Then Naomi broke it by saying, "So, you're just passing through?"

Anna looked down at her belly and then back up. "Well, I thought . . ."

Rig had never felt more awkward. "I'll just be—"

"Don't you go anywhere," Naomi said fiercely to him. Turning back to Anna, she said, "Are you *kidding* me?"

Chapter Seventeen

Keep your knitting out where you can see it. A little wool warms a house.

—E.C.

It wasn't the best opening line she'd ever given her sister, but then again, she'd said worse. She knew she was staring, but she couldn't help it. Couldn't believe it. "Sorry. But you're . . . you're so—"

"Fat?" Anna rested her hand on the high, round slope of her belly. "Pregnant."

"I'd noticed. Hey, can I sit? I walked here from the bus station."

Naomi waved her onto the couch and tried to formulate an appropriate sentence. The bus station. Of course. Where else would her prodigal sister spring from? "You couldn't call first?" She hated the tone of disapproval that already radiated from her words, but she couldn't take them back. Besides, she couldn't *approve* of something like this. A baby wasn't the same as a new tattoo.

"I tried to call, but I think I have an old number for you. It said the line was disconnected." Anna scooted backward, using her hands to push herself deep into the couch.

"I've had the same number for a year."

"Huh."

"How did you find the house if you had the wrong phone number?"

"I asked at the diner in town. They knew who you were and gave me directions." Anna's bright blue eyes were soft. When Naomi was about thirteen or fourteen, visiting her mother's house, she would read to her little sister, ten years younger than herself, and Anna's startlingly sapphire eyes that she'd inherited from their mother had looked just like they did now.

Anna went on, "It must be nice, living here, where everybody knows you." She paused. "Yeah?"

Naomi dared a glance at Rig. He leaned comfortably against the bookcase as if he didn't mind being suddenly thrust into an awkward family situation.

"Living in a town like this means that two people have found me tonight based on word of mouth from the diner. That makes me nervous."

Anna shook her head. "This is the kind of place where you always wanted to live. You love it." She spread out her arms and then rested them on the backs of the couch cushions. "And look at your house! It's gorgeous! So big and roomy!"

Inwardly, Naomi groaned. There was only one translation for this—Anna wanted to stay. She'd probably run out of all other options, and it fell, just like it always had, to Naomi to pick up the pieces.

Only this time the piece in question was pregnant, and that might be more than Naomi could handle.

"Anna, I'm glad to see you," started Naomi. "But—"

"Oh, no buts, please, not right now." Her words were quick. Almost desperate. "Can't we just enjoy seeing each other? Can we have dinner tonight?" Anna gestured to Rig. "He can come, too. We can order in pizza or something. I don't want to get in the way . . ."

She was already in the way. How had she possibly managed to break up the only kiss Naomi had ever had in Cypress Hollow? Her timing was truly a force of nature.

Rig stepped forward and stood next to Naomi. He threaded her fingers with his. "Man, Anna, I'm so sorry, but we already have plans across town. And we should probably be getting going, shouldn't we, honey?"

Honey. As if she didn't already have enough to worry about. But Rig was giving her an out, and she'd be damned if she'd pass it up. For one brief second, she squeezed his hand back and allowed herself to feel its warmth. "Yeah, we're, uh, probably late."

"We are." Rig nodded firmly.

Anna's face clouded as she looked at Naomi. "I can stay here, can't I?"

Naomi took a deep breath.

"Please? I'll stay right here on the couch. I'll nap. I might use the bathroom but that's only because my bladder is the size of a walnut right now. I swear I won't touch *anything*."

Dropping Rig's hand, Naomi knew she was beaten. There wasn't a good way to say no. There wasn't any way to do it without sounding like the biggest asshole in the universe, and while her sister probably already thought of her that way because of the last time she'd tossed her out after her then boyfriend had hocked Naomi's laptop, Naomi didn't actually want to jeopardize any time that she might actually get with her sister.

Real time. She wanted that. And maybe this time Anna had finally changed.

Yeah, right.

"Fine. But just stay out here. Or you can lie down in the guest bedroom, first door down the hall on the left." Was that cruel, to confine her sister to two rooms? "And you can raid the fridge although I don't think there's much there."

"God, I'm starved. Thanks."

Naomi cringed as she imagined what she'd come home to—spaghetti sauce on the counters, dirty pans in the sink. She doubted the MO had changed. "But clean up, okay?"

"Of course I will." Anna's voice was warm, and her bright blue eyes were just the slightest bit wet around the lashes. "It's so good of you to do this. I've missed you so much."

What was she doing? Had she accidentally agreed to more than her sister just waiting in the house for her to come back?

She probably had. And against all her better judgment, Naomi felt a quiet hum that she hadn't felt in a long time—the warmth that she always felt when her sister was safe, and close by. "Damn it, Anna." She bent down to the couch to hug her sister. Anna smelled of sweat and stale, fried food, and very faintly, the sweetness of roses. "I've missed you, too," she said.

Chapter Eighteen

The definition of travel knitting is whatever project you can fit in your purse.

—E.C.

In front of the house, Rig tossed Naomi the extra helmet from the back of his Harley Sportster. "Here you go. I'm betting you don't have your own."

"I'm sorry. What?" She shook her head, making her curls bounce. God, he loved looking at her hair.

"You don't mind taking the bike, do you?"

"A bike is a bicycle, and I don't like them much. *This* is a motorcycle," she said.

"You're *smart*," Rig said. It felt good out here in the cool, clear air, good to get away from the tension he'd felt but didn't quite understand inside the house.

"And you're a smart-ass. I don't ride motorcycles."

"You can't? Or you don't?"

The slight furrow between her brows grew more pronounced, and Rig wanted to raise his thumb and rub it away. "Both. Oh, lord, my father would have killed me."

"You always did what your father told you?"

She leveled a cool glance at him. "Yes."

"Well," said Rig, "It's a good thing you don't have to tell him, then. You don't need to know anything but how to hold on to me. Lean in the direction of the bike, follow my body. You can do it."

He didn't watch to see if she'd follow his lead in putting on the helmet—he knew she would. For whatever reason, Naomi Fontaine wanted to get the hell away from her sister, and even though he didn't understand where it was coming from, he wanted to help her. And sure enough, after he snapped the strap in place and straddled the bike, he looked over to see her pulling her helmet down. Then she put her hands on his shoulders. He felt her nervousness radiating down to her fingertips.

"Wait," she said, her voice small and muffled under the helmet. "Should I leave? Leave her alone like this?"

"Do you want to stay?"

Slowly, the helmet shook back and forth. "That's what's awful. I don't want to. Not right now. I need time to think . . ."

"Get on, then. You're going to love this. Just don't touch that pipe there," he said and pointed to it. "It could burn you. But that's the only thing you have to be careful of. I'll take care of the rest."

"*Now* I'm nervous." But she scrambled on behind him, and wrapped her arms around his waist, thighs and arms clamped tighter than he'd expected her to. Even though her fingers were curled like sharp claws, almost painfully so, he reveled in the way she felt. God, she was good behind him. She fit on his bike perfectly, and he wasn't surprised. When he'd cruised past his place and picked up the extra helmet, hoping that she'd come with him to the party, he'd imagined she'd feel exactly like this.

Only, unbelievably, she felt better.

He started the Harley and felt her respond to its purr. Her legs gripped his a little bit harder, and he thanked God for motorcycles.

The ride to the MacArthur ranch was fast and sweet, no traffic on the narrow highway. They wound their way under the eucalyptus trees, past the live oaks on the rolling hills that were already brown from the summer sun. The air smelled of warm dust and clean sunshine, with a hint of salt from the ocean, now invisible over the hill to the west. The sun, low now in its seaward dive, poured light like honey over the countryside. After five minutes, Naomi had relaxed her death grip on his sides, and she was almost sitting all the way up. Her hands rested on his hips, lightly. The way they should. He took another curve and felt her lean with him, perfectly in sync.

Damn. She had no fucking clue how hot she was. One more time, he reminded himself that she was a complication he didn't want. Didn't need. No way was he getting caught around the axel.

But that didn't stop him from wishing the ride would never end.

There were more than twenty cars already parked out on the county road just down the road from the ranch. Rig pulled the bike in behind a Ducati—someone had nice taste.

Up at the curve, a knot of people had gathered on the road. Rig heard light laughter, followed by good-natured shhh-ing.

He took Naomi's helmet from her and placed both on the bike. Her cheeks were flushed bright pink, and her eyes were sparkling, glinting the color of sea-glass shards. "That was *amazing*. That was . . . wonderful. I didn't think I'd like it, but then I *did*." She pulled her fingers through her hair, trying to smooth it down. Her blue T-shirt was pulled a little sideways—he should have insisted on that jacket, she'd get cold later—and she had dust on the knee of her black pants.

He'd never known he had a type, not until he looked at her.

"Is it always like that?"

"What?" he asked, unable to tear his gaze away from the curls that still defied her efforts.

"Riding. Is it always that great?"

He answered honestly. "No. That was pretty spectacular."

She nodded. "The warm coast before sunset, through the countryside? That was amazing."

It hadn't been the view that had made it his favorite ride ever, but he wasn't going to tell her that. "Yep." He gestured up the road. "Come on. Don't want to miss the surprise."

Naomi looked down at herself, as if for the first time. "I can't go like this."

"What?"

"What the hell was I thinking? I was just so desperate to get away from Anna. I look like I've been cleaning the kitchen. No, wait, I look worse. I look like I've been scrubbing toilets. I have a hole right here, see? Over my belly button. How on earth would I get a hole there?"

He reached forward to touch the hem of the offending shirt she was holding out. "It's a tiny hole," Rig said, running his thumb over the fabric. "No one will notice." And he absolutely couldn't help it, even if he'd tried, when he let the back of his fingers touch the soft skin of her stomach, for the most fleeting of seconds.

Her lower lip dropped, and her eyes met his. Sun motes danced between them in a last shaft of warm light. Time slowed until he had to tell himself to breathe.

The moment shattered as Toots Harrison saw them. She let out a squeak and then called, "Yoohoo! You made it! I can't believe we got the new doctor *and* the shy doctor, too!"

They thought she was shy? He'd call Naomi other things: reticent, maybe. Jumpy. Nervous. But shy wasn't on the list of things he categorized her as.

Toots went on, loud enough for everyone to hear, "Now march! The time is now, and don't forget, don't shout surprise until Abigail actually opens the door. We want Lucy to *die* of surprise. Mildred, don't drop the cake! Bart and Jonas, you have all the wine? Owen, you have the plates? Everyone, go, go, go!"

As the cheerful mob tumbled forward, Rig caught Naomi's hand. He felt seventeen again, unable to stop touching the girl he liked. And shit, she made him nervous. He half-expected her to shrug him off. They were in public, after all. Anyone could see.

But she didn't. She even looked up and caught his eye for a split second, and then, astonishingly, she winked. He wanted to drag her into his arms and restart that searing kiss that had been so cruelly interrupted, damn the fact that they were surrounded by just about everyone who was anyone in town.

Naomi stumbled over a rock and Rig steadied her. Then he wished for more rocks, so that she'd lean against him again.

This was completely ridiculous.

And so much damn fun.

At the mailbox the group turned en masse into the driveway, and moved past a small purple outbuilding. A huge ancient house, painted white with dark green trim, looked as old as the trees around it that stood to their left, and to their right was a smaller, matching cottage with a hanging sign that read ELIZA's in curling script. The sun was now far enough down that they could see into the shop, and a slant of golden light illuminated two women leaning over a large table, holding what looked like squares, moving them back and forth. Everyone ducked and giggled like children.

"Shhh! They'll hear us," hissed Toots. She climbed up the steps of the cottage slowly, avoiding creaks. "Ready?" She banged on the front door with her fist.

A pause. Everyone held their breath. Rig's fingers tightened on Naomi's and she squeezed back. His heart raced in a way that he suspected had nothing to do with the party.

"*Surprise!*"

Lucy Bancroft stood in the open doorway, her mouth hanging open. She didn't say a word—she just started laughing. Great heaving laughs turned into gales of hilarity as the group poured up onto the porch and then into the store.

Owen Bancroft, a local handyman Rig had met at the hardware store when he'd been shopping for wood stain with Jake, lifted his wife, Lucy, up, his hands at her waist. She whooped at the top of the lift, and then she seemed to melt down Owen's body, ending up in a kiss that Rig looked away from. Now *that* was a kiss. And he'd be lying if he didn't admit to himself that the kiss reminded him of the woman whose hand he was still gripping. The thumb he touched was the one he'd bitten earlier, so lightly. . .

Startled by the intensity of the thought, Rig dropped Naomi's hand and turned to shake the hand of the man next to him.

He barely heard himself as he spoke automatically. "Rig Keller," he said. "New in town."

The man, who was tall and wore a wool newsboy cap—and actually got away with it—shook his hand. "Jonas Harrison. Lucy's brother. I own the Rite Spot in town."

Rig tuned in. Sure, the one bar downtown. He needed to check it out. No doubt he'd end up with a couple of patients who only liked to really talk if they were tucked into a dark, private booth. "Good to meet you."

But as Jonas spoke about something his brother Silas was building, Rig tuned out again. He was only registering one thing: where Naomi was at all times. If someone had covered his eyes suddenly, he'd be able to walk to her exact location, as if he had sonar. She bumped around the room, looking at loose ends. Soon he'd go rescue her, but he had a strange feeling she needed to scope out the room for herself.

It was gorgeous, he'd give the store that. Jewel-toned yarn lit up the dark wooden shelves, and skeins of yarn in colors he'd never even dreamed existed were piled high in baskets around the tables and the soft armchairs that were scattered around the room. Janelle Monáe's *Metropolis* played in the background, and people jiggled their hands and their feet in time to the rhythms.

Right now Naomi was behind a tall shelf of yarn. She'd been there a little while, actually, without moving. Almost as if she was hiding.

But she was probably just looking for the yarn she needed next. Rig assumed that all knitters collected yarn, like his mother had. She'd had almost a whole closet full of yarn when she died, and they hadn't known what to do with it after Dad had his heart attack and moved in with Jake. He had a feeling that perhaps they hadn't done anything good with it. They might have just thrown it all out, and now he realized that they probably could have asked around. Surely some charity or another needed yarn, right? It hadn't even crossed their minds as they got rid of most of Mom's stuff.

Maybe that's why Jake couldn't let a thing go. Too hard to make decisions.

Rig was hit with an insane desire to buy Naomi all the yarn she needed, all the yarn she could ever want: the softest, nicest stuff in this place. Anything that made her smile.

He tuned back in just as Jonas said, "Romo?"

"Excuse me?"

"You know Elbert Romo already?"

The old man walked up wearing what looked like a green flight suit, a bit ratty, but patched and clean.

"Course I do. He's the one who introduced me to Dr. Pederson. New look for you there, sir?"

"Howdy, son. Not a new look, just one I'm thinking of bringing back into fashion. Plus, if you get tired when you're at home, you can say they're pajamas and call it good." Elbert shook Rig's hand with such vigor Rig wasn't sure his neck wouldn't suffer a minor case of whiplash. "We was just discussing you yesterday over at the bookstore. Have a few questions for you, if you don't mind."

Uh-oh. Whether this was investigating his private life or the ever-popular game of What-does-this-rash-look-like-to-you, Rig knew he wasn't getting away from Elbert anytime soon. He'd be stuck here while Naomi roamed free as she pleased in the store. No one asking *her* personal questions.

Eh. If he got a query about Elbert's junk downstairs, he'd pull Naomi in for a consult. Just for fun.

Chapter Nineteen

When knitting with a friend, the laughter is worth the dropped stitches.

—E.C.

Naomi touched a skein of baby alpaca, a gorgeous royal purple, soft as air, but she thought only of Anna.

Anna was pregnant. And what had Naomi done? Bolted. It was as if she'd taken a page from Anna's book—her little sister was usually the one running away from confrontation. Naomi was the one who stuck around, even when she felt like hiding.

But not tonight. She'd fled, on a *motorcycle* of all things. And she didn't want to go back. She was a terrible sister.

A man spoke from behind her. "Lost in thought, or just tryin' to figure out what to make next?"

Naomi jumped and turned. She recognized Cade MacArthur, Eliza's friend Abigail's husband, having treated him once, and from seeing him in Tillie's with the ranchers, his daughter Lizzie clinging to his Wranglers, little Owen dangling from an arm. She knew much of the yarn in the store was spun of the fiber from sheep raised on this ranch.

"Oh, sorry." Naomi put back the skein she'd been fondling.

"Why? It's a good place to do it. I'm Cade, and I saw you once, didn't I? Cade MacArthur."

Naomi shook his hand and said, "I know." *Crap.* "I mean, yes, how's that knee? And call me Naomi?"

Cade smiled. He had bright green eyes that actually sparkled. She'd never seen eyes like that besides Eliza Carpenter's. He was her great-nephew, after all. It felt good to see those eyes again, as if she was seeing Eliza. "Knee's better than ever. Should it click so much going downstairs, though?"

Naomi's jaw dropped. "*No.* You need to come back in soon and—"

"Kidding, just kidding. It's just fine."

"Oh," breathed Naomi. Of course. It was a joke. "This is a gorgeous store."

"Thanks. Abigail does a good job. You two friends?" He picked up a sloppy skein and retwisted it as if he knew what he was doing.

Naomi felt the words she was going to say stall in her mouth. She knew Abigail. Kind of. She still wouldn't expect Abigail to know her, though, even with a botched store visit and the deathbed meeting. And they weren't friends, although Naomi could imagine that everyone in town wanted to be able to lay claim to Abigail's friendship.

Then she realized she'd been silent too long. *Shit.* If this was the office, if he were her patient right now, she'd know exactly what to say, instead of staring into this panicked blankness—

"Well," said Cade, scuffing the floor with his boot, "anyway, enjoy." He wandered toward a group of other men, and Naomi's hands went stiff, flexing outward. Why did she always have to be *uncomfortable* with people all the time? Would she ever grow out of it? When she was fifty, maybe? At seventy would she know how to do that casual banter that everyone else seemed born able to do?

She moved toward the back, keeping the smile firmly in place, as if she was happy to be there, as if she was ready to talk to anyone.

The one time Naomi had been in Eliza's, she'd been so flustered that she hadn't taken any time to look at what the stock was like. Something about its organization—how the colors of yarn went up the wall and how shop sweater models hung in unexpected places, the fluid nature of the design and the way that voices were muted, all sounds smoothed over so that conversation became a pleasant hum—soothed Naomi in a way she hadn't felt in a long time, and she felt her heart rate drop back to a more normal zone.

Naomi didn't even *need* yarn. She had plenty. She had an old suitcase that was full of yarn she intended to turn into scarves, and more than that, she had two places in her spare room where she kept enough yarn to make two sweaters, for when she got around to trying. For God's sake, her shawls were wonky enough, with their wandering motifs and dropped stitches. Even though Eliza Carpenter had told her that it wasn't worth worrying about mistakes, that no one would notice them, Naomi had stared at Eliza lying there in her narrow hospital bed and she hadn't believed her. If that was actually true, then when she looked at her friend and patient Eliza, she shouldn't be able to see how the cancer had ravaged her body—she should just be able to see how lovely, smart, and kind a person she was before she died.

That was crap. Eliza had been sick as hell. Naomi saw it, and treated her, treated her right into the grave. Eliza's death had affected her more than any other patient, and she'd never figured out why that was, exactly. She'd lost babies before, in tragic circumstances. She'd lost so many patients to disease she'd given up keeping score.

But Eliza had been different. It was as if Eliza had loved her— Naomi shook her head and picked up a green ball of something incredibly soft and stared at the label, unseeing. Well, who was to say she hadn't? Eliza loved everyone. After all, Eliza had told her about this town, had talked about Cypress Hollow for hours as they knitted together when Naomi was off shift, with nowhere better to go.

Eliza had put her feet on the path that led her here, to a yarn store on Eliza's old land, named in her memory.

She put the green ball back and picked up a dark gray mohair skein that had tiny streaks and flashes of color spun into the softness. From a distance, one would never see the color, but here, in her hand, the sparks looked like tiny, colorful secrets. She put it to her nose and inhaled its musty sweetness and let the yarn rest against the soft piece of skin just above her lip. It was as soft as a breath. Naomi needed this yarn. Keeping it in her hand with no idea of what she'd make with it, she moved farther down the aisle to where it curved. Oooh, this spot was nice; surrounded on three sides by shelves, she was alone and hidden. She took a deep breath, and just for a moment, she let herself pretend that the people out there on the other sides of the shelves were her friends, that they were looking for her, waiting for her.

Naomi peeked through two shelves and caught a glimpse of Rig smiling, talking with Lucy Bancroft's older brother and Elbert Romo. Rig looked like he fit right in—he threw his head back in a laugh, and even from where she was, she could see the dark stubble on his chin, at his jawline, the broad sweep of his cheek up to his eyes that crinkled with the grin. God, he was sex on a platter, wasn't he? Women must shoot their numbers on paper airplanes at him as he rode by their towns on the Harley-Davidson.

Naomi whacked her shin on a wooden drawer that was sticking out, full of overstock yarn.

"Shit," she whispered, and bent over to rub the knot that was quickly forming.

"I can't believe she's here, actually out of her office. Do you think she wants to learn how to knit?"

Naomi froze, still bent over.

"Doubt it. She doesn't look like the type. Well, you saw who she came with. I'd say *he* has something to do with why she's here."

Naomi peeked again through the shelf. Three women sat on low settees, all knitting, and leaning forward as they gossiped. She recognized one as Molly Flood—Naomi had bought her house from her last year. Then she'd treated Molly once for laryngitis. She'd never come back in, but they usually smiled at each other when they passed on the street, and Molly had sent her a bottle of Cypress Hollow red wine for Christmas. The second woman was Janet Morgan, a businesswoman whom Naomi often saw holding court in Tillie's, a cowboy-looking guy hanging on her every word. Everything about Janet looked expensive, from her impeccable eyebrows to the red-soled high heels she wore. The third woman looked familiar, but Naomi couldn't place her—she was a knockout with masses of long, straight red hair and huge blue eyes. She looked like she'd be good in a Victoria's Secret campaign.

They were the popular girls. Naomi could tell just by looking at them, and she felt herself curl into a small ball inside. But she kept eavesdropping.

"He's a hunk, all right," said the redhead. "I'd like to interview *him*."

"Oh, Trix. What about your reporter's code of ethics or whatever that is?"

That was it, now Naomi could place the third woman: Trixie Fletcher, reporter for the local paper. The one who'd had that small mocking laugh in her voice as she'd taken down the copy for the blood sugar check.

"What my boss doesn't know doesn't hurt him. And sometimes I really get the goods." Trixie smirked. "We're talking inside edition, if you know what I mean."

Molly's needles flashed. "There must be more to your interview techniques. You're a smart woman, don't sell yourself short."

"With those legs, darling?" drawled Janet, who was knitting much more slowly than the other two, her needles moving almost luxuriously. "She couldn't sell herself short if she tried. Legs for days—we *hate* you, kitten."

Trixie leaned forward again. "There's a story here, though. I can feel it. Big-time doctor from the Gulf, ultrasuccessful, running his own private practice out of his car, leaping off helicopters to aid injured workers, the guys on oil rigs bringing us the stuff that makes our nation great, slumming it here in little old Cypress Hollow at a small practice that he could probably afford to buy with cash? Only one other doctor in town, excluding the ones at the ER ten miles up the road, and she's a lonely cat lady. I'm seeing a *Modern Love*–style piece, only it wouldn't have a happy ending."

"Don't be mean," said Molly. "We don't know her well."

Naomi blinked, her eyes hot. She didn't have any cats.

Janet pulled out more yarn to use, stretching it slowly above her head and letting it drop. "She might even be a knitter, chickens. You never know. And then your mind would change about her, wouldn't it, Trixie?"

"She's no knitter. We'd know. She'd have come to knit night at least once. She would have *had* to buy yarn here—there's no other place to go. She's just an uptight, stuck-up city girl who doesn't really fit in here." Trixie jerked a stitch tight. "Shit. I dropped something somewhere."

"Careful." Molly looked around and Naomi ducked farther into the Malabrigo so that she couldn't be seen. "She's here somewhere. I'd hate for her to hear."

Trixie said, "Always the peacemaker, Molly. I'd tell her to her face she was stuck up. Always coming in Tillie's in the mornings, never saying hello to anyone. You know they hold that table for her every day just because it's the farthest from the other customers? Keeps her out of the way so she can just *watch* everything like she does."

Naomi felt like she was going to throw up. That's what they

thought? That she was awful? Horrible? The ball of sparkly gray wool she'd been holding turned sticky in her hand, and when she set it down, trying not to breathe, it had left bits of mohair on her palm.

She'd thought she just came off as shy, if anything. That had happened before, and she'd thought it would just take time. It wasn't that she didn't want to talk—she just wasn't good at the fake small talk. But they just plain hated her. *That's* why she was always left alone. The surprise of it hurt, too. It felt so . . . high school.

"What are you girls gossiping about?" Lucy Bancroft leaned over Janet's shoulder.

Naomi peeked one more time. She had to get the hell out of here, but she couldn't move—she had to hear the rest.

"Happy birthday, darling," drawled Janet. "You'll be happy to know I've enrolled you in the champagne of the month club."

Lucy whistled. "Hot damn! I love it. Thank you." She kissed Janet on the cheek, and then said, "Spill."

Trixie said in a whisper designed to carry, "Talking about the girl doctor. And how we'd like to trade her in for the new, über-hot boy doctor we have in town now."

Lucy frowned. "Naomi Fontaine? You know she's here somewhere, right?"

Trixie pouted. "You don't even know her."

"I've ordered some pretty obscure medical texts for her in the past year while she was researching patients' symptoms. And we've gone out for coffee a couple of times. We're friend dating. I like her. Says what she means."

"Well," said Janet in her normal booming voice, "shy is so difficult for people to deal with. I can't imagine being shy."

Lucy grinned. "We know. You were born naked and—"

Janet cut her off. "*Glorious.* I was naked and glorious. Oftentimes, I still am. Ask Tom over there." She pointed at a man in a cowboy hat talking to Abigail at the cash register. He turned bright red as the women looked at him.

Lucy said, "I think he heard you."

"Oh, darling, I meant him to," said Janet, stroking the tip of her needle.

Lucy straightened and waved at a woman across the room. "Well, quit talking smack. It's my party, and I don't want any hurt feelings today. And now I'm going to go give Elbert Romo a piece of my mind about not putting down the toilet seat in my store."

Lucy was too late to prevent hurt feelings. Way too late. Naomi tried to suck in a quiet breath, but it came out as a gasp. She'd gone past hurt feelings a while ago, and now she was all the way to broken ones.

They *hated* her. With the possible exception of Lucy, they despised her. No wonder she didn't have a single friend in town. She'd thought everyone was just formal. That it would take time. That being around the townspeople would eventually make her one of them. Instead, they'd been keeping her quarantined at her own table, lest she infect the rest of the residents with her . . . her what? *What* did they hate about her?

Out. She had to get out, get away. There was nothing more for her here at this party. Yes, Toots had been sweet, but she was practically the official town greeter. She'd probably bring a welcome basket to a newly paroled murderer. Naomi wasn't anyone special.

She scooted down the aisle of yarn, which had remained blessedly empty until now—no one to witness her humiliation, thank God—and she bumped into Rig as she turned the corner. Two more steps and the women would be able to see her. With any luck at all they'd have no idea where she'd been.

Rig wasn't moving. Naomi, desperate to get out of the aisle, walked into him, hoping that by invading his personal space, maybe even pushing if she had to, that he'd get it, and move. She didn't trust her voice to be able to ask him politely to get the fuck out of her way.

Instead, it felt like walking into a tree. A warm, tall, really firm-chested tree. He didn't budge, didn't even blink. Instead he caught her upper arms gently, wrapping his fingers around them. He waited until Naomi looked up at him and said, "Where's the fire, Doc?"

"I can't—I have to—let me go." She cleared her aching throat. "I've got to get out of here."

"Too much yarn? You're overwhelmed by the selection? Personally, I think if you've seen one yarn ball, you've seen—"

Naomi put everything she had into the one word. "Please."

His eyes went from mildly amused to concerned to something resembling ferocity. He turned so that he was beside her, and put his hand against the small of her back.

"Let's go," he said. "I'll handle it."

"No," she said over her shoulder. Somehow, it was desperately important that *she* handle this, not him. But she let him keep his hand on her back. That she would accept.

They made their way out of the yarn aisle and over to the main area, near the register, where most of the partygoers had congregated in small groups. Naomi looked at her phone and said loudly, "Well, dang it! Isn't that a shame?"

Abigail MacArthur, jiggling a baby on her hip and writing out a receipt with her free hand, looked up in alarm. "What is it?"

"Medical emergency. In town. We have to go."

At least five voices asked in unison, "Who?"

Rig's fingers pressed more firmly into her back, moving her toward the door.

"I mean, just out of town," said Naomi. "Tourist in an RV. Ambulance is on its way, but they'll need a doctor to transport, and since we're together on his motorcycle anyway, we're both going. Better two doctors than none."

She looked at Abigail, directly into her eyes. "What a nice party, though. Thanks for having me." Then she turned to Lucy, who stood near a display of needle gauges. "And happy birthday. I hope it's your best year ever."

She sounded good. Normal. Damn, she was proud of herself. Even if she still wanted to cry.

To a chorus of *What a shame* and *Be careful,* Rig steered her out of the crowd, onto the porch. He made excellent drive-by small talk as they passed people, murmuring good-byes that he made sound like they were both being polite.

"We'll see you soon," he said. "Can we just slip behind you here? Thanks, you take care, too."

Naomi didn't even glance in the direction of where Molly, Janet, and Trixie were still sitting. She couldn't.

Once out at the driveway, under the star-studded night sky, Naomi started to catch her breath. The air was cool, and smelled of hay and salt. Screw those women. She didn't need them. She didn't need anyone, never had, no one except her father, and look how far that had gotten her. "About that," she began.

"Don't worry about it. I'd already diagnosed gallstones and a case of gout. Glad for the excuse." The gravel crunched under their feet companionably. Up on the county road, they didn't speak until they reached Rig's motorcycle.

"So," he said. "You've got to get to that 'thing' you mentioned earlier? Should I drop you off wherever that is?"

"I lied. I don't have a thing." He knew already, Naomi figured.

"And you don't mind riding the bike again?"

"Only if you go as fast you can." The words on her lips surprised her, and she pulled on the helmet so hard she hurt her ears.

Chapter Twenty

Knitting with five needles at once is not as dangerous as it looks. And people will think you're even cleverer than you are, which is always a nice thing, isn't it?
—E.C.

The harvest moon still hung low in the sky, and Naomi stared into its face as they rode eastward into the country. The farther they went, it seemed, the faster he drove. And the faster the motorcycle went, the slower Naomi's heart rate felt. It was as if touching the danger, feeling the ground whipping by below them and the slight sting of the air against her bare forearms, allowed her to forget herself and think of nothing but the way Rig felt in front of her: hard, strong, in total control of where he took them, and for those few minutes, Naomi let him be in charge. She let herself feel as if they might ride all night and leaned her cheek against the cool leather of his jacket.

Spread far down below them to the right was a sparkling night panorama—the yellow moon behind them, lighting the fields that stretched right to the ocean's edge. Small collections of light flickered in valleys, groups of two or three homes, surrounded by nothing else but moonlight. And the ocean itself . . . It spread as far to the north and south and due west as her eye could see. There was no fog, rare in and of itself on a summer night, and moonlight glinted on the water, flashes of silver that existed for only a split second, then reappeared somewhere else.

And down there was a town where almost no one liked her. Naomi blinked hard and tilted her head up to the stars, the air cold at her exposed throat. It hurt. She hadn't even *known* they didn't like her. That was the worst part: feeling this stupid, the shock of it.

Much too soon, Rig cruised down the hill into town and pulled onto her street, then up to her house. He put one foot down, rocking the motorcycle to rest as its engine coughed to a stop.

Naomi didn't move. She stayed resting again Rig's broad back, and whispered, "Damn."

She felt his laughter more than she heard it: a rumble that moved from his lower abdomen up to his chest. Naomi's hands had been resting lightly on Rig's hips, and she let herself feel the denim fabric for another heartbeat before she sat up and away from him. Then she slid off the bike, feeling graceless as she hopped backward to avoid touching the pipe Rig had said was hot. She took off her helmet and her head felt so light that it might float away.

Inside, Anna waited for her. It said something awful about her that she wanted to stay out here with Rig, just a few more minutes. But she didn't want to go in, not just yet.

He sat on the curb and patted the concrete next to him. "You wanna tell me what happened back there?"

"When?" Playing the dumb card wouldn't help, but it bought her an extra second or two while she sat down next to him.

"At the shop, when you freaked out."

"I didn't . . ." She couldn't tell him the truth. It was too pathetic.

"You did." He leaned so that he could lift her hand and tuck it into his.

And suddenly, with that touch, Naomi wanted to tell him. She felt as if she could. "I overheard some women talking about me. They weren't nice, and it kind of confirmed something for me."

"What?"

"That I don't fit in here. That instead of just being ambivalent about my presence, which is what I thought, they actually dislike me." The words felt as if they were twisting their way out of her mouth. She closed it tightly to prevent more from coming out.

The streetlight above them gave a metallic *clink* and went out. A curtain twitched across the street, and Naomi knew Mrs. Strufend was watching them, making sure they weren't planning on stealing her 1972 mint green Cadillac.

But instead of protesting, which Naomi expected Rig to do, instead of telling her she must have misunderstood them, he asked, "What are you going to do about it?"

Naomi took her hand back, and shoved it through the curls that kept blowing annoyingly into her face. "*Do* about it? I can't change the way they feel. Psych 101, you remember. I'm not responsible for their emotions."

"Oh, cut the crap," Rig's voice was a drawl in the dark. "You've done something to earn their dislike. If it's something you want to continue, then fuck 'em. And if what you've done is something you want to change, then change, and see what happens with them."

"I didn't *do* anything," muttered Naomi as she plucked a sad piece of grass from behind her and examined it. She really should water more often.

"So what didn't you do?"

Shit. He was on the money, and she didn't like it.

"Well, I didn't come into town and pretend to be the next best thing, trying to be everyone's friend." She let the implication remain only in her tone. "I didn't josh with everyone in Tillie's or join every committee they asked me to. I didn't have time. I thought people would meet me in my practice—I thought that's how I would make friends." Her throat tightened with sudden tears, and Naomi was horrified. She didn't cry in front of anyone. Certainly not her new business partner who happened to be stroking her shoulder in a way that was both comforting and devastatingly hot.

She cleared her throat and tried again. "I thought that slowly, I'd become part of a group, like I was down south. I miss them. I miss my friends. But they're too busy with their own work to come up, and God knows I haven't been able to find the time to go south. It's been a year already . . ." She folded her arms on the tops of her knees, and then put her head down, swallowing as hard as she could to try to keep back the awful lump that rose in her throat. "They said I was stuck up." She groaned and buried her head farther.

Rig didn't say anything immediately, which further increased Naomi's agony. But his hand massaged back and forth along her shoulder blades, a warm, reassuring touch. He wasn't trying anything with her. He more than likely never would, not after this meltdown. And that was fine. Wasn't it?

"You probably haven't failed. Not completely," said Rig finally. "You're just a little . . . awkward."

"Thank you." Naomi turned her head to the right to stare at him. "And you're no help. The town already loves you."

"You forget I had an in—my brother. Everyone loves a firefighter."

Naomi rubbed her head back and forth on her folded hands. "No, I think it's you."

He scooted the final inch closer, so that now their sides were touching. He stared across the street and she saw him blink as Felix, Mrs. Strufend's gigantic great Dane pressed his nose against the glass at the top of her front door. "Wow. But hey, what about me?"

"What?"

"*Why* do you think they like me?" Rig cocked his head to the side and waited, seeming intent on her answer.

Was he fishing for a compliment? It sounded like it, but Naomi didn't think that was his purpose. He didn't really seem like the kind of guy who needed affirmation. God, he felt good next to her. So warm, as if he were giving off warmth like a heater. Naomi had to physically restrain herself from pushing back into him. She'd climb in his lap if she could.

But she couldn't. Naomi gave herself a mental shake, and then considered his question.

"Truthfully?"

He nodded. "Yep. Truth."

"Because you're The Guy."

A slight furrow dented his forehead. "Huh?"

"You're tall. You're the right age. You have cheekbones practically as broad as your shoulders. You're a *doctor*, for goodness' sake."

"So are you. So what?"

"It's different. You drive a motorcycle. You worked on oil rigs. You're a man's man, doing a man's job."

"No way," Rig said. "You can't reduce this to a gender argument."

"I can and I will. That's what it's about. They don't talk to me, put me at my own stupid table at the diner, hold out until they're practically dead hoping Pederson is coming back, but you waltz in, and you're accepted."

"You're saying that's because I'm male."

"And tall. And okay looking."

Rig threw his head back and laughed up into the night sky. "Well, at least you think I'm okay looking."

He was better than okay looking, but she wouldn't say it. She wouldn't give him that satisfaction. Naomi lifted the shoulder that was touching his with a slight up-down motion. "I guess."

She wanted to touch him more. With a wild desperation that didn't fit in her body, she wanted to kiss him. To feel his mouth on hers again, to determine if the heat that had flared between them would happen again.

No, no, no. *No.*

He had to leave. She'd lost her mind, riding out with him. And they had to be at work on Monday, ready to go, working together, side by side, professionally.

Abruptly, Naomi stood. "Thanks for the ride, then." She busied herself with brushing off the seat of her pants.

Rig looked surprised but stood with her. "Yeah. Okay." He threw his leg over the bike and looked at her, his eyes intense in the darkness. "I had a great time tonight."

Naomi kicked at a pebble. "Thanks," she mumbled. She wanted to run in the house and bury herself in the afghan on the couch, but she knew another problem was waiting for her inside.

He gave the kick that would preface the rumble of the bike below him. But instead of a roar, she heard a click. Rig kicked the starter again. Still nothing.

"What's going on?"

"Hell if I know. Old bikes like this . . ." Rig's leg jerked again, and this time, there was a loud *bang* and a rattle that seemed to jerk his whole body, followed by another pop.

"Whoa!" Rig leaped off the bike and stood next to her on the curb, watching as it smoked.

"I think it's on fire," he said. "Whoops."

Chapter Twenty-one

I've studied a little Zen in my time. Knitting is the oppo-site of a koan, I think, but it has the same grace.
—E.C.

But no flames rose, and the smoke or dust, whatever it had been, dissipated, leaving just the smell of burning oil and a faint *tink-tink* from the engine.

Naomi waited a beat while he stared at the bike, unmoving. Then she said, "Isn't this where you hit the dirt with a wrench, getting grease on your hands? Further proving the town right about you? You know, *Zen and the Art* and all?"

Rig shook his head. "I love riding, but I don't know a damn thing about engines. Of any kind. I know how people work. That's about it."

Naomi felt a flutter in her stomach.

Rig stuck his hand in his front pocket and pulled out a cell phone. "I'll just call my brother."

Standing on opposite sides of the motorcycle, Naomi watched as he dialed, then listened as he gave his brother directions. "Quit it. Just get here." A pause. "Shut up." A click as he snapped the phone shut. "Smart-ass. He's on his way. He's not far."

There was an electrically charged pause. Should she invite him in? Naomi dug her nails into her palms. Need hit her, hard. A ridiculous desire to test him. To test herself.

Rig kicked a booted toe into the edge of the gutter and kept his eyes down. The quiet grew louder.

She would figure this out. Naomi only knew why she was moving a second before she came around the back wheel. She didn't give herself time to form an argument. Coming face-to-face with Rig, she grabbed the front of his leather jacket in both hands.

In the moonlight, his eyes widened, and the beginning of a smile crept across his mouth.

"What—?"

"I just have to try this again," Naomi said. This would be scientific. A controlled study. In Portland, it had been . . . In her living room, it was . . . no, she must be remembering wrong. One more try, then.

Going up on tiptoe, she pulled herself up to his mouth. She didn't go slowly. The kiss started up right where it had left off earlier, as if no time had passed. Her head swam, and she held on tightly to her intention. This was a test—she was in control.

Rig met her intensity, wrapping his arms around her waist, drawing her against him, hard. His tongue rasped against hers, and Naomi kept track of who was in charge of the kiss. She was, no, he was . . . No, she definitely was. No question.

He sucked on her lower lip, then breathed into her mouth, and she inhaled him, wanting to draw him into her, down inside where her need started, growing with each flick of his tongue. She was shocked to feel her knees shake, and pressed her thighs to his while at the same time, she leaned out, taking a juddering breath. She needed cool air in her lungs to come back to herself.

More. She should push this further. Just to see. His head dipped toward her again. Releasing his jacket, feeling herself supported fully by his arms around her waist, she wove her hands into his hair, dragging her fingers down his neck, back up to the base of his skull so she could pull his kiss against her harder. Rougher.

Getting air was difficult again, and she heard the ragged edges of his breath match her own. Forgetting her study of the kiss, unable to stop herself, she dropped her hand down to the front of his jeans, pressing against where she could feel him straining. He bit off a curse against the side of her jaw and leaned more heavily into her, bucking again at the touch of her hand.

"Naomi . . ."

"What?" she whispered, dipping her tongue into the corner of his lips, just where they met. He tasted sweet and metallic. She couldn't get enough.

"You have to . . ."

"Have to what?" A heady feeling of power coursed through her as she felt his sides shake with a need that matched hers. Yes. This was what she wanted.

"Stop. You have to stop."

Naomi pulled her head back and looked at him. The moonlight bathed his high, broad cheekbones, and she could see that they were flushed with warmth. Good. Her whole body was superheated, and she wanted his to match.

"Why?" she asked. A little more of the kiss wouldn't hurt. Just testing. She told herself she could keep it together. She knew she could. If she figured out exactly how dangerous he was for her, she could control her responses.

"Because," Rig said, and leaned forward to graze her cheek with the stubble of his chin. His voice was intense, pitched low and directly into her ear. "If you don't, my brother is going to drive up and find me fucking you against the bike."

And just like that, Naomi lost control of the situation. The image crashed through her mind, her naked legs wrapped around his hips,

Rig thrusting into her—her knees, already shaking, felt as if they were made of liquid, like the rest of her. She clung to him, her mouth open. She couldn't find the words, the right words . . .

Rig drew the lobe of her ear into his mouth, and then said, "And if I do that then the woman across the street"—Naomi peeked at Mrs. Strufend, who was gawping at them through her kitchen window—"will probably have a heart attack, and we'll have to save her, and I don't feel like saving anyone but you right now."

Naomi turned her head and took a deep breath. "You're right. We *have* to stop." She managed to push her way out of his arms and stumbled backward a few steps. Her lips felt swollen, burned by stubble, and she put her arms out, as if something were nearby to steady her.

The streetlight clicked back on, and lit him like a spotlight. His hair stuck out on the side where she'd had her fingers in it, and his bottom lip shone, wet. He looked like he should be smoke jumping, not ferrying a coworker home.

She'd been playing with matches, forgetting he was a fucking volcano. Holy Christ. She barely restrained herself from panting.

Naomi couldn't let that happen again. How ridiculous. Thank God it was Friday and she wouldn't have to face him in the morning.

Already, now that the heat of his body had been removed from hers, the cool air was giving her a chill. Goose bumps prickled her arms. His chest was rising and falling like hers. *Damn it.* She was struck by the completely irrational urge to fly back to him, wrap herself around him so tight that they both went crazy, and at the same time, she wanted desperately to run inside. Away from here. Away from *him*. Oh, but God, she'd forgotten yet again that her home was occupied by her pregnant sister. Damn, damn, damn.

"I'm sorry," she mumbled, looking anywhere but at his moonlit eyes. A shooting star grazed his shoulder.

"I'm not," he said. His voice was sugar on gravel. "I'm glad as hell."

A car's engine sounded in the distance. A wild feeling of gratitude rose in her chest. "Is that him? Your brother?"

"Probably."

"Thank God."

The car, a small black Jetta, pulled onto the street and then drew alongside them. The window went down, and Jake Keller's head came out the driver's-side window.

"All three of us needed an outing. Hope you don't mind."

Chapter Twenty-two

At some point, you'll drop all your notions in the worst place possible, as we all do. Just gather as many stitch markers as you can—the ones you can't pick up will help a knitter later.

—E.C.

Rig's father gave a cheery wave, grinning like the five-year-old Milo who sat behind him. For God's sake. His brother had brought the whole damn family.

"Hey, you two." Jake got out of the car and gave Naomi an assessing look. Then he turned to his brother and winked. "What's wrong with your bike?"

Apparently Jake had forgiven him for the argument about the photo album yesterday. Good. That was something.

"You had to bring everyone?" said Rig.

"Sure!" said Jake. "We were bored. Milo couldn't sleep. Thought we'd come help Uncle Rig."

Rig's father unfolded himself from the front passenger seat into the street, stretching and sighing as he did so. "Your car is cramped, Jake. You should get a new one the Keller men fit into."

The situation was turning even more embarrassing than Rig had imagined it would be to have his brother rescue him. Frank approached Naomi, who stood in place with a quizzical expression on her face. Was she wondering if he'd ordered reinforcements?

"Frank Keller, at your service," his father said, holding out his hand.

"Dr. Naomi Fontaine, nice to meet you."

His father leaned forward, took her hand with both of his, and then bowed to kiss her knuckles. She'd been kissed by two Keller men tonight, Rig realized. Naomi giggled, a cute-as-hell sound Rig hadn't heard before. He made an immediate vow to get her to giggle for him. There was no way his father was getting away with it if Rig couldn't.

"I don't know what's wrong. It just kind of blew up," he said to Jake.

"Blew up? Motorcycles don't—" The firefighter in his brother looked concerned. "You both all right?"

"Fine, fine. I think it threw something, which pissed something else off."

"You never were the mechanic in the family." Frank released Naomi's hand and tapped himself proudly on the chest. "I rebuilt my Volvo's engine last summer. It's at Jake's house, runs like a dream."

"The horn honks when you use the turn signal," Jake said.

"That's just electrical," snapped Frank. He turned back to Naomi and beamed. "The engine purrs. And you, my dear, look lovely tonight."

"Don't hit on Rig's date, Dad," said Jake. "It never goes as well as you think it will."

"Well, thanks for coming to get me," said Rig. He wasn't above begging. This had just turned into the most uncomfortable date he'd ever been on. "Naomi, I'll have the shop pick up the bike in the morning."

"You're leaving it here?" asked Jake.

"What, you think you can fix it with your mechanical prowess and mind control? Got a toolbox on you, bro?"

Jake shrugged. "Guess not."

"So let's go."

"I have to pee," piped Milo, poking one hand out the open window.

Rig groaned. "Can't you wait, buddy? Five more minutes? Just till Dad drops me off at my place? You can pee there."

"Now." Milo stood firm on the matter. And when Keller men made up their minds, Rig knew there was no swaying them.

"Naomi, would you mind if we . . . ?"

"Of course not," she said briskly. "Why doesn't everyone come inside?"

"I meant me," Rig said. "I'll take Milo in by myself." But it was too late. Jake and his father were already headed up the walkway. He got Milo out of his car seat, and his nephew shot ahead. All of them were inside the house before Rig finished closing the car door.

A second later, Naomi's face appeared in the living room window, just in time to watch him stumble over a sprinkler head in the lawn as he made his hurried way to the front doorstep. Great.

"You coming in?" She held the screen door open for him.

"Don't mind me," he said.

"I won't," she said. But she smiled, and Rig got stuck all over again on how pretty her mouth was when it moved like that.

He shook his hands out as if the motion would help him clear his mind. Jake had already disappeared, presumably to the bathroom with Milo, and Frank was leaning forward, taking a close look at the pictures Naomi had up near the hallway. Rig hadn't noticed them earlier—he'd only really looked at the large print of the poppy.

These pictures were different; they were family photos, mostly black and white. They were hung haphazardly, some a little crooked, at all points on the wall, in frames that didn't match. Rig's mother would have had a heart attack. Once, he'd seen her use a level while hanging her shopping list on the fridge. He'd teased her, but she'd just told him she liked order.

Naomi, as proven by the pictures, and the piles of professional journals next to the couch, piled so high that several of the piles had toppled over, wasn't like his mother. At all.

Not that he would compare them.

Whatever.

He had to admit, the photos looked nice the way Naomi had hung them. Homey.

Frank pointed a finger, almost touching the glass of one of them.

"Dad," hissed Rig.

"Who is this, my dear?"

Naomi stood next to Frank. "That's my father and mother when they were still married." She smiled, a small private grin. "He wore that suit for years, said it was the best one he ever had made."

"Where are they now?"

Rig watched Naomi's face fall. "Dad died when I was seventeen. He was a doctor, too. Mom's still in L.A."

"Oh, my dear. I'm sorry about your father," said Frank. "Which one do you most resemble?" He leaned in again. "Your father. I can see it clearly."

Naomi nodded, appearing satisfied. "My sister looks like our mother, I look like Dad."

"And this is your grandmother?" Frank pointed to a photo of an elderly woman seated, smiling, on a sand dune.

Naomi laughed. "No, that's Eliza Carpenter. I wish she was my grandmother. But no, just a friend."

Frank said, "Was it taken here?"

Naomi smiled. "No, she *was* from here, but she was my patient in San Diego. I broke her out of the hospital one afternoon, and we went wandering. Eliza taught me how to go down a dune that day. She told me to listen carefully, and I thought she'd have some safe way to do it, a way to preserve the sand and ecology or something, so I concentrated. Then she said, 'You must throw both arms in the air and run down, as fast as you can, screaming as loudly as possible.' Then she held both of her canes up into the air, and wobbled down the dune, hollering the whole time. She watched as I ran down and gave me an eight for performance, and a ten for volume." Naomi laughed, and touched the frame of the photo, her eyes wistful.

Frank nodded, his eyes happy. "Sounds like a smart woman."

"All right, Dad, as soon as Jake—"

"Hi." The voice came from behind them. Naomi's sister, Anna, walked out of the dim hallway and into the bright living room. She wore red pajamas that barely covered her stomach and a fluffy red robe. Rig wondered if they were her own clothes or if she'd borrowed them from her sister.

Naomi would look hot as sin in red.

Anna rubbed her eyes and, her belly notwithstanding, looked about thirteen years old. "What are you all talking about out here?"

Frank looked startled. "Oh, dear, I hope we didn't wake you up."

"You did," Anna said with a smile, "but it sounded nice out here. Interesting."

Naomi said quickly, "This is Frank, Rig's father. His whole family is here, actually. They're using the bathroom. Then they're leaving, and you and I can talk." She paused. "Are those my pajamas?"

So they *were* hers. Now Rig had a visual of Naomi moving though her house at night in the red silk.

"Bathroom?" Anna ignored the question and plopped onto the couch, yawning. "Why?"

Jake came out of the side bathroom, ushering along Milo, who held his hands in the air and flapped them.

"Air dry," said Milo. "Air dry!"

Naomi said, "Isn't there a towel in there?"

Rig nodded. "Milo likes to air dry. Even when he gets out of the bath." He still thought it was one of the funniest things his nephew did, and he did a lot of them, careening naked around the house after his bath, thumping wetly off walls and furniture.

Milo sped up, like he always did when air drying, and he zoomed around the living room. On his second lap, he jumped up onto and then off of the couch where Anna sat.

"Milo!" said Jake. "Come here. Stop."

Milo kept running, but he stayed on level ground.

"Sorry," said Rig to Anna. "That's my nephew, Milo. And this is my brother, Jake."

Anna pulled the red robe around herself more tightly and said, "Well, hi. I didn't know it would be *this* much fun out here."

Jake said, "He's crazy. Gets that from his uncle." Milo stopped running and started spinning like a top.

"Unfair," said Rig, but he was barely listening. He watched Naomi's face, how it lit up at the sight of her sister, only to fall, so quickly, as her eyes fell to her sister's stomach. There were a lot of emotions that needed to be dealt with, and the women couldn't start until all the Kellers left.

Milo stopped spinning and staggered sideways, running into Anna's legs. She reached forward, moving awkwardly with her belly, and caught him under the arms. "Come up and sit next to me, big guy."

Rig waited for Milo to struggle, to pull away like he always did when he was placed in one spot and told to stay. Rig knew it wouldn't fly, especially from a stranger.

But Milo looked up into Anna's eyes, and then down to her belly. He crawled up next to her. "Is there a baby in there?"

Anna nodded. Naomi watched her sister with a guarded expression Rig couldn't read.

"Yep," said Anna. "It's a baby girl. You must be really smart. How did you know?"

"Mrs. Misty at day care has one in her tummy, too."

"Well, you're very smart to figure it out."

Milo nodded, put his thumb in his mouth, and curled up against Anna. Damn. Milo didn't cuddle with strangers. Maybe it was a knocked-up thing.

Jake said, "Don't suck your thumb, Milo. And we should go. Let's get out of their hair."

Anna put her arm around Milo and drew him closer. "You don't have to go. Or is Milo's mother always sure you boys are dead on the highway if you're late?"

Naomi gasped. "Anna!"

Jake opened his mouth, looking like he had something to say but only managed, "Well . . ." before he stopped speaking.

Rig would have to clean it up somehow. "She—"

Milo unstopped his thumb from his mouth and interrupted him. "My mom died a really long time ago. When I was little."

Anna's eyes went wide. "Oh, God. I'm so sorry."

"Why?" said Milo, but Anna was looking at Jake.

"I didn't mean to—"

Jake waved his hands, but still appeared mute.

"But you did," said Naomi sharply. "As usual."

Anna's eyes filled with tears, and she stood up from the couch and rushed down the hallway into the darkness. A door slammed.

Rig swung around, thinking he could say something to ease the situation, smooth it over. Jake was going to be more hurt than he would let on, and Naomi would probably be embarrassed by the whole thing. Dad, of course, would be oblivious, as usual.

As he turned, his elbow hit a tall standing lamp and sent it pitching to the left. He jumped, grabbing for its pole, but missed and sent it flying farther. Just before the lamp crashed to the ground, it thunked a tall gray pot, decorated with an owl, that sat on a side table.

With a huge smash, the pot hit the hardwood floor and exploded into shards of ceramic. A coarse, heavy dust spilled from the broken container.

This Frank noticed. He jumped back and said, "I was nowhere near that. What *was* it?"

Heavyhearted, Rig stared at the dust rising from the floor. There was only one reason to keep a pot full of ashes.

Naomi visibly paled. "Dad," she whispered.

Chapter Twenty-three

Double decreases are awkward with all their slipping of
this and that. Better just to knit three together through
the back loops and call it a day. No one will ever notice.
—E.C.

Frank perked up. "That's your father? That's a lot of ashes. Was he taller than he looked in that picture?"

Jake gathered Milo up into his arms. "We'll be out in the car." They disappeared out the front door before anyone else could move.

"Shit, Naomi," said Rig. "I didn't mean to—oh, God. Is that really—?"

Naomi nodded, her mouth twisting miserably. She was going to have to . . . sweep Dad up.

"I'll get the broom," she said.

Rig leaped forward. "No, let me do it. Please?"

She shook her head. Dammit, she would *not* get emotional about this. Not right now. There would be time for that later, when the house was empty again.

Except for her sister.

A moment later, she brought the dustpan and brush into the living room. Rig still looked shell shocked. "I'm so sorry. I can't imagine . . . but your sister said that to Jake, and then I was just going to say something, but I hit the lamp instead—"

God. Her sister and the comment about Jake's dead wife. The house was full of dead people, wasn't it? At least Jake didn't have to sweep anything up.

The ash was both fine and gritty at the same time. Some of it stayed heavy as sand on the floor, and some flew up into the air like dust. Naomi tasted it in her mouth and bit her inner lip to keep from crying.

She wished Rig would just go. But he wasn't getting it—he just stood above her, staring down at her with those impossibly sad, apologetic eyes.

Frank raised one hand and said, "Lovely to meet you, my dear. My regards to your . . . " His eyes fell to her brush. " . . . family." He slipped out the front door, quietly closing it behind him.

Naomi finished collecting everything into the dustpan, and then she had no clue as to what to do with it. Was it okay to put the ashes into a plastic bag? Was it disrespectful?

Rig spoke again, "Will you at least let me buy another urn? Was that one sentimental?"

"No. My mom gave it to me, actually. Thus the owl on it. I always kinda thought it was funny I stored Dad's ashes in there. It'd rile her if she knew." She smiled at the thought and then felt sadness at having to sweep up her father's ashes. It warred with anger at Rig for creating the whole mess in the first place. But he hadn't meant to. Just like Anna hadn't meant to throw the bomb into the middle of the room.

"I'm sorry about my sister," said Naomi. "She's so used to charming everyone she meets that . . ." *When it comes to men she wants to flirt with*, she thought. Jake was Anna's type, she knew. Tall, dark, and probably emotionally unavailable after a traumatic loss. With a kid to top it off. Great.

"She was fine. She didn't know," said Rig. "Jake's a big boy. He knows that people will ask him questions."

Naomi looked down again into the dustpan. "I don't have any idea what to do with this now."

He considered it with a serious expression and then said, "You don't want to store that in anything like a cup or a bowl. Nothing you eat from. Just as a matter of politeness, of course."

She blanched. "Of course. Do you think a bag would be okay?"

"Do you have a vase?"

Her mind went blank. "Like, for flowers?"

"It seems like a nice place to be until you get a new urn, and the flowers won't mind later. They'll like it."

What a morbid conversation to be having. What a macabre thing to be *doing*. But it had to be done, and preferably before Anna came back out. Naomi didn't want to have to explain to her sister what had happened when she'd left the room. Even though it wasn't *her* father who'd hit the floor, it still wouldn't be a pleasant surprise for a pregnant woman who was probably supposed to be taking it easy.

"I'll get one from the kitchen." But she was still holding the now-heavy dustpan. She didn't want to set it down. . . .

"Tell me where it is. I'll get it."

"Upper-right cabinet, next to the sink. There's a dark-colored one—maybe that would work." If it was the dark vase, they couldn't look through clear glass and see Dad, what was left of him. Oh, God.

As he went into the kitchen, Naomi noticed that there was still dust on the floor, the finest bits that the brush hadn't picked up. It was between the slats of the hardwood. It would probably take a vacuum cleaner to get it up.

She sat on the couch, as carefully as she could without jostling the contents of the dustpan. She didn't even want to breathe too hard, lest she cast any more of the dust upward.

Rig came back. "Is this it?" he asked, holding up the dark vase. It was a shorter, squatter vase than any of her others, and it would be a fine temporary holding place. She could fashion a plastic-wrap lid later.

Naomi nodded.

"You want me to hold it? While you . . . pour?" he asked, sitting next to her on the couch.

Nodding again, Naomi held the corner of the dustpan to the lip of the vase. Carefully, she tipped it, pouring the ash as slowly as she could.

"Would your dad at least have thought this was funny?"

Naomi didn't look at Rig, just kept pouring. "Well, yeah. He wouldn't talk about it much, didn't really talk about anything, usually. Just work." *Maybe that's where I get it from.* "So he didn't laugh much, but when he did, his laughter boomed like thunder. I loved feeling it in my chest."

"That's a nice memory." Rig cupped one hand around the top so that nothing escaped.

It was kind of him to do that, she thought. He was a nice man.

And it was completely, terribly wrong that she heated up this way when she looked at him, warmth pooling between her thighs when she remembered how he'd kissed her. He had the dust of her *father* on his hands, for God's sake.

Naomi stored the vase carefully on the same end table and took the dustpan and brush through the kitchen and out onto the back porch. She'd shake them off in the morning, when she was more clearheaded. Now, she just wanted to get Rig out and away, then she wanted to talk to her sister, then she wanted nothing more than deep, oblivious sleep.

In the living room he stood, shoving his hands deep into his pockets. "Long day," he said.

"Obviously." Crap, it sounded like she was mad. But she wasn't angry with him anymore for breaking the urn, she really wasn't.

Rig didn't flinch, though. "I'm going to go," he said, jerking a thumb in the direction of the front door. "They're out there waiting for me."

How had she forgotten all about the other Keller men? "Yeah, that would be good."

This time he did flinch. "Again, I'm sorry." Then he just stood there, not moving.

"I guess I'll see you on Monday, then," she said.

They faced each other. Naomi didn't know whether she should put out her hand to shake or not. That would be the polite thing. The professional thing.

Therefore it was the right thing. "Well, good night."

Rig looked surprised at seeing her hand, but he shook it brusquely. "Good night," he said.

When she shut the door behind him, she felt a wild urge to either laugh or cry, and she wasn't sure which one she felt more like doing. She turned, leaning her back against the door, staring into the living room that just moments ago had been so abnormally full of people.

And her house still wasn't empty. One person remained, the only person she'd ever avoided more than her mother.

Anna.

Chapter Twenty-four

Grace is knowing when to bind off.
—E.C.

A nna?" Naomi didn't want to just push open the guest room door that stood ajar, but her sister hadn't responded to the light tap she'd given on the wood. The room was dark, no lights on. Anna couldn't possibly have gone to sleep already, could she?

"You still in there?" Would she have slipped out the back door? Without saying anything?

Sure she would. She'd done it before. Naomi entered the room and flipped on the light switch. "Anna?"

Her sister, still wearing the red robe, was lying on her back on the bed, one arm slung over her eyes. "What?"

"We need to talk."

"I guess. Can we do it in the morning, though? I can't even begin to tell you how tired I am. I was on the bus for two days, and that's no place for a person who has to pee every seventeen seconds." Anna sighed. "It's just that everything kind of hurts. And I'm exhausted." Her voice wobbled at the end of the sentence, and Naomi ached to give her something: a hug, maybe, or a kiss on the top of the head. Even a pat on the knee would do. She took a step toward her sister, but Anna rolled so that she was on her side, facing the wall.

Rather than addressing her sister's back, Naomi went to the window and pulled the curtains over the already-shut blinds. Where was she supposed to start? She didn't have a textbook for this, no class had ever prepared her for it. She should ask about the baby's father. How it had happened. Was her sister in love? Had she been left by someone? Had she done the leaving? Was Anna hurting?

Instead, she asked, "How far along are you?"

Anna said nothing.

Naomi tugged the last curtain closed impatiently, and was rewarded for her distractedness by having the curtain rod jump its hooks, the curtain slithering to the floor as she tried to grab it. She always forgot this rod was tricky. Dang it.

"Anna, you have to talk to me. I'm letting you stay—"

"Big of you," her sister muttered.

"Excuse me?" Naomi felt heat in her forehead as she fought with her temper. "The least you can do is answer a couple of questions before you fall asleep."

"Fine." With a thunk, Anna rolled over onto her back again, and folded her arms over her stomach.

"Seven months, I'm guessing?"

"Twenty-nine weeks, actually," said Anna.

"Wow. How do you feel?"

"About being pregnant?"

"No, physically." Shoot, she should have said yes. That would have been good. Naomi kicked herself.

"Physically, great. I'm an ideal pregnant person. I haven't had a second of morning sickness, I don't get overly tired, unless I cross the country on a bus, and my back doesn't even hurt. My feet are getting swollen, that's the only thing that's bothering me lately. That and I'm getting to the point where I can't see them."

"You're carrying well," said Naomi. She brushed some nonexistent dust from the bureau.

"If by that you mean I'm not a fat cow, I beg to differ. I've put on thirty pounds."

"You were underweight before."

"Thanks," said Anna in a sour voice. "Didn't take you long to start criticizing. Should I tell you where the dad and I met? Would you believe a pool hall? Or should I tell you we met in the can? Or better, in jail?"

With a tone sharper than she intended it to be Naomi said, "Quit it. This is exactly what I expected from you."

Faster than Naomi would have thought she'd be able to, Anna sat up, swinging her legs wide over the edge of the bed. "What? Knocked up? Broke? Begging for help?"

Naomi didn't answer her. Besides, the answer was obvious.

Anna got the same sad, stubborn look she used to get when they were kids, the one she got when things weren't going her way. Her mouth turned down, and her eyelids dropped over her blue eyes. When they were young, their mother would fall for it, caving in to her demands for chocolate and new toys.

"I'm keeping the baby," Anna said.

"Okay," said Naomi, feeling proud of herself that she didn't utter the first thing that came to her: *What the fuck are you thinking?*

"You don't mean that."

Naomi shrugged. "It's a pretty innocuous word. *Okay.*"

"You're going to want me to give it away, I know you will. You don't think I can do this, but I can. I've changed."

Naomi had heard this before, most recently the last time Anna had come to visit, which had been when Naomi was still in San Diego. She'd had a plan that involved something with a friend's hydroponics start-up and had needed a loan. The business was supposed to be completely legal, and the reassurances that a check would come the first of every month, paying Naomi back in installments, had sounded heartfelt, and Naomi had actually believed her.

She'd never received one check.

"No, I've *really* changed."

Naomi pulled open a bureau drawer. She patted the T-shirts that she'd left inside it—she should really sort them and get rid of the old ones. If Anna stayed, she'd need room . . . What was she thinking? Anna couldn't stay. No, make that Anna *wouldn't* stay.

"Have you found religion?" asked Naomi, slamming the drawer shut.

"No."

"Addicted to any substances, herbal or otherwise?"

"I don't even eat chocolate because I don't want the caffeine buzz for the baby."

Naomi frowned. "You can eat chocolate. There's no problem with that. Are you employed full-time? Or even part-time?"

"No." Anna's voice was small.

Leaning on the bureau's sharp edge, Naomi said, "Tell me how you've changed."

Anna's eyes met her own. "I'm a mother."

"Oh, please. You have a fetus inside you," said Naomi. "You're not a mother until you've changed four diapers between midnight and three A.M."

Anna's hands curved protectively around her belly. "I have a baby inside me. *My* baby. And I don't know how, but it's all going to be okay." A pause. "For once."

Naomi turned to the side and readjusted the position of the alarm clock on top of the bureau. Owl shaped, it hadn't worked since the batteries died six months ago. It reminded her that she should call their mother. But God, she didn't want to be the one to break the news that Maybelle was going to be a grandmother, and that she wasn't even getting a son-in-law in the bargain. To her mother, Anna, even with all her faults, was perfect. It would be too painful to be the one to knock her off the pedestal. Anna should call her herself, when she was ready.

The owl clock *was* kind of cute. It worked for a nursery-cum-bedroom. She should put new batteries in.

Maybe this would be okay.

She spoke slowly. "You didn't get to see the living room floor after Dad's ashes were scattered all over the room."

Anna covered her mouth with her hand. Muffled, she said, "Your dad's *ashes*? You're kidding me."

"Rig knocked over the urn."

A snort was heard under the hand. "That's awful."

Naomi nodded. "They were in an owl vase until he broke it."

A small, delighted scream. "You're kidding. Mom would plotz. I can't believe I missed that. That's even more awful than me simply not knowing Jake was widowed."

"Way worse," Naomi agreed.

A giggle escaped from Anna. "Did you pick him back up?"

"Rig helped. He felt awful." Naomi didn't think the smile she was trying to subdue would be respectful to her father. But really, it *was* funny, seen from the outside.

"I bet he did," said Anna. "What's the story on him? He's hot."

Naomi fiddled with the green lamp that she always had trouble with. "If you can't get this to shut off, then just unplug it here at the base. I'll get another one that works so you can have a night-light. You always liked reading in bed."

She knew what her words meant. And she knew that her sister might not even stay the whole night, let alone more than a few days. Naomi didn't want to get burned again. Hurt. She was done with all that. When she'd washed her hands of rescuing her sister that last time, when the hydroponics business turned out to be nothing more than a large grow operation that left Anna busted and sitting in jail for four months, she'd felt good, if sad, about the decision to avoid her sister as much as possible in the future.

This, right now, wasn't avoiding. This, probably, wouldn't be smart. But Naomi met Anna's hopeful eyes and, for once, didn't look away first. "I have some of your old books in the garage. I'll get them out tomorrow. And I have a gift certificate a patient gave me for the Book Spire. It's a nice store. I'll dig that up and you can have it." Naomi pulled her hair back from her face. "If you want it."

Anna's smile was like sunrise. "Yeah. I want it. Thank you, Naomi."

"Right." Naomi was out the door in the space of a breath. "Watch the toilet, jiggle the handle if it runs."

She escaped into her own room, and drew a breath that shook in her chest. "Oh, wow," she whispered.

Family. Living under her roof. In Cypress Hollow.

Suddenly, in what felt like the space of a heartbeat, Naomi knew she wanted this to work. There was nothing she could do about Anna freaking out and running off. She knew that from too much past experience. But God, she wanted her sister here.

Now, to just keep from blowing it herself.

Chapter Twenty-five

*Do your best. No one can demand a master sweater from
a novice knitter, and tell those who do that I said so.*
—E.C.

The weekend was a quiet one. Naomi took Anna shopping for
maternity clothes after she realized her sister was sleeping
in one stretched-out shirt while the other one hung in the
bathroom drying.

She had to admit that it was nice spending time with her sister.
Since Anna was ten years younger than she was, born when Naomi
was living with her father, she'd never seen that much of her sister
growing up. And the one year she'd lived with them, after Naomi's
father died, Anna had been only seven. But even then, her sister
was like unexpected sunshine on a dark day. Everyone wanted to
be around Anna. Naomi hadn't been jealous, really. She'd just wondered how Anna did it.

In the dressing room of the only local clothing store, Marzies,
Anna charmed the clothing retailer over the changing-room door,
flattering Mrs. Gonzales's taste in clothing, and when Mrs. G.'s husband tromped through the store, she flattered her taste in men. She

ended up earning Naomi a discount on the pile of clothes she paid for, and Naomi learned that not much had changed in her sister's methods. She distributed radiance as if it was talcum powder.

And she was still the opposite of Naomi, at whom Mrs. Gonzales only glanced when she took her credit card.

They'd gone into the Book Spire, but Naomi hadn't gotten to introduce Anna to Lucy Bancroft, as she'd been looking forward to. Instead, Anna walked right up to the counter and asked Lucy what she recommended. Lucy lit up and spent the next half hour discussing the newest fiction, the best romances, the scariest romantic suspense.

Abigail MacArthur came in while they were there, and Naomi only realized she was hiding from her when she found herself in the kids' section. She had no kids to buy books for—although she would, she supposed, soon enough.

This was stupid. The three women stood at the counter chatting. She could hold her own in a polite, cheery conversation, right?

She walked over, her hands stuck in her pockets so she didn't ball them into nervous fists.

"Hi," she said to Abigail.

"Naomi, I thought that was you. And your sister, just look at her! Are you excited?"

What a strange thing to ask, Naomi thought. Apprehensive, yes. Worried, sure. "I'm . . . hoping for the best."

Anna rolled her eyes and went on talking to Lucy about the newest Sophie Littlefield and Juliet Blackwell books.

Abigail said, "Oh, there's nothing to worry about. She'll be a great mom, and you're going to love being an aunt."

Naomi bit the inside of her lip. How could Abigail say that? She didn't know either of them, especially not Anna.

"I'm sure you're . . ." Naomi had no idea how to finish the sentence without offending anyone and was grateful when Abigail went on.

"I have to tell you that from the first moment I saw you in town,

I've thought you looked familiar." Abigail's smile was so friendly. So open. "We've never had a real chance to talk. You moved here from San Diego, isn't that right? I used to live there, too. Did we know each other there? Is that possible?"

Now was the time to tell Abigail she'd been the doctor to witness her grief at Eliza's bedside. How did she do that gracefully? "Um . . . Actually, I was—"

Abigail waved a hand. "Isn't that silly? It's a big city. Of course we would have remembered before this. It's just those gorgeous green eyes you have, I feel like I remember them. Funny, huh?" She winked at Lucy. "I'm a sucker for green, though. My husband, Cade, has green eyes, and both our kids got that from him. Hey, how's your new friend? Rig, right?"

Naomi choked and tried to turn it into a cough. "Oh, he's not a *friend*. He's a coworker. At the office."

"Right," said Abigail. "The new doctor. But you sure looked good together the other day at the party . . ."

"No." The word came out too loud, but it was too late, she'd said it, and as usual, she couldn't retract it. Had they really looked good together? She blushed so hard her skin hurt.

Abigail nodded, clearly thrown. "Well, it was nice seeing you. Lucy, I'm going to go. Thanks for the book—I'll let you know what I think."

With a flurry of hugs all around—Naomi was startled into stiffness by the quick, tight squeeze she received unexpectedly—Abigail was gone.

And while Lucy and Anna went over to the maternity section of the bookstore, Naomi leaned against the end cap of the self-help section. Well, she'd blown that one, but good. That had been her opening. It had been what she hadn't even known she was waiting for. She'd almost said, *Yes, I was a friend of Eliza's. I was her doctor. Isn't it a small world?*

Wouldn't they have a laugh about it?

Or, and she thought this was more likely, Abigail would just be pissed. It had gone too far—Naomi had taken too long to tell her. It was too late. She'd missed the window now for sure. She'd swallowed the words again and closed the door on that revelation. It couldn't happen now, not after she'd basically denied by her silence any connection at all. Damn it all to hell. It wasn't like it should even *be* a secret. An accidental one, yet another example of how normal human interaction got confusing, how everyone else seemed to know the correct way to barrel through. Now, even though it wasn't, shouldn't be, a big deal, she'd have to continue keeping her silence. At least she knew how to do that.

Back in the car, Naomi asked, "So. What are you going to do next?" Her voice sounded too loud.

Anna sat straighter in the passenger seat. "What do you mean? About the baby?" Her right hand rested over her newly outtie navel.

"You should probably eventually tell Mom you're here."

"I'll call her."

"When?"

"Soon."

Naomi shook her head. How could she put this delicately? "You need to get a job."

Anna wrapped both arms around her belly protectively. She scowled. "I'm huge. I can't work."

"You're the healthiest pregnant woman I've ever seen. You could probably work in the fields picking strawberries if you wanted to."

"You want me to pick *fruit*?"

"No, of course not." Naomi came to a stop too quickly at the light, and the car rocked. "But you can do something to occupy yourself and make some money at the same time until the baby comes."

Anna folded her arms as much as she could and slumped farther in the seat.

"What about a receptionist position? You've worked in offices before."

"I *hated* offices. Women are so political and none of them ever liked me. They'd talk behind my back, make things up. You work alone. You can't even imagine how awful it is."

"Okay, so what about dog walking? It would be good exercise, and there's a woman in town who does it, maybe she needs help."

"I'm allergic to dogs." Anna pulled a tissue awkwardly out of her pocket and wiped her nose.

"Since when?"

"Since . . . the idea of dog walking came up. Too stressful."

Anna thought dog walking was too stressful? Naomi wished she could be paid for hauling a pack of mutts around a dog park, instead of treating people for illnesses they didn't always recover from. She clicked her ring against the steering wheel.

"Where did you get that ring? I've never seen it before," said Anna.

"A friend."

"Oooh!" Anna bounced in her seat, happy to change the subject. "A tall friend? A friend with benefits?"

"A woman friend." Naomi paused. "A good one. She's dead." The words hurt. "Back to the job. Really, we have to think of something."

Anna deflated. "Do you even *like* having me here?"

Naomi did, but she didn't know how to say it. The loving, fiercely protective feeling she got when she looked at her baby sister seemed impossible to speak about out loud. She held it inside and only allowed herself a nod.

"Did Mom put you up to this?" Anna looked sad. Even when she was at her lowest, Anna retained an angelic radiance about her, one that made Naomi want to pick her up and tuck her into bed, soothing her brow until her countenance relaxed again.

Naomi hit the gas and sped around a small red car that was trundling along the waterfront, obviously a tourist. "Are you kidding me? I haven't talked to Mom."

"You haven't? Why not? Don't you two talk all the time? About me?"

Naomi snorted. "Mom would like that. You're her favorite topic."

"Really?" Did Anna actually look pleased?

"You know you are. All she does is think about where you are and what you're doing and how she can change you."

"She hasn't learned yet," said Anna. "You can't tame a wild horse." She gave a comic neigh.

Naomi disagreed but didn't say so. She *did* want her sister to change, but only for the good. To settle down, to figure out her life, to stop being so impulsive. "Mom only wants the best for you."

Anna nodded. "Sure. And she wants the best for you, too. It doesn't mean it has to be the only song in her repertoire. She loves us, Naomi, but she doesn't know us."

The comment felt unfair, but Naomi didn't have a way to respond. "What about Whitney's Bakery? I saw a sign that said she was looking for—"

"What about your office?" asked Anna.

"Mine? Oh, no." Naomi let an old woman and her seven tiny dachshunds cross the street, even though there was no crosswalk.

"Why not? You're busy, right?"

"Not that busy. I already have office help."

"Maybe if you had more help, you'd be busier."

Naomi doubted that. She couldn't even imagine what Anna might do to their carefully filed system. "No. You're not . . ."

Oh, God—she sneaked a look at her sister . . .

Anna's face crumpled.

Shit. She'd done it again. "Anna, I'm sorry. I only meant that you're not experienced enough in medical reception. That's all."

"No," said her sister, sticking her chin out. "I'm not good enough. That's what you meant. You didn't have to say it for me to hear it."

Anna didn't speak to her the rest of the way home, and when they pulled into the driveway, Anna raced as fast as she could into the house, leaving Naomi to carry all the bags. Fine. She deserved it. As she put the bags onto the couch, she heard Anna slam the door of the guest room with a thud that made the pictures on the living room wall rock.

Naomi moved to where Eliza Carpenter's book *The Road Not Taken* was lying next to the couch. She closed her eyes, flipped the pages, and placed her first finger carefully down.

> *Sometimes when we knit for family, we knit problems into our work—problems that we predict, expect, and bring in ourselves. It's not the knitting's fault, you already know that. Knots appear in the work. Stitches you know you didn't drop race to the bottom as if they were on fire. It's okay* not *to knit for family sometimes. To knit for yourself. Often, when you're done, you'll end up giving the work to someone you love anyway.*

Naomi carried her knitting basket to the kitchen table slowly, as if her bones ached. Something inside her hurt, that was for sure. It felt as if her heart was bruised, even though the doctor part of her brain mocked herself for indulging in the thought.

Or maybe it was just her hands that ached, missing having the yarn in them, as if knitting was a physical need.

Spreading the soft lace on the table, Naomi leaned forward against her forearms and picked up where she'd left off. Knitting back. Just like in life, going back was always the same. It was when the pattern changed as it was moving forward that Naomi ran into trouble. It was good that she'd decided to make this for herself.

"Damn," she said softly, to no one.

Chapter Twenty-six

Technically, the act of knitting looks a lot like relaxing.
Sometimes, that's the furthest from the truth.
—E.C.

Days fell into a rhythm at the office—Bruno was good at divvying up the appointments, and when Naomi passed Rig in the hall, she only thought about the kisses every once in a . . . okay, she'd admit she thought about them a lot.

Temporary loss of sanity, that day. Could she blame it on the fact that she'd been thrown because her sister had just arrived? That she was confused by it and had latched on to him because of it?

Considering that Anna hadn't shown up until the end of their kiss, probably not.

But the last month had been smooth at the office. Rig was a good doctor. The patients loved him. Bruno adored him, and actually grinned when Rig came in every morning. She'd seen Rig leaving with Peter and Bruno on Friday afternoons, on their way to the Rite Spot for a drink, and she longed to invite herself along. She even practiced the words, under her breath, *Hey, wait up. I'll come, too.*

But she didn't say it. She worked instead, and when she wasn't working, she fussed over Anna, who still hadn't told her who the father was, who still hadn't gotten a job, who still wouldn't say what her plans for her life were.

Naomi had ideas about all of these things, but she tried not to dump them on her sister every time they were in the kitchen together. She bit her tongue, holding back 80 percent of the advice she wanted to give her. It was a little easier between them when they were knitting in the living room together—she'd taught Anna the basics of garter stitch, and now Anna was going to town on a simple baby blanket, made of soft, washable wool Naomi had picked up at an incredibly uncomfortable visit to Abigail's shop. Abigail had acted normally, of course, because some people were able to do that. All Naomi could think of was whether Abigail thought she and Rig had something going on at the office.

Because they didn't.

Not at all.

Today it was lunchtime before Naomi saw Rig. He wore a crisp tan-colored button-down shirt, a tie, jeans, and cowboy boots— would the man ever wear work pants? A white coat at the very least? Rig looked like a cowboy at a wedding. The only thing missing was his hat. He was bent over the back desk where Bruno placed recent lab results. He looked good, the taut muscles of his back delineated through the thin cotton of his shirt. She could practically see the muscles ripple, and she had to admit that his rear end looked amazing from this vantage point. And how he managed to look like that in regular clothing was beyond her. It must be something about the corded muscles running up his neck . . . the width at his pecs . . .

No. She wasn't looking at him. Not like that.

She cleared her throat. Rig turned, jumping a little.

"Hi, there."

Rig shook his head and smiled. The way that dimple in his left cheek pulled in when he grinned made Naomi's ribs feel tight, as if she could almost get enough air, but not quite.

"Hey, how are you?" he said. "Get some rest over the weekend?"

Why? Did she look like she hadn't? It was true, she hadn't slept well. Again. She put a hand up to make sure her hair hadn't come down.

"Yeah, great. Lots." Her mouth felt tongue-tied. Did he ever think of those kisses, too? The way her lips had felt, the slick rasp of his tongue touching hers . . .

Bruno interrupted her inane thoughts, thank God, coming back from reception. He carried a stack of opened mail.

"Have you seen the bill from PG and E? The one they said was late? You said you had the canceled check, right?" asked Naomi. Bruno started to answer but Rig interrupted.

"You look different. What happened?" Rig sat on the edge of the filing desk. Naomi wished he wouldn't—it was organized so that she knew where everything was, and desks weren't for sitting on, anyway.

Bruno beamed and set the bills down on top of the morning's lab results. "We talked."

"Dude," said Rig. "And?"

"I was right. He bought a ring."

Were they *gossiping*? Naomi felt suddenly left out. "Peter did?"

Her voice was too loud. Not casual enough. She didn't have a desk to lean against, like Rig. She crossed her arms, knowing she looked stiff, but unable to figure out how to soften her stance.

"Umm," said Bruno. He fiddled with the edge on an envelope. God, she'd been his boss for over a year now, and he still couldn't trust her with his personal life?

Well, truthfully, what did he know about hers? What did anyone know about hers? Nothing. Which was just about what she had to say when it came to his. Her stomach hurt.

"Good," she said lamely. "Good for . . . you." She walked toward her office in defeat. Let Rig handle it. He knew how to talk to people, to care about them. She just knew how to fix them, only knew how to care when the person in front of her was a patient. So far today she'd seen an arm in a cast, a raging case of strep throat she'd given antibiotics for, and one case of whooping cough that she'd have to keep an eye on. Just normal, small-town aches and pains, people who needed simple care—she prayed they'd felt the connection she had when they were in the room with her.

It felt like the only real connection she had these days.

Rig and Bruno let her go, not stopping her. Naomi heard their dropped voices, and she wondered what Rig was learning about the man who had been her right hand for a year now. Falling into her father's office chair, she touched the light purple flowers of the African violet on her desk. In the last year, she'd never watered it, not once. She'd trusted Bruno to take care of it. Paid him to do it.

Damn.

She had to go over some charts anyway. Screw eating. Naomi wasn't hungry for lunch. Pulling out a stack of files she needed to update, Naomi lost herself in work for the next half hour.

She didn't notice the time until Rig rapped on her partially open door and stuck his head in.

"Hey, Naomi?"

"Yeah?" she said, slapping together the file folder she'd just finished. A completely nonprofessional rivulet of heat ran from the top of her head to her groin at the sight of him.

"I just gave Bruno the week off."

Her thoughts about the way the underside of his jaw looked, and what it would taste like, dissolved. "You what?"

"He needed some time off. I thought it would be good for him to go get ready to see Peter, and then have some real time to spend with him."

Naomi could only repeat herself. "You what?"

"They've got big plans. Engagement is a serious business." Rig grinned.

"But . . . we *need* him. He does everything around here."

Rig twirled the retro globe she'd picked up at an antiques shop a while ago. He stopped it, his finger landing on what looked like England. "So he had the time, right?'

"He has time on the books, yes."

The globe spun. Rig poked Guatemala. "And he needs it. We can answer phones and clean the head for a week."

That wasn't it. Naomi looked at her nails. "I wish I'd been the one to give it to him. He hardly ever takes time off, even when I've asked him to." If Bruno needed time off, he deserved it, more than anyone she'd ever worked with. He was loyal to a fault, and he was great at his job. She leaned forward. "*How* much time did you give him?"

"It's Monday today. I gave him the rest of the week. He didn't want more."

Folding the corner of her desk calendar, Naomi paused. Then she said haltingly, "Was he . . . happy? About that?"

"He hugged me three times. He said he was going to check in with you but I said that I was giving him a direct order to get the hell out. Nicely. As one of his bosses."

A chime filtered through the back office, indicating that someone had come through the front door.

"You going to get that or should I? That might be a walk-in," said Naomi, crossing her arms in front of her.

"They'll wait till we're done here," said Rig, folding his arms to match hers. "We've been needing to talk. Are you avoiding me because of what happened between us?"

How could he be so direct? Naomi had been prepared to ignore the fact that Portland had ever happened, that their flirting here had never occurred. They were just going to work together. Like adults.

She looked at her desk calendar. Almost a full month had passed without them referencing what had gone on between them. Not exactly the lifetime she'd hoped for.

"Of course not."

"I think you are," he said, his voice calm.

Naomi gripped the armrest of her chair and bit the inside of her lip.

Rig went on, "You hate the fact that you kissed me and almost lost control outside your house that night, and you're going to do everything you can to avoid thinking about it again. That's without even mentioning Portland."

She heated, instantly. He was being ridiculous. She didn't hate the fact that she'd kissed him, she hated the fact that now she couldn't get away from him. Kissing him had shown terrible judgment. How had she not thought it all the way through? Naomi was nothing if not a planner. She looked down at her desk again and saw, on the right-hand corner, a list of her lists. Taking care of things, that's what she was good at. Getting things done. Helping people feel better physically. That was her job.

"Come on," said Rig. "You can't deny we have great chemistry. We have to at least admit it to clear the air."

"Chemistry. Yes. That's what it is." Naomi grasped at something she could name, categorize. "A physical response to external stimuli."

Rig laughed, a low, rich sound. It wasn't fair that he had that kind of laugh, the kind she wanted to wrap around herself. "Yeah. Kissing lowers cholesterol, did you know that?"

Naomi did, actually. "It uses thirty-four facial muscles."

"One hundred and twelve postural muscles, most important, the orbicularis oris muscle." His eyes dared her.

"It's also a good vehicle for transmitting diseases."

Rig's dark eyes danced. "Stress reducer."

"Vestigial premastication technique."

"*Hot*," he drawled, daring her with his gaze.

The word hit her like a blow. And damn, had he gone to school to learn that look? That intense focus that made her feel like he was seeing no one but her . . .

She stood, feeling warmth flood her kneecaps. She would *not* sway. This was ridiculous. "If you're not going to check the reception area, then I am. Since we have no one to help us."

Sweeping his arm forward, Rig motioned her to go ahead of him. "I'll go, too."

"Fine."

It *wasn't* fine. He was behind her now, and she was aware of only one thing: his scorching gaze resting on her rear end.

Chapter Twenty-seven

Knitting lace is a dance of air and fiber, intricate in motion, diaphanous in nature.

—E.C.

Elbert Romo stood on tiptoes at the desk, trying to peer over it. But he was so short, even with his bushy gray buzz cut standing at attention, and the desk was so tall that he looked like a child trying to peer into a high candy counter.

"There's no one out here! Where's Bruno?"

"He's on vacation," said Naomi.

Elbert's bushy eyebrows jumped. "I didn't know he was going on vacation," he said.

Neither did I. "He had some things to take care of."

"And we're here now," said Rig. "What can we do for you?"

Elbert smiled widely at Rig and said, "Well, now. You're gonna love this, Doc."

Again with the Doc thing. She'd never be called that, not with that level of affection. Naomi looked at the ground.

Elbert went on, "Every year we have a contra dance here in town. New England line dancing, only we do it here on the West Coast and have a live band, and the whole town comes, and it's just like old times, when I was a kid on the ranch. It's a week from Saturday. Dr. Fontaine, you've never been, have you?"

Naomi opened her mouth to speak, but Elbert went on without waiting for an answer. "It's a great time. Only this year, we're looking for donations from local businesspeople like yourself. We generally use the Eagles Hall, but because of the bathroom flood that Pete Wegman caused this week, they're still gonna be repairing the woodwork. We on the organizin' committee gotta find somewhere else to have it, fast, and we'll need money to rent the place. So I'm askin'—"

Naomi interrupted, her heart in her throat. "You can have it here."

Elbert looked around the office and laughed. "I don't think you know how many people I'm talking, ma'am. I mean, Doctor."

"In the health center." A restless feeling of excitement filled her as she crossed the room to the connecting door. "In here. Look."

Elbert and Rig followed her into the massive room. Both were quiet as she flipped on the lights.

Spinning to face Elbert, she said, "Here! Look at all this room! We can clear the tables and push them to the side, and you can put your refreshments on them, and you can have the raffle over there, by the desk, and the rest of the room for dancing with the caller and the band at the back!" Oh, yes. It really *could* work. It was completely unlike her to do this—something without planning, without knowing if it was *really* the right thing to do, but it felt good. Exciting. She wanted this.

Elbert gave her a look that was difficult to decipher until he spoke. Slowly, he said, "How did you know there was a raffle?"

Crap. She *had* been to the dance last year, when she first moved to town. It had sounded so wholesome, so very Cypress Hollow. Several times while they'd knitted together, Eliza had spoken of the annual town contra dance in a way that made Naomi ache with longing.

But going to the dance had been excruciating. She'd entered the Eagles Hall during a song, and everyone seemed to know just which way to turn. Even though the caller had been telling them what to do, Naomi didn't even understand the language he'd been using, "Alemán left and round you go." The dancers whirled in long lines that twisted around each other more intricately than the yarn in her lace shawl did. At the end of the song, she'd wondered if she'd be invited to dance, but she'd hung back, too nervous to step forward. In what seemed like seconds, people had switched partners, men asking women to dance, the women nodding or laughing in acceptance, and they'd re-formed, dancing again, Naomi still alone in the darkest corner of the room.

She'd escaped before anyone had said even one word to her.

She said to Elbert, "Raffle? Oh, just a good guess. Everything this town does includes a raffle, am I right?"

He nodded, then looked around the room. "It's big, all right. And damned empty. What do you use this for again?"

"The free health center, where people can come for . . ." Her voice trailed off. "We don't use it for much, I guess."

Maybe it was time she started to admit that.

Naomi took a deep breath and watched Rig reexamine the room. He tugged on his chin in a way that made Naomi forget momentarily about the center and wonder what he'd look like with a beard instead of that light layer of stubble.

Probably incredible. Probably even more rugged than he did now.

Damn. He'd said something while she was staring, and she'd missed it, too busy watching his mouth move to listen.

Elbert answered him, "Well, that's something I don't think anyone ever asked about. Dr. Fontaine?"

"I'm sorry," she said. "What was that again?"

Rig smiled at her as if he knew what she'd been thinking. "I was just asking Elbert here that if you donate the use of what's technically your space, then would they also allow me to donate a little something."

Elbert rubbed his hands together, his deeply lined face delighted.

"I'm pretty invested in getting a good reputation in town," said Rig, "and while Naomi's been here awhile, I'm new. I'd be delighted to provide the drinks and snacks out of my own pocket."

Elbert beamed. "I *knew* there was something I liked about you, Doc."

"Great! We're doing the dance," said Rig. He grinned at her conspiratorially.

Naomi smiled back as her stomach did a small flip.

Yes. They were.

Chapter Twenty-eight

Sometimes the only way through a necessary project is to treat it like a job. Show up, do the work, go home and rest. It will get done, eventually. (If it's not necessary, though, and you're not enjoying it, hurl it into the bin and do a little celebratory dance that you're well shed of it.)

—E.C.

Rig and Naomi conferred with Elbert for another fifteen minutes, laying out plans. Rig kept getting distracted, however, by watching Naomi as she moved around the room. Excitement flooded her face, and he realized that this health center meant everything to her. He'd kind of guessed that already, but it was evident in her rosy red cheeks, the way she laughed out loud in delight when Elbert said that she could call the winning raffle number. She was finally getting to use the space for a real something, and Rig loved the sparkle in her eyes.

He heard the front-office bell chime and hurried through the center into the office. Naomi's sister, Anna, entered, her blue eyes wide as she scanned the room.

"Hi," she said.

"Is everything okay?" asked Rig. "Your sister's in the other room."

"Yeah, yeah." Anna looked around and then said, "I just wanted to see her office. I've never been here before."

"Good lord, girl, you're fit to pop," said Elbert as he and Naomi came into reception. "You sure you should be standing?"

Anna smiled. "I'm fine. I've still got almost a month to go."

"You sit there," Elbert said. He pointed to the bench seat next to the window. "Shouldn't tire yourself."

Some of the happiness left Naomi's face, and concern moved in. Rig fought an irrational urge to pull her into his arms until the crease on her brow disappeared.

"Are you all right? What's going on?" Naomi asked.

Anna frowned. "I was just bored at the house."

Naomi started to say something, but Elbert interrupted.

"Bored! You're bored, and you have a person in there?" He pointed to Anna's belly. "My lord, child, you should sit around and do things with it. Play it classical music. Read it Dostoyevsky. There's so much to *do*! You're just gettin' started!"

"Do you have kids, Elbert?" asked Rig.

"Nah, I never had any. Never settled down with one woman, though I thought about doing it a few times. One almost got me once, but I paid the fine and got away. Got nieces and nephews, though, and that's better. Didn't have to pay for their college, did I?"

Rig nodded. "I have a five-year-old nephew. Milo. Best little boy in the world."

"Good age," said Elbert. "What about you, honey? Boy or a girl?"

Elbert's face softened when he looked at Anna. In the red, flowing blouse with the smocking around the neck and her white maternity skirt and red canvas shoes, she appeared to be glowing. She was the picture of health—an advertisement for motherhood. Naomi pulled her white coat closer around herself and clicked the pen in her pocket. Rig could almost hear her comparing herself to her sister. He wished she wouldn't. They were apples and oranges, these women. Did Naomi know that?

"A girl," said Anna. "A very big girl. At least I think so, anyway. I haven't had them confirm it. I just know."

"Well, that's all right then, isn't it?" Elbert grinned and Anna laughed back at him, but Rig couldn't tear his eyes away from Naomi. Her hair, piled up like that, how did it stay? The pale rose of her cheeks against the white coat, the slenderness of her waist compared to the lush curve at her breast that even the boxy coat couldn't hide . . .

What was *with* him? He felt like he was thirteen.

That was it. His hormones were driving the bus, that was all. This, too, would pass, right? It was a regular old crush. He'd had plenty of crushes in his life; they took a little while to get over, but then he'd feel fine. It would be funny to look back on it, the time that he and his partner had a brief flirtation.

Happened to everyone, right?

The thought made him feel lighter. Happy. Content to just watch her. No pressure.

Elbert clapped his hands. "Well, then!" He raised his hand. "Young lady, take care good care of yourself."

Anna nodded. "I will."

He let himself out, and Naomi turned back to Anna.

"Anna went job hunting again this morning," Naomi said, not quite meeting Rig's eyes. "How did it go?"

Anna groaned again. "Awful. It was horrible."

Naomi frowned. "Why?"

Anna pointed at her stomach. "Because people don't want *this* as a representative of their business. I was asked three times what my husband did for a living."

Naomi displayed the surprise Rig felt. "They can't ask that! I think there are rules against it."

"But they did. And I don't care—if I got a job somewhere, they'd learn the truth. I'm having a bastard. Single mom. All of that."

Rig started poking around in Bruno's computer, trying to figure out how to tell who was coming in this afternoon. "Do people even use that word anymore? *Bastard?*"

"The guy at the tire shop who was looking for a receptionist sure had the word in his mind. I could practically see it hanging there in neon."

"Please," said Naomi. "That's ridiculous. You're smart, and talented—"

"And in four weeks, if I make it that long, I'd need at least a month off. No one wants to train someone just to have them leave." Anna looked at the blue carpet. "And who knows how long I'll be here, anyway?"

The sentence felt weighted, leaden, and it served to drain Naomi's face of the last remaining bit of light Rig had seen in the center.

"What if you work here?" asked Rig.

"What?" said Naomi and Anna in unison.

"Hey, we need someone. Bruno's out on unplanned vacation, and we have patients coming in"—he glanced at his watch—"ten minutes. Three of them, if I'm reading the computer correctly. I think he overbooked by one."

Anna sat forward, hands clasped in front of her belly. "I'd love to work here."

Naomi shook her head. "No. Bad idea. I'm sure there are plenty of other—"

"Jobs for pregnant whales?" Anna said. "There aren't. I hit every place that was in the paper today. They all looked at me like I was crazy."

"She'd just be sitting here," said Rig, "saying hello to patients when they come in. We can show her the basics, and then Bruno can clean it all up when he comes back next week."

"And then what? You want her to work for just a week? That's less than she could do somewhere else . . ."

"I need help with my office. Someone to help me go through the files, figure out what I should keep and what I can toss of Pederson's. And we really need someone to work on the storage unit."

Eagerly, Anna said, "I've done that kind of thing before. I assisted an archivist in Maine while I was there last summer."

Naomi stared at Anna. "I didn't know you were in Maine." She paused. Looked at her feet. Rig waited, hopeful. This could be good for the two of them. He crossed his fingers to match Anna's.

"I suppose it would be okay . . ."

"Yes!" said Rig. He held up his hand and Anna high-fived it. "You're hired! Now come back here, and I'll show you how to answer the phones and transfer them if the calls need to come to us. I know how to do that much. I'm not sure how the intercom system works, because Bruno always initiates it, but Naomi can show us both."

Rig wasn't sure who looked more nervous, Anna or Naomi, but it was going to be okay. It'd be great. They'd see.

Chapter Twenty-nine

Believe in your fingers, in your nimbleness, in your willing-
ness to invent.

—E.C.

A nna did well, surprising Naomi with her creativity when
it came to figuring out Bruno's systems. Four hours later,
by the end of the afternoon, she was actually filing. Naomi
hadn't wanted her to, at first, sure her sister was putting the files in
the wrong places, and that they'd never see the paperwork again.
But when she watched over Anna's shoulder, she was getting all of
it just right.

She was proud of her sister. Another good call on Rig's part.

Rig.

Every time they'd passed each other in the narrow hall, he'd
caught her eye and smiled. He held her gaze for a second too long
each time, just long enough to make her feel breathless, then he'd
walk past, opening the door to his next patient, greeting them with
warmth and enthusiasm.

He was professional. He was good at his job, as good as she hoped
she was.

And he was distracting the hell out of her.

And now it was almost closing time. She had no more appointments, and at this point, she didn't think they'd get any more walk-ins.

She heard voices from the front, and pushed open the door to find Rig's brother, Jake Keller, leaning on the counter, laughing down at Anna. He was in full fire-service uniform, all dark blue with white buttons, his boots as shiny as his badge.

He straightened when he saw her. "Hey, Naomi. I was just telling Anna here how sorry I was about barging in to use your bathroom a while back. Between my dad and Milo, we have to stop every fifteen minutes, I swear. Just stopping by to see my brother now. How's he fitting in around here?"

"Patients seem to like him."

"They just think he's good looking. Runs in the family, you know. Not always that much going on upstairs, though." Jake grinned.

"They're probably thinking about downstairs anyway," Naomi said without thinking.

Jake snorted and Anna giggled while Naomi felt her cheeks burst into flame.

"I mean, you know, those jeans and all. I don't mean *I'm* noticing. Or if I was, it would be purely on the professional . . . shit." She wasn't going to be able to recover—she was only making it worse. "I'll go get him for you."

"I already paged him." Anna tapped the intercom with authority, as if she'd been using it for years.

"Speak of the devil," said Jake on a laugh.

As he entered the room, Rig's eyes met Naomi's again for a split second, and a look that felt like a shiver passed between them. She crossed her arms over her breasts as her nipples tightened. How did he *do* that?

"Hey, Jake. What's so funny?"

"Just your pants, man."

Rig took it easily, saying only, "Doesn't mean much from a man dressed in wool."

Naomi tried to lean on the counter casually, like Jake was doing, and almost lost her balance, ending up wheeling her arms and whacking her wrist on the wood.

"Naomi!" said her sister. "Are you all right?"

"Fine," she said. "Of course I'm fine. Are there any more patients today, Anna?"

"Nope. You're done, and it looks like Rig is done with his last, right?"

"Mr. Swenson is buttoning himself up as we speak."

Jake nodded. "Mr. Swenson. We've responded to his house a couple of times." He gave his brother a look. "Is it for—?"

Rig pursed his mouth and didn't say anything.

"Ahhh. It is. He's a strange duck, isn't he?"

Laughing, Rig loosened his tie, working it back and forth. "God, I hate these things." He stripped it off, undoing his top shirt button. "Better," he said.

It *was* better. He looked more relaxed already. Actually, he'd just gone from looking like a cowboy at a wedding to someone about to rope a steer. Naomi wished she had an equivalent piece of clothing to loosen, one that would be like letting her hair down.

Well. She guessed she could just let her hair down.

Naomi tugged at the three bobby pins that had been holding her curls into a loose bun at the back of her neck, and then slipped the pins in her white coat pocket. She felt her hair tumble to her shoulders, and she tousled it with one hand, hoping it didn't look ridiculous after being up all day. Anna and Jake talked about the merits of a hamburger joint just up the coast. Jake said something about a case of shigella that had recently cropped up at a taco stand, and that no restaurant could be trusted. Anna said, "Where's your sense of adventure? You must have plenty of it inside that uniform somewhere."

"Adventure's overrated. I like safe," said Jake.

Naomi glanced at Rig.

Oh, he'd noticed her hair all right. He had both his hands in his pockets, and he leaned against the entryway wall, right next to the tasteful lamp she'd installed when she'd come to the practice. It cast a light glow in the room, very feng shui. But Rig didn't look subtle or tasteful or any other adjective that might describe a soothing reception area.

Rig burned. His eyes smoldered. Naomi swore she could feel his heat from six feet away. His body radiated a fine, hot control and his eyes raked her body, starting at her hair and going all the way down, pausing at her breasts and then again at her waist, and then back up. She sent the look back; she knew she did. Even though she didn't want to. She shouldn't, God knew she shouldn't.

Naomi couldn't breathe. Again. He was becoming hazardous to her health. At this rate, she'd need an albuterol inhaler by nightfall.

Anna laughed and Jake said something back to her. They both sounded as if their voices were underwater—her ears listened only for Rig.

For fuck's sake, she *had* to get over this. Get her life back. She couldn't work in a place that she feared would burn down just by the way they were looking at each other.

A thought crossed her mind as she dimly heard Jake bring up garlic fries.

What if she just slept with Rig again?

The idea shocked and soothed her at the same time. Rig was her coworker. Her new, ridiculously steamy coworker, but still her business associate. Naomi had always been very clear about keeping her personal life very separate from her work life.

But her work life *was* her personal life now. There wasn't any real separation, so really, what could it hurt? They'd done it once before, and it had been . . . great. Yes, she could admit to herself it was the hottest sex since—well, maybe since ever. Unless she was remembering that night wrong, which she might be. And given the frequency with which she got laid, she really might be getting the facts mixed up.

Her last boyfriend was what, four years ago now? Franco had been a manager at the Italian restaurant she frequented, and the reason he'd become her boyfriend was because he didn't really care if she talked or not. They made love, ate, and slept. Lather, rinse, repeat. She'd been fond of him, but she wasn't in love with him, and the worst part of their breakup had been no more free puttanesca. As it were.

Rig contributed something to Jack and Anna's discussion and laughed. How was he keeping up with both conversations? He turned his eyes back on Naomi and her core overheated. She was going to be sending up smoke signals if this kept up.

One thing had always been sure, no matter how long the dry spells between taking men into her bed: she'd known what she was doing. Like all things, sex was better after she'd studied it. After an uncomfortable, unsatisfying experience at eighteen with a boy who was as inexperienced as she was, she'd taken out books from the college's library and deconstructed various sexual positions, reading about which was better for whom, and why. She'd rented porn movies and watched them, blushing the whole time, in order to learn what sounds women made and how men moved—she kept in mind that they were actors in a multibillion-dollar enterprise, and she never expected the pizza guy to deliver anything but pepperoni—but the movies still had things to teach her.

Sex was just bodies in motion, and Naomi understood how bodies worked. No big deal. Treating a patient, learning to achieve an orgasm: both were just getting parts to work right. So why wouldn't she be able to manage a second one-night stand with Rig if it meant she'd be able to file it safely away afterward under "Completed"?

Naomi studied Rig. Thank goodness he was looking at his brother and she got a few seconds to drag her gaze all over him.

Her eyes moved to the front of his jeans and she flushed with heat again. He was a big guy, she probably remembered that much correctly from their one night together. Mmmm.

Then Rig caught her. He caught her gaze red-handed as it traveled upward again, and his amused expression told her he knew exactly where she'd just been staring. Crap. She couldn't even take a deep breath to steady herself or he'd notice.

"You going with them, Naomi?" Rig asked.

"I'm sorry?"

"The Smokehouse," said Jake. "Your sister has convinced me to try a burger that may or may not end up being heated to a safe temperature. I do have life insurance, after all. Rig can take Milo if I *die*." He shot a pointed look at Anna, who laughed, a pretty pink color high on her cheeks. "I can't go to the one on the coast, since I'm on duty—have to stay near the firehouse. But the other one, on Fourth Street, we could all go there. They have thirty different flavors of milk shakes, I do know that."

Naomi said, "No, thanks. Not hungry." She was too wound up from thinking about Rig to think about food.

"Butterscotch," said Anna with a grin. "I've always loved a butterscotch milk shake."

He nodded. "They're hard to find. I happen to know the Smokehouse has great butterscotch shakes."

"Oooh," Anna purred.

Were they flirting? Naomi had been so firmly entrenched in her own plans that she'd failed to notice that Jake and Anna were grinning widely at each other. It looked like Jake was over Anna asking where Milo's mom was.

"What time do you get off?" Jake asked Anna.

Anna looked at Naomi questioningly. "I'm not sure . . . What else needs doing?"

"You can leave, that's fine." What else was Naomi supposed to say? Be careful? Anna was already knocked up—how much more trouble could she get into?

Jake gestured at his uniform. "I might look a little official for a burger, but as long as I stay within running distance of the firehouse in case the siren goes off, I can go. Rig, you coming?"

Rig also declined. "Naomi and I have to go over plans for the contra dance. We're hosting." He sounded proud, and Naomi's toes curled happily.

"Oh, great, you're doing that?" Jake looked pleased. "The whole department always goes and passes the boot for donations."

Anna came around the desk slowly, a hand on the top of her stomach. "I'm ready, then."

"Guess we'll catch you later," said Jake.

"Hey, why *did* you come by?" said Rig as Jake held open the door for Anna. The noise of cars passing on Main Street poured in like water.

Jake leaned in and spoke so that Anna, already outside, couldn't hear. "Was going to ask you about Dad's medication. But then something more important came up. Catch you later." The smile took over his whole face before he ducked out and the door shut. It was quiet again.

Naomi straightened the magazines on the low table, just to give herself something to do. Was she going to go through with this? Could she? *Should* she? The idea had taken root, and she couldn't think of anything else.

Yes. She would. Do it and get over it. Once and for all.

"So, great idea," Rig said. He was too close, suddenly right behind her. She hadn't heard his footsteps moving across the carpet.

"What?" She pushed a curl out of her face.

"Hosting the dance." He was just an inch too close.

Naomi stood straight and looked at him. Yep. He was with her on this one. She'd take the lead. That way, maybe she'd be able to keep it.

"We should talk about it some more."

He smiled, easily. He had *no* idea how easy it was going to be. "Over dinner?"

"What about at your house? Can you cook for me there?"

Rig blinked. Yep. She knew he hadn't seen that coming.

"Sure," he said. "I make a mean take-out pizza."

Even better. She would get laid *and* get fed, because she hadn't been planning on letting him have too much time to cook.

"I'll be there in an hour," she said.

"You eat meat?"

"Do I ever," she said. Was that a blush creeping onto his face? Good. She would *not* go red. She would do this. God, her heart was beating triple time. Making the shift from office mate to object of desire was something people did all the time, right? No reason for these nerves.

"You're different," he said. "What's changed in you?"

"Nothing," she said. "Just looking forward to our . . . dinner."

Chapter Thirty

*Cheating on your knitting, casting on when you shouldn't,
is illicit, delicious, and very hard to resist.*

—E.C.

In the drugstore, Naomi stood in the aisle that thoughtfully provided a one-stop shopping experience for every nether-region over-the-counter experience possible. Condoms, spermicide, jelly for before. Pregnancy tests for the oops after. For in between, douches (Naomi shook her head in disapproval), yeast infection treatments, and a whole range of sanitary supplies—pads, pantiliners, and tampons. All the down there corralled right here.

She looked over her shoulder in each direction. Naomi knew Zonker, the pharmacist, pretty well from phoning in prescriptions. She'd overheard a rumor once that his unfortunate nickname came from an ill-fated college experiment with psychotropic drugs, but had never known whether to believe it or not. He always looked presentable at work in his scrub whites, but she had seen him once at Tillie's on a Saturday morning wearing a Deadhead shirt, so there might be something to it. He did seem a little dizzy, but then again, he was married to Margie, who staffed the counter and was a well-respected member of the Baptist church. She never wore anything lower cut than a turtleneck. Naomi certainly couldn't see her taking anything more than an ibuprofen every once in a while, let alone allowing Zonker to listen to Jerry in her house.

And dammit, if there was any other place to buy condoms within a thirty-mile radius, she would. But this was a rush job. She hadn't been able to grab them from the supply cabinet before she left—Rig had been in there, and she'd rather have died than reach around him. She'd already been home to change, and now she was on her way to his place, and if she'd spent any time thinking about it, she'd have done those the other way around. It would have looked more innocuous to be caught buying condoms while wearing the street clothes she'd worn under her white coat than it did while wearing a low-cut red silk blouse, short skirt, and red high heels.

She looked around again furtively. Good. Still no one in sight.

God, there was a dizzying array of choices. Racks and racks of colors, types, and styles. Should she buy extra large, with the intention of flattery? She struggled to figure out how large was extra large. No way was she riding a horse with a loose saddle.

But then again, Rig was above average. Naomi felt a rush of heat between her legs at the thought, and then the same rush hit her brain.

She was going to sleep with Rig. Again.

And Naomi didn't think she'd ever been this nervous about sex before. What was wrong with her? She forced herself to pick up and examine a matte black box. Was this supposed to be the manly purchase? Black so no one would think he was buying tampons, which came in the pink and yellow boxes? Good grief.

It was just sex. Enjoyable mutual stimulation, after which she'd grab her bag and head home, satisfied, primed for sleep.

Right. She bit the inside of her cheek so hard she squeaked.

Pick a box, any box. How about the one with the ribs? Naomi honestly couldn't remember if she'd ever used condoms made "for her pleasure," and her eyebrows lifted as she read the copy. Really? Now, she knew a woman's insides were sensitive, but structurally speaking they didn't have as great a number of nerves as did other places, like fingers. How on earth would a woman be able to feel minuscule ridges made of an uber-thin, flexible membrane?

She picked up another, cheaper box, and held them together for comparison. The ribbed kind was four dollars more than the regular box. Screw that.

She flushed. She *was* going to screw that.

"Excuse me, do you have any idea where I'd find laxatives?"

Naomi jumped and wheeled on her heel and, to her extreme horror, found herself face-to-face with Frank Keller, Rig's father. While she was holding a box of condoms in each hand.

To his credit, he also looked unnerved.

"Well, dammit," he said. "I thought you worked here. I don't have many secrets, but talking about my bodily functions with pretty ladies is something I prefer to keep on the down low. But *look* at you." Frank took a step back. "You're all dressed up! Let's forget what I asked you about. What are *you* here for? I thought Jake said you and Rig were hanging out tonight."

Dumbstruck, Naomi looked at her full hands. They might as well have been lit up with a flashing sign that read *Sex Sex Sex!*

"Ah," said Frank. "Well."

Naomi nodded, feeling as red as the fire extinguisher on the wall behind Frank's head.

"How 'bout we pretend that we never saw each other right here. But I do have a question for you." He ducked his head. "How about we meet on aisle three? Nothing embarrassing about candy."

He turned his back, heading away, giving Naomi time to hang up both boxes and take a deep breath. Good God.

In aisle three, Frank held up a bag of miniature Reese's peanut butter cups. "I like 'em better tiny like this. More flavor."

"Ah," said Naomi, still trying to figure out if there was any way in hell she could just disappear. "So what was your question for me?"

Rubbing his knuckles over the top of his bald head, Frank said, "Well, you see, I've got heart trouble. Nothing major, just a little ticker damage from a heart attack I had about five years ago. Had another one six months or so ago."

"How are you feeling right now?" Please, Lord, don't let him fall out in the pharmacy right before she had a date with his son.

"Nah, don't worry about that. I'm fit as a fiddle. Scratch that, I don't like fiddles. Screechy. I'm fit as a banjo."

"Are you under a doctor's care? Your son's? Do you carry nitro-glycerin with you?" Naomi asked.

"That's the thing. Pederson was my doctor, and I never really liked the guy anyway. I refuse to let Rig treat me because then he'll tell Jake, who worries like a little girl stuck on top of a jungle gym. My nitro's expired. I need some more. Just to carry with me."

"And . . ." She was going to make him say it.

"I thought maybe you'd write a 'scrip for me."

Naomi didn't say anything. It was an outrageous suggestion. She didn't just prescribe medicine that a patient said he needed without seeing a chart, a history, without running tests.

"Come on. It's not like I need OxyContin or something. Cypress Hollow doesn't have a big black market for nitro. And I'm just a little worried." He patted his shirt pocket. "The pills I carry here have been expired for more than a year."

"But . . ."

Frank shrugged expressively. "Eh. I know. They're probably just fine still, huh? Yeah, that's what I thought. Thanks, kid."

Naomi drew in a heavy sigh. "You're something else, you know that?" She rummaged in her purse for the emergency prescription pad she always kept with her. She'd never had to use it before.

Frank perked up, his shoulders going back. He ripped open the bag of Reese's and took out a mini wrapped chocolate. As if she'd heard it from across the store, Naomi saw Margie's head peek around the end of the aisle. She stared disapprovingly at Frank, who ignored her while Naomi finished scribbling her signature.

His mouth full, he said, "You're the bee's knees, kiddo."

She pulled off the sheet and waved it under his nose. "I'm only giving you this if you promise to come see me this week."

He snatched the paper and kept chewing. "Gotta be a time when Rig's not there. I'm not going to worry him, or worse, Jakey."

"Give back the prescription."

Sticking it in his pocket, he nodded. "Fine, fine. I'll come in."

Naomi shook her finger, feeling like an ineffective schoolteacher as she did so. "You better. Or I'm going to tell on you to Rig."

Frank's grin swept over his gray stubble, brightening the dark eyes that reminded her suddenly of Rig's. "You might be good for him, you know that?"

"Wh-what?"

"I saw you two in your house that night he knocked your father all over the ground. I saw something there. You both got some loneliness, I think."

Naomi would bet she'd been lonely longer than Rig had. And if she didn't get rid of Frank, that wouldn't change anytime soon. She needed those condoms. Any condoms. She waved her hands as if shooing a chicken. "Go on, take that to Zonker."

He held out the bag of chocolate. "Want one?"

She couldn't help laughing. "You haven't even paid for that yet."

"Planning ahead. I'm always planning ahead. By the way, those ribbed ones are for crap. Don't bother." Naomi gasped as he trundled down the aisle. "Have fun, Doc!"

Five minutes later, her plain old vanilla condoms purchased from a scowling Margie, Naomi had planned ahead, too. Her heart pounded so hard she wondered if she shouldn't have picked up some nitro herself.

Chapter Thirty-one

Knitters have an instant connection in the same way readers of the same author do: "Oh, yes, you know about that, too? Oh, you understand me!" Revel in it.
—E.C.

As Rig slid the take-and-bake meat lover's special into his oven, he wondered what the hell had gotten into Naomi.

Not that he was complaining. Any woman who looked at him like she did, well, that was okay by him. The way she'd shaken down her hair in reception—he'd gotten hard just looking at her. And then, when she'd looked down at the front of his jeans . . . *That* was the confident Naomi he'd met in Portland. Gone was the tongue-tiedness, gone were the nerves and the impression that she was hiding something, keeping a secret that he didn't understand.

Hell, if she wanted to play, he'd play. He'd had dalliances with women in the workplace before, and while they hadn't been anything really special, he knew he could handle it. Lisa, the lab tech who did most of his processing when he was on the rigs, she'd been nice. And after it was over, they'd still been friends. And Patty, at the hospital during his internship—well, they'd made good use of the broom closet when the janitors were off cleaning. The women in his past were nice. Simple. He'd been lucky, he knew. Well, Rosie had been uber-complicated, but that might have been the problem with her.

Rig didn't know if anything was simple with Naomi. She sometimes seemed nervous as a cat in the rain, and other times, with her patients, she came across as assured, calm. Friendly. In control.

Which was the real Naomi? Who was she when she closed her bedroom door? When she was really, truly alone? Why was it that he suspected that somewhere, under those jangled nerves of hers, there was a roaring fire in a hearth banked against winter? *That* was the danger of her. Rig wanted to uncover that heat, but at the same time he was terrified of finding it, terrified that if he did, he wouldn't be able to walk away. Not that he was going to get hung up on her, he reminded himself. Just the opposite. Type A was Rig's blood type, and that's about all he understood about it. She was too driven to be with, he could see that a mile out, not that he was looking. For anyone.

The doorbell rang, and he set the timer quickly. Fifteen minutes, and they'd eat.

"Hey, you," he said as he opened the door and let her in. "Come in," he tried to say, but his voice choked on the words.

Damn. Naomi wore a loose red shirt cut with a low V that flowed when she moved, showing off a nice little peek at the top of her cleavage, and a black short skirt that moved with her in the best way. And red fuck-me heels. He'd known those legs were under there, but now that he saw them again, all naked like that . . . Rig wanted to put both hands on either side of her face, draw her in for a white-hot kiss, then run his hands down . . .

He had to get a grip.

Naomi smelled perfect, too, of a sweet, light perfume, something that went right to his head and made him dizzy.

"Welcome," Rig said as she looked around. He saw it with new eyes—he was tidy most of the time, but he'd never quite gotten around to unpacking all the way. His table and chairs were out, so there was somewhere to sit, but the tiny one-bedroom apartment didn't have room for much more than a small, two-seater couch that his brother had stored in the garage, and a TV that he never watched. Boxes were still stacked in the small hallway, full of stuff that he'd packed away before he went on the rigs, junk that had been in storage all these years. Finally he could start going through them, but he hadn't been motivated to start yet. He'd lived without whatever was in there for this long, so why bother now?

"Still settling in?" she asked.

"Sort of. Pizza should be ready soon."

"Smells good in here." She brushed the top of a stack of books with her fingertips.

It did smell great, the scent of the pizza warming had just filled the room. This was going to be a good night, even if he wasn't quite sure what was going to happen.

"So," she said, turning to face him. If he got a little closer to her, he might be able to look down that awesome shirt, just the tiniest bit.

And that's all it took to feel thirteen years old again. *Cool your jets, man.*

"Come sit in the kitchen. I've got a table in there. You want a beer?"

"Do you have wine?"

Shit. He should have thought of that. "No, I'm sorry. Fresh out."

"Beer's fine, then."

Rig handed her a bottle, and she drank from the neck, a long pull. He loved looking at the line of her throat.

"So," he said. What was this feeling? Was it really nervousness? Rig was both amused with himself and chagrined. Nervous. Sheesh.

The metal table legs wobbled as she put her bottle down, and he straightened one so that it wouldn't collapse altogether. "Sorry about this. It's old. It was my dad's, but my brother didn't have room for it at his house."

"I like it. It's kitschy." Her smile was more familiar as she said it—she looked more like the woman he'd taken out on his bike.

"About the dance . . . ," he started.

"Thank you for backing me on it," Naomi said. "I can't believe I'm going to do something with the town. Something real."

He shook his head and took a swig of his beer. "It'll be a better way to get people into your center than putting out those dusty old brochures, those ones that tell people how to wash their hands. Why do you *have* those in there, anyway?"

"I don't know," she said. "I agree that they're boring," She met his eyes, and his gut knotted in that way that kept happening when she was around. "And I hate boring. That's not me."

"Yeah, I've already picked up on that," he said. "I wouldn't call you that."

"What *would* you call me, then?" It sounded so much like a line a girl would say in a bar that he almost laughed. But she was serious. Naomi gave the smallest, sexiest smile he'd ever seen. She leaned forward infinitesimally and he felt himself drawn to her like iron to her magnet. Her green eyes were flecked with bits of hazel brown and tiny sparks of yellow. He wanted to lose himself in them. And the way her mouth was tilted up like that . . . He was going to kiss her and embarrass them both if she kept this up.

"Interesting," Rig said, his voice gruffer than he'd meant it to be. He stood and checked the pizza even though he knew it still had some time to go. Leaning back against the counter, he was as far as he could physically get from her and still be in the kitchen.

Naomi frowned. "What does that mean?"

"It means I don't . . . get you."

She grinned, that loose, easy smile, and he couldn't help smiling back at her. "I get you, though."

"You do? Tell me."

Holding the bottle against her cheek as if she was hot, she said, "You like women. You have one in every port. Or on every rig, as it were."

He frowned. It wasn't true. "Where would you pick that up from? Have I given you that impression?"

"No," she said, sliding that heated gaze over him again. "But it would be all right if you did."

"It would be okay if I was a user like that? That's not cool."

She looked surprised, as if she'd lit a candle and hadn't expected him to blow it out.

"I'm not, by the way," he continued. "A user."

"That's . . . fine," Naomi said, her voice breathy. She fiddled with the old napkin dispenser that had come with the furnishings. She popped a napkin out, folded it, then unfolded and refolded it again.

So she was nervous, too.

Good. It wasn't just him.

She uncrossed her legs and stood, going to the window that looked into the side yard. Shirley's flowers bloomed in planters, spilled from boxes. "It's gorgeous out there," she said. "Do you spend time in the garden?"

He nodded. "It's a good place for a book. And I hung a hammock out there that's good for pretending to read while you're really on the way to napping."

She glanced over her shoulder at him in what seemed like surprise.

"Yes," Rig said. "I read."

"Sorry." She gave an apologetic smile. "I just see you as the kind of guy who, if he's not working, he's out working on his motorcycle—"

"We've already established how bad I am at that."

"Do you have it back yet?"

"I got it taken to the garage. They haven't gotten back to me on repairs yet. They're a little slow."

"Oh." She touched the glass with the tip of her finger, as if testing it. "But yeah, I see you being outside."

"Not reading."

"What do you read?" she asked. It sounded curious, not challenging.

"Everything. Mostly I like to pick up old—"

"Wait," Naomi said, turning to face him. It felt like she'd made a decision, but he didn't know what it was regarding. "Let me guess."

Rig cocked an eyebrow. "You won't get it right."

"Old Louis L'Amour westerns. And John D. MacDonald. The ones you can get by the bag at used bookstores."

He gaped. She'd gotten it exactly right. "Did you—I must have some lying out?"

"Nope."

"At the office? Did I take any there?" He thought for a second. "No, I didn't. The one I'm reading is in the bedroom, and that's where I put my boxes of books. How did you do that?"

"Even if you're not outside working on your bike, you're still a man's man. Tough."

"Would a man's man be pleased that you said that? Would he preen like this?" Rig lengthened his neck and bugged out his eyes.

She laughed. "You're not going to read science fiction—too close to the science at work, too cerebral for relaxation. You're not going to read romance, obviously. And most current crime novels are probably too long to carry comfortably in a pocket, which is where I'm guessing you sometimes carry your books. The smaller, older paperbacks are perfect for that. I personally love the westerns, and I like the older romances, myself, the regency ones. They tuck into just about anything, even a small purse or the pocket of my white coat."

"You're good," he said. "And you're exactly right."

She dropped into the chair again and propped her elbows on the table. "I've read every single Louis L'Amour, everything he ever wrote. What's your favorite?"

"I'll do better—I'll bring out the box."

Ten minutes later, when the oven beeped, Rig barely heard it. Old western novels littered the table and they pawed through them, exclaiming and holding them up. If this was a way to have a date, Rig fully approved. Why hadn't he ever done it this way before?

Because no woman had ever understood his penchant for thrifting old books, or his need to stop at every yard sale in case a rare John D. MacDonald was lurking in the bottom of a box of DVDs. Sure, he read some new stuff, plenty of it when he was in the mood, but nothing beat drinking a beer in the hammock, reading a yellow-paged western until the book dropped out of his hand and his eyes slid shut against the sunset.

He pulled out the pizza, sliced it quickly, slid a few pieces onto plates and put one in front of her.

"It's not fancy," he said, "but it's good."

"The best," Naomi said.

It *was* good pizza, his favorite in town so far, and Naomi seemed to agree with him. She put away slices as fast as he did, three in under fifteen minutes. Most women said they liked pizza and then claimed to be full after one slice. He'd never understood that. He and Naomi barely spoke around the pepperoni, but damn, it felt good just being near her.

After they'd killed the medium pizza, Rig handed her a second beer and took one for himself. They moved into the living room as if there was a plan.

There wasn't. He wished he had one.

"Now what?" he said. "We're supposed to be talking about the dance, right?"

She nodded, slowly. "Yep."

He thought about kissing her. He wouldn't, though, even if she looked so good he could barely take his eyes off her. That red shirt was so silky, moving with her like water clinging to her skin.

"Right." He coughed. "Like I said, I know you can rent things like soda fountains—and if you tell me a couple of your favorite restaurants, we can get it catered."

"I like that." Naomi sank into the small couch, putting one arm over the back, crossing her legs so that those heels, and the long, curved line of her leg, were all he saw.

Standing, feeling awkward, Rig said, "What else do we need?"

"It's just drinks and food, right?" She waited a beat, her green eyes locked on his, long enough for Rig's pulse to speed up. Then she went on. "Easy. You and I can handle the drinks section—we can make a big sign that says—Oh! 'The doctor is IN.' You know, like the booth in Charlie Brown?"

Rig laughed. "That's good."

He sat next to her. It was really the only place in the small living room to sit. He *had* to get real furniture at some point; there just hadn't been a reason to do so until now. He was careful not to brush her knee, but he felt the warmth of her body near his, smelled the sweet light perfume, and got that strange zooming rush in his blood again. If it weren't completely inappropriate, if she hadn't made that clear last month, when she'd shaken his hand while saying good-bye, Rig would kiss her. Right now. Hard.

" . . . a list?"

"Excuse me?" He'd lost track of the conversation at some point.

"Should we make a list?"

"Oh. Yeah." He'd misread her in the office. Misread her badly. Pizza and beer was very friendly. It was what pals did. Coworkers.

Did pals lean their knees against each other like they were doing, though? He'd thought it was an accident, that she'd pull her leg away any second, but it stayed there, resting on his. Just that lightest touch was enough to render him speechless. He hoped he didn't have to say much more than that "oh," because it was possible he'd forgotten how to speak English.

She went to his head like no alcohol ever had. He practically had the spins.

Leaning forward, she reached across him to the coffee table, where he had a pad of paper advertising some drug company or other and a pen. He held his breath. Lord, she was practically in his lap. If he were sixteen and in a movie theater, this would be his version of yawning so that his arm would come down around her shoulders. The only difference was that that she'd come up with it first.

And at the last moment, before she settled back into her spot, Naomi turned her head and brushed his lips with hers.

"Thanks," she said. And then she did it again.

Her lips pressed chastely against his, drew away. He opened his eyes and, while the touch of her mouth was light, he was damned if she wasn't looking at him with something akin to pure lust. Just about what he was feeling, actually. Those green eyes of hers, just the color of the Gulf at sunset, when the blue had worn off and the dark night was rolling in.

He should put the brakes on before the car even got rolling. "Should we—maybe we should start with things like cups? Napkins?"

"Nah," she said as she wound an arm around his neck. Now she really was in his lap.

"Plastic forks?"

"Plastic's fine."

"So . . ." Should he pull away? Why wasn't she moving away from him, scooting off him? Instead, she stayed exactly where she was.

Her fingers reached up to play with his hair, sending shivers down his spine. Could she feel how hard he was under her? She had to be able to. He should move, should do something . . .

Rig forgot what he was supposed to do as she kissed him again. This time it wasn't chaste, it wasn't closed mouthed, and it wasn't casually friendly. This was for her, he could feel it. This was what she wanted, as much as he did.

Sweet hell. He'd give it to her, then. He kissed her with all the heat that he'd stored inside, ever since she'd let down her hair in the reception area, ever since she'd walked in here with those red fuck-me heels.

When her mouth parted under his, his tongue stroked hers as he plundered her mouth with his. He sucked the delicious plumpness of her lower lip and heard her gasp, a tiny inhalation he gloried in. The temperature of her skin soared right along with his, and he didn't know how he was going to get enough of her.

Rig didn't think it was possible.

Chapter Thirty-two

All lace looks different by candlelight.
—E.C.

Naomi started out totally in control. But what was supposed to be a sexy romp turned heavy in seconds. She couldn't breathe when he was kissing her, and she didn't want to breathe when he wasn't.

Bad sign. It was a very bad sign.

She could feel him under her, hard as a rock, ready. And she could feel herself, slick and heated. She wanted one thing, but this wasn't the way she wanted it. Naomi had planned on guiding him, leading him, turn by turn, as they both shook this insane wanting out of their bodies for once and for all.

But it seemed like he'd arrived at this ready, and it was seriously throwing off her concentration.

Damn. The arm that he'd been using to hold her on his lap trailed down her spine until he was touching the small of her back. While he did that thing with her bottom lip again lightly, that lick-suck thing that made her insides melt, he lifted the hem of her silk shirt, moving his fingers across the sensitive skin he found. The heat of him was so intense that she felt a fine trail of sweat break out wherever his fingers touched.

Naomi tugged her lip back and tried to regain her focus—she sucked his tongue, so soft, so wet, as she moved against him. She ground into his hips. For the love of God, if she just shifted six inches, if her damned panties were off and gone, she'd slide his zipper down, and he'd be in her, and she'd . . . God . . . Who *was* she? Was this what she'd . . . Her brain stilled and focused on the most important thing—the way his fingers slid up her spine again, and then—

If he'd just bring that hand at her back up and around, like that, until it was under her shirt, pushing her bra aside, touching her nipple just like *that*, yes.

Naomi wasn't sure which one of them gasped as she pulled her head back to look at him again. His dark eyes were even darker now, stormy, his lids half dropped, a satisfied look on his face as he tugged gently on her nipple. The touch sent an electric jolt to her groin and she arched her back, pushing into him again. His eyes grew even blacker, and he sank the fingers of his other hand into her hair, pulling her mouth back up to his.

"Tell me to stop," he growled against her mouth.

"No." Naomi ran her hand down his side and tugged his shirt up. "You can't." His skin underneath was so soft, a fine layer of hair covering a hardness underneath, the muscles matching the ones in his forearms.

"Do you know what you're saying?" His voice was low.

"Take me to bed."

He pulled away one more time. Naomi didn't think he'd pause like this for much longer. Thank God. "And you're sure? I want to know that you're with me in this."

"Oh, yeah." Boy, did he not know how with him she was. She'd come over for this. Why, then, did she feel like she wasn't keeping as tight a rein on things as she'd thought she would? Why was her breathing this ramped up, catching in her throat, when he wasn't even in her yet? From just his kiss and a light touch?

She slid off his lap, careful not to hurt him—good lord, he was big—and stood. She wobbled on her left heel and tried to make it into a sexy sidestep. Curling her first finger in a come-hither gesture, she winked.

"Wanna show me your bedroom?" Crap. It came out sounding silly. Rig's laughter showed he obviously thought so, too. But he stood and pulled her close, flush against him. He dipped his head to her ear, touched the lobe with a flick of his tongue and whispered, "Okay. I'm going into my bedroom. You going to come, too?" The double entendre made her knees wobble again. Damn heels. She was never wearing these again.

Rig led her forward through the door on the right, the one room she hadn't yet seen. He reached left and turned on a desk lamp that gave off only a soft glow. Through the dimness she saw a large bed, the simple brown quilt kicked aside. A low bookcase ran along the wall under the windows, and two boxes sat near the bed. She could see from where she stood that they were filled with more of the old paperbacks.

Two black-and-white prints hung above the bed, one of an oil derrick shot in bad weather—the rain clouds hung low, the deck of the rig was ominous, almost frightening. The other had been taken from the same vantage point, but on a sunny day. Naomi couldn't believe how cheery—pretty, really—an oil derrick could look.

"Those are great," she couldn't help saying. It wasn't part of her seduction technique, but he grinned when she said it.

"Thanks. They're both taken from a helicopter on the approach in."

"Wow." In the second, bright one, she could see a gull in the upper-right-hand corner, swooping away, on his way out of the picture. Naomi pointed at it. "Is that you?"

Rig turned her in place, his hands on her shoulders. "No one's ever seen that in there before. But yeah."

For a second, as he looked at her, Naomi felt giddy. As if he was her first crush. As if she'd gotten an A for getting the answer right to a test question she hadn't studied for.

"Please," she said, trying to keep her voice from shaking, trying not to let him see how tangled her emotions were. She knew she was here to accomplish a goal. And even though she couldn't remember the point of it anymore, Naomi knew it was the most important goal she could remember having in a very long time. She stepped closer into the circle of his arms and said, "I need you."

"Whoa," laughed Rig, pulling her closer. "You're not shy." He dropped his head, his mouth nuzzling the soft place in the crook of her neck, just above her shoulder. She shivered.

No, in this, she couldn't be shy. This she knew. Stepping back, she pulled her shirt up over her head, slowly, so that he could discover that the red lace demibra matched her heels. He murmured something, and his hands came forward to touch the soft skin between her breasts, but she shook her head.

"Not yet," she said.

"Ah, I get it. You're running the show."

"Yes, please." And she'd give him a show, all right, if her heart didn't stop first. She unzipped her skirt, sliding it slowly down her legs, then stepped out of it.

She stood there, in front of Rig, in her red bra, matching panties, and red high heels.

This was where she'd predicted she'd feel in control. Powerful.

Where the hell was that feeling? Why did she have the shivers, deep in her stomach, a quivery feeling that in about a second he'd be able to see? Why this incredible nervousness? She wanted to run to the bed and pull the covers over herself. *Damn* it.

Rig stood in place, watching. He liked what he saw, she could tell.

That intense heat poured off him in waves, warming her, lessening the inner shivers.

She would *act* like she was brave, then. Act like everything was normal. This was just sex, right? They both understood the human body as a mechanism and the clinical state of arousal: part A fit into slot B, add friction, achieve pleasurable state of relaxation. As she moved to sit on the bed, she told herself he could be anyone.

But he was Rig. That was the difference.

She draped herself over the bed in the most seductive pose she could imagine, her knees crooked, left ankle draped over right ankle to show her shoes to best advantage. She sucked in her belly, inclined her head, and patted the spot next to her.

"Want to join me?"

Rig shook his head as if to clear it. "I'm still getting used to what I'm seeing."

"Don't you like what you see?" Big, brave words. Now she was getting the hang of it.

"I do," he started. He paused. "But I'm not buying it."

She straightened a little, heart racing. "What are you talking about?"

He put one knee on the bed, just below her foot, and half knelt. "This isn't you. The only time you've really been you since you got here was when we were talking books, and when you saw my photography." He gestured to the prints above her. "This sexy-siren thing? It's working for you, and goddamn, you look amazing, but I'm just going to keep waiting until the real you shows up again."

Naomi sat all the way up. Why couldn't this be the real her? How dare he presume to know who she was? And what she wanted?

Especially since she didn't even know what she wanted this very second. To make love to him or to run out the door? She was torn between desires, although since she was dressed for only one of those activities, she didn't bolt. Yet.

"Who hurt you?"

She pulled back, her libido screeching to a halt. "What?"

"Who made it hard for you to trust anyone else? What makes you keep all those secrets inside?"

She pulled a portion of the sheet over her to cover the lace bits. "I don't know what you're talking about."

"Someone did a number on you. Was it a boyfriend? Ex-fiancé? Is that the ring you still wear?" He pointed at her right hand.

Naomi snorted. "Of course not. You're imagining things."

"Isn't that an engagement ring?"

"Maybe it was once, but never for me. A friend I loved gave me this." She rubbed the circlet with her thumb and hoped it would help ground her.

"Your family, then. Your dad then, when he died. Where did that leave you? How did you recover from that?"

Naomi shut her eyes. This was too intense. She hadn't expected this onslaught of questions. Where had her father's death left her? Alone, a package to be handed off to a mother who wasn't pleased she'd have to house it for the last year before she turned eighteen. Her boyfriend at the time, with whom she'd never gone past third base, dumped her since she'd be too far away down 405 to be worth driving to. She'd had no one. Even her friends hadn't called her after she moved, as if they hadn't known how to talk to her anymore.

The worst part had been her mother, though. To be seventeen and to feel unwanted, unseen, like that. . .

She pushed the feelings down and prayed they hadn't played across her face. "I was fine. I was studying premed by then, on my own. I wanted only one thing."

"Love?"

Naomi shook her head, hard. "To be a doctor."

"Oh," he said, his voice a rasp. "There you go with the secrets again. I don't believe you."

"I'm not asking you to." Naomi rearranged the sheet around her and didn't meet his eyes. She almost didn't recognize her voice as she continued to speak. "If you don't protect yourself, you get hurt."

"Darlin', that's no way to live life. And I *will* get to the bottom of your secrets, Naomi. But you can hold on to them right now." Rig came all the way up on the bed, easing her down, pulling the sheet back off her. "I have other things in mind."

Then, while she still wasn't sure what she was going to let him do, he bent over her, flicking his tongue into the dip between her breasts. He licked his way up to the underside of her jaw, then nibbled her cheek, grazed her forehead, and worked his way back to her mouth, all the while holding himself above her, not touching her with anything but his mouth.

Keeping his lips on hers, their breathing mingling, he said in a dark, low voice, "You want me inside you."

She gasped against him. Yes, she did. That's what she'd come here for. To get it out of the way already, to get her brain back into working order when it came to him.

"But that's not the way I work," he went on.

All her senses went on even higher alert as he drew back and looked down at her.

"You just lie back. Relax," said Rig.

Oh, no. This wasn't the way it was supposed to go.

"And now," he went on, "I'm going to take off your bra even though you probably don't want me to."

He was right, she didn't. It would help with keeping the upper hand if she stayed a little bit dressed, she knew it would: men loved a woman in lace. But his hand went to the catch between her breasts, and with one quick snap, the bra came open. Her breasts spilled out, hitting the cool air, her nipples immediately stiffening.

"Now, I'm going to lick you." He put one hand on her right breast and flicked the nipple with his finger. "Here." He gave her left nipple the slightest twist. "And here."

His mouth came down, and he made good on his word. And while he bit and sucked, teased and taunted, his hand roamed her body, dipping into the top of her panties, trailing up to her other breast, then back down to touch her inner thighs as if testing their softness, their willingness to part for him.

When she regained a few seconds of sense, Naomi twisted her fingers into his hair, stopping his mouth from kissing the sensitive skin just below her breast. She could still get herself back in control of the situation. She knew it. If she could just tamp down this need . . .

Oh, thank God. Rig sat up and tugged her panties down. She lifted herself to make it easier and then wriggled her legs, pushing the underwear down with one high heel. He helped her work it off, and then, to her surprise, he took first one of her shoes, then the other one, off. They dropped to the hardwood floor with a clatter. Didn't he like the way they looked?

But at least he was going to do as she wanted. He'd get a condom and then he'd be . . .

Rig moved down her body, placing slow kisses on her belly button, her hip, the outside of her thigh. Then he put himself between her legs, yes, that was it, but oh, God, he was too far away. Not there. That's not what she wanted. That would be *way* too much.

"Rig." The voice that she'd meant to be commanding came out as a squeak. "Not that, I need—"

He interrupted her as if she wasn't speaking. "Now I'm going to lick you here." He touched her inner folds with a finger, running it slickly up to her clit, and then back down. "Oh, Jesus, Naomi. You're so wet."

No. That's not what she wanted. That wasn't . . .

Naomi lost all ability to think in clear sentences the second he moved between her legs, his tongue touching her, licking her, pushing into her slowly and then retreating. He made broad strokes and tiny little ones, hard ones, and gentle, teasing ones. She writhed, holding on to the bedpost behind her. She moaned—she couldn't help it. He was driving her out of her mind.

With just his tongue Rig took her right to the edge—her legs were shaking, her stomach muscles quivering. In another second, she'd—she'd . . . He stopped, lifting his head to look at her. God, if he stopped now—she needed—

"Now I'm going to make you come." He lowered his head, his tongue sucking, pulling, flicking until Naomi started to pulse. Then, as she came, he put two fingers inside her, right where she needed it, right there, God—he slid up her body, keeping his fingers inside her, using his thumb to continue the pressure his tongue had been giving her, and he whispered in her ear as she came around his hand, "See? I told you so." He laughed, his chest shaking against her, a deep, happy laugh.

How did this happen? How did he take over her plan? Why didn't she care more? Instead, she reveled in the feeling of coming down, rolling against him so that she was flush against his body.

"You're still dressed," she said. "How did that happen?"

"I wanted to give you something, rather than taking." He slid his fingers out, and she took a quick, indrawn breath with the aftershock.

"So now you're going to take off your clothes?" Maybe she could still regain her footing.

"Nope. I'm just going to lie here until you fall asleep." He laughed again, and Naomi thought fleetingly that she'd never had anyone laugh at her in bed before, but the way he laughed made her feel amazing.

She could make him feel amazing. too, if he let her.

"What about this?" Her hand reached down and pressed against the erection that strained at the front of his jeans.

Rig growled. "Let's leave that alone, or I'll forget I'm trying to be a gentleman."

"I'm naked in your bed. How is that gentlemanly?"

"You want me to show you again?"

Naomi smiled, suddenly inexplicably shy. "No. I couldn't."

"Oh, I bet you could."

He slid down, not heeding her pleas to stop, and when he got to the right spot, his mouth took her the same way. Naomi started shaking again and didn't stop for a long, long time.

Chapter Thirty-three

Don't be afraid to jump in with both feet and make the biggest splash you can. It's a good way to block your finished objects, anyway.

— E.C.

When she woke up, it took Naomi a half second of panic to figure out where the hell she was. The room was dark, and she was perfectly warm from the top of her head all the way down to the tips of her toes.

Rig.

She felt one long tremble rock her as she remembered what he'd done to her, how high he'd taken her, and how hard she'd crashed into his arms. He'd stayed true to his word—he'd kept his clothes on and made it purely all about her.

Naomi had felt treasured. Beautiful. Sexy. Safe.

She was still in his arms, lying on her side, her left arm and leg draped across him as he lay on his back. He breathed deeply and evenly.

God, she'd screwed up. She had to get out of here.

Naomi carefully lifted her arm and leg off him slowly so that she was also on her back. She held her breath for a moment. He didn't stir. She lifted the quilt that she'd been half under and slid out in one even motion.

Once her bare feet were on the floor, she began looking for her clothes. She found her panties in a ball near the bookcase, and her skirt where she'd left it at the foot of the bed. Her shirt was still on top of the box of books, but no matter how hard she looked, she couldn't find her bra.

She'd just have to leave without it.

Rig made a low, guttural noise as he rolled to her side of the bed, and Naomi froze. With all her heart, she wished to be out of here. She stood stock-still, holding her breath. That big, muscular arm that had held her last night wrapped itself around her pillow and dragged it under his head. Then he relaxed and sank back down under the covers.

Out, out. She crept to the bedroom door, thankful it already stood ajar. She crossed the living room, her heels dangling from one finger. Their tippy-tap would certainly give her away. The front door was a challenge, but one that she took quickly, unsnapping the dead bolt, twisting the smaller lock. Even if he woke now, she could still make her getaway if she moved fast.

In the garden, she paused, almost not breathing. Her ears strained to hear anything from inside. Nothing. Thank God.

Turning, she almost bumped right into Shirley Bellflower.

"Where's the fire?" Shirley said and grinned.

Naomi couldn't think of a single thing to say. It was Shirley's yard, after all. Dammit.

"I see you're dressed for a walk." Shirley pointed at her heels, still hanging from her fingers, and she cast a glance at the red silk shirt that she possibly had buttoned wrong.

"Yeah. I was just . . ."

"Honey, you don't have to make up a story. Nothing wrong with a walk of shame. I think he's a nice guy, and you've always looked like you deserved some fun. You've been busy lately. This is good for you."

Shirley looked tired, her face more drawn than Naomi remembered it being.

"Sit," Naomi said, ignoring every muscle and nerve in her body that was urging her to flee. "Here, on the bench. Sit a minute. We haven't talked in too long. Tell me how you are."

Shirley sat, but it was with effort. "Fine, just fine."

"Really?"

Stretching her arms in front of her as if she was uncomfortable, Shirley waited a beat and then said, "You askin' as a doctor?"

Should she say no? "As your friend."

"You usually don't see me without my face on, that's all," Shirley said lightly.

"Anything wrong?" Naomi kept her voice soft, but she caught Shirley's eye.

Finally Shirley said, "Seein' a new guy. I didn't tell you about him yet . . . We were up late last night." A smile crept across her face. "Now I'm fighting a migraine, but I don't want to let on, 'cause I have to get to work soon."

"Can't you take the day off?"

Shirley shook her head. "Nope. No can do."

"You can't use a sick day?"

"Waitresses don't get sick days. At least not this kind of waitress. I build up vacation time, but I blow that every year on a cruise, and I've already been to the Mexican Riviera this year. If I'm out, I'm not making tips, and that's how I keep this property afloat. That, and renting the back house out to lover boys like him." She jerked her thumb in the direction of where Rig was sleeping.

"Well, come see me, then. We can talk about medication. Prevention. How long have you been getting the migraines?"

Standing slowly, Shirley said, "Ever since my husband died, years ago. I get them on the anniversary of his death. No exception."

Naomi stood with her. Grief could trigger migraines. And she knew that sometimes not working wasn't an option. But . . . No. She wouldn't give the lecture she normally gave, the one about taking care of yourself before anyone else—with Shirley's shoulders slumped like they were, it didn't feel like the right thing. She just wished that she knew what to do. Goddammit, what would she do in the office with a patient she was trying to help?

Then she remembered. A hug. Friends hugged. She'd forgotten that.

She bent awkwardly at the waist and put her arms around Shirley's shoulders. At first, the woman jumped, seeming utterly surprised. The hug was rigid. It didn't feel like it was working. Naomi should let go.

Then Shirley made a noise in the back of her throat and dropped her shoulders. She reached up, letting the sides of their faces touch, and wrapped her arms around Naomi. The hug was tight, strong. It felt important. Naomi held on even though her heart rate skittered into overdrive. Shirley needed this.

And Naomi herself felt long overdue.

After a moment, Shirley dropped her arms and pulled away, sinking back into the garden bench.

It was astonishing. She looked like a different person. So gray earlier, there was a slight hint of color to her cheeks now. The tension that had been in her eyes was completely gone. Smiling up at Naomi, she said, "So, you and the doc, huh? Say, have you met Frank, his father?"

Confused, Naomi said, "I've met him, yes."

Shirley nodded. "Yeah," she said. "Nice guy."

Confused, Naomi *really* didn't know what to do now. But she settled on a smile that felt real, and Shirley returned it.

"Don't work too hard," said Naomi.

"Thanks, Doc," said Shirley.

Chapter Thirty-four

Sometimes I feel made of laceweight merino, so happy I could float away on a whispered breath.
—E.C.

O ut in her car, Naomi sank into the seat and snapped on the belt. She'd hugged a friend. She lifted herself in the seat so she could see her face in the rearview mirror. A happy-looking woman looked back at her. Her brown curls were messy, of course, and there wasn't a trace of the eyeliner or lipstick she'd worn last night. But she looked . . . happy.

Shirley had called her *Doc*. Okay, Shirley was her friend, but still. Someone had called her *Doc*.

She grinned at herself in the mirror and laughed, before suddenly feeling sheepish.

He'd brought this out in her. Rig, who had never even removed his clothing last night, had found this part of her. Or at least, being near him brought it closer to the surface. Naomi loved this feeling.

And, she decided, as she started the car, it scared her. She hadn't driven their actions last night like she'd thought she would. He'd been as active a part of their seduction as she had.

Naomi should hate that. It should make her feel almost sick with nervousness. There was no doubt about that. He hadn't lost his mind like she had hers, so it was unequal. If she could take care of that, the draw to him would undoubtedly lessen. But she didn't have to *reject* what happened last night just because she had a good time.

A really freaking amazing time.

She drove toward her house. It was a gorgeous, rare day of summer with absolutely no fog pushing in from the ocean. Crystal clear, deep blue, and flat as a sheet—the water looked like something from a tourist postcard. *Hi, Mom, Wish you were here.*

Naomi drove past a taco truck that she'd seen before but never stopped at. The sign, Los Mariscos, was cheery, and a pot-bellied man stood waiting for his food.

She was starving, she realized. The sense of unexpected buoyancy reacted with the happiness, and it seemed to make her hunger even stronger. She was ravenous.

She pulled over and started to get out of the car. Damn. She'd probably need shoes to cross the dirt to the truck.

Her red strappy heels certainly didn't feel right, or good, to put on. But she wobbled her way up to the ordering counter of the truck where the open window was up high, and she had to crane her neck to read the even higher menu.

"Hi." The man peering out the truck's order window had a broad, florid face with a nose as wide as a spoon. His eyes were friendly, and he looked at Naomi with curiosity. "You want breakfast?"

"I can have breakfast?" Naomi had thought it just sold tacos.

"'Course. Everything?"

"Then heck, yeah."

The day was getting even better. She leaned on her car in the warming sun, waiting, and tilted her head back. A block away she could hear the ocean, a low, dull roar that sounded almost exactly like the freeway had when she lived in San Diego. Two seagulls in the parking lot squabbled over a dirty tortilla.

"Hey," called the man. He held out her burrito. "Have a good day, pretty lady."

It was foil wrapped and huge. Naomi could tell it was going to be fantastic. "Thanks."

Back in her car, she realized she felt like a different person from the one she'd been the day before. And she was too sleepy to examine why. She needed home, a shower, a pot of coffee, and the incredible-smelling burrito, and she'd be able to face going in to the office.

Where she'd face the man who'd had his fingers and—oh God—his tongue inside her last night. Naomi felt heat rush through her again.

What with Rig last night, and hugging Shirley this morning, she was on a roll. Who knew what wild and crazy out-of-character thing she might pull later? She might jump out of an airplane. Or even call her mother of her own volition! Naomi grinned at the thought.

But that whole Rig thing. She was going to keep a lid on it, unless she knew exactly what she was doing. He'd almost gotten to her last night. She knew it, could admit it, if only to herself. And that made her nervous.

She stepped happily into her house, pleased that it would be just as she'd left it, rules of order maintained in her friendly jumble, clutter corralled so that she understood it. Order, perfection, peace. They were all integrally linked, and Naomi loved the feeling of—

Oh, crap. She didn't love the furniture in the living room being moved so that the couch now faced the fireplace. She didn't love the sink being full of dishes. She didn't love the look of the pan on the stove that had apparently boiled over and hadn't been cleaned up. Oh, *Anna*.

At least she had her bedroom. Her sanctuary.

She opened the door, and pulled back the curtains to let in the light. Something groaned under the covers.

Naomi screamed. Whatever it was in the bed screamed, too, and burrowed farther.

Anna.

Ripping back the coverlet, Naomi said, "What the *hell* are you doing in here?"

Anna squeaked again and then gave a weak giggle. "You scared me," she said. "Why did you scream?"

"Because, unlike you, I'm not in the habit of finding strange people in my bed."

Anna sat up slowly, scooting backward so that she could rest against the headboard. "That's just rude."

"I know." Naomi felt immediately guilty. "I apologize. Cheap shot. But you *scared* me."

"You?" Anna pulled the sheet over her belly and up to her chin. "There was a *mouse* in my room."

She was already calling it her room.

"I don't have mice," Naomi said. "Did you actually see one?"

"Well, no, but I heard something scritching under the bed, and then it sounded like it ran along the baseboard and into the hall."

"So whatever it was, and I doubt it was a mouse, wasn't even in your room anymore?"

Anna's eyes were round. Guileless. "But what if it came back?" She sat up straighter as Naomi opened her tiny closet. "Where were you, anyway? I kept expecting you to kick me out of bed when you came home." She pointed to the window, where sunlight was streaming around the slits in the venetian blind.

Naomi tugged a hand through her hopeless hair. Did she still have time for a shower? It didn't matter if she was late, she needed one, if only to rinse the smell of Rig off her body, to wash the two of them out of her mind. "I was out."

"With Rig? I knew it! I fucking *knew* it." Anna's face was smug. "I think you make a good couple."

Naomi couldn't help but laugh. "You've seen him twice."

"Three times. Hey, are you blushing?" Anna crowed. "You *are*. Like a schoolgirl!"

"I'm not. It's just warm in here. And anyway, aren't you supposed to be at work to open in," Naomi looked over Anna's shoulder at her alarm clock, "twenty-five minutes?"

"Oh, shit!" As much as an almost-full-term pregnant woman could, Anna hopped out of bed and darted into the bathroom.

Well, there went Naomi's chance of hurrying.

She took her burrito out to the back porch. In between bites, she worked on the shawl, which was actually growing—Naomi could finally see some progress. At the end of each full repeat, her brain was always confused with the change, all the sudden K2togs and SSKs that followed the rows of plain garter stitch, but at the present moment, she understood these increases and decreases. She was starting to be able to read the lace. A little bit.

While she ate and knitted, she studied the backyard. She loved it out here, all flowering shrubs and native plants that she'd put in instead of the grass that had been here when she moved in. She'd hired a landscape company to do the heavy lifting, but she'd chosen and put in the plants herself, and since they were all drought-resistant native plants that flourished in their coastal clime, she barely ever had to water. She just weeded a bit every few months, and let the garden go. Naomi had thrown out a wildflower seed bomb in early spring, when they got most of their rains, and now her favorite California poppies nodded their heads next to forget-me-nots and Indian paintbrush.

The burrito was delicious. Naomi took her time with it. She breathed. In. Out. Early sunlight filtered through a few puffy clouds, and the day promised to be warm. A perfect beach day.

She felt more alive than she had in longer than she could remember. Her sister was living in her house, and Rig was tangling her brain waves like a ball of laceweight rolling on the floor, and Naomi didn't want to be anywhere else.

Chapter Thirty-five

*Reward yourself for good behavior: if you finish a sweater,
make a quick hat. If you finish a challenging piece of lace,
cast on for chunky cables. Remember to treat yourself
well.*

—E.C.

Rig woke to disappointment that felt like a giant storm swell
rolling under his bunk. Naomi wasn't there next to him, she
wasn't curled in his arms like she had been all night. It wasn't
that much of a surprise, honestly—he should have guessed she'd run
at the first light of dawn, but he'd hoped that he'd awaken with her,
and that he'd be able to convince her to stay a little longer.

Instead, all trace of her was gone save for the lingering sweet scent
that still hung in the air like a ghost.

Oh, and the bra that was stuck under the door between the bedroom and the bathroom.

Rig laughed and gently pulled it free. Red lace, with that under-
lining of black . . . was it silk? Whatever it was, the bra was pretty,
but looking at it, Rig could only think of what had been inside it last
night. What he'd taken out of it.

The thought hit him like a punch.

Slow down, Keller. It had been a really long time since he could think of a girl he wanted to wrap back up like a sexy package—the bra, the panties, the long red silk shirt—just so he could take them off and start touching her again.

Danger. The signs were obvious.

Now was about reconnecting with his family. Taking the time to rebuild his relationship with his brother. To be a good son and uncle. To help the Keller men with their grief. Someday he'd find his own soul mate and settle down, but it wasn't time for that yet. And Naomi wasn't his soul mate. Obviously. She was a highly driven professional career woman, a little too tightly wound for him to consider anything more than a dalliance of the sort they'd had last night.

She also made tiny mewling whimpers of pleasure when he stroked her with his tongue, noises that made him harder than he'd ever been. She hadn't seemed highly driven or wound tight last night. God, he ached right now, just thinking about it.

For a little while, maybe he'd continue to ignore the signs. It was like driving in a foreign country—you didn't need to understand the directions just to stay on the road. He left the house, shutting his door with a click. Had Naomi kept her shoes off while she flitted through the garden to the street? Or had he just slept through the noise of her leaving? He checked to see if Shirley was in the garden, as she sometimes was early in the morning, but she wasn't, and her car wasn't in the driveway. She was working at Tillie's, then.

He felt a half smile on his face. He touched the lace of Naomi's red bra in his coat pocket. It was going to be a great day, and he had the best job in the world.

When he stepped into the office, chaos swirled like a storm. Three people were in line, two of them looking furious. Anna was behind the reception desk, her hands up in the air as if she was being robbed.

Naomi was scuttling around behind her, filling her arms with files, setting them down, then grabbing more papers. She looked out and met his eyes. For a moment, he felt her remember the night before— he saw a flare of heat in her emerald eyes—and then her face went blank.

"You're late," she said. "We need you back here, *now*."

"Coming," he said. And then to the woman in line who looked the angriest, he said, "Good morning. Yellow's a great color for you."

The woman's shoulders relaxed and she smiled. "Well, thank you." She ran her hands down the velour jumpsuit she was wearing.

He pushed through the door into the back area. Naomi stopped in her tracks and stared at him.

"I thought *I* was going to be late, but you're even later than I was. You know it's nine thirty already? And we've had patients since before nine? I've been doing everything I can, and I've seen two so far, but Anna is so far behind in what she has to do that I'm afraid nothing's going to get done at all. She hasn't even started phoning in prescriptions, or sorting lab results, and if Bruno was here everything would be fine, but he's not—" Her voice broke off, and she frowned even harder. "And that's your fault. So is hiring Anna. We are *better* than this here."

"You were in such a good mood last night."

A hint of rose crept across her cheeks that made him long fiercely to cross the room and kiss her senseless.

"Yeah. I was." Her voice was softer. "I was even in a good mood this morning, but not since the office exploded."

"I'll help. You take a patient back, and I'll help Anna sort it out."

Naomi puffed air out of her cheeks. Then she said, "That's very reasonable. Thank you."

He laughed. "That looked like it hurt to say."

Her eyes looked wounded. "No. Your idea is a good one. I'll go get Mr. Cruz."

Damn. He hadn't meant to hurt her feelings. Maybe he could make her laugh instead. "Oh, Naomi?"

She stopped, one hand on the door to reception. "Yeah?"

"You left something at my house." He pulled just the strap of her bra out of his pocket so that she could see it.

"Oh! You shouldn't have . . ." Naomi stammered. "Dammit. Give it to me," she said, crossing the room in three quick steps. She snapped it out of his pocket, ran to her office, opened the door, and threw it in. He pictured it landing on her desk, draping from her lamp, and smiled.

"Do I get a reward?" he asked as he went to help Anna.

"Oooh!" Naomi sounded both angry and amused, like a child being teased with a toy just over her head. He liked it that he could make her sound like that. She needed to relax more, obviously, and good God, if that wasn't a worthwhile way to spend some time, he didn't know what was.

Chapter Thirty-six

*If you have a sick feeling about the edge, or the cast on,
or even the yarn itself, trust that feeling. You're always
right.*

—E.C.

N aomi stretched and looked out her office window. Once Rig
had jumped into the fray, the rush had eased, and the work
flow had been manageable. No matter what, it would have
been a busier day than normal, a summer cold going around that
had every mother worried. It would play itself out, and in the mean-
time, Naomi took a lot of temperatures and discussed the color of
sputum with concerned parents. She herself was fighting a stomach-
ache, probably from the way it tightened up every time she saw Rig.
Just one time, as they'd passed in the hallway, she'd met his dark
eyes. Instantly, she'd felt that deep, internal heat flare to life, and the
amused look on his face told her he knew what he was doing to her.

She'd made an iced coffee in the break room and retreated to her
office, dousing her feelings with chilled caffeine.

Anna had finally caught on to the rhythm—that, or instead
of filing things, she was just throwing them out. Naomi doubted

the latter, though. She knew her sister was smart. She'd just never been . . . very focused. Now that Anna was sitting at the desk, Naomi found it more difficult not to get her hopes up that she would stay. But she had to remember: this was temporary. It always was with Anna.

Naomi tilted back in the chair

Her heart still ached for the baby. God, what kind of life was her sister going to give an infant? Why couldn't Anna have used birth control, like a sensible, sexually active woman? Abortion this late was unthinkable, of course, but earlier on? When she was only a month or two along? Surely her sister had considered it?

Outside on the sidewalk, a tiny old woman moved at what must be slower than a snail's pace, leaning on her walker. At one point her head dropped onto her chest, and she stood there, swaying. Naomi stood up halfway, ready to run outside if the woman dropped, but after what appeared to be a micronap, she raised her head and moved on, one inch at a time.

What kind of life had that woman had? Was it one full of love and laughter, kids and grandchildren? A husband who adored her? Or was Naomi looking at her own future, alone, slowly making her solitary way down a concrete sidewalk?

She ran her fingers along the arms of her father's office chair. As always, touching the pleated, worn leather soothed her in a way usually only knitting did. When she was a child and begged to be taken to her father's office, he'd perch her in his chair when he left the room to see patients. He'd let her draw on his prescription pads with the thin blue pen he favored. "Sit there. Draw me something."

"What should I draw?" she'd ask.

"Something good. Something you like."

She'd draw a stick figure in a white coat and dress, a gigantic stethoscope around her neck, and high heels.

Her father would laugh when he came back and pretend to misunderstand. "I don't wear a dress! I don't wear heels." He was waiting for her answer, and she knew the correct one.

"No, Daddy, that's *me*. I'm going to be a doctor, just like you. And sit in a chair like this one. And have a nurse and my own thermometer." Thermometers, with the way the mercury slid up and down, had been magical to her.

"You shall have as many thermometers as you like, my little monkey. Now, scoot over and let me sit there."

Naomi brought herself back to the present, her fingers still tight around the leather arm of her chair, and checked on the woman moving outside again. She'd gone another seven feet, and Naomi hoped she didn't live more than another block or so away or she'd be out there all month.

At least he'd known that was what she wanted, to follow in his footsteps. He'd done everything right, and damned if she wasn't still trying to live up to him. The chair, and a few of his old medical texts, were all she had left of him.

And God knew, he'd never had an office romance. He'd be horrified if he'd ever known that was exactly what she was doing.

Was last night just an aberration? Naomi could try to think of it as that. She'd had a plan—it hadn't been a good one, and it hadn't worked.

Why, then, was she completely unable to stop listening for Rig's boots in the hallway? Being with him had scrambled her circuits, and electricity was zapping around, but charging the wrong areas. Well, she supposed they were the *right* areas, sometimes . . . Spinning a pencil in her fingers, she watched as the old woman finally turned the corner and was out of sight.

Rig. She sighed again, knowing she sounded like a crushed-out teenager. Sinking farther into the chair, she spun the pencil so hard she lost control of it, knocking herself in the chin with the lead.

She stood quickly, crossing the room to the bookcases, and, randomly, pulled out her father's *New England Journal of Medicine,* from the week of September 9, 1984. This was where the game had begun, so many years ago. This was why she'd kept such out-of-date magazines for so long.

Late at night, as a child, waiting for her father to come home from work, unwilling to phone her mother who was so busy with Buzz and the new baby, she'd flip through the pages of his medical journals while asking a question in her mind. If the divined passage answered it, then she'd done it right. If it was a garbage answer, she'd have to study the section and learn it, to make up for playing such a silly game.

Nowadays it worked a little better with Eliza's books. But this was all she had here at the office.

Closing her eyes, Naomi flipped the pages of the journal. *What would Daddy have thought of Rig?*

Carefully, carefully, she let her finger trail down a page, and then stop. She opened her eyes.

> Professionalism is the most important part of gaining a patient's trust. Little things, like a firm handshake, and addressing them with their correctly pronounced surname, can go a long way toward inspiring a useful doctor/patient relationship. Even professional cloth-ing—correct, pressed, the expected white coat—can translate into trust.

A knock came at the door. Rig entered, wearing a green button-down shirt and jeans. His stethoscope was shoved halfway into his back pocket instead of being hung neatly around his neck, and his hair stuck up as if he'd just run his fingers through it.

Oh dear. That *was* what her father would have said. But he'd never had to deal with anything like this. She slid the journal under a pile of files on her desk.

Thank God she'd put her bra back in her purse after lifting it from the desk where she'd flung it.

"Hi," she said. Would he be able to tell she'd just been thinking about him? Thinking about last night?

"Hey." His voice blew on the coals she'd thought she'd banked inside. She wanted him to say more.

But he didn't. Rig kicked the door shut with his boot, and came around the desk. Without preamble, he threaded his fingers behind her head, bringing his mouth down to hers. He kissed her hard.

Hot.

Long.

When he finally drew his head back, Naomi's spine had somehow gone to jelly, as if the dura matter had heated, just like the space between her legs. She felt as if she was flying, but at the same time, the spinning sickness at the pit of her abdomen was back, too.

Rig growled, "I've been wanting to do that all day."

Naomi looked up into Rig's face. She wanted to press her cheek against the long curve of his jaw, now faintly stubbled. She wanted to say something that would stun him. That would let him know that she was still in control, something sexy that would prevent him from noticing that he undid her with every touch.

She opened her mouth to speak.

And instantly threw up, barely leaning over to make it into the trash can in time.

Chapter Thirty-seven

Children are often more adept than we expect them to be when it comes to learning the important things: walking, talking, knitting, and then reading. Best if done in this order.

—E.C.

Two nights later, at his brother's home, Rig wondered for the fiftieth time how Naomi was doing. It was hard to keep his mind off her—she'd been so instantly sick yesterday afternoon, and so damn horrified. He'd offered to take her home, but she'd refused. He thought he'd seen the sheen of tears in her eyes, but she hadn't given him a second chance to look as she'd run out of her office carrying her purse. She was gone in what felt like seconds, and she'd been out sick today. He and Anna had handled it in the office, but just barely, and Anna had said she'd been in her bathroom most of the night.

Frank was obviously waiting for an answer from him, and Rig tried to focus. "Dad," said Rig, "Milo barely reliably ties his shoes. And you think he's going to be able to play chess?"

Frank humphed as he thumped the pieces of the heavy old chess board that he'd dragged out of his bedroom into the backyard to the picnic table. "He's already five. He has to learn sometime. I showed him the basics the other night and he seemed to get it. We'll play after dinner."

Milo dropped off the branch he hung from and raced over to his grandfather. "I can play! I can play!"

Rig laughed and looked down at him. "You can? Can you tell me the rules?"

Milo shrugged. "It's just like checkers only the pieces jump crooked. Duh." He zoomed away again, his arms up in the air. Screeching, he turned the corner to run to the front gate. He'd be back in a minute.

Rig took a deep breath and let it out. The sun was dropping in the west, and he could see, just over his brother's fence, the fog bank approaching. It wasn't here yet, but he could feel a hint of cool mist being pushed in his direction. In the yard, two robins hopped on the edge of the perpetually empty birdbath; Megan had loved birds, but Jake always forgot to fill the bath with water. Maybe a nice gift would be turning it into a fountain—Rig bet Jake would like that, and Milo would love being able to splash his hands in it.

He should check on Naomi. Did she need anything? Being sick sucked.

Jake came out from the kitchen carrying two boxes. "Pizza tonight. I'm too tired to grill."

"Pizza's always good," said Rig as he looked at his brother. Two dark blue circles were pressed under his eyes, the kind that used to be there for months on end after Megan died.

"Milo!" Jake yelled. "Dinner!"

Another screech followed by maniacal laughter was all they heard.

"He wants to be the Joker this week," Jake said. "It's his new thing, but all he knows how to do is the laugh. It's creeping me out." As he handed Rig a beer, he smiled, but it didn't seem real—it looked like one of those that he'd had for the first two years after Megan died, the smile that never reached his eyes.

Frank grabbed a piece of pizza and leaned back in his deck chair. The piece of ham he grabbed with his teeth fell onto his shirt. Shrugging, Frank kept eating.

"Dad, you've got—," Jake started, waving his finger.

"Saving it for later," said Frank. "Mind your own business. Now if you'll excuse your old man, I have to listen to Rachel Maddow's podcast. I missed it this morning." With that, Frank stuck the cords of his iPod into his ears, and climbed into the hammock, leaning back in the thin evening sunlight. He closed his eyes, chewing all the while.

"So what's up?" Rig asked.

"Nothin'," said Jake. "How 'bout you?"

"Don't give me that." Rig took his first, perfect, ham and pineapple bite. It had been a good week for pizza eating, that was for sure. "Something's wrong, and you'll have to tell me or I'll give Milo two of the candy bars I have in my car for just these kinds of emergencies."

He didn't see or hear Milo approaching but he felt the tug at his elbow.

"Candy bar, please." He tilted his head back and to the side, grinning a patently fake grin.

"Is that the Joker look? Because it's freaky," said Rig. "Not now, buddy. Get some pizza."

"Candy bar, please." He rocked his head back and forth, the same enormous smile plastered on his face.

Jake snapped, "Knock it off. Eat pizza or go to your room."

Milo jumped, his smile falling. His shoulders slumped. "Fine," he whispered. "Candy later?" This was said more hopefully, and Rig could see him inhaling slowly, just in case a fit was required.

Rig nodded hurriedly. "One piece of pizza equals a candy bar if your dad says it's okay."

Jake raised one shoulder and dropped it. "Fine. Whatever."

After Milo had whooped and run to sit under the oak tree with his slice, Jake finally sighed and said, "Don Barger's wife died last night."

"Shit, Jake. Was he on duty?"

Jake nodded. "He'd grabbed Milton's shift—he's been looking for overtime lately. Medical bills. The hospice nurse was with her."

"Shit," was all Rig could say.

"They didn't call 911, obviously, because it was hospice, but they called Don on his cell. We took the rig out of service and spent the morning there with him. Bunch of us stayed over after the shift. Left there about five, just as her mom got there." Jake's voice cracked. "They have two kids. Ages seven and nine. Girls. And oh, God," he leaned forward, pushing the pizza box away, putting his elbows on the table and burying his eyes in his palms. "The girls are old enough to know what happened. I don't think I've ever seen anyone cry that hard in my life, and their dad could only hold one at a time."

A tremor rocked Jake's body. "I held Lacy, the seven-year-old. For an hour, I held her and told her it would be okay. But it won't be, Rig. It's never, ever going to be okay again. And she has to learn that the hardest way possible."

Rig slid forward on his chair, holding his pizza in one hand, the other outstretched. Fuck. Of all the calls for his brother to go on . . . "Jake—"

His brother sat up and rubbed his eyes, hard. They shone brightly, but the wetness was gone. "All I could be was as tough as I could be. I told him the truth, though. He wanted to hear it. I told him it was going to be awful. He just looked relieved someone was telling him something he could believe. I think everyone had been telling him it was going to be fine, that she would miraculously recover or something. Damn, Rig. His eyes . . . were the worst I've ever seen. I wonder if I looked like that?"

It sounded rhetorical, so Rig didn't answer, just took another swallow of his beer. Yeah, Jake had looked exactly like that when Megan died. It had been almost unbearable for Rig to look at him. He glanced at Frank to see if his father had heard any of this, but he still had his earbuds in and his eyes were closed.

"I'm sorry," Rig finally said. "But I'm glad you were there for him. Not many other people could go through that with him, not like you could."

Jake nodded. "I guess I've been pretty fucked up for the last few years, huh?"

Rig almost laughed. It was an understatement. But who reacted well to the loss of a love? No one, that's who. "You've been doing just fine."

From under the tree, Milo made a *whoop-whoop* noise, like a fire engine clearing its throat. Jake looked startled and turned in his chair, ready to run toward his son. Then Milo kept eating. Jake's shoulders relaxed.

"He's fine," said Rig.

Jake picked up his beer bottle and drank. "Yeah, but for how long is he going to be fine?"

It must be hell to feel that scared, all the time. But that's what love did to people.

He wondered if Naomi was okay. If he should check on her.

Jake cleared his throat. "Changing the subject. You got your eye on your office partner?"

Rig took a bite of pizza to put off answering and ended up biting the inside of his mouth so hard he tasted blood. "Shit."

"What's your problem?"

He used his tongue to prod the wound. He'd live. "Bit my cheek. And yeah. I guess I do."

"Have you slept with her?"

"Easy, Trigger." How much should he admit to the man who hadn't gotten any in three years?

"Because I bet Dad five bucks you'd already slept with her. Am I right?"

"You had a *bet* on me?"

"Hell, player, if you've got it, use it. Dad actually agreed, but he was mad at me for using the last of the toilet paper without changing the roll, so he bet against me."

"I'm not answering the question." His brother didn't need to know the details.

"Sweet. That's a yes. Was it fun?"

Rig leaned back so that he rocked on the back two legs of his patio chair. He couldn't help admitting, "Yeah."

His brother frowned. "If that back leg slips, you'll crack your head wide open."

Thunking back to the ground, Rig sighed. "I'm fine. I'm not going to hurt myself."

Jake looked like he was going to say something else, then he shook his head and finished his beer.

"What?" asked Rig.

"Nothing."

"I swear to God, Jake, leaning back in my chair is not the same as jumping out of an airplane with no parachute. I'm fine."

"It's not that," Jake said.

"Then what?"

"You think she could be your Megan?"

Rig sucked in his breath. "What?"

"I saw the way you looked at her in your office. Naomi's not just a good time, am I right?"

"You and Dad have another bet?"

"No." Jake's voice was softer. "I was just wondering. If she could be that one for you."

"No way, dude. Megan was good at everything. Naomi is . . . She can barely speak to people unless she's in the office. She hides, and I don't know why. Her house is cluttered . . ." Rig's voice trailed off. He could list the reasons he couldn't be with Naomi, but they didn't seem to matter when he said them out loud. Each bullet point, actually, was tugging a smile from him. Sometimes she wasn't able to string two sentences together, and he'd seen magazines on her floor that were four years old.

But she was so warm. So lovely. She just didn't know it.

Nah.

Naomi wasn't his Megan.

That was the party line, anyway. The one he was working really fucking hard to remember, the one he forgot whenever Naomi was near.

"Nope," he continued lamely. "She's just going to be a friend. Co-worker. Hell, she's my boss, if it comes to that, until Pederson's out and I buy in." He needed to change the subject, fast. "What about you and Anna? How was your burger run the other day? I didn't have a chance to grill her at work today. Get it? Grill? Burger?" He grinned toothily at his brother.

Jake didn't smile. "You want to know if she's *my* next Megan?"

"No!" Rig hadn't even considered that she might be. "She's pregnant. Not sure if you noticed that."

"Only when her stomach got to the Smokehouse five minutes before the rest of her did. But you know what? It was nice being around her. Made me remember what Megan was like when she was carrying Milo. Remember how she loved those butterscotch shakes? She used to have two or three a day of those from the Smokehouse. Anna had one, and while Milo and I ate our burgers, she went and got another one. Eating for two, I guess." Jake smiled.

"Uh-uh. No way. You're not dating a woman about to give birth."

"Who said anything about dating? I'm not dating."

But Jake's voice wasn't convincing.

Frank chose that moment to pull out his earbuds and join the conversation. "What about that girl Anna you took to get burgers? A girl and a burger sounds like a date."

Jake said, "It was just food, Dad."

"You couldn't even help me teach Milo chess, you were so amped up."

Rig watched, fascinated, as his brother turned red.

"He's too young for chess," said Jake. "Gonna give him migraines or something. Stress."

"It's all right for you to date, son." Frank rubbed the gray stubble on his chin and then passed his hand over his eyes. "Just because I don't doesn't mean you shouldn't."

"You loved Mom," said Jake.

"You said she was the only one you could ever love," said Rig. "You couldn't get out of bed for almost six months."

"Your mother was a saint," Frank snapped. "But that's not the point. The point is, life goes on. We'd all do well to remember that."

Rig looked at Milo, who was now lying under the tree, looking up into the branches. "So are you telling us you're going to start dating? Should I make a profile for you on Match.com?"

Frank shot him a sideways look but didn't answer him. "Jake, someday you'll find someone you can love again."

Jake shook his head. "There won't ever be anyone like Megan."

"And I'll never find another woman like your mother." Frank scowled.

There was a silent moment when Rig could feel tears in the back of his throat, threatening to break through. "Well, it's a good thing I'm not going to end up like you two."

Dammit, he could tell by the look that passed between them that they didn't believe him.

He wasn't sure he believed himself.

Time to change the subject. "So," said Rig. "*Die Hard* tonight?"

"Yeah." Jake stood, collecting the paper plates they'd eaten off of. "That'll do."

Frank stood slowly, holding on to the ropes of the hammock for support. "I like that Bruce Willis kid. He's gonna be someone, I think."

Rig rolled his eyes and then smiled at his father. "Yep. Bet you're right."

Milo, who'd been in the house, slid open the back door and yelled, "Hey! I got a lady here!"

Laughing, Rig turned. "You what?"

But Milo really did have a woman by the hand. Anna followed him out, her face a mask of concern.

Jake was the first to find his voice. "Anna?"

One word flashed through Rig's mind: *Naomi*.

Anna's eyes found his. "My sister said if you weren't home you might be here. She gave me directions." She glanced at Jake. "I hope you don't mind."

Jake said, "Of course not."

What if she was hurt? A traffic accident? A fall? Did they have much violence here? A mugging? He was finally able to croak, "What? What happened?"

Anna said, "She's really sick. Like, *really* scary sick. She said food poisoning, but when I came home tonight, she'd passed out, and it took me the longest time to get her to wake up. She wouldn't let me call 911, just said that you could get what she needed."

Shit. Food poisoning didn't normally make people pass out. "How was she when you left?"

"Locked in the bathroom. Can you go?" Here she looked at Rig, "Can you check on her?"

Rig was moving before he could form conscious thought. "Are you coming with me?"

"Stay here," said Jake.

Rig and Anna both stared at him.

He went on, "What if she has something that's contagious? Think about the baby. Just stay until Rig diagnoses her."

"Jake," said Rig. "If she has something contagious, then Anna's bringing it here. Aren't you freaked out about *that*?"

Jake shrugged. "Milo's tough."

It was surprising enough to make him pause, even while his brain screamed *Get to Naomi!*

Frank wandered past, seemingly unsurprised to see Anna. "Old Fashioned, my dear?" Then he looked at her belly. "Ah. I'll go light on the bourbon."

Jake said, "And Dad's too pickled to catch anything. We'll be fine. I'll take care of her until you get back." He turned to Anna. "Do you like Bruce Willis?"

Anna rubbed the top of her stomach. "*Die Hard* is only, like, one of the best movies ever."

"Can I have your house keys?" Rig held out his hand toward Anna. "Just in case."

Something like fear, a feeling he hadn't had since swinging over the edge of a derrick to get to a trapped patient, rippled down his spine.

She had to be okay.

Chapter Thirty-eight

Sometimes, the knitting gets the better of us. It's okay to ask for help. You'll be needed at some point, too.
—E.C.

Naomi opened her eyes to the sound of someone calling her name. Cold, she was so cold. Her teeth chattered so hard her vision shook. And everything hurt, every cell of her body screamed for relief.

"Naomi!" The man's voice was sharp. Loud, in the small bathroom, echoing off the tile floor.

The pain was the worst. As every cramping spell waxed, she could barely breathe, and she choked around the anguish until the cramps waned again.

"Naomi, honey."

Why was there a man in her bathroom? More specifically, Naomi wondered as she started putting things together, why was *Rig* in her bathroom? Oh, *no*. No one should be in here. A vast, horrified feeling of embarrassment swept over her, and tears leaped to her eyes.

"No, no, no, no. Out, please *out* . . ."

"Naomi, sugar, tell me what happened."

She barely heard the endearment, she was so wrapped up in the awful thought that he was in her bathroom, and she knew it must not smell as fresh as a bathroom could. She knew she *herself* must not smell very good.

Damn, damn, *damn*. "I told Anna to get you, didn't I?" Naomi worked herself to a sitting position, shaking off his offer of help. They had to get out of here. To her bedroom, at least. Why the hell had she asked for Rig?

"She said you needed help."

"I'm fine," Naomi said. She stood, feeling like a newborn colt, unable to trust her legs. Rig's arms came out to catch her as she wobbled.

"Don't need you."

"You don't, huh?" Rig stepped back as she walked toward her bed.

A cramp twisted her gut again—she knew it was just pain, she had to get to her bed, but the gasp she let out must have jolted Rig, because his arms were around her before she took a second step.

"I'm helping you to the bed, that's all."

"I'm okay," she lied.

"Then you won't mind if I do this. Yes, that's right, easy does it." Rig held on to Naomi's elbow as she sat down slowly on the bed. She tipped, landing on her pillow, and he pulled her legs up so that she was lying on her side, facing him.

"Am I as green as I feel?"

Rig smiled. "You're actually a little more yellow. Mixed with a slight tinge of blue around the eyes."

"Attractive."

"I'll say." Rig said it like he meant it, and Naomi felt something move inside her that had nothing to do with food poisoning. Her heart did that slow somersault again as he grinned at her. Oh, hell. What should she do now?

He knelt so that he was eye to eye with her. "You think it's food poisoning?"

Naomi nodded, moving her head gingerly.

"We both ate the pizza the other night . . ."

"Burrito . . ."

"What burrito?"

Oh, it hurt to even think about it. "Breakfast burrito at a taco truck."

"Uh-oh. We should get you tested, you know."

Naomi turned her head so she could bury it in the pillow. "No." She knew what he meant, and she'd be damned if she gave him a stool sample. She'd light her feet on fire first. She rocked her head back and forth.

"Yes."

"Never," she said into the pillow.

She felt her side of the bed sink as he sat down beside her. "Oh, don't make me move like that."

His large cool hand covered her upper arm. It felt perfect, just what she needed. That blessed coolness . . .

"You're burning up."

"I was just freezing a minute ago." And now she was on fire. She closed her eyes and muttered, "Oh, God."

"Am I interrupting your prayers?" asked Rig, his tone light. "Because I can go and sit in the kitchen till you're done."

"I'm not praying."

"Okay."

"Except maybe for death."

"It'll come to all of us."

"That's your idea of a bedside manner?" she managed before another wave of nausea flooded over her. Death didn't seem like the absolute worst idea in the whole world.

Rig ran his hand down her arm to her wrist and back up again.

She lifted it so he could cover more area. There, yes, the more he touched, the more she felt soothed. Relieved.

"You have a headache?"

Like cymbals of red-hot metal clanging in her brain. She nodded and then regretted the motion.

"I'm guessing shigellosis," Rig said.

"Yeah." Short sentences seemed to help, and they were all she could manage around the short gasps of air she was trying to drink, to swallow, as if they would ease the pain.

"I saw Z-Pak at the office—I'll be back in twenty minutes."

"I can get it later," Naomi said.

Rig laughed. "You're not serious. You wouldn't make it two blocks. You can't drive, and you can't walk."

"Then I'll tough it out. I'm not going to die." She clutched the edge of her afghan—the only one she'd ever made. The purple yarn cut into her fingers, and for one second she believed herself.

"You're a doctor." Rig's voice was serious. "Don't be an idiot."

She would not, *could* not let him take care of her. She'd asked for him—she could send him away. Naomi had spent a long time taking care of herself. She was good at it. She didn't need this now. It would practically be an admission of failure, wouldn't it?

She was just a little sick.

Just then, a shiver shot through her, pain slipping from her head into her stomach, everything seeming to get worse all at once. Rolling over on her stomach, she groaned. *Please, God, don't let me have to go back to the bathroom. Not now, not while he's here.* If she could just get him to leave . . .

"Yes. Z-Pak." The words were all she could manage before doubling over again, breathless.

"I'll be back soon," Rig said, his voice tight.

Fine. Whatever. Just as long as he left now. Naomi squeezed her eyes shut and tried to pretend she wasn't crying, that those weren't tears leaking from her eyes.

Rig reached forward and took her hand. His was cool and dry, huge against hers. She cracked open her eyes to see if the spinning had stopped, and her gaze was caught by how the light of her lamp illuminated the fine, golden hairs on his arm.

For one second, she felt normal. Wonderful. The feeling of her hand in his, and then, when she looked up and caught his dark, worried gaze—she felt as if she'd forgotten why she was lying in this bed. The last time they'd lain down together had worked out pretty crazy terrific. Was that only the night before last? She closed her eyes again, feeling a tear run across the bridge of her nose.

Then there was the softest touch on her head, just for a moment, as if his cool hand had rested there before moving away. Then, above her shoulder, where her neck was bare, she felt his lips, the slightest touch. Her door shut, and he was gone.

Naomi wobbled upright and touched the place on her neck where he'd placed the kiss. She felt dizzy. Then she staggered to the bathroom again.

Rig managed to get the Zithromax into Naomi, and it stayed down long enough for a first dose. Before she fell asleep, she asked him through a yawn, "Where's Anna?"

"Jake texted me. She fell asleep on the couch. I told him to keep her there. I've got things under control here."

"Thank you. But you really don't have to stay."

"I know I don't."

Then she shivered again.

He kicked his shoes onto the floor and pulled her closer to him, then moved the blankets up over them both. Wrapping his arms around her tightly, he whispered, "There. Is that better?"

She nodded against his chest. "The last time I let anyone see me sick I was seventeen. Back with my mom."

"Moms are good for that."

Even sick, Naomi managed a snort. "She gave me a robe and I promptly threw up all over it. She threw it out, brand new." A pause. "I just wanted my dad. He loved me."

"Mothers are hardwired to love," said Rig. "Maybe she just wasn't very good at showing it."

"That's the thing," said Naomi, and her voice was the saddest he'd ever heard. "I think she's a good mother. To Anna. She and I just never saw eye to eye, that's all. It felt like we didn't share a language. She was looking for a little charmer, a performer, someone to dress up. She got that in Anna. Me, I was nothing like her. I disappointed her." Another shudder rocked her, then Rig heard a deep breath, and her breathing slowed, growing regular and heavy.

Naomi fit against him like she'd been made for him, as if the mold that his body had been cut from had originally been a part of hers. Over the course of her restless night, Rig had the opportunity to hold her in many positions: sitting up, lying down spooned, cradled on his chest. Every hour or so, he helped her miserably to the bathroom, and then she'd come back to bed, even more tired than before. No matter how he held her, she dropped instantly back into sleep as soon as her eyes closed.

And even pale as she was, face shiny with dried sweat, her curls tangled as if they'd been in a blender, Rig's heart twisted when he looked at her. He pressed kiss after kiss into her temple, her forehead, her cheek, and when he did, she snuggled closer to him, her arms wrapping around his neck or his arm, whatever was closest to her. He wasn't sure if it was just because she was sick, but he hoped not. He loved it.

Rig looked at the way the lamplight fell across Naomi's cheekbones, putting her lips into shadow. She was still felt feverish—the

next time she was awake, he'd force more Gatorade into her, even
if she protested. And in the morning, he'd go buy some chicken
broth and bring it back to her. Maybe some saltines. She wouldn't be
eating much of anything for at least the next three days, he guessed.

And damn it all if he didn't want to be there for every second of
her recovery. And afterward.

He closed his eyes. Shit.

Go to sleep, Keller, he told himself, but sleep was hard to find. She
seemed to be using it all, and for that he was glad, but every time
she made a small noise, moved the slightest bit, he went on notice,
ready to help.

God, he wished he could snap his fingers and make this go away.
If she wasn't a little better when she woke up, he would haul her ass
in for IV fluids. Or if she threw a total fit against it, which he could
imagine her doing, he'd bring the IV pole here.

Even in sleep, Naomi's mouth was twisted, as if she felt the abdominal pain. He couldn't help it—his index finger moved as if of
its own volition and touched that perfect bottom lip. He stroked
it softly, just for a second or two, and her mouth relaxed under his
touch. Her lips parted and she sighed against his finger. He felt himself grow hard and shifted left so that if she woke, she wouldn't
know. Totally fucking inappropriate. A boner at a time like this—
what an eighteen-year-old move. Rig felt himself blush in the dimness. Ridiculous. Thank God she was asleep.

Naomi made a soft sound, and then a sound of stifled pain, rolling to rest against his arm and shoulder.

It was going to be a long, long night. And he wanted to be nowhere else in the world. Rig knew he was in trouble, and he was
going to have to deal with it at some point. But not tonight.

He closed his eyes and willed sleep to find him.

Chapter Thirty-nine

*Don't regret a moment spent knitting, even when you're
ripping out hours, days, of work. It all meant something.
It always does.*

—E.C.

N aomi woke in a pool of sunshine. She opened her eyes warily.
Something was, or had been, very wrong. She just couldn't
remember what it was.

She stretched. Oh, God, her stomach felt like she'd been kicked
in the gut by a furious horse. The back of her hand stung, and her
head felt light. The bedsheets were tangled around her. But the windows were open, and a warm summer wind blew through the room,
tickling her nose with the scent of dusty jasmine and mown grass.
Something told her she should feel much worse than she did.

Shigellosis. It had dropped her much harder than a normal touch
of food poisoning would. But now she felt better, and suddenly . . .
she felt hungry.

It might have had something to do with the smell of toast wafting
in through her open bedroom door, but she was ravenous. Everything Naomi thought of to eat—bread, bananas, cereal, ice cream,

steak—sounded like the best idea she'd ever had. Knowing her body was probably lying to her and that she should take it easy didn't prevent her stomach from rumbling hungrily, loudly. Anna must be home. Maybe she'd make Naomi some toast, too.

She stood, careful to hold on to first the nightstand, then the door handle. Making it to the kitchen was more difficult than she'd thought it would be. The hallway she'd always thought short seemed a million miles long. At some point, she'd changed her pajamas to the ones with the cherries on them, and the crazy thing was, she didn't even remember doing it.

How long had Rig stayed with her last night? Had he helped her change? She'd remember *that*, wouldn't she?

She turned the corner to enter the kitchen and almost ran smack-dab into the tall man who was leaving the kitchen in a hurry. Naomi wasn't able to stifle the scream.

Rig—of course it was Rig—yelled back, "Hoooo! Damn! You scared me!"

"Me?' Naomi pulled out a kitchen chair and sat down slowly, propping herself against the table for support. "What are you doing here?"

"What does it look like?" He pointed at the tray resting on the kitchen countertop. On it was buttered toast on her favorite blue plate, and a glass holding something that looked like Gatorade. A pill was on a napkin, and a banana was halfway peeled, ready to be picked up and eaten. A red rose was at the top of the tray—she recognized it as one of hers from the overgrown garden.

"That's for me?"

Rig nodded. "I was going to bring it to you in bed before I split, see if I could tempt your appetite, but now that you're there, just stay." He set the tray down in front of her.

Naomi picked up a piece of toast and considered her stomach. It twanged, but didn't lurch or roll. And the bread smelled so good . . .

she took a bite, chewing slowly. Rig watched with what looked like approval.

After a couple of bites and a swallow of the noxious sports drink, she asked, "Where's Anna?" She'd need her to go in and cancel her appointments for today, or see if they could be shifted to Rig. She was still in no shape to go to work. Naomi knew she could be stubborn, but she wouldn't play around with this. You didn't mess with shigellosis, and she was glad she'd taken yesterday off.

The back of her left hand burned, and she looked down at it. Holy hell—there was an access hole and the remnants of tape left on her skin.

Naomi looked up at Rig, who was leaning against her refrigerator, watching her eat. "You gave me an IV?"

He nodded.

Naomi felt her head swim. "*When?*"

"Yesterday. You were pretty delirious. It was that or take you in to be hospitalized, and I figured you'd hate that."

"You mean last night? I totally don't remember."

"No, yesterday. In the afternoon. I told Anna what to bring me, and she did."

Math, numbers, days . . . Nothing added up to the right thing. "But I got sick two nights ago, right?"

"Four nights ago. It's Saturday. I've spent the last three nights with you, and I missed as much work as I possibly could to be here. And you're doing well to be moving around as much as you are now. So eat, and then go back to bed. I've got a project I'm working on this afternoon, but I want to make sure you're okay before I leave."

Naomi sat back in the wooden chair, feeling the top rung dig into her back. She'd lost *days*? Was that possible? But the more she thought about it, the more things started trickling back into her mind: Rig, holding her for long hours as she shook with cold; his hands around her as she swayed back to the bathroom; a cold washcloth that felt just right; the look of Rig's jaw at dawn, profiled against the light.

Also: Anna's face, worried, then hurt.

"What did I say to Anna?"

Rig grimaced and, as if buying time, poured himself a cup of coffee. Turning back to face Naomi, he said, "It wasn't great."

Naomi put a hand to her cheek. "What did I say?"

"You should probably ask her." He pulled the other chair out and spun it so that he could sit backward on it and still face her.

"Is she at the office?"

Rig glanced at his watch. "It's Saturday."

"Has she been . . . here? With me?"

Rig looked almost apologetic. "She didn't want to stay."

Oh, dear. So, apparently, when sick, Naomi had said things she didn't mean to. An echo of a memory sounded in her brain . . . Anna's shocked face . . .

"You can't remember *anything* I said to her? Did I mention the baby?"

Rig gave a careful nod. "You did."

Another memory rocked Naomi, making her feel sick all over again. "Did I . . . ask why she didn't get rid of the baby when she found out?"

His lips folded into a line that told her the answer.

"Shit, *shit*. What did she do?"

"She left. Thought it would be better if you healed up before you had a real conversation. I tried telling her that you were feverish, and too sick to make sense, but she wasn't listening by that point."

Naomi slumped in her chair, ignoring how much her body hurt. "I'm a horrible, horrible person."

"No, you're not."

"I hate myself."

"You said that, too," said Rig.

"Wow." Shoving her fingers through her hair was a mistake. "Where's she been staying?"

"The first night, when you asked for me—"

"I did?"

"She stayed that night at my brother's house after she fell asleep on the couch. He's got a spare room, the one I used to crash in when I visited. The next night she was going to stay here, but that's when you went squirrely, so she went back over there."

Naomi felt like she'd been hit by a tractor. "Your brother . . ."

"I'm sure he didn't mind. Your sister's a nice girl, Naomi."

"Who's pregnant. Almost due. What if she'd had the baby, early? And I was still sick . . . Oh, God . . ."

Rig pushed the toast plate a little closer to her. "But she didn't. And don't forget, Jake's a paramedic. She's in good hands."

"What did I miss at work?"

"Not much. It was slow."

Naomi shot him a look.

"Okay, I handled it. All right? Anna and I handled it." He laughed. "Just barely. It was the blonde leading the blind. We didn't have a freaking clue where anything was, *who* anyone was. But we got it all done."

"Thanks."

Rig inclined his head. "What are almost partners for? Heard from Pederson, he'll be retiring officially in a month. I'll buy in then, if you still want me."

Naomi looked dumbly at her plate. Of course she wanted him.

That was the problem.

"Oh, and your mother called."

It was getting worse and worse. "What did she want?"

"To talk to you about Anna, but I said you were out of town and that I was house-sitting."

Naomi smiled, in spite of herself. "Genius."

"She sounded friendly."

"That's the key word: *sounded*."

Rig folded his arms. "You called out for her, you know."

Naomi gaped. "I didn't."

"You did. Tell me again what's wrong with her?"

Sighing, Naomi took another nibble and then rested her wrist on the table, looking down at the access point on the back of her hand. "It's not like she's a monster. She doesn't eat kittens for breakfast, as far as I know. She's just been so busy worrying about Anna for so long that she didn't realize she never worried about me."

"You were the good girl."

Naomi nodded. "And worse, I was a Daddy's girl. I've played second fiddle in her heart my whole life. She didn't have to deal with me except every other weekend from the time I was five until I was seventeen. And she liked it that way. She never . . ." She paused. Then she made herself continue. "She never even tried to get to know me." It was silly, Naomi knew, that this secret truth hurt so much to say out loud.

"And your dad was everything to you. Must have been hard to lose him so young."

Naomi bit her lip. "Yep." God, it felt weird to tell him. And what was stranger, she wanted to tell him more. "But it's okay. Ninety-nine percent of the time it's fine. Then, the only time in my adult life I get really sick . . ." Her voice trailed off, and she was horrified to feel tears fill her eyes. "Then apparently I cry like a baby for my mama. Go figure."

There was a small pause. Then Rig said, "I loved my mom. My brother and my dad and me, we worshipped her. It was terrible when she died—none of us knew how to live without her. I guess Jake's always been the more sensitive one, and I'd always teased him for it, but we had to be there for each other after she died. Sometimes I'd cry harder than he would." He paused again. "But it seems that even if your mother blew it with you, she did okay by your sister, right? Seems like Anna turned out just fine." His gaze was open.

"Well, there's that whole thing where she's pregnant? Jobless? Itinerant?"

Slapping a red fabric napkin against his leg, Rig said, "So she's knocked up. She'll get a baby out of the deal, and that's always a nice thing. Babies are cool, don't you think?" He didn't give her time to answer. "And she has a job, with us. She has a place to stay when you're not fighting, and when you are, it sounds like she has a second place to stay. Jake seems pretty happy with the whole thing, and apparently Milo loves her. Won't quit hanging from her arm like a monkey. And I'm sure my dad is fussing over her and making her eat comfort foods like macaroni and cheese and Vienna sausages."

How did he make it sound so easy? How did he make *everything* seem so easy? The chair he sat in seemed dwarfed by his long legs, his broad thighs. Thighs that Naomi was remembering snuggling up against. He hadn't—

No, he hadn't. She'd know. She would remember that. Looking into his eyes, she saw he knew what she had wondered, and he gave his head an almost imperceptible shake. "I just took care of you," he said.

"Why?"

Rig's coffee cup stopped halfway to his mouth. "Why? It's obvious."

"It's not."

"You didn't have anyone else."

Chapter Forty

Once you've learned the math for a set-in sleeve cap, you can solve the problems of the world. But once you've learned it, please share it with me, because a raglan is just so attractive and easy that I've never bothered to learn it myself.

—E.C.

The next morning, Rig left Naomi sleeping. She'd asked him to get her knitting needles and a book called *Eliza's Road Not Taken* from the living room for her after he'd fed her one scrambled egg, but she hadn't gotten very far into either knitting or reading. She looked adorable, though, sleeping on her side, the book propped open in front of her, her knitting clutched in her left hand. The food seemed to be staying settled, and Rig left a note saying he'd be back as soon as he could be.

Rig didn't want to be away from her.

Damn, he *was* in big trouble.

But forewarned was forearmed, right? A crush was easily dealt with. No big deal. But every time he told himself the no-big-deal line, Rig bumped into something, or stubbed his toe, or dropped his sunglasses.

As he pushed through the door at Tillie's and found his eyes drawn to the back booth where he'd seen her for the second time, he had to admit that this Naomi thing was seriously messing with his head.

But he could handle it. *No big deal.* Instantly, he tripped over Elbert's cane, which had slipped to the ground. He caught himself, hoping no one had seen his windmill.

Shirley greeted him with a grin and a quick peck on the cheek.

"Sit at the counter, honey? Sunday morning's busy 'round here."

Rig looked at Naomi's empty booth. "Can I sit there? If you don't mind? I've got a couple of people meeting me."

She flapped her hand. "Just opened up. Have at it. I'll bring you coffee in a second."

As he eased himself into the crooked booth, Rig thought about how many times Naomi had sat here over the last year. Alone.

He didn't want her to sit here by herself anymore.

Rig watched Shirley fly around the room, coffeepot in hand whenever she wasn't carrying plates. Another younger waitress was also working today, but Shirley ran circles around her. He looked out the window, toward the beach. A young redheaded woman wearing a white half apron leaned against the brick wall of the Italian restaurant, watching the low surf and smoking a cigarette. Two skateboarders heading for the boardwalk rolled past her. She grinned and said something to them and they laughed as they skated past.

It was a nice little town. And man, it was different than moving from one platform to another, always a different sick bay, always an offshore medic who thought he knew everything, always a hundred new guys, faces he didn't know. Here, it was just him and Naomi and Bruno. And now Anna. He admitted to himself that he'd do just about anything to keep Anna working at the office with them after the baby came. Last week, he'd caught Naomi looking at her with pride. She'd probably never admit it, but he knew she loved having her sister so close.

And that was her problem. She'd never admit it. For a woman who felt so much, so deeply, she sure was closed off to her emotions. Or at least that's what Naomi would have him think. But he'd seen her eyes when Anna had gasped, right after the abortion comment, and even while sick, Naomi's expression had been stricken. She'd felt that to her core.

And when she'd talked about her mother, those weren't crocodile tears she'd turned away to hide. They'd been painful and very real. She *felt* things, especially that distance from her mother. That much was sure.

Getting her to talk about her feelings more, that's what he wasn't sure he'd be able to do.

He sipped his coffee and waited, listening to the chatter of the diner as it swirled around him. It sounded like it had his first day in town: Mildred argued with Toots about something related to the upcoming contra dance as Greta knitted quietly and watched both of them. Elbert Romo sat at the counter as an ambassador of goodwill, greeting every person who entered. Officer Moss chatted with Old Bill and kept an eagle eye on the parking meters in front. A firefighter who worked with Rig's brother nodded to him—Rig had forgotten his name but knew he made a mean lasagna. In the side room just behind his head, Rig could hear the ranchers talking. Cade MacArthur barked a laugh and startled baby Owen into crying. Lucy Bancroft, carrying a stack of magazines to a back table, smiled at him.

It felt so good to be part of it all.

The front door opened, and Anna entered the diner. She was followed by Bruno, and Rig realized they didn't know each other yet.

That was okay. They would. Rig waved. He needed to talk to Anna, but that could wait until he could get her apart from Bruno—later, when they were working, he'd get her by herself.

Bruno sat down heavily across from him. "Iced tea," he told Shirley, who was pulling up a chair to place in the aisle for Anna.

"Because there's no way you're getting that belly behind that table, honey. Milk for you?"

Rig made the introductions, saying, "Anna's saved us this week, Bruno. I hope you enjoyed your vacation, but thanks for coming in today. I need you both." As Anna settled herself, pulling as close to the booth as she could, Rig asked her, "How's it going at Jake's? Milo terrorizing you?"

"Nah," said Anna. "He's sweet. I read to him before he goes to sleep. He's cuddly then—not so much at other times."

"Watch out, or my brother's gonna fall for having a woman in his house." Rig laughed and waited for Anna to do the same.

She didn't. She turned pink instead.

Oh, Jesus. "Jake's not . . . giving you any problems?"

Anna shook her head, smiling down at her lap.

Whoa. Jake, serious about anyone, let alone a woman who was about to have her life turned upside down by an infant—he needed to talk to his brother, the sooner the better.

But right now, he had more pressing things to take care of. "I know it's Sunday, so thanks, you two, again. We can get a shitload done today."

Anna pulled the paper napkin from around the silverware and tore off a piece of it. Rolling the paper in her fingers, she said, "I'm still mad at her."

"I know," said Rig.

"And really hurt."

Bruno patted Anna on the shoulder. "It's big of you to help Rig out, then," he said.

"It is," Anna agreed. "Plus, I know it'll be satisfying to see her face when she hears I helped anyway."

Rig leaned forward. "Okay, so here's the deal—" He broke off as he saw his father enter the diner and greet Old Bill at the front.

Well, heck. Frank hadn't been invited. But he could help if he wanted to, even though he'd probably just end up getting in the way.

Rig raised his hand to gesture his father over, but Frank didn't see him. Instead, he went directly to the open stool next to Elbert who patted him on the back as he sat. Frank pushed the menu out of his way and turned his mug right side up, ready for coffee.

And then Rig watched in utter stupefaction as Shirley leaned over the counter to kiss his father full on the mouth.

Chapter Forty-one

If you are too sleepy to knit, take a nap. Better, indeed, if you can double your knitting under your head and nap in a puddle of sunlight. Best, if a cat purrs next to you while you snooze. Oh, the joy of life.
　　　　　　　　　　　　　　　　　　　—E.C.

Monday morning, Naomi hauled herself into the office. She was feeling more tired than anything else, a deep, bone-level exhaustion, but the pain had lessened now, and she thought she could pull off a half day if she took it slowly.

She sat in her office, the window propped open to let in the summer fog, and logged in to her e-mail. God, even doing that much, just remembering her password and typing it in, felt like a huge task.

Her ears strained to hear Rig's footsteps in the hallway. She didn't think he'd been in yet when she arrived, and she hadn't seen him since yesterday afternoon when he'd come by for a brief moment. He'd dropped off a container of chicken soup and a box of saltine crackers, saying something about getting back to a project, before he ran off again. He'd asked if she'd be okay without him that night.

He'd sounded like a friend when he asked. A nice guy.

As if he hadn't spent a whole night last week driving her out of her ever-loving mind with his tongue. As if he hadn't held her while she was sick, for four nights straight. As if she hadn't fallen asleep with him kissing her hair and woken to his arms tight around her. There had been times when she hadn't wanted him to touch her at all—when she was sicker than she'd ever felt before, and just the thought of someone near her made her feel even worse. Those times, he'd gone to sit on her porch, or he'd made a run to the store to bring her something else that might sit easily in her stomach, although nothing had, and when she was ready, he was there again to hold her until the next wave passed.

Naomi clicked blindly through her e-mail. Nothing important, nothing she had to address right now.

She'd have thought she wouldn't have wanted anyone to see her like that, sick, weak, at her most unattractive. But she'd wanted Rig there. He'd made things just a little better. And that had been un-expected. And good.

She'd gotten to the point where she could almost admit she'd needed him.

And then she'd gone and blown it all by being impossibly rude to Anna. No wonder he hadn't wanted to stay yesterday. Maybe he was too disgusted with her, too, like she was with herself.

Anna—would she even come into the office to work today? Was she still staying with Jake? Or somewhere else? Naomi had tried her cell phone, over and over again. But she must still be too furious to even speak to her. Naomi didn't blame her.

She'd blown it, in the worst way possible.

Naomi sighed and rubbed her eyes.

Work had to help.

Why, then, was she finding it impossible to figure out what to do next?

Across her office, on the chair next to the door, was her knitting basket. She'd brought it to work this morning even though she normally never brought it here. Someone might see it, might guess her silly secret. But today Naomi had needed to keep the shawl close. Her fingers almost ached to have the yarn in her hands. She'd made considerable headway on it while she'd been sick, once she'd been able to sit upright for any length of time without wanting to throw up.

And in the basket next to the shawl was Eliza's book *Silk Road*. Knowing it was ridiculous didn't stop her from checking to see that there was no one outside her door, and then moving to pick the book up, to close her eyes, to jab at the page.

"A mother's love can be transmitted through stitches—a sweater made by a mother is worth ten of any other kind."

Damn. Even Eliza was out to get her.

As she lifted her eyes from the page, a voice said, "Sweetheart!"

Her mother stood in her doorway, her stepfather and Bruno behind her. Bruno's eyes were wide and he mouthed a silent "I'm sorry" at her over their heads.

Her mother was wearing an obviously expensive royal blue silk shirt and black pants that hung perfectly, the cuff breaking at just the right point over her patent-leather black pumps that probably cost more than all of Naomi's shoes put together. Her eye makeup was flawless, deep plums and soft pinks, the skin around the corners dewy fresh. She'd probably had a little something done.

"Hi, Mom." Oh, God, now what? Maybelle was going in for the hug, though, so Naomi met her in the middle. Her mother's arms didn't feel familiar. It was like suddenly hugging a teller at the bank—foreign and much too intimate.

"Hey there, kid," said Buzz. He was in a gray suit that looked a little tight, and his hair was more silvery than the last time she'd seen him. His smile looked genuine, and Naomi wondered if she was expected to hug him, too, but instead he held out his hand. Naomi shook it gratefully.

"Wow, Mom." Naomi leaned on the wall. Standing unsupported was too tiring. "I have to admit I'm surprised to see you."

"Well, Anna finally left us a message saying she was in this one-horse town," Maybelle said. "I can't believe it, the one time I don't pick up the phone. Buzz knows I *always* pick up the phone, just on the off chance it's her. It never is. But that time, of *course* it was."

Buzz said, "Your mom just wanted to see her. So we thought we'd make a quick road trip."

Naomi bit the inside of her lip. They hadn't come to see her in the year she'd lived in Cypress Hollow. Then she managed, "It's nice to see you both."

Maybelle said, "Where's Anna? We stopped by your house, but it didn't seem like anyone was there."

"I'm not sure—"

"I haven't seen her in almost ten months, did you know that? That's too long for a mother to go."

Naomi just said, "Of course. I'll track her down and we'll have dinner tonight."

"Sweetheart, you're so pale. Maybe we'll all go for a makeover later? And where, for dinner?"

At that moment Rig came out of his office—Naomi hadn't even known he was in yet. How long had he been there? What had he heard?

"Naomi, are we still on for barbecuing at Jake's tonight?"

Naomi's mouth dropped open as her mother stepped forward with a hundred-watt smile. "Maybelle Maubert, Naomi's mother. My husband, Buzz. And you are?"

"Dr. Rig Keller, newest staff member." He gave Maybelle a knee-numbingly smoldering grin. "You should both come to dinner, too. I know my brother Jake would be glad to meet you, and Anna will be there."

"You know Anna?" Maybelle brightened ten more watts. "Are you dating her? Wouldn't that be wonderful?" She looked over her shoulder at Buzz. "If she was dating a doctor?"

"Mom, they're not dating." Naomi felt like she was losing any small hold she'd had on the conversation.

"No. I'm not dating Anna. I'm dating Naomi," said Rig.

"Oh, holy Helen," said Naomi. She moved past her mother into the back office where three chairs sat next to the lab work area. "I have to sit down."

"You're dating *him*?" Maybelle sounded thrilled. In a stage whisper, she said to Buzz, "She's dating a *doctor*."

"Mom!" Naomi rubbed her face. "I *am* a doctor."

Maybelle blinked. "I know, darling. Of course."

Had Rig really just told her mother they were dating? When in reality all they'd done was . . . Well, okay. They'd done a lot. Dating. Huh.

And God help her, she wanted so much more. She kept her hands on her cheeks, cooling them, not daring to look the only place she wanted to: at Rig.

Smoothly placing himself in the conversation again, Rig said, "So, seven o'clock? At Jake's?"

Maybelle snapped to attention. "What does your brother do?"

"He's a captain with the local fire department. Very important to the town. Anna and he are close," said Rig.

"A fire captain," said Maybelle. "Oh, yes. We'd *love* to meet him."

Rig nodded. "I'll go print out driving directions. Where are you staying?"

A small part of Naomi withered in despair as her mother turned to look at her.

"At Naomi's, of course," Maybelle said. "Where else?"

Chapter Forty-two

The click of a knitter's needles is the metronome of her life.

—E.C.

In Jake's backyard, Rig pulled all the chairs Milo had used to make a fort back to the picnic table, and he realized that the tingling he was feeling in the tips of his fingers wasn't the first indication of poor circulation. It was just good old-fashioned excitement. Maybe—no, probably—she'd seen what he'd done with her health center while she was sick.

God, if she didn't like it . . .

But what wasn't to like? He'd worked his ass off in there for the last two days, and while he wished he'd been around to see her open the door and discover what he'd done, he couldn't wait to hear what she thought.

And maybe tonight they'd get to talk about Jake and Anna. Sure, Anna had been sleeping in the spare room, and Jake said he was in his own. And Rig didn't have any reason not to believe Jake, but there was something in his eyes when he looked at Anna that made Rig hold his breath.

He wanted Jake to be happy. To date. To have a good time. He wanted those things for both his brother and his father.

But Jake was stressed out just trying to take care of himself and Milo. If a baby was thrown into the mix? Rig couldn't imagine Jake changing diapers while trying to keep Milo from climbing to the top of anything tall nearby, while trying to balance being in love with a real woman and a dead woman at the same time.

And Dad, sneaking around with Shirley? Why hadn't he told them? Shirley was awesome. She was great. Strong. Vibrant. A good landlord.

Why did Rig feel worried, then? How had Naomi handled it when her mother remarried Buzz? Had she been resentful? Her father had still been alive, though. Maybe it made it somewhat easier, although he wasn't sure.

Rig's frown turned into a half grin thinking of how nonplussed Naomi had been when he'd said they were dating. It had made him want to grab her hand, kiss her right there in front of her mother. He hadn't—he'd restrained himself. But it had been difficult.

Milo raced past his legs. Did he ever just walk? He seemed to have wings on his heels.

"Uncle Rig, watch!"

But Milo had pulled open the screen door and was inside the house before Rig could figure out what he was supposed to be looking at.

Jake brought out a store-bought potato salad and put it on the picnic table. "I still can't believe you invited a whole party here without asking me."

"This from the man who knows everyone? You love a party."

Jake groaned. "Do not. I don't even like people. You're the one with the dang people-loving gene."

Rig laughed. "You're the firefighter. You're the one who goes in and saves people every day."

"Yeah, well, you're the doctor. You—"

"Just give them bad news or good news." He thought of news he'd delivered today—a possible diagnosis of multiple myeloma for a mother of three girls, very bad news. And an hour later, he'd been able to tell Pete Wegman the news that his biopsy had come back benign. "And I can't really do anything about the results. They're just the way they are. At least you sometimes get to do CPR."

"Well, thanks, Dr. Feelgood."

"Anyway, you ready to be introduced to your girlfriend's parents?" Rig was pushing, but he wanted to.

"I'm a little nervous, I guess."

Even though it confirmed that his guess was right, Rig felt surprise. "She's been here how many nights now? Five? And you've been hanging out with her for what, two weeks? Maybe?"

Jake turned, clutching a bouquet of forks. "Yeah?"

"You're way into her."

Jake shrugged in acknowledgment. "So what if I am?"

"So, just be careful." Rig felt the lid of the grill. It was heating up fast.

"Whatever, dude. I'm fine." Jake stalked back into the kitchen. A scream from Milo came floating out the living room window, followed by hysterical laughter.

A second later, Milo flew out of the house, raced around Rig's legs three times, and then ran back in the house, screaming something about Superman and frosting that Rig didn't quite catch.

The screen door banged again, and Rig looked up. Anna wobbled her way carefully down the two steps to the porch, smiling.

"Hey," he said.

"Hey yourself."

"You did okay today?"

She lowered herself into a wicker chair. "Yeah. I like the papers. It's quiet over there." This morning Bruno had sent her over to the storage place to start dealing with Pederson's unarchived papers. It was safer there, anyway—they hadn't had to worry about the sisters running into each other at work.

Now they'd run into each other here. In front of their mother. Rig hoped this wasn't the worst idea he'd ever had.

Anna laughed. "I probably shouldn't tell you, but instead of lunch I had a nap in one of the aisles. Nice and cool. I just couldn't keep my eyes open."

"And we're paying you for that?" But Rig smiled back at her. He didn't mind. She deserved a break, and damn if she hadn't done a shitload over the weekend, unpaid, helping him with the center. "I hope you ate lunch, too."

"Of course I did. I'm not into missing meals right now." She rubbed her belly. "This little gal won't let me."

"You know it's a girl, huh?"

"Yep."

"We could tell you for sure, you know. Anytime. Your sister could do it, give you the ultrasound. We have the technology." He smiled to soften his words.

But Anna shook her head firmly. "No. I got the only ultrasound I needed in the city already. I didn't want them to tell me, and I don't want to know now."

"Okay. Fine by me."

"Hey, who's coming to this shindig, anyway? Jake wouldn't tell me, just said there would be more people coming."

Oh, crap.

Anna caught his look. "Naomi. I *knew* it. Look, we'll work it out when we feel like we're ready to work it out. I still don't want to see her."

"Um," started Rig. "Well . . ."

The screen door opened again. First came Naomi. She was dressed simply, as usual, in a white linen blouse and jeans that fit her better than jeans should be allowed to fit. That curve of her hip just begged for his hand to . . . Oh, that way lay madness. He couldn't think about that right now.

Just behind her, looking ecstatic, came Naomi's mother, Maybelle, followed by Buzz and Frank. Maybelle didn't look anything like Naomi, although he could see the resemblance between the blond Anna and Maybelle's strawberry-tinted hair.

Anna's eyes widened as she saw her mother, in exactly the same way Naomi's did when she was surprised. "Oh, help," she whispered weakly.

"Gang's all here!" shouted Frank, who probably had no idea who the company was. "Isn't this *great*?"

Maybelle looked at Anna. Her mouth formed a perfect O. Whoops. Looked like Mama didn't know her baby was knocked up. Maybelle coughed, a strangled, choking sound, and looked at Naomi.

Then she clutched Buzz, said something inaudible to him, and fainted dead away.

Chapter Forty-three

Excitement has its place in knitting, too. Does anything really compare to cutting your first steek? Downhill skiing, perhaps, if one does it during an avalanche.
—E.C.

Mother down!" yelled Anna. "Alert, alert!"

Naomi raced to help Maybelle, and she and Rig reached her at the same time. Buzz had caught her as she fainted and was lowering her to the ground.

"Easy there," said Rig, reaching to roll Maybelle onto her back on the wooden deck. "Go slow."

Naomi pushed his hands away. "I've got it," she said. "Thanks."

Maybelle's closed eyes twitched underneath her eyelids as Naomi tilted her mother's head back to make sure her breathing was even. She wouldn't *automatically* assume her mother was faking.

"She's fine," said Anna in a bored voice. "She just didn't know I was pregnant and now she's trying to make it all about her."

Maybelle's eyes twitched again. Naomi, now suspicious, raised her mother's hand so that it hovered above her face, an old ER trick. She released it, and instead of whacking herself in the face, which she'd do if she were unconscious, her hand fell to the side, slowly.

"You're awake, Mom. We know it."

Maybelle's eyes flew open and she glared at Naomi.

"I can't believe you just faked fainting. In front of a doctor and all." Naomi pointed at Rig, who knelt on the other side of Maybelle.

"I did not fake fainting. It was just a very fast, very sudden spell. Thank *goodness* it's over now." Maybelle sat up and fanned herself as Buzz leaned over her, still looking concerned.

"Alert, alert!" Milo screamed the words as he raced between the oak tree and the old unused clothesline.

Naomi stood, her legs feeling rubbery. "I'd better sit . . ."

"Here." Rig ushered her to a chair next to her sister. "Just sit here and rest. You want a soda? Something stronger?"

Naomi thought about her stomach. It felt better than it had in days, but she didn't want to test her system. "Water, please."

"Me, too," said Anna. "If you don't mind."

"Me, too," said Maybelle weakly.

"Three waters," said Rig. He went inside the house.

"Mom," hissed Anna. "Seriously?"

Maybelle pointed a finger at Anna. "Who *did* that to you?"

Jake and Frank shot a look at each other. "We'll help Rig," they said, and the two men nearly tripped over themselves going through the screen door. Buzz looked up in the treetops, and then back slowly. "Yeah, maybe they need . . ." He, too, was gone.

Anna sat up, her back remarkably straight for a woman in her ninth month. "He doesn't matter."

"Was it that firefighter? Jake? Is that little hellion his, too? Because if he's going to let you bring a bastard—"

"No!" Anna said the word loudly. Good. Naomi wanted to let them have it out. She didn't want to be part of this unless she had to be. Although Naomi had to admit that knowing Anna had kept the pregnancy from her mother made her feel a little bit better. She was the only one Anna had trusted. She was the one Anna had come to.

And then she'd chased her away.

"It's not Jake. Jake's just a nice guy." Anna smiled. "A really nice guy."

"How could you not *tell* me?" Maybelle pressed her hand against her chest. "Oh, Naomi, I think I'm having palpitations."

"You are not," said Anna. "And this is exactly why I didn't tell you. I'm doing this my way. On my terms. Neither you nor Naomi have any say in this."

"Hey," said Naomi. "I'm not like her."

Anna's eyes were fierce. "Well, you kept acting like her, even when you were sick. Especially when you were sick. That's why I left."

Naomi closed her eyes for a minute. The pain was intense, as bad as being sick had been. She was *not* like their mother.

Maybelle shook her head sharply. "What do you mean? How I act? I'm your mother. I get to act any way I want."

"That's the problem, Mom," said Anna. She held out her hand in a pleading gesture, then let it drop on top of her belly. "You *don't* get to. You have to be nice."

"I'm always nice. Daddy calls me his spun sugar." Maybelle's hand fluttered up to make sure her perfectly coiffed hair was still in place.

Anna spoke as if Maybelle hadn't. "I mean nice as in genuine. If you're not, I won't be around you. Naomi, that goes for you, too."

Naomi turned in her seat so that she was facing Anna and pulled a curl forward so she couldn't see her mother at all. This was important. This mattered so much that her heart physically ached.

"Anna. I'm so sorry. I was completely wrong in what I said, and in the judgmental way I acted toward you. I want to be there for you in any way that you'll have me. I want you in the house, and in the office, and I can't wait to meet the person you're bringing us. As your sister, and as your friend, I'm so sorry."

Anna dropped her eyes to her stomach and looked back up at Naomi. "If you ever tell me what to do again, like *that*, I'll—"

"You'll sock me in the arm and tell me to jump off a bridge. And move all my furniture and lose my gas and electric bill. And sock me again."

"Will you listen?"

"If you hit me hard enough." The words were light, the tone wasn't. Naomi held out a hand, and Anna squeezed it, hard.

"Okay, then," said Anna.

Okay? Did Anna need more? She'd apologize all night if she had to. Anna smiled.

Okay was all she needed. Naomi felt lighter as happiness swelled inside her throat, pushing tears to her eyes. She blinked fast, and then jumped as Milo hurtled himself into her lap.

"Hey, buddy."

"That's your sister?" Milo demanded.

"Yep. And that's my mom." Naomi pointed at Maybelle, who was squirming in her seat, obviously trying to look penitent.

"Where's *your* mom?" Milo asked Anna.

She gestured to Maybelle. "Right there. We have the same mom. Because we're sisters."

Milo said, "You're luckier than me, I guess. With a mom and a sister and everything. But I have Spiderman!" With an accidental sharp elbowing to her ribs, Milo leaped off Naomi's lap and ran inside, with the rest of the men.

Maybelle wriggled forward and said, "Anna, honey, I'm sorry, too. It's just that you being pregnant means that . . ."

"You're old enough to be a grandmother?" Anna said.

Naomi couldn't help smiling at the way her mother's face crinkled in dismay.

"Maybe the baby can call me something else. Not Grandma."

"How about Granny?" asked Naomi, keeping her voice neutral.

"Oh! Stop it, both of you. Anna, sugar, when we're at Naomi's tonight, I want to have a private talk with you. Just me and you, cozied up. I want to make sure you know—"

Anna sighed. "I'm not staying with Naomi anymore."

Naomi felt her hopes fall. *Dammit.* Well, she'd work on a bigger, louder apology. She'd do just about anything so that her sister would know how sorry she was.

"It's not that." Anna knew what she was thinking. "I'm just better here. And Jake likes having me here. I'm helping with Milo, so Frank can take it easier on Jake's workdays, and Jake worries less about them both when I'm here and he's at work. Maybe I'll come back and stay with you when he gets sick of me. But for now I'm good."

The look on Anna's face was soft. Oh, God. This was worse than Naomi had thought.

"But come on, your room is all set up there. I'd love to have you back."

Anna shook her head. "No, you wouldn't. You could barely stand having me there."

"That wasn't the way it was . . . I was just confused. I'm not anymore. I want you with me. What about when the baby comes?"

Anna raised her gaze to the screen door. Jake stepped through, Rig, Frank, and Buzz behind him.

"I want her to stay. The baby, too," said Jake. "For as long as she'll have us." And something in his voice made chills run down Naomi's back. He looked at Anna as if she was something he couldn't believe, something he didn't deserve. Anna looked back, and a whole conversation flowed between them, in front of Naomi's eyes.

They were in love.

Oh, whoa.

"So," Naomi said, as quickly as she could. "Enough about where people are staying. We can talk more about that later. So is it burgers or steak tonight?" She'd talk to Rig afterward about their siblings—

neither of them could possibly know what they were getting into. It was way too fast, for either of them. Right? But the time for that wasn't now.

"Steak," said Rig. His voice was distant. "I'll put them on now."

Anna said, "Did Naomi see what you did at the clinic?"

"What you both did?" said Jake. "You worked *way* too hard on that. It could have been bad for the baby, Anna. You should take it easy for the next week or so. Keep your feet up."

Anna shot him a look that was both tolerant and amused. A *loving* look.

"The clinic? What?" Naomi was confused. Her poor, unused health clinic that she hadn't even opened recently because she'd been sick? God, she still had to pull it together for the dance on Sunday. At least she had all week to do it. Hopefully she'd feel even better tomorrow.

"I guess she didn't see it," said Rig. He kept his eyes on the grill.

"What did you do?"

Anna laughed. "You should take her there after dinner."

Rig looked at Naomi, and as their eyes connected, Naomi felt a flutter of something she didn't want to name. She crossed and then uncrossed her legs.

"Yeah," said Rig. "Maybe I will."

And the tone in his voice made Naomi felt better than she had all week, and even though her mother was in town, Naomi felt a flicker of hope. She didn't even know what she hoped for. She just knew she did.

Chapter Forty-four

If a man complains about your stash, ask him how many
guitars he has. He has a collection of something, too.
—E.C.

I t was, of course, an uncomfortable dinner. How could it have
been anything else? Frank cornered Naomi over by the roses,
going on about how grateful he was for the nitroglycerin, and
how he'd come see her soon, as soon as he had some time free. Then
he'd begun to talk about Shirley, the waitress at Tillie's, which just
served to confuse her, and she extricated herself and went back to
the group again.

At the table, Rig also mentioned something about Shirley, about
how they couldn't hope to serve dinner the same way she did at
the diner, and Frank's eyebrows flew upward, but nothing more
was said. It seemed as if everyone was talking about one thing, but
meaning another. Maybelle talked about how difficult her first pregnancy was, and what a joy it had been to carry Anna, ten years later.
Jake and Anna shot superheated looks at each other, as if only the
company being present was keeping their hands off one another.

The second Buzz, the last one eating after three helpings of steak and potato salad, put his fork down, Naomi stood. No matter what Rig had to show her, she needed to go.

"Well, thanks a lot. Let's do it again sometime. Now, I'd better get going. Still recovering, you know . . . Mom, Buzz, I'll leave the back door unlocked, and you can just settle yourselves in—"

Rig stood. "Can I show you something before you go home?"

Feeling a sudden pang of worry, Naomi said, "What did you *do* at the clinic?"

He moved toward the front door. "Can't tell. Just gotta show you."

Anna said, "Go on, it's cool. You'll like it."

It was a way out of here, out of this sticky, uncomfortable dinner full of unexpected land mines, and soon she could go home and drag the shawl into her room and knit herself to sleep. Exhaustion was wearing on her, and her shoulders slumped as she left the house. She made a halfhearted attempt at pushing her shoulders back and standing up straight as she turned to look at Rig.

He was closer behind her than she'd known he was. He sure moved quietly for such a big guy.

"I have the bike," he said, facing her. He lifted his hands and gently rubbed the tops of her shoulders, right where her muscles were most tense. "Or are you too tired? We can do this another night."

She let her head go limp and rolled it from side to side. She pretended his were just any fingers, that he wasn't making her shake inside. "Can't we walk? It's not that far. I'll be fine."

He leaned forward, and his voice was a low rumble that made Naomi nervous. "You're still just getting over being sick. Ride with me."

The last three words were said in such a deep register she felt, more than heard, them. Had he meant to make them sound so sexual? Looking up into his face, she decided, yes. He had. For a second, oddly, she felt like she was about to sneeze, a delicious foreshadowing of something she didn't want to name.

"Yeah," she said, feeling suddenly daring. "Okay. Yes."

The ride was fast and short. Naomi, feeling like an old hand, wrapped her arms around Rig's waist, and felt his muscled back against her chest through their T-shirts. He'd given her his leather jacket to wear—it hung long and open on her, while he rode with his arms bared to the wind. He took one lap down Main, around the gazebo, and back up past the dunes. He rode up for a moment onto the sidewalk that led to the pier, and he paused, as if considering whether or not it was worth it. A *whoop-whoop* from the cop car in the parking lot convinced him to back the bike up. Naomi laughed, bringing her arms tighter around him.

"Let's go," she called up to him, even though she felt as if she could ride all night. Unfortunately, her insides weren't agreeing with her, and she knew she'd probably have to walk home. But the discomfort had been worth the delicious butterflies the ride had given her. Or that he'd given her. How could she tell the difference?

He nodded, and a minute later, they pulled up in front of the health clinic.

"It looks the same," she said, dismounting and shaking her hair out from the helmet. She tried not to notice how his eyes glowed as she did so. Running her fingers through her hopeless curls, she examined the building more closely. The same small stenciled sign in the window, but . . .

"Curtains! You hung curtains!"

"It's hard to tell in the dark, but they're green and sheer, so it lets in the light and kind of makes it looks softer inside. That was Bruno's idea."

Naomi looked at him in surprise. "Bruno's been in on this?"

"Everyone was. We only had a few days while you were sick to pull it off."

She unlocked the door and stepped inside. Then she lost her breath.

The room had been transformed. The dance studio's old mirrors were still up, but now they were covered with a gauzelike orange fabric that moved and shifted subtly as air from the door changed the current in the room. The tables she'd had lined up along all the walls were gone, except for one at the back, which was covered with all the literature she'd compiled.

Rig said, "You can still do whatever you want. This is just a suggestion. Keep on looking around."

Instead of the wooden chairs she'd bought from an office-furniture sale, two long brown leather couches were placed at opposing angles, with a large, sturdy coffee table between them. Two separate gathering areas were delineated by groupings of small, deep armchairs with tables set next to them.

It looked so inviting. So warm. How the hell had he done this? Naomi looked up and saw that the fluorescent tubes that had hung down, ugly in their brightness, had been replaced by simple track lighting. It was still light enough, but it felt softer. Everything felt gentler.

It was as if she'd laid out a plastic card table with some cubed cheese on it. Then he'd come along and made it a long wooden dining table, with a tablecloth, candles, and imported Camembert when she wasn't looking.

Naomi took a few steps and touched the back of one of the armchairs.

"I can't afford this," she said.

"You don't have to. This is my donation to your center. My tax preparer assures me I'll be able to write it off somehow. She's magic."

"But . . ." Naomi's words trailed off and she looked to the left and saw something that looked like . . . "Is that—that looks like a knitting circle."

Rig slapped his thigh and laughed, a huge, rolling boom that filled the space. "I told her you'd like that."

"Told who?"

"Anna. She helped set it up."

"Anna?" But her sister had been furious with her when she'd been sick. She'd still done this? Naomi felt something hard and cold inside her start to melt.

"Come look." He held out his hand, and too befuddled to do anything else, she took it.

"See," he pointed. "Five armchairs, but I made sure they're light-weight, so you can drag them around and move them if you want to get more knitters in here. Special lights so it looks like you're knitting during the daytime even at night, like now. Racks," he pointed to the wall, just under the window. "For knitting maga-zines. I bought as many as I could from Lucy at the Book Spire, but I got subscriptions to them, too. Empty baskets, here, so people can set their projects down and come back to them. And yarn to sample over there, with spare needles. I picked it all out at Abigail's shop. Anna gave me that idea, too."

"But—" Naomi shook her head. "But there are already places in town for people to knit. Abigail's store. And they have knitting les-sons sometimes at Lucy's bookstore, I've seen the fliers. How are we supposed to bring people in when—"

Rig cut her off. "You're bringing in a totally different market. You're targeting the woman in this town who's sick, who needs someplace to go where she can talk about being sick with other people who won't tell her to look on the bright side. As far as I can tell, this whole town is addicted to knitting. I saw some old men playing chess on the pier, and one of them was knitting while he did it. I've never seen such a knit-crazy place, and you should be able to harness that for healing." He took Naomi's hands and looked right into her eyes. "I really think you could have something here. We just need to get the people who need it to come see what it is. And we'll be one step closer when we host the dance on the weekend. We can push the couches out of the way, and look, that can be where we put the band."

She looked at him, feeling a huge space in her chest, not sure what to do with it. "But . . . how do we know . . . ?"

He held up a pair of needles. "Do you always know what you're making when you cast on?"

She nodded firmly. "Of course."

He pulled out an arm's length of a green variegated wool. "What if you don't?" Using what looked like a modified long-tail cast on, he started moving the yarn over one of the needles, building stitches.

"You'll end up with something ugly. Something not useful," Naomi said, fascinated by watching him. The move looked simple— the stitches loading onto his left needle as if he really did know what he was doing.

"How do you know that's what you'll get?" Rig asked.

"I just do." Naomi perched on the edge of an armchair. "Without a plan, you end up floundering."

"Not always," said Rig. He started knitting across the stitches, fast, large loops of the yarn. He held the yarn in his left hand, and threw, so different from her own careful, tight stitches.

"Well, you're not like most people," said Naomi.

"I never said I was." He sat in the chair directly across from her. "Some people like different."

He was, perhaps, the fastest knitter she'd ever seen. She stared, and within less than five minutes, five peaceful, quiet minutes, she watched him create no less than three inches of something flat and wide.

Finally breaking the silence, she said, "So you'll organize these knit-ins?"

"Sure," said Rig. "But I don't think we'll have to worry. They'll set themselves up, I think. When I was at Abigail's, I told her about the idea, and two women in the store thought it was great, and could already think of people who were in recovery from different things who would want to come."

"But Abigail doesn't . . . we're not friends."

Rig gave her a confused look. "Why would you say that? Did someone tell you that? Did *she*?"

Naomi had the grace to blush. "We had a . . . an odd conversation one day. She thought she remembered me from down south. But . . . " *I didn't tell her she was right.*

"Do you routinely say hello to people in town? Smile at them in Tillie's?"

"I try. I really do. But sometimes . . ."

Rig didn't pull any punches. "Not saying hello looks stuck up."

"I'm not. You *know* I'm not stuck up. I've just been so . . . worried."

"I know that. But maybe they don't. We'll change that."

The use of *we*? Did he mean it? Should she let him?

Rig went on, "I've set up two yoga classes a week, a beginners level and a level one. The rugs over there," he pointed to the cheerful, colorful rugs that hadn't been in the room the last time she'd looked, just like all the other changes, "will roll up and move to the side. I figure we can fit about fifteen people in per session."

"And you'll be teaching these classes?"

"Toots Harrison. She's already agreed."

Naomi was torn between being furious that he'd set this up without consulting her and thrilled that someone would be using the space. "I told you, I'm not into alterna-medicine." But her voice held no heat, she knew, and she dropped her eyes to the floor.

"Yoga is good for the body. Most people don't consider it quackery anymore. You should try it sometime. You could use it."

Naomi's voice was light. "Yeah, whatever." She watched him knit for another minute. It must be almost five inches already.

For once, her hands felt fine being still. She didn't feel the need to have the needles in her hands, if she could see his. "Anything else you want to admit? While we're at it."

Rig glanced at her and then back down at the knitting.

"What is it?" Naomi knew there was more.

"Acupuncture. Tuesday afternoons, drop in, drop out."

Naomi took a deep breath. "You have an acupuncturist lined up for this? Let me guess, Toots?"

"She's only an amateur. I'm pretty sure she wouldn't fit under our liability insurance, although she did offer. No, it's her teacher, Herb Dansk, who's actually licensed. He's donating his time."

"Wow." Shouldn't Naomi be annoyed? This was what she'd said she didn't want, after all. She searched herself and found nothing but curiosity and a sudden, desperate warmth that had nothing to do with the temperature of the room.

The knitting was longer yet. He was as fast with the needles as he was on his bike. "Is it a scarf?" Her fingers twitched to feel the fabric he was making.

"No idea."

"It has to *be* something."

Rig looked at her. "It already is. It's exactly what it's supposed to be."

Naomi's head swam in a sudden wave of dizziness that felt different from the dizzy sickness she'd had all week. He was serious. He really meant it.

She moved before she thought, before she lost her nerve. She went to him, putting one knee to the outside of his, the other on his other side until she was straddling him. This time, she wasn't sure of herself. Last time she had been, and she hadn't gotten her way. She'd received something else, something she'd barely even processed yet.

This time, she had no idea how it would go, and for once in her goddamn life, she didn't need to know. She just knew that she'd never seen anything she needed more in her whole life than this huge man, sitting here in front of her, in a room he'd helped her create, knitting.

And Rig kept knitting in the small space between them. His big hands made the needles look small, and they had to be a size nine, at least. Their mouths were a breath apart now as she sat on his lap. She felt him rise underneath her, hard, heated. But he just smiled.

"Hi, you." His voice was a low rumble that fit between her ribs.

"Hi," she whispered.

"Whatcha doing?" *Click, click, click.*

"Hoping to God you'll kiss me."

Chapter Forty-five

Knit through everything.

—E.C.

His reaction was instant, primal. He dropped the needles and yarn between them and lifted his hands to the back of her neck. Pulling her in hard with complete assuredness, he took her mouth, and she gave it to him. She was supposed to be here, she knew it. She could feel it.

He bit her lower lip, softly, then traced it with his tongue. His hands moved from behind her head, traveling down her back.

As his hands tugged out the bottom edge of her shirt and slid upward, as one hand cupped her entire breast, as his fingertips dipped past the lace edge and brushed her nipple, Naomi realized she had no idea about anything anymore. Everything about the man was a surprise, including the way he pulled her shirt over her head.

Half a second later, Naomi panicked. The window faced Main Street. There was no way in hell . . . Oh. She'd forgotten about the new green curtains he'd put up.

Rig laughed underneath her. "They're sheer, but they'll protect you."

"From what?" Naomi's knees drove farther into the space between his thighs and the arms of his chair, and she pushed against him.

"From the eyes of the street. Not from mine, though." Rig's gaze roamed her upper body, lingering on the cherry-colored lace of her bra, running down to her navel then back up to her eyes. His hands rested lightly at her waist, spanning it. Underneath her, she felt power. Coiled. Ready to spring.

If she chose him, she could have him. Naomi knew that. But she wouldn't be able to control him. Or even her own responses.

She should really get up, move away, put her shirt back on. Break this contact . . .

Rig slid his hands down her waist to the top of her hips. He pulled her body down at the same moment that he pushed up against her.

Holy shit. He was shockingly hard under the bulge of his jeans, and Naomi lost her breath again. Conscious thought wasn't far behind it as their mouths met again in a kiss that tasted of rain and fog and a strength that Naomi had never tasted before.

Rig's hand raked between them, and something metallic clattered to the floor. The knitting.

"Did you . . ." What was she trying to say over the panting, around the heat? "Will you lose your stitches?"

"*Fuck* the stitches." Rig drew her down again and kissed his way up her neck, trailing his teeth against her sensitive skin, up to her ear, lightly biting it before drawing the lobe into his mouth.

Naomi pressed into him again. She should stop. This wasn't the best idea. Sitting up, she pushed against his chest. "Um . . ."

His eyes were dark heat, flames blazing through his lashes. He reached one hand behind himself, and pulled the T-shirt over his head in one motion, tossing it in the same direction he'd thrown the knitting.

Holy Christ. Ridges of muscle and lines of definition skated across his abdominal obliques and then disappeared into the top of his jeans.

Her thoughts went up in smoke. Instinctively, she leaned forward, running her hands over him, touching each muscle. She dropped her head and kissed the side of his neck, then moved her mouth along his clavicle. Her fingers danced down the central line of his stomach, then dipped into his navel. Rig gasped, and she smiled. He was sensitive there? Wait till she got lower . . .

She undid the fly of his jeans and, leaning forward, putting her head on his shoulder, slid her hand into his shorts And then her eyes widened. He was hard, wide, and hot as hell.

Naomi wanted it. She wanted *him*. Normally at this point, she'd know what to do. What moves to make. But instead, tiny tremors rocked her, taking away her ability to decide what would be her best move, what would be to her best advantage. She couldn't do the sexual math, couldn't hold the formula in her head.

Rig's hand wrapped around hers, stilling her. "Dammit, woman, you could make me come by touching me like that."

Naomi felt herself get wetter at the sound of just his voice. She let him draw her hand away.

He leaned forward and whispered in her ear. "Be with me here. Bring your heart with your body."

The words shocked her. Her heart? But she'd already . . . Couldn't this be just sex? And what about him? She bit her bottom lip.

Rig watched her and grinned. Obviously, he knew exactly what asking that of her meant. Then he pushed up against her again, their jeans grinding a glorious, heated friction. She felt the muscles in his thighs contract and moved against him.

It felt like a butterfly was lodged in her throat. "Okay."

His laugh was more like a growl as he stood, lifting both of them. He kicked the knitting farther away and opened the fly of her jeans with a flick of his fingers. Pushing them down, he lifted one of her feet, then the other, and she shuffled out of first her shoes, then her pants. For one moment they stood in front of the curtained window, looking at each other, Rig in only his jeans, fly open, his chest rising and falling as hard as hers was, she in only her bra and panties.

Rig seemed to be waiting for something. For her to do something, and she had no idea what it was, but she made the best guess she could, and reached back to unclasp her bra. Her fingers shook so badly she thought she might have to ask for help. For the love of God, could she not retain one small shred of self-control? In giving it up, did she have to give *all* of it up?

Finally, she let the bra slip with a whisper to the ground, and Naomi thought she heard him take a quick breath, but when she looked up at him, she couldn't tell what he was thinking. Yes, he'd wanted her a second ago. No, he wasn't stopping her from taking her clothes off. But he was still waiting.

All she had left on were her panties, and she pushed them off her hips, down to her knees, then let them drop. She nudged them away with her bare toe.

She still didn't understand what showed on Rig's face. Something . . . it had to be lust, right?

Oh, God, what if it wasn't? She started to shiver all over. What if she'd just made a fool's mistake? What if he was about to ask her to put her clothes back on? What was he *waiting* for?

She could think of only one thing left to try. "Please," Naomi said.

It was the right thing to say. His eyes got darker and she sensed his muscles moving under his skin, coiling, ready to spring.

"Please," she said again. "Oh, Rig, please. I need you."

He was on her in the space of a second, his arms tight around her, lifting her against him, pushing her back until she hit the leather of the sofa. Then he pushed his own jeans and shorts down, then off.

Rig was huge, and ready, and how he already had the condom in his hand, she'd never know because she hadn't seen him take it out. Without lifting his eyes from hers, he rolled it on. She knew that he was going to be inside her within seconds, and every fiber of her being screamed for him to move faster.

He smiled, suddenly, and the eyes that had darkened so much lit up, sparkling. "You're incandescent."

She gasped, her nerves on fire. The leather behind her was cool, and she opened her mouth to his. He kissed her deeply, thoroughly, and then reached down to slip one finger inside her wetness, as if testing her to see if she was ready.

She was. She writhed against him, trying to pull him down with her arms, her legs. But he stopped her, pressed the tip of himself against her heated flesh, just at her very opening. When she pushed forward he pulled back. He drew his mouth away from hers so that he could look into her eyes again.

She wanted everything. She *needed* him, God help her. Him, his body, his heart, his mind, and she finally found the words she needed, the words she'd been trying to find since he showed up in her life for the second time. "Please, Rig. You. I just need you." The words shocked her, making her ache inside, and there was only one way to fix it.

His eyes sparked heat, and he agreed with his body, sinking into her with one sharp thrust. Once inside, he held himself there, waiting one more time.

She whispered the very last of the breath she'd been holding, "Please."

He rocked her then, his rhythm urgent, every stroke filling her farther, harder, deeper. She had nothing left but the thought of him, the feel of him, and in his eyes she saw only herself reflected back. She rode against him, and they fit each other as if they'd been waiting for this, only this. He slipped the finger that had been inside her into her mouth, and she sucked—he moved even faster. His lips moved against her ear, whispering gasped words she couldn't quite hear but understood. Time collapsed against itself, and Naomi lost any thought but where she was in her climb, and what he felt like as he lifted her there. And when she came, she came around him, clenching so tightly he moaned into her mouth, groaning as he pushed harder, faster. The orgasm spiraled around her, and kept going, stretching out until he was roaring above her, his bottom lip wet from her tongue, the corded muscles at his neck strained, his eyes never once leaving hers.

"Please, please, Rig, please . . ." she whispered, not knowing anymore what she was asking for, just knowing he was giving her everything she needed.

He sank down, covering her body with his, stroking her face with the backs of his fingertips. His voice, when it reached her ears, was a low whisper. "I needed you, too, Doc."

Chapter Forty-six

Joy is a finished object that fits.
                                                    —E.C.

Rig felt her start to wake and didn't move a muscle. It was all he could do not to slide back a bit, just a few inches, really, and slip into her again. He was ready to go, had been since minutes after they'd stopped earlier. She did something to him, made his blood race and churn in a way he'd never felt before.

This thing, whatever it was with Naomi, was deep. And it was scaring the shit out of him. It was probably something he needed to stop, actually. Put some kind of kibosh on it. But he didn't want to be anywhere else, and he sure hadn't kiboshed anything earlier, when he'd been sunk into her, buried in her as far as he could go . . .

And besides, he thought, *how do you put the kibosh on love?*

Holy Christ on a cracker. The thought paralyzed him.

He was in love?

Well, damn, that would explain a lot of it. How his heart felt twelve times its size when he was near her, and how it got even larger, beat faster, when he touched her. How she made him re-think that whole bachelor-forever thing, because a life with Naomi would be better than any kind of life without her. But jumping off helicopters during storm surges over the Gulf hadn't scared him more.

Fear made him momentarily dizzy. No wonder Jake acted the way he did. Rig could see himself being crazy terrified of losing Naomi.

She gave a small sigh and frowned in her sleep. Then her eyes flew open.

"Holy shit," she said, frozen underneath him.

He laughed. "Hi to you, too."

"I didn't . . . I don't . . ." She stuttered to a halt and put one hand over her eyes, biting her lower lip.

While he longed to do the same, he didn't—he just lifted her hand to peek under it. "Me, neither. Don't worry."

"But we *did*."

And her voice sounded so like herself, smart and controlled, noth-ing like she'd sounded earlier, that he laughed again and hugged her against him.

"You're incredible," he said.

"We're both crazy." She stood, pushing against him, still buck-ass naked and gorgeous as anything any sculptor had ever carved. He loved the way her hips flared, the way her breasts swayed, the way her curls dropped over her bare shoulder.

"Yeah, probably." And really, he agreed. It was crazy to feel like this about Naomi Fontaine. But it was a little late for reasonable thought.

"What did we *do*?"

"You want me to show you? I can remind you."

She stamped her foot, which was probably more ineffective than she realized, as her breasts bobbed. He longed to taste them again.

"Oh, lord," she said and started pulling her clothes on. A crying shame, really, that her body ever had to be covered. He watched, unashamed of the way his body was reacting.

"You!" She snapped her fingers toward his obvious arousal. "Down, boy. We have to get out of here." But her eyes lingered below his waist, and Rig's blood pressure rose again.

"Why don't you come sit on my lap?" He gestured.

"We should go," she said, but there was hesitation in her voice, still hoarse from the sounds she'd made earlier.

"It's our place, though. Your center. You can do whatever you want to here. And you *should* do whatever you want to."

Naomi covered her breasts ineffectively with her hands and moved forward slowly. "Oh, God. We're holding a dance here. Not a lap dance."

"Then give me just a kiss." His heart beat in a syncopation that he didn't recognize, that he'd never felt.

She leaned over him, letting her hands rest on his shoulders. Then she dropped a light kiss on his mouth. Rig brushed her perfect nipples with his fingertips, and felt her tongue skim his lower lip. Goddamn, he couldn't get any harder. Hadn't she just used him up, not even an hour ago?

Naomi's hand touched his hardness, and he felt her smile against his lips. Maybe, just maybe—

There was a rap at the window inches from the couch.

"Shit!" Naomi jerked backward and grabbed her shirt from the floor, pulling it over her head. "What the *hell* is that?"

"Don't worry." Rig swiveled on the couch so that he was facing the curtain. Through its sheerness, he could just make out the figure of someone standing at the window, looking in.

"I thought you said you couldn't see in here through those!"

Rig shook his head. "I didn't think you could."

"Yoo-hoo!" It was a high, female voice.

"Shit, shit, shit." Naomi hopped in front of him, yanking up her jeans. "Shit!"

With the sofa hiding the most outrageous parts of his naked-ness, Rig leaned forward and pulled the curtain aside an inch. A woman with long red hair waggled her fingers at him. "Hi!" she called, her voice coming clearly through the glass. She was wearing a short electric blue skirt and a matching blue jacket and had at least six necklaces strung around her neck. Her heels were high, and her lipstick was bright.

"Who the hell is that?"

Naomi looked green at the gills. "Trixie Fletcher. Reporter. *Shit.*"

"Crap." Rig pulled on his jeans and shirt. "Are we decent?"

"Why? You can't talk to her. No way."

Rig nodded and moved toward the door.

Naomi continued protesting as she wrestled with her shirt, her arms flying over her head. "We can't. Don't you dare. She'll know what we were—"

Rig opened the door a crack and said, "Yeah?"

"Trixie Fletcher, with the *Independent*." She had a trace of lipstick on her teeth, and Rig suddenly loved the fact that Naomi never appeared to wear anything more than Chap Stick on her naturally pink lips.

"Yeah?" he said again.

She peered over his shoulder at Naomi, who was suddenly mirac-ulously clothed. "I just thought you should know that the curtains are so thin that if the lights are on in here, which they are, I can see the freckles on your shoulder, Naomi. Main Street can be busy, and the smokers outside the Rite Spot tend to wander when they're out here. I wondered what they were doing down here, and I shooed them off when I found out."

"Shit," said Rig.

"Just thought you should know." She waggled her fingers. "Toodles!"

He locked the door behind her and turned slowly to face Naomi. *Shit, shit, shit.*

Her face was pale as she sat in an armchair and pulled on her shoes. "So we just performed for all of Cypress Hollow."

"I didn't know—"

"You said that you did! I didn't buy or put up those curtains, *you* did! I trusted you! And now the whole damn town will think I'm a whore."

Holding up his hands, Rig moved forward slowly. "This isn't the eighteenth century. People have sex."

"Not. In. Business. Windows." She glared. "Maybe in Amsterdam's red-light district, but not in Cypress Hollow." Tugging her hand through her mop of curls, she stood. "I should have known better."

"It's not your fault."

"Aren't you embarrassed at *all*? This is your town, too, after all. You'll be able to walk into Tillie's tomorrow with your head up? She's a reporter, for Christ's sake." Naomi took the long way past him on her way to the door, moving around the low footstool as if she was trying to stay as far from him as possible.

"It was just sex, Naomi." It wasn't—the words hurt to say. But he had to make this better somehow. "No one will care."

Her eyes, as she pulled open the door, were bruised. "I care. I hate people knowing my secrets."

"Wouldn't it be okay if I wasn't a secret?" Rig hoped she'd say yes. She *had* to say yes.

But she just said, "I'm walking home. By myself."

And then she was gone, the snap of the door latch reverberating in the large room, leaving Rig standing barefoot, more alone than he could remember ever feeling before.

Chapter Forty-seven

Sometimes, though, we have to admit we made the wrong choice: the wrong yarn, the wrong color, the wrong size. Sometimes we knit for the wrong person. It happens to all of us, at least twice.

—E.C.

I t was a foggy walk, but Naomi didn't feel the chill—her emotions kept her warm as she walked the familiar sidewalks. Anger—he should have known better. Embarrassment—what was to keep townspeople from gossiping about her? Sadness—she wasn't really sure where that was coming from, and she pushed it away. Naomi was good at that.

She'd already had enough to do in this town just trying to be accepted as a good doctor, but now they'd never, ever trust her. Sex in public, good God. In view of the local bar. She curled her fingers tightly, the nails biting into her palms.

But . . . it *had* been amazing sex. With an amazing man. At Naomi's core, she felt a flare of heat, remembering the feeling of Rig being inside her, his eyes focused only on her.

No. She reached again for her anger, her feeling of betrayal, and walked faster.

In front of her house, she got her keys out as quietly as she could, praying they didn't jingle. She'd forgotten about her mother and Buzz staying with her until she saw Buzz's white truck parked in front of the house, taking both the parking spaces.

She did *not* want to talk to Maybelle right now—she wanted to take a shower, wash Rig's smell off her body so she'd stop having that dizzy, floating sensation whenever she thought about how he'd touched her, how he'd made her body feel.

And how he'd made her heart feel.

She shut the door behind her, willing the latch to click silently. Instead it shot home like a bolt with a loud *snick.* Naomi waited.

And it came: "Is that you?" Maybelle's voice called from down the hallway.

"No, Mom," Naomi said. "It's not."

"Very funny." Maybelle entered the room wearing a long pink nightgown that looked like it was made of nylon. It clung to her hips and belly, and there was no way Naomi would ever have imagined her mother wearing anything like it.

"I'm scarred for life, Mom." Naomi opened the bathroom door and tugged her fuzzy red robe off the hook. "Cover up, would you?"

"Oh, honey, it's Buzz's favorite."

"I don't want to know that. Good night, Mom." Naomi went into the kitchen, hoping her mother wouldn't follow her. No such luck, of course. Maybelle trailed behind her, her eyes wide and innocent.

"What's wrong? How did things go with Rig?"

"Fine." Naomi poured herself a glass of water. What did her mother know? God forbid they'd driven down Main on the way home and looked at the health center's windows . . . It wouldn't have been on the way, not from Jake's, but would they have . . . ? Oh, lord. "Why do you ask?"

"I just wondered. I sensed a real chemistry between you two."

Naomi drank her water too quickly, and some of it went down the wrong way. She coughed, and then managed, "Oh."

"Are you choking?" Maybelle pounded her on the back.

"Mom, stop!" Naomi kept coughing.

"Do you need the Heimlich? Put your hands to your throat, and I'll go get Buzz. He knows how to do it."

"Mom. You can't choke on liquid." Naomi coughed again and tried to stifle it.

"I'm sure you can." Maybelle sniffed.

"I'm the doctor, Mom. You can drown, but liquid eventually goes down. I don't need the Heimlich."

"You may be the doctor, but you don't always have that much sense."

Her mother had just found out that her sister was knocked up, and she was the one getting the criticism? "It's late, Mom. Is Buzz asleep?"

Her mother smiled slyly. "I gave him the old knockout one-two."

"Jesus! Mother!" She'd have to buy new sheets for the guest bed. Naomi closed her eyes. Maybe if she pretended she were somewhere else . . .

"And anyway," Maybelle continued, "I don't mind setting a good example for you. You and that Rig, what's the story?" She sat at the kitchen table and looked at Naomi expectantly. "Will you get me some water, too? Please?"

No getting around this one. Naomi accepted her fate.

"Here," she said, setting the glass of water on the table.

"Now sit down, yes, right there. I want to hear everything about Rig. He's very handsome, isn't he?"

Rig was the best-looking man Naomi had ever seen, and even more, he was the *best* man she'd ever known. Kind, and smart, and completely unbothered by what other people thought. Ridiculously hot. And he cared about her. She could feel it.

And by tomorrow, everyone in town would know she'd screwed him in a window. Way to create a connection with the locals.

She reached for her knitting, still in its basket where she'd left it on the kitchen table. Thank God for the lace. It might keep her from going stark raving insane during the next few moments she had to spend with her mother.

"Have you had sex yet?"

"Mom." Naomi pretended to search for a dropped stitch when it was actually a simple knit-back row.

"Fine. Don't tell me. But this is what I have to tell you, darling: don't wait too long. You need to get a man like that on the hook, and catch him. Pull him into your boat before—" Maybelle stopped speaking and looked down into her ice cubes. "You can keep it from him that you're not perfect until you snare him."

Naomi exhaled sharply. "You sound like a magazine article from the fifties. Do you really believe that? Did Buzz think you were perfect when you got married?"

Maybelle nodded, confidence exuding from every tight pore. "He thought there was nothing better than me. I've still never once farted around him."

Naomi winced. "That doesn't sound healthy."

"Healthy for the relationship, though. And that's what I'm trying to say to you. Keep the romance alive, keep that spark, make him wonder a little, never show him all the mystery. A little suspense adds spice." She shot a sharp look at her daughter. "And get your hair done. You've got a little gray coming in now, haven't you? You get that early silver from me, poor thing."

Naomi moved the salt shaker, a little pink girl owl, away from the pepper, a little blue boy owl. Since she hadn't known her mother was coming to town, most of the owl things were put away. At least these were out.

"That's a game, Mom. I don't want that."

"Not a game so much as a clever plan. Nothing wrong with that, right? Didn't you have a plan when you wanted to be a doctor?"

Of course she had. But Maybelle wouldn't know much about that plan. Her father had been the one who had plotted and schemed with Naomi late at night while she was in high school, critiquing her college entrance essays, and planning which college campuses to visit on school break. After he'd died, even though no one else she knew worked full-time through medical school, she had, picking up whatever waitressing job would provide her with the most flexibility. She'd worked as hard as she could, at everything.

"Of course I had a plan," said Naomi.

"There." Maybelle tapped the top of the table with her French-manicured nail. "That's what I'm talking about. No different from when you were in college. You were so *good* at things then."

"And now?"

Maybelle took a sip of water and looked up at the ceiling.

"Okay, Mom. I think I'll—"

"No, don't go. I have more to say."

Naomi should have known she wouldn't get off so easily. Her head ached, throbbing in time with her heartbeat, but she stayed at the table. Just a few more minutes, a few more stitches, and then she'd be able to cry in bed. "I'm sorry I didn't tell you about Anna. But I'd just found out and—"

"You *should* have told me. I'm furious with you about that. But no matter who that father is, I know one thing: it's going to be a gorgeous baby. I can't even imagine what I'll feel, holding my perfect little grandchild. I wonder if I can talk her into coming home with me this time . . ."

"Are you kidding me?"

Maybelle looked at her hot-pink-tipped manicure.

Naomi went on, feeling almost frantic. "I don't get it. I've never done anything right on your terms in my whole life. I've been screwing up, left and right, from the moment you left me with Dad. At least he loved me, just as I was. You've always pushed and *pushed* me. Now that Anna's knocked up, you're supporting her? You're not going to be mad, even a little bit? But you're mad at me for not telling you, when it wasn't my job in the first place?"

"I just—"

"What, Mom? You just what?" Nothing her mother said could change the fact that she was always going to play second fiddle in her mother's estimation, and yeah, that hurt. Like hell.

"I just never expected any more from her." Maybelle's words were flat, without affect.

The words shocked Naomi into closing her mouth, into swallowing the retort she hadn't quite come up with. Finally she managed, "What do you mean?" But she knew. In a small, ashamed part of her heart, she wondered if she'd felt the same way about Anna as her mother had. God, she hoped she hadn't. But it was possible.

Maybelle sighed heavily, and it sounded real. "It was the same with me, you know. When I got pregnant with you. She's just repeating her mother's mistakes."

"But you were with Daddy."

Her mother laced her fingers together so tightly Naomi could see her knuckles going white. Again, she remained silent.

"Mom. You were with Daddy. It was totally different from the situation Anna's in."

Maybelle met her eyes, and with a thunk, Naomi felt something drop heavily into place.

"You weren't with Daddy."

"I couldn't . . ."

"You couldn't *what*, Mom? Tell me the most important truth of my life?" Naomi took a deep breath around her tightening chest. "Who was he, then?"

"Naomi, I can't just . . ."

"You *have* to." Naomi had never felt such a combination of shock mixed with grief. If the one person who'd ever really, truly loved her wasn't her father, then where did that leave her in the world? Who was she?

Nobody.

Maybelle, looking more miserable than Naomi had ever seen her look, said, "He was a young man I met while I was traveling, trying to see the world. He was married to a woman he loved but who didn't love him. He already had a son. When he found out I was pregnant, he said he couldn't see me again. He cut off everything."

"I have a *brother*?" This was just too much. "Where is my . . . father now?"

"He died. A long time ago."

"Oh, good. Just like my fake dad. How did you know? Were you keeping track of him the whole time?"

Maybelle looked like she was about to cry. Her fingers still fought each other, the acrylic ends clicking, an echo of Naomi's needles that, astonishingly, were still moving. "Facebook."

Naomi let out a sharp-edged laugh. "Are you serious?"

"Not that long ago, an old friend of a friend put together a list of the people we'd been traveling with that summer. He wasn't on it, and another friend asked why."

Naomi would never have a chance to know him. She'd never meet him. Naomi stopped knitting, finally, and wound the leading yarn around her fingers, wanting them to go as white and bloodless as Maybelle's knuckles. "Do you know where my . . . brother is?"

Maybelle bit a nail tip between her teeth. "No, I'm sorry. I haven't tried to find out. And honey, you have to understand that Daddy is still your father. He was that, in every single way," Maybelle said, panic rising in her voice.

"Except he wasn't my father. Ever."

"He *was*. He loved you so much, Naomi—I wish you could know how much—he was there when you were born. He chose you as his from your first breath. He held you first. Before I even did. He claimed you as his."

"Daddy was the one thing that buoyed me up in the face of your indifference. Why didn't you tell me? What possible excuse could you have had for keeping the most important thing in my life a secret?"

"You loved your father. If I was bad at being your mother, I could always rest easier knowing I'd given you the best father in the world." Maybelle paled even further. "I know you think . . . Anna told me. But—"

"Anna told you what?" A fear crept into Naomi's heart that she didn't know how to name.

"That you've always thought you were second best to me."

Naomi's blood felt icy. "Where did she get that information?"

"She said Rig told her. When they were working on a surprise for you. But, honey—"

"Stop." Naomi let the right needle go. "Stop for a minute." She'd told Rig in confidence, when she was sick, her secret belief that her mother loved her two daughters very differently. It was something she'd never said out loud, until she said it to him. And he'd gone and told *her sister*? Anna had of course run and blabbed it to their mother, which made it a million times worse.

"Is that why Anna called you? To talk about me? Not to tell you that you were going to be a grandmother?"

Maybelle flinched. "What matters is that she called. And that I came. And now I can tell you that you're wrong; even if I've never been good at showing you, I do love you as much as I do Anna."

"Words, Mom. That's all those are." The feeling of betrayal was like a scalpel, one slick, fast cut letting the blood spill out. She stood, throwing her shawl onto the table with a metallic clatter and *shush* of wool. "No matter what you tell yourself, you never, ever loved me like Anna. No matter what I was or how well I did. Your love for me was different. Conditional. Contingent on my being the good daughter, on my grades, on my being the one who never screwed up. And now I finally get it."

"No, you don't—"

"You must see my biological father in me." Naomi wondered how it was that when her entire world was shattering around her, she could think about this so clinically. So rationally. So like her father would have. Her father had always said to take herself out of the equation when dealing with patients. Now, she was the patient, and when she took herself away, she could see the situation clearly.

Her mother had abandoned her in all the ways that counted. "When you divorced the man I thought was my father, you made me live with him. Someone I wasn't even related to."

"You *wanted* to. You chose him over me. You *always* chose him over me. And Daddy chose you over me, too."

Naomi gritted her teeth together and spoke through them. "But he wasn't my father."

"He *was*," said Maybelle stubbornly. "In every single way that counted."

Something else struck Naomi with the weight of a bat. "He was from here. My real father."

"Your real father was Daddy."

"My *biological* father. Oh, God, that's why you hate Cypress Hollow so much. You passed through here before I was born. Maybe nine months before?"

Maybelle pressed her fingertips to her eyelids, and then covered her mouth. She nodded. "I didn't want to have to come here to visit you. To remember."

"You always loved Anna. Totally. But never me, not that way."

"Never the same way, no," said Maybelle. "But parents don't love their children exactly the same. Equally, yes, but in different ways. And I have *always* loved you."

Scanning her mother's face, Naomi knew her mother thought she was telling the truth. But that wasn't enough. She pulled her shawl up off the table by the working yarn and clutched it as if it could save her.

"Does Buzz know?"

Maybelle bit her lip. One huge tear rolled down her cheek and then was matched by another. And another.

"I see," said Naomi. "He does. Of course. Please, for the love of God, does Anna—"

"No! Of course not. And I don't want her to know how alike we are. I'm . . ." Maybelle's voice trailed off. "I'm ashamed. Please, Naomi?"

Naomi laced her fingers through the holes, bringing the mass between her hands. Her mother was ashamed of her, on top of everything else. Naomi was the symbol of a mistake made years ago. It made so much sense, now that she knew. She looked at her mother one last time. "I don't have to agree to do anything you ask of me. Ever again."

Once in her room, the door safely closed and locked behind her, Naomi buried her face in her pillow and put another one over her head so she couldn't hear her mother's sobs. Maybelle was only crying about revealing a secret.

Naomi had much more to mourn: today she'd lost a real father, a pretend father, an unknown brother . . . and the man she was involved with had gone behind her back, betraying her.

Oh, Rig. It was because of him that she now knew the truth. That her world was upside down. The weight of it hit her like a bullet, ripping and tearing her flesh.

She wouldn't forgive him.

Her own tears came then.

Chapter Forty-eight

We will always have wool in our fingers, and everything comes down to these small stitches that march forward, resolutely.

—E.C.

The first thing Naomi did at the office the next morning was to go over her patient roster for the day. She was a professional. She ignored the fact that her hands shook on the keyboard—it was lack of sleep, that was all.

Good. She had fifteen minutes before her first patient.

That would be just enough time to let Rig know exactly what she thought of him.

Knocking only once before she swung his office door open, Naomi entered. Rig looked up. The surprise on his face changed quickly to pleasure, and for a terrible second, Naomi forgot what she was going to say. She could only remember the feel of his arms around her, his mouth on hers, the shivers she couldn't control . . .

The green curtains, so sheer they hid nothing from viewers on the street.

Anna chose that moment to pop her head in as she walked by.

"Good morning, you two. I'm going for a coffee run, or really, a coffee waddle. Do you want anything?"

"No thanks," said Rig politely.

Naomi could only shake her head. Anna was next on her list, but first, most important, was Rig.

"Okay, I'll be back soon, then."

She waited until Anna was down the hall before she pushed Rig's door shut. She supposed it could have been called slamming, but she didn't actually mean to. Not really.

"Hi, you," said Rig, his voice sweet gravel.

"You told Anna." She was proud she controlled her voice so that it didn't shake.

"About last night? No, of course I didn't. If she knows, it's because of those damned curtains, and I've told you I'm sorry about those, but I'm happy to apologize again." His smile was slow and rich. "I'll apologize any way you want."

Naomi folded her arms in front of her and took another step forward. "You told Anna what I told you about my mother."

He blinked. "Oh. Yeah. I thought she might know how to make you feel better, and she knew your mother would come."

"So you knew Anna would tell her." It was even worse than she'd thought.

"She said she might. It's what she thought would be best."

"You *plotted* with her about it?"

Rig sat heavily in Dr. Pederson's old chair, the leather creaking under him. "I'm sorry, Naomi. I was worried about you, and you were so sick. Anna said she knew your mother loved you, and that maybe it would be good for you to hear that from her."

"It was awful. Horrible. Not only did the fact that she *has* never loved me the same as she loves Anna come out, but so did the fact that the man I thought was my father was never actually related to me. The same man she gave me to when she remarried." The sharp, slicing pain cut into her again. She met Rig's eyes, choosing to ignore his look of bewilderment. "Your betrayal was bad enough. I spoke to you in confidence. I *trusted* you."

"And then to have your mother's betrayal follow so closely." Rig's voice was gentle, as were his eyes. "Of course you're upset."

"Upset?" He had no idea. How dare he *agree* with her? "I'm so far beyond upset the word doesn't even seem to apply."

"I'm sorry, Naomi." He stood and came around the desk toward her.

Scrambling backward, Naomi almost tripped on a pile of books on the floor. She raised her hands to hold him off. "Don't touch me."

"Okay, okay. Don't worry."

"Don't worry? I'm now officially worried about everything. The town probably hates me. I didn't even dare go to Tillie's this morning."

"I went. I got a couple of high fives, but no one actually said anything. And Shirley wasn't there, so I couldn't get the real scoop."

Naomi's vision blurred as she shook her head. "High fives. You're kidding me, right?"

"I don't know what they were about. Could just have been guys saying hello . . ."

Naomi groaned. "I'm going to kill you."

"Before you kill me, will you accept my apology? I'm deeply sorry that I betrayed your confidence. I acted in a hasty manner, and I didn't think it through. I know you're a private person, and I should have known better. I'm sorry, Doc."

"Don't you *Doc* me." She pressed her fingers to her temples in a vain attempt to dull the headache. "It's done. Whatever it was between us is completely over. The trust is gone."

A frown cut a deep furrow in Rig's brow. "Naomi. I just said I was sorry. And I think your mother's revelation is definitely a huge betrayal, too. You want to talk about it?"

Naomi's laugh was hollow. "With you? No way."

"I'm a good listener."

"Yeah. You're good at listening and then sharing my secrets."

He took another step forward, moving into her space. "Naomi, what's it going to take to get you to believe that I'm truly sorry?"

She just shook her head. Nope, she couldn't think of a thing. "I just had to tell you that we . . . that whatever this was, we're done." She couldn't scoot any farther back—he had to stay away. If he touched her . . .

"So that's it?" His voice was rough.

"What do you expect me to do?"

Rig raised his hand as if he would reach out to her, and she felt herself flinch away. He noticed, and the pain in his eyes was obvious. But then he just rubbed the back of his neck and said, "I expect you to be angry and then to accept a heartfelt apology and move forward. Like a grown-up."

"You're calling me a child?"

"If the kid's shoe fits . . ."

"I can't believe this."

"You?" Rig's face matched his tone—shocked and hurt. His eyes darkened like a sudden storm over the ocean. "I can't believe that you aren't seeing this for what it is. I made a mistake. But that's because I was thinking so hard of how to make your surprise special. Fixing up the center was a big deal, I knew, but helping fix an actual, emotional problem between you and your mother was even bigger. That was more important to me. And I thought it would be to you, too, even though I was wrong."

"See? You were keeping secrets from me, too. What if Anna had told me about what you did with the center? How would you have felt?"

Rig sighed and jammed a fist in his hair. The way it stuck up afterward reminded Naomi of how he'd looked when she'd woken in his arms during her illness. "A surprise is different from a secret.

Did you ever stop to think about that? It's okay to keep secrets when you're planning a surprise for someone. Your problem is that you hold emotional secrets inside about everything, locked away in the darkness. You don't let people in. You don't let anyone get close, and my God, that's what this life is for. Letting people in. Living with an open heart. I thought you were letting *me* in, and I'm not talking sexually, although that was beyond amazing. But now you've shut me out again."

"That's not fair—" Naomi started.

"No, what's not fair is letting me get close to you for a second or two, and then pushing me away like this."

"I have to—"

"You don't. That's a lie you're telling yourself. But when you find out you're wrong about this, you can lock that knowledge up, too. Add it to your box of deep, dark secrets."

"You don't understand." Naomi felt a desperate longing for . . . what? Rig's arms around her? No.

Rig's cell phone beeped, and he pulled it out of his pocket while stepping backward, away from her. "I guess there's only one secret you don't know about me."

Naomi felt herself pale. How had this become even more broken than she'd thought it was? "What?"

His words fell heavily into the room, his voice raw with emotion. "I fell in love with you. Now lock *that* away, because I'll be working on getting over it as soon as possible."

Something shattered in Naomi with an almost audible *snap*. Darkness folded in at the edges of her vision.

Then Rig made a strangled noise in the back of his throat as he stared at his phone. He snapped it shut and ran out of the room without saying another word.

"Rig?" Naomi followed him. What had his phone said? Something even worse than what had just happened? Was that even possible?

He'd already exited the side door at a dead run when Bruno caught her in the hallway.

"The ER just called," he said. "Rig's dad was just brought in, code three. They're working him now."

"As in *working*?" CPR couldn't be in progress. No, please, *no*.

Bruno nodded. "You'd better go."

Chains couldn't have held her. Naomi flew.

Chapter Forty-nine

For a friend who must be in the hospital, knit cashmere socks. They will remind her that she is loved.
—E.C.

The floor was buzzing—the three nurses on duty looked swamped. A motor-vehicle accident victim was in one bed, his head bandaged, blinking rapidly. An older woman clutched her stomach in another bed, crying quietly. Naomi felt an urge to go to each one, but kept moving, kept looking.

Frank lay in the farthest bed, his eyes closed, his skin gray. The back of his hand was already bruised from the lines the nurses had prepped.

Naomi felt her knees go weak with relief. He was alive.

Jake and Rig stood next to their father. Milo, sitting on the metal chair next to them, looked at Frank with wide, startled eyes, a green plastic dinosaur dangling from his right hand.

Rig barely glanced at Naomi. "How is he? What the hell happened?"

"Shirley Bellflower happened," hissed Jake.

"I heard that," said a voice from behind Naomi. Shirley stood just outside the pulled-back curtain, dressed in what looked like a black peignoir that had been stuffed into jeans. The black material puffed out at her waist, and Naomi tried not to notice that it was obviously she wasn't wearing a bra. "I didn't *happen*. Don't forget, I'm the reason he got here at all." But her voice belied her words—it shook, just like her hands.

Naomi felt like she was putting together a puzzle, but half the pieces were turned over, so she couldn't see the pattern.

"You're right," snapped Jake. "You *are* the reason he's here. If he'd been home where he should have been, if he hadn't been grabbing a morning quickie at your house, this wouldn't have happened."

Rig stepped forward so his body was partially between them. "Jake. Just tell me."

Rolling his eyes, Jake said, "Dad was with Shirley, here. And they apparently wanted to have some fun with blue pills, if you get me. He went out in her kitchen, hit his head on the way down. I talked to Lucy Bancroft, who was staffing the ambulance today, and she said he coded briefly on the way in." Jake's voice was strangled. "They had to zap him back."

"He coded?" A vein beat in Rig's neck so hard Naomi could see it pulse. "*Viagra?*"

Frank's eyes fluttered. "Don't tell Shirley."

Shirley looked at Naomi and clasped her hands in front of the black lace tie at her navel. "They keep saying that. *Coded*. What is that?"

Naomi said, "His heart stopped."

Shirley gasped.

"But obviously," she hurried to say, "the defibrillator worked. He's here."

"Oh, God," said Shirley, her face drawn. "I didn't know about the Viagra. I swear. I just thought he was—"

"Don't say it," warned Jake.

Rig already had the blood pressure cuff on Frank's IV-less arm, and kept his eyes on the screen. "So what next?"

"They're giving him Activase, talking about a stent. Operating in a few hours, probably."

"Who?" Naomi asked. It mattered here—in a town this size, they didn't have their pick of surgeons. The ones they had regularly rotated on and off duty, and Naomi trusted some more than others.

"Hayashi," said Jake.

Milo mumbled, "Hayashi hayashi hayashi," as he pulled the leg off the dinosaur and then snapped it back on.

"Is he good?" Rig looked at Naomi, and the emotion written in his eyes took her breath away. He loved his father.

Goddamn. She loved *him*.

She felt her right knee dip with the realization, and it felt like she was physically dragging herself back into answering the question. What was the question again? Oh, yeah. "Hayashi's the best. You couldn't have better."

Naomi loved Rig. She dropped her gaze to the rumpled blanket covering Frank's legs. Was it all over her face? Could he see? Was there ever in the history of the world anyone with worse timing than hers? His father had stopped breathing earlier tonight. She'd broken up with him right before he admitted he loved her.

Oh, God. She had to get out of here. "I'm going to—"

Rig interrupted, saying, "Where did he get the Viagra?"

Frank spoke again, not opening his eyes. "Mexico. Internet."

"Dad!" said Rig.

"Frank!" said Shirley. "Honey, you didn't need that. You'd be a sex pistol no matter what."

Jake groaned.

An image of herself, holding condoms in the drugstore, flashed in Naomi's mind. "Viagra and nitro don't mix," she said. "Worst combo ever."

Rig shook his head, fiddling with the blood pressure cuff. "He's not on nitro. He suffered hypovolemia last time, so they took him off it."

Naomi's thoughts stalled briefly, whirred, and restarted. "I refilled his prescription. He asked me to."

"Excuse me?" Only the beep of the heart monitor and the hiss of the cuff broke the silence in the small, fabric-enclosed area. Rig's jaw worked.

"He . . . said he was out, that his was expired. He didn't want to worry you two. He was supposed to come in to see me last week, but he didn't. We talked about it last night at dinner."

"*Shit.* He'll need a transfusion before the surgery, then. Goddammit. He wants the nitro for the angina, but he can't be on it. Period. And mixed with Viagra, we're lucky he's alive." Rig's face was stone, his jaw rigid. The eyes that had heated her last night were now cold as liquid nitrogen. "How could you have—I can't believe you'd put my father in jeopardy like that."

"I'm—"

Rig glanced at his father as if to determine whether he was listening or not, and then said in a thin, tight voice, "What kind of doctor *are* you?"

"I'm a—" Naomi's voice broke. She was a good doctor. She knew she was. Just because she'd made a mistake . . . a critical mistake that had threatened, *was* threatening the life of the father of the man she loved . . . "I didn't mean any harm."

"But the phrase you're obviously forgetting is, *do* no harm." Rig's words cut the air.

Jake's voice was as cold as Rig's. "You should go."

Shirley grasped her forearm. "I'm sure she didn't mean—"

"He's right. Go," said Rig. The fury pulsed from his body, but she could also see, deep in the blackest part of his dark eyes, a pain she'd never before witnessed, a pain darker even than what she'd caused him earlier.

Naomi bit the inside of her lip so hard she tasted blood. The air she breathed tasted crystalline. Shards of ice filled her lungs, and she couldn't move. What kind of a doctor *was* she? For Christ's sake, she knew better.

"*Go.*"

"It was just—but he said . . ." She stumbled backward, the curtain rings clinking over her head.

Jake snapped the fabric shut and she heard Rig say, "Don't worry, Dad. We're here." A nurse stepped around her, chart in hand. A phone rang, unanswered.

She'd never known that hearts could actually break. Naomi had always thought it was a poetic description for something that was most likely sentimentality mixed with stomach upset. But when he pulled the curtain closed, Naomi's heart shattered into hundreds of fragments, the shrapnel of his words twisting through her body. No surgery, no treatment in the world would fix her. She knew it was too late for her.

For both of them.

And God only knew how Frank would fare.

Naomi turned and fled.

Chapter Fifty

*Don't argue with a friend over which stitch is better —
you are both right, and your friendship is more important
than any petty knitting belief (except your belief in the
three-needle bind-off — it's always the best choice, and it
might be worth fighting for).*

—E.C.

Christ, Rig was sorry he'd told her he loved her. It was true, which made everything worse, but he wished he'd at least kept his big fat mouth shut.

The fog still hung heavily over Main Street, darkening the interior of the office, and Rig scowled as he unlocked the front door and flipped on the lights in reception.

He'd thought, for a moment, that Naomi could be the one. That she was his Megan. That she was what his mother had been to his father.

But that didn't mean he'd ever have to tell her that he'd thought it.

Bruno wasn't in yet, and Rig went through the motions of opening the office. Naomi wasn't in, either—he'd beat her in all week. She'd barely been there at all, which suited him fine. They'd exchanged e-mails about the catering firm that was coming to the clinic on Saturday, and she'd said she would be in charge of setting the place up for the dance.

Good. He'd done enough work in there for her. It was bad enough that he'd have to go to the dance at all, but since it was supposed to be a promo for the partnership as well as her damn health clinic, he needed to be there.

The front door banged shut, and Bruno shuffled in, looking like he'd just woken up.

Rig put on a smile that he didn't feel. "Morning, bright eyes."

"Yeah, you, too. How's your dad today?"

"Better. He should get to go home after the weekend. I started both coffeepots."

"God bless."

Rig said, "Anna still working in the dead files?"

"She'll be out there for a while, I think. Lot to do."

Rig nodded and wondered how often his brother would make an excuse to go see her while she was working. Pretty damn often, he supposed. Anna had come with Jake a few times to see Frank, and Frank had loved it, flirting with her as well as a man could do while hooked up to two IVs, and lying on his back.

Bruno moved to go around him toward the break room, and Rig trailed behind him. There was something he wanted to ask, but he couldn't think of the right way to bring it up.

He watched as Bruno filled his mug, added what looked like fifteen spoonfuls of sugar, and swirled nondairy creamer into it with a wooden stir stick from a box in the cupboard.

Bruno took the first sip and met his eyes. "I feel like I'm squashed on a slide, and you're waiting for me to squirm around."

Rig shook his head to clear it. "I'm sorry. I didn't mean to stare."

Bruno shrugged. "It's okay. A guy as good lookin' as me . . ." He waved his coffee cup in the air dismissively. "Used to it."

Rig smiled and then said, "Do you think Naomi is a good doctor?"

Standing straighter, Bruno said, "Why?"

"Do you?"

He nodded. "I do. I've worked with her long enough to say with authority that she is."

"Have you ever seen her be reckless?"

Bruno snorted. "Her? Never. She couldn't be reckless if she won the lottery. Thinks too much. Keeps too much in her head."

Rig pulled out a metal chair at the small table and folded himself into it. "Is that what it is?"

"What happened?" Bruno towered over him.

"She almost killed my dad by giving him something that, with his medical history, he can't take."

Bruno's eyes widened, but he just took another swallow. Deliberately, he said, "Then she didn't know his history. Dr. Fontaine may not be all touchy-feely like you, but she's good. She knows what she's doing. I've never seen her screw up like that."

"She didn't know the history because she didn't think it was important enough to get." Rig gripped the leg of the table and jiggled it—somewhere, a pin was loose, and the table squeaked as it rocked.

"You sure about that?"

"Pretty sure."

"That's why you two are giving each other the silent treatment."

"Part of it." Also, he'd told her he loved her, and she'd broken his fucking heart. "I'm waiting for her professional apology, but I'm pretty sure that's not going to be enough."

Bruno frowned. He opened his mouth and then snapped it shut again. Then, speaking so quickly that his words almost ran together, he said, "If it comes down to picking between you and her, you should know that I choose her. My loyalty is with Dr. Fontaine. And if she screwed up, she's probably taking it harder than anyone else ever would. But everyone makes mistakes. You made two dosing mistakes already this week on prescriptions that I fixed when I sent them in."

Rig gaped. "You what? You can't just—"

"One was *take for 100 days*, I made it 10—100 days of Cipro would be pretty bad—the other was *take twice a day, in the mornings,* and I made it morning and night, since that drug has a twelve-hour spacing. I initialed each change, so you'd know it was me if it came up. But what you wrote was just plain wrong, and I know your scatterbrainedness has got something to do with the fight you're having with her. But you have to remember, she's a technically skilled doctor. She knows how to fix people who are sick."

"So do I."

Bruno shook his head. "You know *how*, but you spend an awful lot of time chatting with your patients, time that could be spent like she does, in research, or double-checking your work."

"Taking time with patients, getting to know them, is part of healing."

"Is having sex with your coworkers on a couch in plain view of the street part of healing, too?"

Rig could actually feel his jaw drop.

Making a *tsssk* noise through his teeth, Bruno paused in the doorway. "She's a private person, something you might not understand. I call it a bad idea to throw curveballs at her like that. Something's bound to break, and while Naomi's strong, she's also more easily hurt than she knows. She may not know her ass from her elbow when it comes to human relations, and we've had our own ups and downs. But she's a great doctor, and I respect the hell out of her. And if you hurt her . . . Well, like I said. I choose her." He left the room, leaving Rig no time to retort.

Fine—Rig was too surprised to say anything back. He'd kind of thought, if push came to shove, that Bruno would back him. Not that he wanted that to happen—he didn't want to divide the office.

But they'd talked together in a way Bruno never had with Naomi, and he'd thought they were friends. Possibly, they were. But Bruno still felt loyalty to Naomi. There was something admirable about that, even if it was goddamned annoying.

A lighter tread behind him.

Naomi.

Without turning in his chair, he knew she'd entered the break room. The way his heart raced confirmed it, the way the center of his abdomen heated, sending warmth up through his chest.

"Sorry," she said. "Just getting coffee. I'll be in and out."

Rig turned. The look of her slammed into him like the huge rogue waves that pounded the platforms during the worst fall hurricanes. White coat, long legs in black pants, clean face, those perfect soft lips. It was a travesty that she pulled her hair back like that.

For just a second he forgot he was furious, forgot how much she'd let him down, and he almost moved to go to her, to wrap his arms around her shoulders and kiss her until they both had to come up for air. To tell her he loved her. That he couldn't be without her. That she was who he'd been waiting for.

And for that split second, he swore he could read the same impulse in her eyes, all of it, echoed.

Then she poured a cup of coffee and pulled a note out of her pocket to read as she stirred the creamer in. She'd shut herself off again, and Rig remembered with a sinking gut that her irresponsible actions had almost killed his father. And she hadn't even *asked* about Frank. Of course, she could be getting info on him from any of the doctors or nurses over at the hospital, but she hadn't asked Rig.

New anger bubbled up, and Rig had no place to put it. "Did you order the stage set up? With the microphone and amps for the band?"

She nodded.

"What about the permit Elbert said we needed?"

"He got it for us."

"And all the drinks—"

"Are lined up," she said, as she walked past him on her way out of the break room. She kept her eyes on the floor.

Rig leaned forward in his chair, and took her wrist as she passed. "Stop."

She did, but when she raised her eyes to his, they were bright green pools of sorrow.

"I just . . ." he started, but he didn't know where to go. He had too much anger to do even one of the things he was considering.

"I am sorry, you know," Naomi said.

The breath left his body in a clean *whoosh*.

"I've never done that before—prescribed anything with no medical history. I could have at least asked you, but I didn't. Frank didn't want you to know, and it felt like I was in on a little secret. It felt . . . fun. Like he was my friend. That was wrong. I screwed up. I know the words don't mean much, but I am sorry."

They were the words he'd needed to hear, and now that she was saying them, Rig was astonished to find that his anger wasn't dissolving instantly. In fact, God, he was so angry now his hands were shaking. He let go of her wrist before she noticed.

"You almost killed my *father*."

She nodded miserably. "Yes."

He needed to go, to get out, to be on the water, to be anywhere but here, anywhere away from where he could smell that sweet rose and iodine smell of her. The last thing he wanted was to have to work with her at the dance. How the hell were they supposed to present a unified business front if they couldn't even stand next to each other while melting down?

"I'm taking the day off," he said, suddenly sure this was what he needed. He'd rent a kayak, or hell, he'd buy one and be out on the ocean this afternoon, paddling hard, pushing every thought of her out of his body.

"You are? We have a full load today," she said.

"I handled it when you were sick. You handled it before I started here. You'll be fine."

Naomi just looked at him, and his fingers physically ached with the need to touch her cheek.

"I can't be around you today," he said.

She looked like she was trying to stop herself from saying something.

"Yeah?" he asked.

"I'm *very* sorry for my mistake. But you're gonna have to learn how to be around me, buddy." She shook her head, and he realized the tears that had welled in her eyes now were from anger. "Even if you hate me forever, you're going to have to do better than this. You can despise me. Go ahead. But me screwing up big time, *one* time, doesn't give you the right to be an asshole in perpetuity."

Didn't it?

"And now," she said, "if you'll excuse me, Hank, *I* have to remain professional. I have sick people who are here to see me. Luckily, I'm fast with my patients. In, out, better, faster. "

She sidled past him, her lips clenched together furiously.

Fine. He'd stay at the practice today. He wouldn't run away. And he'd cut his patient visits short. He'd be the model of efficiency in doctoring, and show her he could have both bedside manner *and* speed. But for now, Rig remained where he was, holding fury in his clenched fists, his heart shredding in a way that he wouldn't, couldn't, examine.

Chapter Fifty-one

There's an end to every knitting project. That much is guaranteed.

—E.C.

Naomi passed another almost sleepless night, torn between quietly crying, silently raging, and dropping into fits of sleep that were torn apart every time she remembered. She didn't know how to mourn the loss of Rig and the loss of the man she'd thought was her father, and it felt impossible to do both at the same time. The pain might keep her from breathing, she thought, even though she knew that was physiologically improbable.

Oh, *Rig.* The molten fury she'd seen in his eyes had scared her, but she'd expected it. What she hadn't expected was that in the depths of her grief and remorse, even while she was still trying to accept her misplaced feelings toward him, she'd been able to be mad at him at the same time. She still hadn't quite forgiven him for spilling her secret about Maybelle to Anna, but she had to admit she was closer to doing so. Regret made her feel softer, more willing to admit that perhaps she'd overreacted. A little.

Telling him to man up and keep working hadn't been planned,

but it had felt good. And he'd listened, and stayed, and seemed to turn over patients a little faster than usual.

Naomi had never had to live—and work—through a broken heart before. All day long at the office, every day this week, every word that she'd managed to speak had felt like a miracle. She'd thought she was pulling it off until Bruno had given her a bear hug before he went home. She'd almost burst into tears on the spot, but instead went into the center and moved the new furniture around for an hour.

The new furniture Rig had bought for her. For her and her dream.

She rolled over onto her back and stared up at a cobweb in the corner of her ceiling. Finally, what seemed like months after she'd gotten into bed, the alarm went off. It was time to face the music, literally.

The dance had been trumpeted in the *Independent* for the last week—Trixie had been surprisingly agreeable when Naomi had called in the small ad, upping its placement for free, placing it on the front page, and writing a nice piece about what the annual contra dance meant to the community.

Community. She would have to face everyone. Even him. And today, she just didn't know if she was strong enough.

For a moment, she gave herself the talk she'd been falling back on, the one that had been getting her out of bed every day. *Dad wouldn't have stayed in bed. He would be up and at 'em, ready for the day, excited about how he'd get to help.*

But her father's health clinic had never hosted a dance.

And he wasn't even really her father, goddammit. More than just learning the truth of her birth, she'd also learned that the man she'd loved the most in her life, the one she'd held all other men up to only to find them wanting, had been lying to her for as long as she'd known him. He'd lied every time he'd allowed her to call him *Dad*. Naomi felt as if she were standing on a pier in a storm, the pilings below her swaying. She couldn't trust herself to stay upright.

Or was it that lying had been his way of loving her?

No, it was too much. Too confusing. Too awful.

Naomi punched the pillow underneath her head and then smoothed it, fantasizing about pulling the covers over her, staying there all day. She heard the shower go on, and groaned. At least her mother and Buzz would be leaving tomorrow. They wanted to attend the dance before they left.

Bully for them.

Naomi knew she still had to have the talk with her mother about who, exactly, her deceased biological father was, but that was a conversation she had put off every time she'd seen Maybelle since they'd had that first, fateful talk five days ago. Tonight, though, she'd talk to her tonight, after the dance.

If she got out of bed, that is, and that wasn't necessarily in the cards.

Instead, without leaving her warm spot under the covers, Naomi reached for the closest Eliza Carpenter book. *Eliza's Road Not Taken* was on the nightstand where she'd last placed it. She flipped to the inside front flap, touching the picture of Eliza and her husband, Joshua. They leaned against the barn wall, both wearing hand-knit ganseys, both grinning from ear to ear. Tears welled again. Dammit. That happiness, that joy radiated by Eliza, even in a picture, was almost too difficult to look at.

She flipped it open, pointing with her finger randomly, hoping, praying that she'd get the answer she needed about how to handle these feelings that threatened to drown her. A painful lump filled her throat as she saw the passage she'd landed on, and she reread the paragraphs greedily, gulping them in as if they were air.

> Joshua laughs at me, sometimes, when I get that old familiar yearning to start a family tradition. Any tradition, large or small. He's never quite understood the need I

have for touchstones, but he humors me, and is patient
when I decide that every year the Christmas tree must
be chopped down while Thanksgiving dinner is cook-
ing. If he had his way, we'd never have a Christmas tree
at all, he cares that little about them, but having grown
up in foster homes where Christmas usually came only
with new socks and a tall bottle for the foster mother, the
holiday means so much to me.

Bless him. Sometimes, late at night, I wonder where my
people are. I'm sure my real mother died years ago, when
I felt that pain that had no explanation—that drop in my
heart's assertion that I could never really be alone—but
is anyone else left?

It's not that I want to meet them. I believe we create our
own family. Joshua is my world, and I know I'm his.
And even though we couldn't have children, when Cade
moved in to help, he took over that spot I'd known was
empty. He is my great-nephew but I think of him as my
son, and he loves me. My knitters, too, are my family.
Our connections run deeper than mere friendship as we
sit together, making our own traditions, building useful
art that will be the foundation for future generations to
base their traditions upon.

But it still hurts occasionally, and I'm always thunder-
struck when the pain resurfaces: they didn't want me.
Was it only she, or were there more of them pushing me
out? Was I a discussion, something to be hidden, closed
over, a chapter never to be reopened? Did anyone wonder
about me? Could they have any idea that I made it to

college? And to Europe, on my own earnings? That I worked my way across the Continent carrying only a knapsack and my needles in a time when women didn't travel alone like they do now? Do they know that I skied the Alps with a Russian, got drunk in a Roman tavern on homemade grappa, herded sheep on a cold Scottish moor? Do they know Joshua feels like he's always the luckiest person in the world that I picked him? Do they know he's wrong? That I'm the one who came out ahead when I fell in love with the man with the most brilliant blue eyes I've ever seen? Do the people connected to me by blood know that Joshua and I built a house together, with our own hands? That every day I wake up with him, I'm happy just to open my eyes and the only thing that makes thinking of one day not being able to do that is my surety that we'll be together again, later?

They know none of this. And after all the thinking I've done, late into many nights, I know better than anyone else that they did the right thing, letting me go. I've been free all my life—a freedom granted me by birth. Joshua is my tie-down to the earth, the yarn that keeps me tethered. Otherwise, I might float right up into the air, coming down only to see what Uruguay is like. Or South Africa. Or Prague.

Love makes a family. And thank heaven for that.

Naomi closed the book and hugged it to her stomach, as if she could press the words into herself by sheer force of will.

Love makes a family. It sounded like a slogan for a bank ad or something equally banal. But knowing the words were Eliza's made them truer, and as Naomi closed her eyes again, she clung to them. Love *did* make Rig's family, she could see it in everything they did for each other—how Rig always preheated his brother's barbecue because Jake, firefighter though he was, would have been nervous about it; how they both tolerated Frank's blasphemous prayers; how Rig hung Milo upside down despite Jake's protests.

Naomi's heart plummeted again to her feet. She'd lost her father once to death. Now she was losing him again. Grief made her shoulders ache. Naomi had spent her adult years trying to get everything right, to be perfect, for him.

And he wasn't perfect. He'd lied for so long.

From the back of her mind, a small, quiet thought arose that perhaps it showed something important on his part that he'd never given Naomi the slightest hint she wasn't truly his.

Even that thought ached.

Naomi sat up and swung her feet to the cool floor. The whole room was cold and slightly damp, as she'd forgotten to shut the window last night against the fog. It felt right, matching the feelings in her heart, her lungs.

A shower. That was next. A really, really hot one—maybe it would finally warm her up.

One last time, before she stood, she flipped the book open to another random page. Just once more. Opening her eyes, she saw that she'd stabbed the epigraph for chapter eight.

Knit through everything.

Tears welled again. Dammit. That wasn't right. She'd try again.

A poke of her fingers into the book. Eyes opened again, she read: *Always be brave.*

Naomi gasped. So be it. Before she got in the shower, she put her shawl-in-progress into her bag. For so long, she'd been trying to prove her worth to a man she hadn't even truly known. So who cared if she asked someone for help with her knitting? Would it make her less of a doctor to appear stupid? Incompetent? Unable to even do a simple craft? She'd ask someone to show her what she was doing wrong with the dang picot edge bind off tonight. If she could build up the nerve.

She stood under the water, and didn't try to determine if the water on her face was salty or not. For a brief moment she allowed herself the fantasy of getting out of the shower, drying off, and going to find Rig, saying whatever it took to make it right again. Forgiving him. Asking him to pardon her. Pulling him into bed with her. Drawing the covers over their heads and staying there, for a very long time. Forever.

Or maybe she'd just go far, far away from everyone who knew she was a mistake.

Oh, God, she wanted to see him again.

Naomi leaned against the cold tiles while the hot water hit the places on her body Rig had touched, kissed, worshipped. Then it felt right to cry, just for a few moments. Later, she'd figure out how to live her life again, but not right now. Naomi would give herself that.

Chapter Fifty-two

When a pattern comes together, when you can finally see how the pieces fit, it makes you feel like a genius. And, my dear, you certainly are!

—E.C.

I t was working.

All of it. It had come together, after a long day of hard work and avoiding Rig, ducking into the office every time he carried something for the party into the clinic. The clinic had been transformed into what, to Naomi's wondering eyes, appeared to be a ballroom. Okay, a western ballroom, yes—there were hay bales along the far wall, under the windows, for sitting on. A low raised platform held the band, which consisted of a fiddler, a bass player, an accordion player, and a guitar player, each of them wearing a cowboy hat. The caller for the dance, Eric, was tall and bearded, his smooth, clear voice telling people to *form long lines up and down the hall, now alemán right, alemán all.*

Rig and Naomi worked refreshments together, as planned. They were doing fine, professional and crisp, until Naomi spun around while reaching for extra napkins and collided full into his chest. She apologized. Rig mumbled something she couldn't catch, and then he handed a flyer on the early warnings of heart disease to a short, stout woman who took it without suspicion.

When Stephens asked her to dance, she looked at Rig, who nodded and finally spoke to her. He turned his face toward her without meeting her eyes and said, "I can handle this part." He gave out two more glasses of wine to the Lempkes and sold a raffle ticket to Mrs. Luby, who said she was on a fixed income so he should make sure she won.

Naomi moved into Stephens's arms, her hand in his work-roughened palm, her arm at his shoulder, grateful that there was no way to keep from smiling when an old cowboy was spinning a girl around and around so fast that Naomi knew if he let her go, she'd fly across the room like an out-of-control top. She didn't know what she was doing, but he made her feel coordinated and graceful.

Elbert Romo, dapper in his new blue overalls that were creased as if he'd just ironed them, cut in as the music turned to a waltz. He smelled not unpleasantly like a cough drop and was just as good as Stephens on the floor. As they spun through the crowd, Naomi felt the grin again creep across her face.

"You're good at this dance," said Elbert as they wheeled past Mayor Finley, resplendent in a yellow sequined gown that made her look like Big Bird in drag. "Who taught you?"

Naomi felt her smile fade. "My father. The waltz was his favorite."

"He did good, teaching his daughter. But I gotta say, you should dance the next waltz with that new doc who's got his eye on you. You two look fine together, and I have to admit, though I'm young for my years, it's possible I'm a little old for you."

Elbert led them backward past the refreshments table, and for one dizzy second Naomi met Rig's gaze. The blood roared in her ears and she stumbled. Elbert caught her, "Whoopsie! It's *one*-two-three, *four*-five-six." He pulled her back on the beat, and she tried not to think how red faced she must be.

And about how much Rig must despise her. She'd never find out how it felt to waltz with him.

"Everyone's here," said Elbert. "You done good."

Naomi dragged her attention back to her partner. "You think they like it?"

Elbert winked. "They do. You see ever'body grinning?"

"You think they'll be back?"

"For another dance? Sure!"

"No," she said. "For clinic services. Like I told you about."

"Maybe," said Elbert, looking over her shoulder. Then he met her eyes. "Maybe so. They seem to like it. But you . . . You gotta be a tiny bit more approachable."

Naomi's heart *kerplopped* into her stomach. "What do you mean?"

"I think you think people don't like you. But they're just treating you with respect. You're a doctor. Hard for a crowd like this, mostly blue collar and local, to get past that white coat you're wearing."

Naomi glanced down at the pale blue chiffon dress she wore. "Even when I'm not."

Elbert swung them past Rig again, and this time Naomi counted her steps and made sure she didn't stumble.

"Show them something they don't expect," said Elbert. "Show them you're human."

"What about all this? Isn't this something?" Naomi glanced at the dancers, the groups of people laughing, the large circle of women knitting in the yarn area Rig had created.

"You're getting closer. But show them *you*." The music ended, and Elbert let her go. He took a step back, and gave a brief bow. Naomi dropped into a curtsy—it felt clumsy, but appropriate. Then she leaned forward spontaneously and kissed Elbert on the cheek.

"That's more like it," Elbert crowed.

Chapter Fifty-three

The best stitches are sometimes the simplest ones. Not everything has to be difficult.
— E.C.

Naomi was the prettiest girl out there, and Rig couldn't keep his eyes off her, and God knew, he'd tried. He'd made deals with himself, promises to go hiking tomorrow, to buy that enormous flat-screen TV he'd been thinking about purchasing, to do *anything* to keep from staring at her as she wove around the dance floor with that old coot, but it was impossible. No matter where she was, his eyes found her.

She was gorgeous, the way she moved, swaying and dipping in time, her curls brushing her shoulders, that old-fashioned light blue dress spinning out, showing an incredible expanse of leg . . . He thought about cutting in—the waltz was one of the few dances he knew.

And then he'd remember all over again why his father wasn't at the dance. Frank was still in the hospital, recovering from the insertion of his stent. He was doing well, and enjoying the opportunity to flirt with nurses every chance he got. Shirley sat at his side during the hours she wasn't at work, sometimes even sleeping in the chair next to him, and Rig could see true affection between them.

What the hell was happening to the men in his family? As he handed a glass of lemonade to Lucy Bancroft and gave a beer to her husband, Owen, he looked over their shoulders to watch Jake leaning solicitously over Anna, who was seated on a hay bale on the opposite side of the crowded room. In between the whirling dancers, he could see that Jake had that look, the one he'd had with Megan. His face was soft, unguarded, and it reminded Rig of the way Jakey had looked when they were kids, when they were falling asleep in the tent in the backyard in summer.

He looked completely happy.

Lucy and Owen were obviously waiting for him to answer something they'd asked. "I'm sorry, what?"

Lucy just smiled and said, "I'll take the table for a while. You should get out there."

"Oh, that's okay . . ."

"Go. Owen, come help me. Let's play bartender. Here, Rig, why don't you take these lemonades over to Jake and Anna? Their hands are empty."

To their encouragement, Rig took off the half apron he'd been wearing for more than two hours, and walked around the edge of the room. His eyes scanned the dancers.

He didn't see Naomi.

Which was *fine*, he told himself. He didn't need to know where she was every second of the night, for cripe's sake. He made his way to Jake and Anna, the lemonade sloshing a little as he handed it over.

"Thanks," said Anna. "I needed something like this. Look, I even brought my own table." She rested the glass on top of her belly.

"Looking almost ready there," Rig said. It was an automatic response, and he heard the distance in his voice. He brought himself back and looked at her. "How are you feeling?"

"Fine," she said. "A few Braxton-Hicks that haven't been fun, and obviously I'm not going to dance tonight, but I'm okay."

"She's letting me take care of her." The pride in his brother's words was practically visible, and Anna lit up like neon.

"He does a great job." They held hands, their fingers laced together.

"Mmmm," said Rig. What else could he say when both his father and brother had gone off the deep end into the whirlpool of love?

"I see Mom and Buzz over there with the snowbird group. Where's Naomi?" asked Anna.

Rig tried to shrug as casually as possible. "Haven't seen her."

"Did you two make up yet?" asked Jake.

Surprise coursed through Rig, and he consciously stilled his jaw, which had clenched automatically. "You think we should? You, of all people?"

Picking up Anna's hand, Jake said, "Hey, I was pissed as hell the other night. She obviously knows better than to medicate a patient without getting a history. But she made a mistake, and she knows it. She told Dad she was sorry, and she personally apologized to me, too. Looked like she really meant it. Didn't she talk to you?"

"When did she apologize to you?"

"Wednesday morning. She's come by the hospital every day at lunch this week. Brought Dad a dirty crossword book yesterday. And a Bible." Jake grinned. "I think she's got his number."

"I . . . didn't know." Naomi had done that? She'd been seeing his father and no one had told him?

"She sits on the bed and holds his hand when Shirley isn't looking."

She sat with Frank?

The image of Naomi slid sideways in Rig's head, shifted into something . . . different. He needed to see her in order to regain his anger. He hadn't planned on falling in love with her. But he could fight it. He was strong. And what she'd done was just plain wrong. She'd committed the cardinal sin: she'd hurt his family. He scanned the room, but still didn't catch sight of her.

Anna leaned slightly forward, pushing her heels into the hay. "I know she's my sister, so I might be biased. But when Naomi does and says thoughtless things, it's because she's so far inside her own world she doesn't really understand sometimes how they translate in the real one. But that doesn't mean her intentions aren't good. She wants the best for people. She always has. That includes your father."

Shit. If he let his righteous rage cool for even a second, Rig knew the mistake hadn't been malicious. Hadn't been planned. Anna was right.

He'd tried ripping Naomi out of his heart as if he was tearing off a Band-Aid. But it wasn't working. At all.

Maybe because it *shouldn't* work. Maybe it didn't have to. Jake didn't hate her, and apparently his father didn't, either. They'd forgiven her.

Something small and warm bloomed in his chest, something he couldn't identify for a moment. The tiniest tendril of hope crept in, took root, and started to grow.

Chapter Fifty-four

Always be brave.

—E.C.

Naomi's heart beat triple time as she approached the group of women, the bag she'd quickly grabbed out of her office slung over her arm. Abigail, Lucy, Trixie, Whitney from the bakery, Janet, Toots, a few more Naomi didn't know—they were all here. They'd found the knitting area, of course, as if they were cats drawn to a winter hearth. Their work spread out over laps, yarn trailing over fingers, balls of wool haphazardly dancing on the floor in time to the fiddle music: all the women knitted while they chatted and laughed.

There was one chair left open.

Naomi walked toward it, then her feet stalled. She could keep walking. They hadn't noticed her yet—

Trixie had. Her perfect red lips parted in what looked like a genuine smile. "Come sit with us," she said. "Tell us how Frank is doing."

Ouch. Was it a dig? Did they all know what she'd done?

But Naomi took a deep breath and sat. Looking around the circle, meeting their eyes, she realized that, no, they didn't know.

No one did. But it seemed as if they were all leaning forward, waiting . . .

"He's going to be fine. He's got to take it easy for a while, but the
surgery was successful, and he's healing well."

As one, all the women leaned back in relief. Needles flew again,
yarn bobbing at their feet.

Naomi reached forward, pulling her shawl out of her bag. She
tried to do it as if it were nothing, which really, she knew, it was.
Just knitting.

The circle exploded.

"Darling!" exclaimed Janet.

"You big *sneak*," said Trixie, a note of admiration in her voice.

"And lace!" said Lucy, her eyes glowing. "It took me forever to
get lace."

Naomi draped the shawl over her lap. Suddenly, it looked as if it
wasn't awful. It was kind of pretty, in fact. She fingered the yarn-
overs and touched the bit of the picot bind off that she'd managed.
"This is taking me forever, though. I don't know if I'm getting it
right."

"Is that the wedding shawl from Eliza Carpenter's third book?"
asked Lucy.

Naomi nodded, biting her bottom lip.

Janet laughed and drawled, "Who's it for, darling? Any plans you
want to fill us in on?"

"*No*," said Naomi but her eyes fell on Anna and Jake just then,
as Jake leaned forward for a kiss from her sister, his hand resting
on the curve of her belly. Anna would look gorgeous in this shawl.
Maybe. . .

Abigail leaned forward to touch Naomi's yarn. She studied the
stitches for a moment. "It looks right to me, but it always feels a little
off until it's done, right? This is gorgeous. What *is* this?"

Naomi took another deep breath.

But Abigail leaned closer, looking at the fiber. She touched the working yarn, her face a question. "May I see . . . the ball you're working from?"

"Oh, it's just—I wound it by hand. I don't have a ball winder or a—what do you call that thing that spins?"

"A swift." Abigail's voice was preoccupied as she examined the fiber. "I recognize the hand of this yarn . . . Who spun this?"

It was time.

"Eliza Carpenter."

Gasps followed her pronouncement, but not from Abigail, who was still staring at the yarn.

"I know I should have made my connection with her clearer earlier, but . . ." What was Abigail *looking* for so intently? Naomi put out her right hand to take the yarn back. Abigail was making her nervous.

But instead, Abigail put the ball in her lap and grabbed Naomi's hand. "Where did you get this?" She touched the small ring.

Oh, God, would they think she *stole* it from Eliza? Thank God she still had the note, but—

"It's the same as mine. Look." Abigail put out her left hand, holding it next to Naomi's. Sure enough, the bands were identical, from their gold circlet to the little platinum leafy stems that held the tiny diamond chip in place.

"How—?" Naomi couldn't make things fit together in her mind for a moment.

"Eliza Carpenter gave hers to Cade a long time ago, even before he met me. It was for his wife, she said. But . . ." Abigail's voice trailed off. She looked into Naomi's eyes.

Then Abigail's filled with tears, and Naomi had never been as surprised as she was when Abigail placed her palm on her face, touching her cheek softly.

"That's where I know you from. The hospital. You were Eliza's favorite. She talked about you, but I was too sad afterward to put it all together. Oh, God. Did you know then? How did you find her?"

Naomi bit her inner cheek. She hadn't found Eliza. Eliza had found her, in her Eliza way.

Abigail went on. "I can't believe I didn't see it before. I look at these eyes every night before I go to sleep. Then I wake up to them. Oh, Naomi." Abigail swept her into the biggest hug of her life, and Naomi still didn't understand.

Mildred and Greta both said at the same time, "What's going on?" Mildred had her iPhone in hand, ready to tweet whatever it was.

"I don't . . . know," said Naomi. "Abigail, what do you mean?"

"I can't believe you didn't tell us this before," laughed Abigail, wiping her eyes. She looked overcome by joy, and she kept hold of Naomi's right hand. "How were you related to her? I got a glimpse of it when I saw that fiber, that's *our* Corriedale, I can tell. And I know Eliza's hand in the spin of it like I know my own. But when I saw the ring, the one I knew she was saving, and your eyes—"

"Eyes?" Naomi interrupted. "What do you *mean*?"

"You and Cade both have your great-aunt Eliza's eyes."

From behind her, Naomi heard a gasp that echoed the one sounding in her chest.

She knew that gasp. She'd heard it a million times in her life, usually when she'd let her mother down somehow.

Maybelle said, "Stop. Don't, please—"

"Mom, what does she mean?"

But the answer came to her, like water flooding over a riverbank. Her eyes resembled Eliza's because they were related. Naomi, who'd always thought she'd known her father, hadn't. Her father . . . must be Cade's father. And that would explain why her mother hated Cypress Hollow, why she'd been so dead set against Naomi moving to the town—there was a resemblance that could be seen, identified.

That made Cade MacArthur, Abigail's husband, her half brother.

She had a *brother*. Her eyes scanned the room, ignoring her mother grabbing her arm, not hearing anything of the words that fell from her mouth.

There was Cade—she could see him through the dancers when they parted. The way he was laughing, with his head back, at that forty-five-degree angle—she did that exact same thing when she laughed hard—she'd seen it in pictures.

Cade was talking to Rig. Anna, her eyes sparkling at Jake, sat next to them on a hay bale.

God, Rig was talking to her brother.

Abigail said softly, "I've always wanted a sister. Trust Eliza to give me one. From out of the blue."

Naomi stood, the lace falling on the ground, unheeded. Their hands still clasped, they crossed the room, hardly noticing that they broke through the dancers' long lines, causing Elbert to almost drop Mrs. Luby. Behind them, Maybelle sputtered.

In front of them, her family. And a man she loved. A future that nothing Eliza had ever written could help Naomi divine.

She'd never been more scared in her life. She'd screwed so much of this up, and she'd been blind to the rest. But her sister-in-law gripped her hand, and she wasn't alone.

Chapter Fifty-five

A revelation may occur to you as you're knitting. If you think you've developed a more clever way to do something, you have. Embrace it, and then share it.

—E.C.

Rig saw them coming. Who didn't? They parted the dancers as if there was no one on the floor, their hands joined, their faces . . . Well, Abigail's glowed, but Naomi's face had about ten thousand emotions on it, and Rig could identify only one: terrified happiness. He'd seen that look once before: when she'd napped on his shoulder in this very room and had woken to find herself in his arms. Her expression had been similar: eyes wide, with a look that said she might bolt at any moment and the same almost smile kicking at the corner of her mouth.

God, he loved her mouth. That same small hope bloomed more, uncurling further in his chest.

If only . . .

Was she making her way to him? Was that the terrified joyful look she had? His heart thumped almost through his chest as she approached. That insane thought pushed through his heart again, apparently not heeding his brain.

Love.

Oh, hot damn.

Pushing past the last line of dancers, seemingly oblivious to the disapproving looks they were garnering, the women tumbled up to them. Abigail dropped Naomi's hand and grabbed her husband's.

"Cade, Cade!" Abigail was breathless.

Cade laughed. "Is the barn on fire again?"

"So much bigger than that!"

Fascinated, Rig watched the way they looked at each other. Cade reached out with his free hand and touched his wife's nose, kindness in his eyes. "Tell me."

Abigail's mouth zipped closed, and she turned to look at Naomi, who also, suddenly, looked struck dumb.

"What?" pressed Cade. "Are you pregnant again?"

That got Abigail breathing again. "*No.* Okay, look at Naomi."

"Is *she* pregnant?" Cade was obviously kidding, but Rig heard it like a punch to the gut. Naomi. Pregnant. With his child.

He couldn't breathe.

Anna, too, sitting next to them, leaning on Jake, tipped her head to hear the answer.

"Stop. Of course not. But look at her."

All three men, Rig, Cade, and Jake stared at Naomi. Rig was pretty sure he was the only one who could read her accurately, though. She was now completely terrified, and it had nothing to do with him. It had something to do with Cade, and Rig's fists involuntarily clenched. He didn't know if Cade had done anything wrong, but on the slightest off chance that he had—their new friendship wouldn't stand a chance. Rig had learned his best moves tossing drunks out of bars onshore, and he'd use them again if Cade had in any way hurt her.

"*Look* at her," Abigail insisted. "Cade, look at her eyes."

Shaking his head, Cade looked embarrassed. "They look like her eyes. Honey, just tell me."

"They look like *your* eyes."

Cade's mouth opened, then closed.

"And like Eliza's."

Nodding, Cade said, "But . . ."

"And look at her ring. It's your grandma Honey's ring, the one she had Eliza keep for her. Eliza gave it to *Naomi*." Abigail lifted Naomi's hand. This all meant something, but what?

Naomi still hadn't said a word, and Rig ached to stand at her side, to help with whatever it was they had to reveal. Catching her eye, he nodded, almost imperceptibly. Something, anything, to help that look of anguish on her face. She could do this, whatever it was. He knew she could.

Naomi saw his nod. She stood straighter and said, "I'm not sure how to say this, exactly. Well, I'll just say it like it is. My mother slept with your father. Thirty-fourish years ago. I think . . . I think I'm your half sister."

From behind them, Anna gasped, "Naomi!"

Cade just stared.

Looking like she might cry, Naomi shuffled two steps backward. "I'm sorry," she said, "to break this news about your father. I don't know how he was with your mother, but—"

"My mother and father never got along, from day one. My mom was MIA most of my life. I didn't know my dad had . . . but I know she . . ." said Cade. His words were clipped, as if he couldn't get enough air to say more.

"I'm sorry," said Naomi again.

But then, in a burst of motion, Cade wrapped his arms around

Naomi in an embrace that enveloped her almost completely. Abigail clapped her hands over her mouth, tears springing to her eyes. Rig felt a wild stab of completely unreasonable jealousy watching another man's hands on Naomi and closed his eyes briefly. *Don't be an idiot.*

Naomi had a *brother.* Then, opening his eyes again, he saw Jake grin as he took Anna's hand. Anna just looked shocked.

"A sister! I have a sister!" Cade whooped. A couple of the dancers missed their steps, and heads turned all over the room. "I always *wanted* a sister." He hugged her again. "Now here's one built in. Right in my own backyard. God*damn* that Eliza! She always knew how to make an entrance."

Naomi still looked shell shocked, her arms stiff at her sides, her eyes wide. "I wouldn't be hurt if you wanted to get a DNA test, to see if we're right. But she did once ask my mother's name—I thought it was just because I said that she'd come through Cypress Hollow. I didn't know she was testing who I might be."

"Look at you!" Cade put his arm around his wife and stared at Naomi. The green eyes that looked like the mirrors of Naomi's danced. "I don't need any damn DNA. Eliza didn't. Even far away, she knew who you were. We're idiots for not seeing it, too."

"*Naomi,*" hissed Anna. "Mom's coming."

Maybelle sailed across the room, dragging Buzz behind her.

"Oh, no," said Naomi. "I can't deal with her. I just—I can't."

Then Naomi did something that split Rig's heart wide open. She stepped away from Cade, away from Abigail, and moved toward him. Without a word, she pressed against Rig's side.

Rig's arm went naturally around her shoulders, and the relief he felt in touching her was like drinking ice water after a long, hot day. Sweet blessed forgiveness. That's what this was. And he felt hers, too. She leaned farther into him, and he dropped a kiss on the top of her hair. Both actions were unspoken apologies, ones he knew they'd articulate later. But now, nothing mattered but the fact that he was touching her again.

Rig longed for so much more. He longed for forever.

"Naomi!" said Anna again. Her voice was sharp.

Maybelle was almost on top of them now.

"Anna, honey, *do something*. Distract her. I don't want to handle her. I can't." Naomi threaded her arm around Rig's waist, burying the side of her face in his shirt, and he barely dared move. He didn't want to be anyplace else. Nothing could break this moment, not the fact that she'd just blown a family secret out of the water, not the fact that her mother was about to topple them all like trees—

"I can do that," gasped Anna. "My water just broke."

Chapter Fifty-six

Baby sweaters: little woolen cubes of delight.
—E.C.

Naomi had always been fast on her feet, quick witted, swift to grasp a situation's severity. It was, probably, the part she liked best about herself.

But even she could barely keep up with the next few seconds.

Maybelle barreled in, her arms already over her head, ready to do battle. "No one listen to another word, unless I say it! Oh, Anna . . . Oh, lord. Oh! Don't worry a bit, my precious lamb. It took seven hours to have you. You've got plenty of time. Someone call a doctor!" she exclaimed, looking over the heads of the crowd.

Naomi and Rig didn't need to talk about what to do next. Naomi went to one side of Anna, and Rig took the other. They needed to get her out of here, away from all the eyes that had already been curious as to why Cade had started hugging Naomi and whooping.

"Jake," said Naomi. "Call 911. Get an ambulance here. We need to get her to the hospital."

Anna's cheeks were bright pink, and she puffed air between her teeth. "I swear I wasn't in labor fifteen minutes ago, and now . . ."

She broke off, unable to speak for a few seconds as Rig and Naomi carefully stood her up and started moving her toward the door. "Now I feel like it's moving way too fast for me. Naomi—I'm three weeks early."

"It's all right, that's no problem. Hang on, sugar. We're almost there. We'll put you in a patient's room until the ambulance is here. Then you'll have a little ride, and then you'll have a baby."

Rig, with his shoulder, knocked open the door that led to the office. "Here, come on. You're almost there."

Maybelle followed behind them, flapping Jake through with her hands. "Naomi, on the other hand, she was my first. They always say first babies are the ones who take a while, but Naomi's never been patient. I had her in thirty minutes from the time my water broke."

Anna gasped as another contraction hit her, and Naomi felt a wave of protectiveness. "Mom. This isn't the time. She doesn't want to hear it."

"Of course she does, don't you, darling?"

"No. I. *Don't*." Anna glared at her mother as Naomi and Rig helped her up onto the examining table. "Nothing. More."

Naomi spun in place to face Maybelle. "Out." She pointed behind her and tried to keep the bubbling anger out of her voice, but it rose up in spite of herself. "I'm going to examine her, and you're going to get *out*."

"Don't be silly. I'm here for the long haul."

"No." Naomi clenched her teeth. "It's just me and Rig here. And Anna."

"And Jake," said Anna. "Where's Jake?" She sat up and then fell back down with a groan.

"I'm here," said Jake as he moved around Maybelle and into the small room.

"Him?" bellowed Maybelle. "You're keeping a man you barely know in here and I have to leave?"

Rig moved forward and said diplomatically, "Maybe when we're at the hospital you'll be able to see her. But this isn't a hospital, and we don't want her to have the baby here."

"Why *not*? Shouldn't you already have everything?"

"We're a doctor's office, not a surgery center."

"Surgery?" moaned Anna. "I get drugs, then, right? Good ones."

"So if you'd just sit in the waiting room," continued Rig, a hand on Maybelle's elbow steering her around, "I'll come give you any information you need."

Naomi felt a wave of gratefulness toward Rig for trying to do the right thing, but from how Anna was breathing, they might not have time for the niceties.

"Out. Now." She would move next to Rig and *push* her mother out of here if she had to. Anna was all that mattered, not her conniving mother . . .

Were those tears in her mother's eyes? "I'm sorry," said Maybelle. "Honey, I'm sorry. I should have told you."

"Told her what?" demanded Anna in a roar.

"Naomi, I know we never got along like a house on fire. We've never really spoken the same language. But you know I love you, even if we don't say it, right?" Maybelle paused, as if she had more to say. She put her hand on Naomi's arm and held on, tightly. "He was the first one to hold you, you know. Even before me. He was in love with you from the very first second you drew breath, Naomi, in love with you more than he ever was with anything else in his whole life, even his work. He lived for you. You know that, in your heart."

Anna wailed, "What the hell are you talking about?"

"Nothing," said Naomi. "Nothing that can't wait. Okay, Mom, out." But somehow, the anger was dissipating, fizzling. What if her mother had just been trying to do the right thing all along? Was that possible? They were two women related by blood who didn't understand each other as well as others did. And that might be okay.

They could talk about it later. Now was for Anna. But as her mother left, head down, Naomi said, "Thanks, Mom. I love you, too."

Maybelle turned, a look of utter relief on her face. She kissed her fingers and blew on the tips, once for each daughter. Then she closed the door behind her.

Showtime. Naomi turned to Anna. "I'm going to give you a quick exam, okay?"

"My own *sister*," said Anna. "Dammit. This isn't quite what I'd planned."

Then Naomi heard Anna's breathing change, and things sped up again. Shit. Anna was fully dilated. And crowning.

"Where is that damned ambulance?"

"Close, I'm sure," said Rig, moving to stand next to her. "Wow," was all he said.

Jake stood at Anna's head, holding her hand, and was so pale Naomi prayed they wouldn't have to pick him up off the floor. He was a firefighter, for Pete's sake. He'd be able to handle this, right? He must have delivered babies a time or three.

But never one that mattered this much, she'd bet.

"Well, this show is sure on the road, huh?" said Rig. Was that a laugh in his voice?

Naomi shot him a suspicious look. Yes, it was. "What's funny about this?"

"Nothing's funny, Doc. But there's gonna be a baby here in a few minutes, and that's pretty damn great."

Joy. That's what it was in his eyes. Naomi drew it in with one long breath, and he gave her a look that made her heart pound even faster than it already was.

"Yep, Anna, you're ready to go."

"I am *not*," said Anna around another contraction. "I'm not at the hospital . . . I can't . . ."

"Hold on, and don't push until I tell you to. Rig, can you round up some paper gowns? And the infant suction pump? Paper towels, too, lots of them. Everything we'll need."

Rig nodded. As he passed by her shoulder, he paused. She smelled of grass and wind. He dipped his head to her ear and said, "Breathe."

He was right. She had to remember to tell Anna to breathe—this was what Rig was good at, remembering what the patient needed, making what they were doing the number one priority.

"Anna, honey, breathe. Don't forget to breathe. It's going to be all right."

"No," said Rig. "I meant *you*. Don't you forget to breathe. It's going to be all right."

And then he dropped a kiss on her lips, a kiss so light and quick it might not have happened except that she heard Jake snort. Rig had kissed her. He'd really kissed her again. Even with the drama in the room, Naomi's heart took flight, and hope, the best feeling of all, flowed through her like a heady, sweet wine.

Then Rig was gone, out of the room to get supplies, and Anna was panting again, and Jake turned his attention to her while Naomi monitored the baby that was on the way out, stat.

"Now, Anna, now. The baby's head is coming, *push*."

With a scream that Naomi was sure the entire dance had heard just a few closed doors away, Anna pushed. The head came out. The eyes were closed tight, the face squinched up as Anna took another breath. Naomi felt tears spring to her eyes that she didn't have time for.

"Good girl, that's exactly right. Now wait, wait . . . Just a second." Naomi, moving quickly, made sure the cord was in the right place.

"I can't DO this," said Anna. "Naomi, I can't." Her voice was almost inaudible.

"Of course you can."

"I can't."

Memories of conversations, times she'd shared with her sister, the good times, flooded her brain. Naomi stood up from her stool and looked over her sister's knees. Her words tumbled over each other, and she spoke as fast as she could. "You remember when you said you couldn't skateboard? And when you said you were too scared to skydive? And that time you said you'd never try to hop a freight train? Or that you couldn't learn Spanish?"

Anna's eyes opened for a second. "So what?"

"Whenever you've said you can't do something, that's right before you do it. That's what I love about you." Naomi sat back down on the stool, her hands in place. "You always do whatever you want to, and you do it just right."

Her sister's only response was a gasp as the next contraction came.

"Now, Anna. It's time now." Naomi hadn't even heard Rig come back in the room with the supplies she'd hoped she wouldn't need, but now he was next to her, his hands near hers, not trying to get in her way, not impeding her work as Anna pushed as hard as a human could. He was just with her. Ready to help if she needed him. Next to her.

Anna pushed.

The baby squirmed completely out—she was perfect and tiny, red and wriggling, and gasping almost as hard as her mother was. Suddenly, Naomi's sister was a mother, and she was an aunt. Before she started the routine that went into place now, checking Anna, tying the umbilical cord, getting her ready for transport when the ambulance finally showed up—she could just hear the siren now—she held her tiniest new relative and watched her eyes open for the very first time. Naomi suctioned the tiny mouth and nose and the child's first cries, an angry catlike mewling, were the sweetest sounds she'd ever heard. Every birth she attended felt like a miracle, but this one made her sure that nothing else would ever be able to compare.

Jake stood next to her, angling to catch a glimpse. "Anna, it's a girl," he said, his voice choked. "And she's gorgeous."

Naomi's eyes caught Rig's, and he dropped a slow wink, a grin stealing over his whole face. Her cheeks hurt from smiling back. Blinking hard, she looked at Jake. This man was in Anna's life.

Much like her father had been in Maybelle's life when Naomi was born.

"Jake. Do you want to give Anna her daughter?"

Jake's cheeks went from pale to bright red. "Y-yes. If I don't drop her." He looked at Rig. "Don't let me drop her."

"You got this," said Rig. "You're good at this part, remember?"

Jake took the baby, wrapped in a paper dressing gown, from Naomi, his hands tentative, but steady. He looked down at her, and a smile to match his brother's lit up his face. Turning to Anna, he said, "Look what you did. You're amazing."

Anna's face was like sunlight.

When Anna had her baby in her arms, after she'd touched her head with wondering fingers, she lifted her face to Jake and said, "What do you think?"

Jake dropped a kiss on Anna's head. "I love her. I think she's as beautiful as her mother."

The words were intimate, but Naomi couldn't help staring at Jake. There, in that gaze, Naomi saw her own father. That look—Dad had always looked at her that way. Always.

That was the look of a father who loved a daughter.

Something caught in Naomi's throat, and as she moved to the sink, she almost stumbled. Eliza had been right, even though she'd sent her to find more of her kin. Blood didn't make a family. Love did.

In a moment, she'd turn from the sink, and Rig would be there. So damn close she could reach out and . . . Her hands started to shake as she washed them again. And she, Naomi, knew she'd found love. She prayed she could keep it, but even if it wasn't returned, she'd had it, at least for a little while.

Chapter Fifty-seven

Love through everything.

—E.C.

The paramedics swept up Anna and the baby while Naomi put together what they had to take and filled out a form that needed signing.

"Please," Anna said, "Let Jake come with us. Please?"

The crew made an exception to the rule—it was Captain Keller, after all—and loaded up at the back door.

"I'll be there soon!" Naomi yelled as the doors shut behind Anna, desperate for her sister to know she was still there. "I'm right behind you."

No lights or sirens, rolling code two since both patients' vitals were good, the ambulance drove away into the night.

"And I'm right behind *you*." Rig's voice was gentle and the night was warm, but a shiver ran down Naomi's spine.

She turned. It was too much to hope that he really meant it, the way she wanted him to. But still, the tiny flutter she felt at every pulse beat wouldn't let her *stop* hoping.

In the distance, Naomi could hear the surf pound against the

sand. Sounds traveled farther at night, she knew, the fog creating a
shell above them. She heard a seagull cry, and a car alarm, quickly
silenced. She could feel the mist making her hair curl, and wished
she didn't still have the paper gown over her pretty dance dress.

Rig leaned against the concrete wall, the streetlight above him il-
luminating the tops of his cheekbones—they stood out stark against
his face. The joy she'd seen in him inside had fled, leaving him serious. Quiet.

She had to tell him the truth. He might never feel the same way
about her—probably still hated her—but she had to say it. She'd live
through whatever came next, she knew that now.

"I love you." Her throat ached as she said the words—they'd been
locked so far inside her that it hurt when she released them. "I know
you don't feel the same way, but you needed to know so we can still
work together. And I'll be fine as a business partner, I promise. I just
needed you to know. Just—that I love you, Rig."

Rig didn't say anything. A vein pulsed at his throat, a tiny motion
she longed to touch, and couldn't.

Well. That was that, then. She'd gotten mixed signals from him
in there, and that was her fault. She would just deal with her feelings, and keep feeling them, and now that they were out of her, in
the open air . . . The pain of it hit her so hard that she almost cried
out. Inside, she'd just get inside and—

He grabbed her by the waist, pulling her so hard against him she
lost all breath, all desire to breathe ever again. He claimed her mouth
in a kiss that said everything she'd ever wanted to hear, his lips moved
against hers in a way that told her exactly how he felt, and if he hadn't
been holding her up, she would have had to reach behind her to grab
the wall. As if she weren't close enough, he pulled her tighter. Thigh
to thigh, her breasts against his chest, his hand tangled in her curls,
scooping her against him, holding her, kissing her, and she kissed him
back, and in the back of her mind, she felt *yes, yes, yes.*

"Yes," he finally said against her mouth.

"Yes, what?" She was desperate to hear it, to hear the words he'd just told her with his kiss.

"I love you so much I thought I'd die if I had to go one more second without telling you." He smiled at her, his face radiant. "I'm so sorry I let you think that you—Naomi, I'm sorry about all of it. For everything I said, if I made you feel that I didn't love you for even a second. I've loved you since I first saw you across that hotel bar, I just didn't know it until recently." He paused for a moment. Naomi could feel him taking a breath and she breathed with him. Then he said, "You're everything I ever dreamed of, and a thousand times more than I could have imagined. You're my heart. You, Naomi. I love you. Just you."

How could a heart contain these feelings? She didn't know how it was possible, but she was grateful, *so* grateful that it could keep beating while she felt them. She kissed him then, standing on her tiptoes, pulling him down to her. "I missed you," she whispered.

"I missed you, too, Doc." Rig laughed then, the glorious sound resonating inside her chest, and her laughter joined his. The sound of their joy bounced against the concrete walls, echoing out in Main Street, and down to the water. As the townspeople filed out of the dance just around the corner, heading home for the night, they heard the sound and more laughter joined theirs, drifting up into the dark velvet night sky. A star winked, and glancing down, Naomi saw the same sparkle reflected in her ring.

Her father would have approved.

Rig kissed her again, and she was home.

Epilogue

Never underestimate the strength of your stitches: your knitting warms the body, soul, and spirit, and your love lives there, between your knits and purls.

—E.C.

Six months later.

The winter night was clear and cold, stars twinkling brightly above the pier, a crescent moon dangling above the far end of the bay as if it had been hung there in honor of the wedding.

And indeed, it might have been.

Naomi pulled the shawl across her shoulders, making sure it draped exactly where it should. It looked perfect with her dress, and she knew Eliza would have been proud of it. Yes, it had flaws and dropped stitches, and yarn-overs where there should have been decreases, but after blocking it had come out perfectly, a drift of creamy lace, just right for a night this important.

There was little traditional about this wedding, and she was glad of it—heart glad and filled with happiness. The white ranunculus she held in her hands trembled, and she made sure she concentrated on where she placed her feet. Tripping now wouldn't do at all.

Ahead of her, Jake walked next to Anna as they moved through the open door. Inside, Naomi could see candlelight bouncing against the high rafters of the Book Spire, and the red ribbons they'd spent the afternoon twining up the aisle looked perfect. The books had been pushed back on their racks, and the pews had been replaced in their original places in the old church.

Good. She wanted this to be as lovely as love itself.

Naomi followed Jake and Anna at a steady pace, wishing her heart would beat the same way. She focused on the back of Anna's red dress and the curve of her sister's arm where she carried baby Josephine, who was also draped in matching red lace. To the left of Jake, Milo hung at the end of his father's arm, annoyed that he hadn't been allowed to carry the baby, but still pleased with his role as ring bearer. The rings were tucked in his tiny tux pocket, and Naomi had checked three times to make sure they were safe.

Ahead, in the church, Rig waited for her.

Her love. Her heart.

Even though she'd sensibly worn flats, she almost stumbled again on a small rock as she thought of the man she loved, the man who had made tonight happen. He'd been the one to think of the Book Spire, to hire the band, to order the food for the reception. He'd been giddy about it all, more excited than even she had been.

It made her love him even more.

Now, it was almost time. . . .

At the edge of the narthex, Naomi took a deep breath. What if he wasn't there? What if, at the very last minute, he'd changed his mind?

But then, there, just to the side of the door that led into the nave itself, Bruno waited.

His face was so pale he almost glowed. Above his red bow tie,

Naomi watched him attempt to swallow three times before he actually did it right. His hands were shaking, but at the sight of her, he smiled a rare Bruno smile.

"You look beautiful," he said.

"And you look more handsome than you ever have."

Bruno gulped. "Really? Do you think so?"

"Truly," said Naomi. "Now, may I have the honor of walking you down the aisle, sir?"

Bruno put out his arm, but before Naomi took it, she rose on tiptoe and kissed his clean-shaven cheek.

"I couldn't be happier for you, Bruno." Then she laced her arm with his, and as the sound of Iron & Wine's "Such Great Heights" drifted out to them, as the guests stood, turning to face them as they entered, Naomi caught sight of Rig, standing at the end of the aisle between Peter and Jake.

Rig grinned and winked just for her. Naomi's heart grew again and she felt the tops of her cheeks flush, like they always did. She gripped Bruno's arm tighter.

And as they made it to the end of the white runner, Peter came forward, his hand outstretched.

"Who gives this man to Peter Washburn to be wed?" Toots wore a purple robe she'd bought on the Internet along with her minister's license, and her voice rang through the church.

"I do," said Naomi, proudly.

"*Well* done," said Toots, beaming at her.

The men walked toward Toots, and Naomi fell back next to Anna. Across from her, Rig sent her the look that made her, literally, weak in the knees. She still wasn't sure how he did it, but Naomi locked her legs and prayed it wouldn't make her faint.

As Toots talked about love, and as Bruno and Peter exchanged vows, Josephine made the tiny whimpering noises that meant she was about to wake up. Anna nodded at her, and Naomi took the bundle that she loved so much, joggling her quietly. From the time Jo had landed in this world, Naomi'd had the special touch, the one that always quieted her.

There was no feeling like the heft of her niece in her arms. Unless it was the feeling of looking at the Keller brothers, standing up for Bruno and Peter—Jake and Rig, serious, listening to Toots gravely, as if the ceremony depended on their memory of it.

In the crowd of guests, Maybelle sobbed heftily. Of course. Their mother was always going to play an audience for all it was worth. Elbert Romo leaned forward and pressed a neatly folded yellow hankie into her hand. But the tears were real: Maybelle had been the first to say it was ridiculous that two men were getting married, and then the first to say (after she and Bruno had discovered a mutual love of Neil Diamond) that she might have been a little bit wrong, and "didn't everyone know that true love knows no gender?" She'd joined PFLAG just to get the T-shirt. She and Bruno had formed an uncommon alliance in the past months in attempting to browbeat Naomi and Anna into marriage. Now that Bruno was getting hitched, he thought everyone else should find the same happiness, and Maybelle came behind him, always echoing his sentiments loudly whenever she was in town, which nowadays was often.

Naomi knew that look Rig had—he was imagining their own ceremony, but she wasn't in any hurry. She had him, and his love, and didn't need to walk down an aisle to prove it. She already had forever.

Jake kept trying to talk Anna into marriage, too, but like her sister, she was also happy to live in sin for the moment. "Why buy the cow when I already get the milk for free?" she asked Jake with a laugh whenever he brought it up.

Naomi caught Rig's eye and watched his gaze go soft—the same look he always gave her when she held Josephine. Someday, they'd probably have one of these little creatures themselves. Someday, she'd probably wear Eliza's shawl and come down an aisle like this toward Rig, while watching those eyes she loved darken with emotion.

There was no hurry, though. For now, their family was big enough. Made of love, bound by love, circled and kept safe by love. Eliza had been right. Cypress Hollow was where she'd been meant to be. With her free hand, Naomi draped the edge of the shawl over Josephine's hand-knit socks.

It was winter after all, and nothing warmed like wool.

A+

AUTHOR INSIGHTS, EXTRAS & MORE...

FROM
RACHAEL HERRON
AND

WM

WILLIAM MORROW

Eliza's Wedding Shawl

Designed by Rosemary (Romi) Hill

Materials: Hand-dyed sock yarn: 450 yards (shawl pictured is
    worked in A Verb For Keeping Warm's "Metamorphosis")
Needles: 1 set US #6/4mm knitting needles
Notions: stitch markers, tapestry needle, blocking wires, T-pins
Gauge: 16 sts/32 rows = 4"/10cm in lace pattern. Exact gauge
    is not important for this project. Please note, however, that a
    looser gauge will result in the use of more yardage.

PATTERN

With smaller needle, CO 3 sts.
Row 1 (WS): knit

Work Chart A one time.

NOTES: When working the first few rows of Chart A, it is helpful to mark the right side of the piece with a safety pin to distinguish it from the wrong side. A marker is placed on Row 1 to mark the center st. It is not mentioned again until Chart C, but must be slipped on each row.

Charts

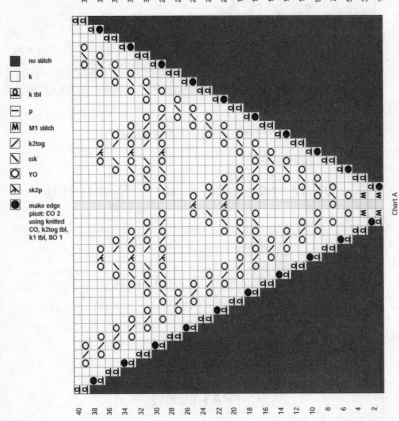

Legend:
- no stitch
- k
- k tbl
- p
- M1 stitch
- k2tog
- ssk
- YO
- sk2p
- make edge picot: CO 2 using knitted CO, k2tog tbl, k1 tbl, BO 1

Chart A

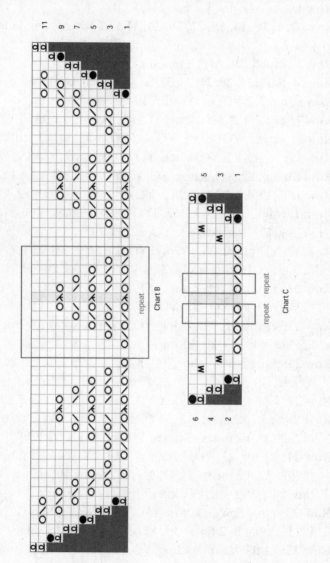

Chart B

Chart C

repeat

Chart A written instructions

Row 1: mp, M1, pm, k1, pm, M1, k1 tbl

Rows 2, 6, 10, 14, 18, 22, 26, 30, 34 and 38: mp, knit to last st, k1 tbl

Row 3: k1 tbl, [k1, M1] 2 times, k1, k1 tbl

Rows 4, 8, 12, 16, 20, 24, 28, 32, 36, 40: k1 tbl, knit to last st, k1 tbl

Row 5: mp, k2, YO, k1, YO, k2, k1 tbl

Row 7: k1 tbl, k2, YO, k2tog, YO, k1, YO, k2, k1 tbl

Row 9: mp, k2, YO, k2tog, YO, k1, YO, ssk, YO, k2, k1 tbl

Row 11: k1 tbl, k2, YO, k2tog, YO, k3, YO, ssk, YO, k2, k1 tbl

Row 13: mp, k2, YO, k2tog, YO, k5, YO, ssk, YO, k2, k1 tbl

Row 15: k1 tbl, k2, YO, k2tog, YO, k7, YO, ssk, YO, k2, k1 tbl

Row 17: mp, k2, YO, k2tog, [YO, ssk] 2 times, YO, k1, YO, [k2tog, YO] 2 times, ssk, YO, k2, k1 tbl

Row 19: k1 tbl, k2, YO, k2tog, YO, k1, [YO, ssk] 2 times, k1, [k2tog, YO] 2 times, k1, YO, ssk, YO, k2, k1 tbl

Row 21: mp, k2, YO, k2tog, YO, k3, YO, ssk, YO, sk2p, YO, k2tog, YO, k3, YO, ssk, YO, k2, k1 tbl

Row 23: k1 tbl, k2, YO, k2tog, YO, k5, YO, ssk, k1, k2tog, YO, k5, YO, ssk, YO, k2, k1 tbl

Row 25: mp, k2, YO, k2tog, YO, k7, YO, sk2p, YO, k7, YO, ssk, YO, k2, k1 tbl

Row 27: k1 tbl, k2, YO, k2tog, YO, k19, YO, ssk, YO, k2, k1 tbl

Row 29: mp, k2, YO, [k1, (YO, ssk) 2 times, YO, sk2p, YO, (k2tog, YO) 2 times] 2 times, YO, k1, YO, k2, k1 tbl

Row 31: k1 tbl, k2, YO, k2tog, YO, k1, [YO, ssk] 2 times, k1, [k2tog, YO] 2 times, k3, [YO, ssk] 2 times, k1, [k2tog, YO] 2 times, k1, YO, ssk, YO, k2, k1 tbl

Row 33: mp, k2, YO, k2tog, YO, [k3, YO, ssk, YO, sk2p, YO, k2tog, YO, k2] 2 times, k1, YO, ssk, YO, k2, k1 tbl

Row 35: k1 tbl, k2, YO, k2tog, YO, k5, YO, ssk, k1, k2tog, YO, k7, YO, ssk, k1, k2tog, YO, k5, YO, ssk, YO, k2, k1 tbl

Row 37: mp, k2, YO, k2tog, YO, k7, YO, sk2p, YO, k9, YO, sk2p, YO, k7, YO, ssk, YO, k2, k1 tbl

Row 39: k1 tbl, k2, YO, k2tog, YO, k31, YO, ssk, YO, k2, k1 tbl

Repeat Chart B approximately 5 times. You can resize this shawl easily by omitting or adding Chart B repeats.

Chart B written instructions

Row 1: mp, k2, YO, [k1, (YO, ssk) 2 times, YO, sk2p, (YO, k2tog) 2 times, YO] *3 times*, k1, YO, k2, k1 tbl
Rows 2, 6, 10: mp, knit to last st, k1 tbl
Row 3: k1 tbl, k2, YO, k2tog, YO, k1, [(YO, ssk) 2 times, k1, (k2tog, YO) 2 times, k3] *2 times*, [YO, ssk] 2 times, k1, [k2tog, YO] 2 times, k1, YO, ssk, YO, k2, k1 tbl
Rows 4, 8, 12: k1 tbl, knit to last st, k1 tbl
Row 5: mp, k2, YO, k2tog, YO, [k3, YO, ssk, YO, sk2p, YO, k2tog, YO, k2] *3 times*, k1, YO, ssk, YO, k2, k1 tbl
Row 7: k1 tbl, k2, YO, k2tog, YO, [k5, YO, ssk, k1, k2tog, YO, k2] *3 times*, k3, YO, ssk, YO, k2, k1 tbl
Row 9: mp, k2, YO, k2tog, YO, [k7, YO, sk2p, YO, k2] *3 times*, k5, YO, ssk, YO, k2, k1 tbl
Row 11: k1 tbl, k2, YO, k2tog, YO, knit to last 5 sts, YO, ssk, YO, k2, k1 tbl

Note that on subsequent repeats of Chart B, the *repeat numbers* in each odd numbered row will increase by two for each repeat of the entire Chart B worked.

Work Chart C one time.

Chart C written instructions

Row 1: mp, k2, YO, [k2tog, YO] to marker, sl m, k1, [YO, ssk] to last 3 sts, YO, k2, k1 tbl
Rows 2, 6: mp, knit to last st, k1 tbl
Rows 3: k1 tbl, k2, M1, knit to last 3 sts, M1, k2, k1 tbl
Row 4: k1 tbl, knit to last st, k1 tbl
Row 5: mp, k2, M1, knit to last 3 sts, M1, k2, k1 tbl

Finishing

Bind off using picot bind off as follows: [mp, BO 2 sts, sl st from right needle back to left needle] to end of row, making 1 picot at end of row. Break yarn and sew end into border so that last picot sits properly.

Abbreviations

BO—bind off

CO—cast on

k—knit

k2tog—(right-leaning decrease) knit 2 stitches together

k tbl—knit through back loop to twist stitch

mp—make picot—CO 2 sts using knitted CO; k2tog tbl, k1 tbl; BO 1

M1—make 1 stitch by lifting the bar between sts, twisting and knitting into the resulting loop

p—purl

RS—right side

sl—slip st knitwise

ssk—(left-leaning decrease) slip 1 stitch as if to knit, slip 1 stitch as if to knit, slip both stitches back onto left needle, knit stitches together, inserting needle from right to left

st(s)—stitch(es)

WS—wrong side

YO—yarn over

For additional pictures/errata, please see
yarnagogo.com/elizasweddingshawl

Khalil Robinson

RACHAEL HERRON received her MFA in English and Creative Writing from Mills College. She lives in Oakland, California, with her family and has way more animals than she ever planned to, though no sheep or alpaca (yet). She learned to knit at the age of five, and generally only puts the needles down to eat, write, or sleep, and sometimes not even then.

www.RachaelHerron.com

Rachael Herron

Close-Knit Reads From Rachael Herron

Wishes & Stitches
A Cypress Hollow Yarn

ISBN 978-0-06-184132-3 (paperback)

"In Cypress Hollow, a lonely woman's life is unraveled
and knit whole again when family secrets come to light
and a sexy man comes to town. Warm and romantic,
another Rachael Herron winner!"
—Christie Ridgway, *USA Today* bestselling author

How to Knit a Heart Back Home
A Cypress Hollow Yarn

ISBN 978-0-06-184131-6 (paperback)

"This novel is a warm-hearted hug from a talented author—
and knitter. It's a sweet comfort read, with an edge of
humor and irony that strikes just the right note. The love
story of Lucy and Owen will stay in your heart long after
the last page is turned."
—Susan Wiggs, *New York Times*
bestselling author

How to Knit a Love Song
A Cypress Hollow Yarn

ISBN 978-0-06-184129-3 (paperback)

"Intricate and clever, Herron's knit-centric novel is as
warm as the sweater pattern it includes! The delightful
Abigail brings both knitting know-how and down-home
sense to this story about picking up the threads of your
life and creating something brilliant."
—*Romantic Times BOOKclub*

**Interact with Rachael online at www.YarnAGoGo.com,
Facebook.com/RachaelHerron, and Twitter @rachaelherron**

Available wherever books are sold, or call 1-800-331-3761 to order.